Hotel Vendôme

www.daniellesteel.com

Also by Danielle Steel

THE SINS OF THE MOTHER	THE KLONE AND I
BETRAYAL	THE LONG ROAD HOME
HAPPY BIRTHDAY	THE GHOST
44 CHARLES STREET	SPECIAL DELIVERY
LEGACY	THE RANCH
FAMILY TIES	SILENT HONOUR
BIG GIRL	MALICE
SOUTHERN LIGHTS	FIVE DAYS IN PARIS
MATTERS OF THE HEART	LIGHTNING
ONE DAY AT A TIME	WINGS
A GOOD WOMAN	THE GIFT
ROGUE	ACCIDENT
HONOUR THYSELF	VANISHED
AMAZING GRACE	MIXED BLESSINGS
BUNGALOW 2	JEWELS
SISTERS	NO GREATER LOVE
H.R.H.	HEARTBEAT
COMING OUT	MESSAGE FROM NAM
THE HOUSE	DADDY
TOXIC BACHELORS	STAR
MIRACLE	ZOYA
IMPOSSIBLE	KALEIDOSCOPE
ECHOES	FINE THINGS
SECOND CHANCE	WANDERLUST
RANSOM	SECRETS
SAFE HARBOUR	FAMILY ALBUM
JOHNNY ANGEL	FULL CIRCLE
DATING GAME	CHANGES
ANSWERED PRAYERS	THURSTON HOUSE
SUNSET IN ST. TROPEZ	CROSSINGS
THE COTTAGE	ONCE IN A LIFETIME
THE KISS	A PERFECT STRANGER
LEAP OF FAITH	REMEMBRANCE
LONE EAGLE	PALOMINO
JOURNEY	LOVE: POEMS
THE HOUSE ON HOPE	THE RING
STREET	LOVING
THE WEDDING	TO LOVE AGAIN
IRRESISTIBLE FORCES	SUMMER'S END
GRANNY DAN	SEASON OF PASSION
BITTERSWEET	THE PROMISE
MIRROR IMAGE	NOW AND FOREVER
HIS BRIGHT LIGHT:	GOLDEN MOMENTS*
The Story of My Son, Nick Traina	GOING HOME

* Published outside the UK under the title PASSION'S PROMISE

For more information on Danielle Steel and her books, see her
website at www.daniellesteel.com

Danielle Steel

Hotel Vendôme

A Novel

CORGI BOOKS

TRANSWORLD PUBLISHERS
61–63 Uxbridge Road, London W5 5SA
A Random House Group Company
www.transworldbooks.co.uk

HOTEL VENDÔME
A CORGI BOOK: 9780552159029
9780552159036

First published in the United States
in 2011 by Delacorte Press,
an imprint of The Random House Publishing Group,
a division of Random House, Inc., New York

First published in Great Britain
in 2011 by Bantam Press
an imprint of Transworld Publishers
Corgi edition published 2012

Copyright © Danielle Steel 2011

Danielle Steel has asserted her right under the Copyright, Designs
and Patents Act 1988 to be identified as the author of this work.

This book is a work of fiction and, except in the case of historical fact, any
resemblance to actual persons, living or dead, is purely coincidental.
A CIP catalogue record for this book
is available from the British Library.

This book is sold subject to the condition that it shall not,
by way of trade or otherwise, be lent, resold, hired out,
or otherwise circulated without the publisher's prior
consent in any form of binding or cover other than that
in which it is published and without a similar condition,
including this condition, being imposed on the
subsequent purchaser.

Addresses for Random House Group Ltd companies outside the UK
can be found at: www.randomhouse.co.uk
The Random House Group Ltd Reg. No. 954009

The Random House Group Limited supports The Forest Stewardship Council
(FSC®), the leading international forest certification organisation. Our books
carrying the FSC label are printed on FSC® certified paper. FSC is the only
forest certification scheme endorsed by the leading environmental
organisations, including Greenpeace. Our paper procurement
policy can be found at www.randomhouse.co.uk/environment

Typeset in 12/15.5pt AGaramond by Falcon Oast Graphic Art Ltd.
Printed in the UK by CPI Group (UK) Ltd, Croydon, CR0 4YY.

2 4 6 8 10 9 7 5 3 1

MIX
Paper from
responsible sources
FSC
www.fsc.org   FSC® C016897

To my adorable, wonderful children,
Beatie, Trevor, Todd, Nick, Sam,
Victoria, Vanessa, Maxx, and Zara,
Joy of my life, music of my soul
You are the delight in my days!
How incredibly lucky and blessed
I am to have you!

All my love,
Mommy/D.S.

Hotel Vendôme

Chapter 1

The scene in the lobby of the Hotel Vendôme on East 69th Street in New York was one of impeccable elegance and meticulous precision. The black-and-white-checked marble floors were immaculate, red runners were rolled out the instant there was a drop of rain outside, the moldings on the walls were exquisite, and the enormous crystal chandelier that hung in the lobby was reminiscent of the finest palaces in Europe. The hotel was much smaller than the one that had inspired its decor, but for practiced travelers, it was remarkably similar to the Ritz in Paris, where the Hotel Vendôme's owner had worked as an assistant manager for two years, during his training in the finest hotels in Europe.

Hugues Martin was forty years old, a graduate of the

illustrious and respected École Hôtelière de Lausanne in
Switzerland, and the hotel on Manhattan's Upper East
Side was his dream. He still couldn't believe how lucky he
had been, how perfectly it had all come together five years
before. His Swiss banker father and equally conservative
mother had been devastated when he announced that he
wanted to go to hotel school. He came from a family of
bankers, and they thought that running a hotel, or working in one, had a seamy quality to it, of which they
strongly disapproved. They had done everything they
could to talk him out of it, to no avail. After four years at
the school in Lausanne, he trained and eventually had
respected positions at the Hotel du Cap in Cap
d'Antibes, the Ritz in Paris, and Claridge's in London,
and even did a brief stint at the famed Peninsula Hotel in
Hong Kong. He figured out during that time that if he
ever had his own hotel, he wanted it to be somewhere in
the States.

Hugues worked at the Plaza in New York before it
closed for extensive renovations, and he assumed that he
was still light-years away from his dream. Then it
happened. The Hotel Mulberry was put up for sale, a
small tired hotel that had been run-down for years and
had never been considered chic, despite its perfect
location. When he heard about it, Hugues put together

every penny of his savings, took out every loan he could get in both New York and Switzerland, and used all of the modest inheritance his parents had left him, which he had carefully put aside and invested. And the combination made the purchase of the hotel possible. He just managed to do it, with a mortgage on the building. And suddenly Hugues was able to buy the Mulberry and do the necessary renovations, which took two years, and at the end of it the Hotel Vendôme was born, to the amazement of New Yorkers, most of whom said they had never even realized that there was a hotel in that location.

The building had been a small private hospital in the 1920s and was turned into a hotel in the 1940s, with abysmally bad decor. In contrast, in its transformed state, every inch of the Vendôme was magnificent, and the service was superb. Hugues had brought chefs from all over the world for their now extremely popular restaurant. His catering manager was one of the best in the business, and everyone agreed that even the food from room service was fantastic. In its first year it had become an overnight success and was booked months in advance now, with reservations made by visitors to the city from around the world. The presidential suite was one of the finest in the city. The Hotel Vendôme was an absolute gem, with beautifully decorated suites, and rooms with fireplaces, moldings, and high ceilings. The hotel faced south, so most of the rooms were sunny, and Hugues had chosen the finest china, crystal, and linens, and as many antiques as he could afford, like the chandelier in the lobby, which he had bought in Geneva at a Christie's auction. It had come out of a French château near Bordeaux and was in perfect condition.

Hugues ran his 120-room hotel with Swiss precision, a warm smile, and an iron hand. His employees were discreet and experienced, had a remarkable memory for every guest, and kept detailed files on each important client's needs and requests while they were there. It had made the Vendôme the most popular small hotel in New York for the past three years. And the moment one entered the lobby, one knew it was a special place. A young bellboy stood at the revolving door, in a uniform inspired by those the *chasseurs* wore at the Ritz: navy pants, a short jacket, a small amount of gold braid on the collar, and a little round hat with a strap under the chin, tilted at an angle. To meet the clients' needs, there was a fleet of willing bellmen, a crew of brilliantly capable concierges. Everyone moved rapidly to serve the guests, and the entire staff was ready to service large requests and small ones. Hugues knew that impeccable service was essential.

The assistant managers wore black tailcoats and striped trousers, once again inspired by the Ritz. And Hugues himself was on hand night and day, in a dark blue suit, always with a white shirt and dark Hermès tie, and he had an extraordinary memory for everyone who had stayed with them and, whenever possible, greeted important guests himself. He was the consummate hotel owner, and no detail missed his practiced eye. And he expected his department heads to meet the standards that he set. Guests of the hotel came as much for the service as the luxurious decor.

As an added touch, the hotel was always filled with spectacular flowers, and its spa was one of the best. There was almost no service the staff wouldn't provide, as long as it was legal and in relatively good taste. And despite the objections Hugues knew his parents had had, he couldn't help feeling that they would have been proud of him now. He had used their money well, and the hotel had been such a success in its first three years that he was almost out of debt. It wasn't surprising, since Hugues worked day and night himself to make it what it was. And personally, his victory had come at a high price. Owning the hotel had cost him his wife. It had been the subject of considerable gossip among staff and guests.

Nine years before, when Hugues had been working at

Claridge's in London, he had met Miriam Vale, the internationally famous and spectacularly beautiful super-model. And like everyone else who laid eyes on her, he had been dazzled by her the moment they met. He had been infinitely proper and professional, as he had always been with guests of the hotels he worked in, but she was a twenty-three-year-old girl, and she had made it clear that she wanted him, and he fell head over heels in love with her overnight. She was American, and eventually he had followed her back to New York. It had been an exciting time for him, and he took a lesser position at the Plaza to be in the same city with her and continue their romance. And much to his own amazement, she was just as much in love with him, and they were married within six months. He had never been happier in his life than in their early years together.

Eighteen months later their daughter Heloise was born, and Hugues was madly in love with his wife and child. He trembled when he said it, for fear of angering the gods, but he always said then that he had the perfect life. And he was a dedicated man. Despite whatever temptations came his way in the hotel business, he was totally in love with and faithful to his wife. She continued her modeling career after Heloise was born, and everyone at the Plaza had fawned over his little girl and indulged her, and teased them about her name. Hugues assured them honestly that she had been named after his great-grandmother and he didn't expect to stay at the Plaza forever, so there was no reason not to use the name. Heloise was two years old when he bought the Mulberry and turned it into the Vendôme. He had everything he wanted then, a wife and child he loved, and his own hotel. Miriam had been far less enthused about the project and had complained bitterly that it would take too much of his time, but owning his own hotel, and one of the sort he was creating, had always been his dream.

His parents had been even less pleased about Miriam than they had been about his working in the hotel business. They had serious doubts that a spoiled, twenty-three-year-old, spectacularly beautiful, internationally known supermodel would make him a good wife. But Hugues loved her profoundly and had no doubts.

As Hugues had expected, it took two years to renovate the hotel. It came in only slightly over budget, and the end result was everything he had hoped.

He and Miriam had been married for six years, and Heloise was four, when the Hotel Vendôme opened, and Miriam had obligingly posed for some of their ads. It added a distinctive cachet that the owner was married to Miriam Vale, and male guests in particular always hoped they'd catch a glimpse of her in the lobby or at the bar. What they saw far more frequently than her mother was four-year-old Heloise following after her father, with one of the maids holding her hand, and she enchanted everyone she met. She had gone from being Heloise at the Plaza to being Heloise at the Vendôme, and became something of a mascot for the hotel, and was clearly the pride and joy of her father's life.

Greg Bones, the famous and notoriously badly behaved rock star, was one of the first guests in one of the penthouse suites, and fell in love with the hotel. Hugues was uneasy about it, because Bones was well known for trashing hotel rooms and causing chaos wherever he stayed, but he behaved surprisingly well at the Vendôme, much to Hugues's relief. And they were fully prepared to meet celebrity needs and requests.

On Greg's second day there, he met Miriam Vale Martin at the bar, surrounded by assistants, magazine editors, stylists, and a famous photographer after a shoot. They had just finished a twelve-page spread for *Vogue* that afternoon, and as soon as they recognized Greg Bones, they invited him to join them. And what happened afterward hadn't taken long. Miriam spent most of the following night in Greg's suite with him, while Hugues thought she was out when he was working. The maids were all aware of where she was and what had happened – the room service waiters discovered it when Greg ordered champagne and caviar for them at midnight. And it rapidly became the backstairs talk of the hotel and spread like a forest fire. By the end of the week Hugues had heard about it too. He didn't know whether to confront her or to hope it would pass.

Hugues, Miriam, and Heloise had their own private apartment one floor below the two penthouse suites, and the hotel security were well aware that Miriam was constantly slipping up the back stairs to join Greg in his suite, whenever Hugues was in his office. It was an extremely awkward situation for Hugues, who didn't want to ask the famous rock star to leave the hotel. It would cause a public scandal. Instead he begged his wife to come to her senses and behave. He suggested she go away for a few days, to stop the madness of what she was doing. But when Bones checked out, she flew to Los Angeles with him on his private plane. She left Heloise with Hugues and promised she'd be back in a few weeks, and said this was something she had to get out of her system, and begged him to understand. It was a heartbreak and humiliation for Hugues, but he didn't want to lose his wife. He hoped that if he let her do it, she'd get over her infatuation quickly. She was twenty-nine years old, and he thought she'd come to her senses. He loved her, and they had a child. But it was all over the tabloids by then, and on Page Six of the *New York Post*. It was a crushing humiliation for Hugues, in front of all of his employees and an entire city.

Hugues told Heloise that her mother had to go away to work, which was something that the little girl already understood at four. The story became harder to maintain when Miriam didn't come home. And three months later, back in London with Greg Bones, Miriam told him she was filing for divorce. It had been the most devastating moment of his life, and although his demeanor with the guests was unchanged, and he was ever smiling and attentive to them, in the three years since, those who knew him well were aware that he had never been the same again. He was far more aloof, serious, deeply hurt, and withdrawn in his private moments, although he put a good face on it for his staff and guests.

Hugues had been the soul of discretion since the divorce. His assistant and some of his department heads were aware of quiet affairs he had had, occasionally with hotel guests or with well-bred or accomplished women around the city. He was one of the most sought-after bachelors in New York, invited to everything, although he rarely accepted. He preferred to keep a low profile, and keep his personal life to himself. And most of the time he was working at the hotel. The hotel came before all else for him, except for his daughter, who came first. He hadn't had a serious relationship since Miriam left and didn't want one. He believed that to run a hotel properly, you had to sacrifice your own life. He was always there, keeping an eye on everything, and working incredible hours, most of the time behind the scenes to ensure the smooth running of the hotel.

A month after her divorce from Hugues was final, Miriam married Greg Bones, and they had been married now for two years and had just had a baby girl six months before. Heloise had only seen her mother a few times since she left. Heloise was sad about it. And Hugues was angry at Miriam. She was too busy in her new life, too obsessed with Greg, and now their child, to tend to their daughter or even see her. Heloise and Hugues had become relics of her past. It left Hugues no other choice but to be both mother and father to their child. He never commented on it to Heloise, but he considered it a painful circumstance for them both.

At the hotel Heloise was constantly surrounded by doting surrogate mothers, at the concierge desk, in room service, the maids, the florist, the hairdresser, and the girls who worked in the spa. *Everyone* loved Heloise. They were no substitute for a real mother, but at least she had a happy life, adored her father, and at seven she was the princess of the Hotel Vendôme. Their regular guests knew her, and once in a while brought her little gifts, and thanks to her father's attention to her education and manners, she was both adorable and extremely polite. She wore pretty little smocked dresses, and the hairdresser did her long red hair in braids with ribbons every day before she went to school at the Lycée Français nearby. Her father walked her to school every morning before he started work. Her mother called her once every month or two, if she remembered.

Hugues was at the front desk in the evening, as he often was when he had time away from other tasks, surveying the scene in the lobby, and greeting guests discreetly. He always knew exactly who was staying at the hotel. He checked the reservation ledgers daily, was aware of who was there, when they arrived, and when they'd be departing. And there was the familiar aura of calm in the lobby as guests were checking in. Mrs. Van Damme, a well-known aristocratic dowager, had just come in from her evening walk with her Pekingese, and Hugues walked her slowly to the elevator as he chatted with her. She had moved into one of the largest suites in the hotel the year before, and brought some of her own furniture with her, and some very important works of art. She had a son in Boston who seldom visited her, and she was extremely fond of Hugues, and Heloise had become the grand-daughter she'd never had, having only grandsons, including one the same age as Heloise. She often spoke to Heloise in French, since Heloise went to the Lycée Français, and Heloise loved to join her on her walks with her dog. They would walk slowly, and Mrs. Van Damme would tell her stories of when she was a little girl. Heloise adored her.

'Where's Heloise?' Mrs. Van Damme asked with a warm smile, as the elevator man waited for them, and Hugues chatted with her for a few minutes. He always made time for the guests. No matter how busy he was, he never looked it.

'Doing her homework upstairs, I hope.' And if not, they both knew she was probably roaming the hotel, visiting her friends. She loved pushing the maids' carts, and distributing the lotions and shampoos, and they always gave her spares.

'If you see her, tell her to come and have tea with me when she's finished,' Mrs. Van Damme said with a smile. Heloise often did that, and they shared tea sandwiches of cucumber or egg salad, and éclairs from room service.

They had a British chef, originally from Claridge's, who was in charge of only their high tea, which was the best in the city, even though their main chef was French, and had been personally recruited by Hugues too. He had his hand in every aspect of the hotel, whether 'front of the house' or back. It was all part of what made the Hotel Vendôme so special. The staff was trained to provide personalized attention, and it started with Hugues.

'Thank you very much, Madame Van Damme,' Hugues said politely, smiling at her, as the elevator door closed. After that he walked back through the lobby, thought of his daughter, and hoped she was doing her homework, as he had said. He had other things on his mind, although he looked so totally unruffled that no one would have suspected the chaos that was going on in the basement of the hotel at that moment. They had had several calls from guests, since they had had to shut off the water to most of the floors half an hour before. They explained that they were doing some minor repairs, and the hotel operators and desk clerks were assuring anyone who called that they expected to have the water back on within the hour. But the truth was that a pipe had burst in the basement, every engineer and plumber in the hotel was working on it, and minutes before, outside plumbers had been called.

Hugues looked calm as he reassured everyone with a smile. Seeing him, one could only assume that he had everything in control. He mentioned the water shutoff lightly to each guest who checked in. He told them that water service would be restored imminently, and asked if room service could send anything to their room. He didn't say it, but there would be no charge for it, of course, to make up for the lack of water and the inconvenience. He had preferred to stay in the lobby himself so arriving guests had a sense that all was in order. All he could hope was that the burst pipe could be located and repaired quickly. They were hoping that room service wouldn't be forced to close; the main kitchen was already swimming in six inches of water, and everyone they could spare had been sent to the basement to help. There was no sign of any of it in the lobby. He was planning to go downstairs himself in a few minutes to check the situation again. And from what he was being told, the flood in the basement was getting worse. Despite all their renovations, it was after all an old hotel.

As Hugues greeted a Spanish aristocrat and his wife, just arriving from Europe, the scene in the basement was one of utter chaos. No one observing the calm appearance of elegance in the lobby could have suspected what a mess it was downstairs.

In the basement men were shouting, the water was rising, and a torrent of water burst from a wall, as engineers in brown uniforms waded through the flood, and were soaked from head to foot. Four plumbers were working on it, and all six of the hotel's engineers had been called back into work. Mike, the head engineer, was close to where the torrent was coming from, and working like a demon to try and locate the source. He had a belt around his waist with a series of wrenches hanging from it, and as he tried one after another, a small voice behind him told him to try the biggest one. He turned in surprise as he heard the familiar voice over the ruckus, and saw Heloise standing there, watching him with interest. She was up to her knees in water, wearing a red bikini and a yellow slicker, and she pointed to the biggest wrench on his belt.

'I think you have to use the big one, Mike,' she said calmly, standing very close to him, with her big green eyes and bright red hair still in neat braids. He could see that her feet were bare beneath the water.

'Okay,' he acknowledged, 'but I want you to go stand over there. I don't want you to get hurt.' She nodded very seriously and then smiled at him. She had freckles and was missing both her front teeth.

'It's okay, Mike, I can swim,' she reassured him.

'I hope you won't have to,' he said, grabbing the biggest wrench from his belt, which he had been about to use anyway. Whatever went on in the hotel, Heloise was always there to see it. And she particularly loved hanging out with the engineers. He pointed to where she should stand, and she obediently went to higher ground and chatted with some of the kitchen staff who had come out to see what they could do to help. And with that the outside plumbers arrived and waded into the rising water to join the others. A number of the bellmen came down to carry bottles of expensive wine out of the wine cellars, and the kitchen staff joined them to help.

Half an hour later, after intense work by both the engineers and outside plumbers, the leak was located, the right valves were turned off, and the plumbers were working on the repair. Heloise waded back in to see Mike then, patted his shoulder, and told him he had done a really great job. He laughed as he looked down at her, picked her up, walked her back to the sous chefs in their tall white hats, white jackets, and checked pants standing just outside the kitchen, and set her down.

'If you get hurt, young lady, your father will kill me. I want you to stay here.' He knew the directive was useless. Heloise never stayed in one place for long.

'There's nothing for me to do here,' she complained.

'Room service is too busy. I'm not supposed to disturb them.' She knew not to get in their way during peak hours.

By then the desk was getting frantic calls. People who wanted to get dressed for the evening were discovering they had no water to bathe or shower with, and anyone calling room service was told that they were extremely busy, and all orders were delayed, but the hotel was offering free wine or drinks. Hugues knew that an event like this could seriously damage the reputation of a hotel, unless handled with grace and poise. He called all of their most important guests himself to apologize and asked the catering manager to send a complimentary bottle of Cristal to each of their rooms, and he was fully prepared to discount the rate for every room affected, for that night. He knew that it would cost him, but it would cost him far more not to. Problems could occur in any hotel, but how they were handled made all the difference between a second-rate hotel and a first-class hotel like the Vendôme, which was what they called a 'palace' in Europe. So far no one was truly furious at them, people were just annoyed, and happy with the free wine and champagne. How they ultimately felt about the inconvenience would depend on how fast it was going to take the plumbers and engineers to make the repairs.

They had to do the best they could that night, and in the ensuing days they would have to make more extensive efforts to replace the broken pipe. Right now, all they needed was water for the hotel, to get service back to normal.

Forty-five minutes later Hugues was finally able to slip away from the front desk and went down to the basement to see what was happening there. Pumps had already been set up to bail the water, and a cheer went up just as he arrived. The plumbers had been able to do what was necessary to circumvent the pipe and turn the water back on. The room service staff were working frantically to deliver bottles of wine and champagne to the guests. Heloise was dancing around in the water in her slicker and bikini, grinning happily minus her front teeth, and clapping her hands. And the moment she saw him, she waded over to her father, who looked at her with a rueful expression. He wasn't happy to see her there, but he wasn't surprised, and the sous chefs she'd been talking to all laughed. Heloise was always where the action was, just like her father. She was as much a part of the hotel as he was.

'What are you doing down here?' her father asked her, trying to sound stern but without much success. She looked so cute that it was hard for him to be angry at her,

27

and he very rarely was, even though he prided himself on being strict. But he could never quite pull it off. Just looking at her melted his heart, and her missing front teeth made her even more irresistible, and she made him want to laugh in her red bathing suit and yellow slicker. She had dressed for the occasion. Since her mother had left, he helped her dress for school every morning.

'I came down to see what I could do to help,' she said practically. 'Mike did a wonderful job. There was nothing for me to do.' She gave a little shrug of her shoulders as her father laughed. People always commented that she looked very European.

'I hope not,' her father said, trying not to laugh. 'If you're the chief engineer now, we're in big trouble.' As he said it, he walked her back into the kitchen, and then went to congratulate his plumbers and engineers for their good work. He was always deft at handling his staff, and they liked working for him, although he could be tough at times. He expected a great deal of them and himself, and everyone agreed that he ran a tight ship. It was his training and what the hotel guests loved; they could rely on a high standard of excellence if they stayed at the Vendôme. Hugues ran it to perfection.

When he came back to the kitchen, Heloise was eating a cookie and chatting with the pastry chef in French. He always made her French *macarons*, and she took them to school for lunch. 'What about your homework, young lady? What happened to that?' her father asked her seriously, and Heloise opened her eyes wide and shook her head.

'I don't have any, Papa.'

'Why is it that I don't believe you?' He looked carefully into the big green eyes.

'I did it all before.' She was lying to him, but he knew her well. She much preferred cruising around the hotel to sitting in the apartment alone doing her homework for the Lycée.

'I saw you in my office making paper clip necklaces when you got back from school. I think you'd better check again.'

'Well, maybe I have just a little math to do,' she said sheepishly, as he took her hand in his own and led her to the back elevator. She had left a pair of red clogs there when she waded into the flood and retrieved them now for the ride upstairs.

As soon as they arrived in the apartment, Hugues changed his suit and shoes. The cuffs of his trousers, and his shoes, were soaked from his brief visit to the basement. He was a tall, thin man with dark hair and the same green eyes as Heloise's. Her mother was an equally tall blonde with blue eyes. The great-grandmother that Heloise had been named after had had red hair like Heloise.

Hugues wrapped her in a towel and told her to change her clothes, and she reappeared a few minutes later in blue jeans and a pink sweater and pink ballet shoes. She took ballet class twice a week. Hugues wanted her to lead the life of a normal child, but he was well aware that she didn't. Without a mother, her life was already unusual, and her entire world consisted of the hotel. She loved everything that happened there.

With a mournful look at her father, she sat down at the desk in the living room, once she was dressed, and took out her math book, and the notebook from school.

'Make sure you do all of it. And call me when you're finished. I'll come up and have dinner with you if I can. I have to make sure everything has calmed down first.'

'Yes, Papa,' she said quietly as he left the apartment to go back to the reception desk and check on things there.

Heloise sat looking dreamily at her math book for a few minutes, and then tiptoed to the door. She opened it a crack and looked out. The coast was clear. He was back in the lobby by then. And with an elfin toothless grin that made her look like a pixie with her freckles and red hair, Heloise let herself out of the apartment and slipped down the back stairs in her jeans and pink ballet shoes. She knew just where her favorite night maids would be. And five minutes later she was helping them push the trolley with all the creams and shampoos and lotions on it, as they turned down the rooms for the guests. She loved turn-down time, when they delivered little boxes of chocolates to each guest, from La Maison du Chocolat. The chocolates were delicious, and as they always did, Ernesta and Maria handed one of the boxes to her, and after thanking them, she helped herself to the chocolates with a grin.

'We had a lot of work to do in the basement today,' she informed them seriously in Spanish. They had been teaching her Spanish ever since she could talk. She had been fluent in both French and Spanish as well as English before she was five. It was important to Hugues that she speak several languages. And he spoke Italian and German too, since he was Swiss.

'So I hear,' Ernesta, the motherly Puerto Rican woman, said to her and gave her a hug. Heloise loved being with her and held her hand. 'You must have been very busy this afternoon,' Ernesta said with a twinkle in her eye, as Maria, the pretty young second night maid, laughed. She had children of her own the same age as Heloise. And they never minded having her join them for their turn-down service to every room. She was always hungry for female companionship and got lonely alone in the apartment.

'The water was up to here,' Heloise said, showing them a place just above her knees. 'But it's all fixed now.' Both women knew there would have to be more extensive repairs in the coming days. They had heard it from the engineers.

'What about your homework?' Ernesta asked her then, as Heloise avoided her gaze and played with the shampoos. They had recently changed brands to a more luxurious one, and Heloise loved the way it smelled. 'Did you do it?'

'Yes, of course,' Heloise said, grinning mischievously, as they pushed the cart to the next room, and Heloise handed her two more shampoos. She followed them on their rounds until an internal alarm went off for her, and she knew it was time to go. She kissed them both good night then and scampered up the back stairs, just in time to get back to their apartment and sit at the desk again. She had just finished her last math problem, when her father walked in to have dinner with her. He had ordered it from room service, as he always did, although later than usual tonight. Her schedule had to be flexible to adjust to his, but having dinner together was a ritual that was important to them both.

'Sorry I'm late,' he said as he walked in. 'It's a little crazy downstairs tonight, but at least everyone has water again.' He was just praying they didn't spring another leak, but things were holding for now, as long as they did the necessary repairs soon.

'What's for dinner?' Heloise asked as she closed her math book.

'Chicken, mashed potatoes, asparagus, and ice cream for dessert. Sound okay to you?' her father asked her with a loving look.

'Perfect,' she smiled at him as she put her arms around his neck. She was the woman in his life, and had been the only important one for the past three years since her mother left. And as he hugged her, their dinner arrived. The chef had added escargots for Heloise, because he knew she loved them, and profiteroles for dessert. It was hardly an ordinary dinner for a child, but it was one of the perks of living in the hotel, for both of them. Hugues had built-in babysitters for her, and they both had all the services that the hotel provided, including gourmet food.

They sat down properly in the dining room of the apartment, and they talked about the hotel, as they always did. She asked him what important guests had checked in, and if any movie stars were coming soon, and he told her a simplified but accurate version of what he had done that day, as she looked at him adoringly. He liked teaching her about the hotel. And with Heloise to love, and the hotel to keep him busy, Hugues needed nothing more in his life; nor did Heloise. They lived in a sheltered world that suited them both to perfection. She had lost a mother, and he a wife, but they had each other, and that seemed like more than enough for now. And in his fantasies about the future, Hugues liked to think that when she grew up, they would run the hotel together. Until then they lived in the hotel that had been his dream.

Chapter 2

Hugues had structured the hotel in the traditional way he had learned at the École Hôtelière and at all the important hotels where he had worked. And he made good use of his staff. He had a back office, which handled all the business aspects of running the hotel, reservations, sales, marketing, and accounting, all functions that were vital to the operation of the hotel. The human resources staff were part of the back office too, and they dealt not only with the employees but with the labor unions, which was crucial. A strike could cripple the hotel. Hugues had picked his staff with infinite care and knew full well how important they were. If reservations weren't diligently handled with minute precision, and carefully kept track of, or if accounting was inaccurate, it could put them out of business. And he kept a careful eye on all the administrative aspects of the hotel. He had a profound respect for how important the back office was, despite the fact that their guests never saw any of those people, but the smooth running of the hotel depended on the competence of the administrative staff, and he had chosen them well.

The front desk and concierges worked hand in hand and were key faces that the hotel guests saw on a constant basis. Without a smoothly run reception desk, and supremely competent concierges, his guests would have swiftly shifted their allegiance to other better-run hotels. Among the many functions they performed, they had to meet the sometimes-exotic needs of their VIP and celebrity hotel guests. They were used to movie stars, who insisted on changing suites three and four times until they found the one that pleased them, had their assistants send long lists of special dietary needs in advance, and required everything from satin sheets to orthopedic mattresses, special items for their children, air filters, hypoallergenic pillows, and masseurs to be standing by day and night. The staff were used to unusual requests and took pride in adapting to their most demanding guests. They were also accustomed to some of the more unpleasant behaviors of their VIPs, who frequently accused the maids of stealing valuable items that they had misplaced or lost themselves. In the past three years, they had not had a single case of real theft by employees, had been able to calm hysterical guests who falsely accused staff, and had proved otherwise in each instance. The hotel staff had learned how to handle difficult guests and take accusations of that nature in stride. Hugues demanded criminal background checks and bonded all his employees to protect the hotel and the guests.

The housekeeping department was impeccably run by another graduate of the École Hôtelière, with a fleet of maids and valets, and a dry-cleaning operation and laundry in the basement. They were responsible for keeping the rooms and suites and hallways immaculate and their guests satisfied, again frequently with challenging demands. All of the personnel who had direct face-to-face contact with the guests had to be efficient and diplomatic, and the rooms had to pass housekeeping inspections that were conducted with military precision. Members of the housekeeping staff were let go if they did not meet the Vendôme's stringent standards.

The department that provided uniformed services was equally closely supervised and included bellmen, doormen, elevator men, valet parkers, and chauffeurs when they needed them, which they did frequently, from a limousine service that they used for many of their guests. They were responsible for getting people in and out of the hotel quickly and efficiently, with the right luggage, keeping track of arriving packages, and getting them to where they wanted to go around the city, to airports, or out of town.

Food, beverages, and catering was one of their largest departments and was responsible not only for room service, and their now-famous restaurant frequented by people from all over the city, but they dealt with all catered events that were held at the hotel: weddings, private dinners and lunches, conferences, and meetings. Food and beverage handled it all, and thus far, extremely well.

The security division was somewhat behind the scenes, but it was another vital service that Hugues relied on heavily to keep personnel in line and guests safe. Jewel robberies had become a common occurrence in many first-rate hotels, and Hugues was extremely pleased that the hotel had experienced none so far. Their staff was extremely vigilant on all aspects of security.

They had a business center, with secretaries and IT personnel available at all times. The spa and health center was one of the best in the city. Engineering and maintenance kept the hotel in working order, whether it was a crisis like the burst pipe in the basement, or something as simple as a blocked toilet or a television that wasn't working. All of it required the attention of engineers. And the other essential department was the staff that manned the telephones to keep communications in and out of and within the hotel working smoothly, taking messages properly, and handling all calls with speed, precision, and discretion.

In all, it was an enormous staff to make the hotel what it was, with Hugues overseeing everything himself. He was proud that he knew each of his employees by name, and his constant presence at the hotel kept everyone on their toes. Running the hotel was a tremendous job, and each piece of the machine, however seemingly unimportant, was actually a vital piece that allowed the hotel to function smoothly and well as a whole. And just as Hugues knew every one of his employees, so did Heloise as she roamed freely through the hotel.

The Hotel Vendôme was not only Hugues's dream but his passion, and other than his daughter, it was his love. There was so much to do there that it was hard for him to focus on much else. In the absence of Miriam, once she left him, the hotel became his wife. He often said he was married to the hotel. He ate, slept, breathed, and loved everything about it. He couldn't even imagine being married again now; he didn't have time. And any woman he got involved with realized very quickly that she was only secondary in his life, if that. He had too much else on his plate – all of which related to the smooth running of his hotel and averting crises before they happened, or solving them quickly when they did – to have time for anything other than breakfast and dinner with Heloise and a few quick hugs in between. The rest of what he did all day required his full concentration and most of his time. Heloise got what was left.

When he arrived at dinner parties, he inevitably arrived late. When he went to the theater, the opera, or the ballet, when taking out a woman, his phone vibrated on his belt all night, and too often he had to leave halfway through the performance to deal with a security issue surrounding a head of state or the Secret Service. They had to clear the floors above and below the floor occupied by a head of state. It was a hugely complicated undertaking, and he needed to make sure that the other guests were not unduly inconvenienced while they were there. It left the passing women in Hugues's life frustrated and annoyed that they could never spend an evening with him without interruptions. It was rare that he could enjoy a quiet evening with a friend, and more often than not, he didn't even try. Women staying in the hotel frequently pursued him, once they realized that he was single and saw how handsome he was. But he was always candid with them right from the beginning that he was too busy at this point in his life to get seriously involved with anyone, and they were liable to be disappointed by the little time he had to share. It was also a clever way to mask how badly he had been hurt by the failure of his marriage, and by Miriam's betrayal when she left with Greg. He had no desire to go through that again, although he enjoyed female companionship once he healed from Miriam, and frequently he couldn't resist a pretty woman, but it never lasted long. There were too many other demands on his time, and Heloise fulfilled his emotional needs better than any romance. She wasn't going to cheat on him and leave him, and she filled his heart in all the ways that mattered most to him.

'I can't compete with your daughter and your hotel,' a famous film actress had complained after dating him for a few months whenever she was in New York. She had been crazy about Hugues and sent him expensive gifts, which he quietly sent back to her. He couldn't be bought, and he knew that what he offered wasn't a fair exchange. All he wanted was an occasional lighthearted evening here and there, and on rare occasions he would slip away for a weekend, but only if Heloise was staying at a friend's. And he never involved her with the women he went out with. None of them was ever important enough for him to do so. And his affairs within the hotel had been discreet and rare. He had learned that lesson before his marriage, and he knew how disruptive it could be to get involved with someone he worked with. His early attempts in his youth had ended badly, and he almost always avoided them now, with very rare exceptions. He didn't want to get tangled up in complicated situations.

All he really wanted was to be a good father and run a great hotel, and so far he was doing well at both. It left little or no time for an important woman in his life. He was essentially unavailable in all the ways most women wanted, and rather than disappoint them, he preferred to engage lightly and move on, or steer clear of them entirely if they were too demanding or intense.

More than one of the women he had had a brief romance with had tried to turn it into more, without success. All that did was make Hugues run faster in the opposite direction. And he remembered all too clearly how agonizing it had been for him when Miriam left. He never wanted to experience that kind of pain again. He didn't consider himself relationship material, and said openly that he didn't know if he would ever be again. To some women that only provided a greater challenge, and they eventually discovered that he meant what he said. He never lied to the women he went out with. He was extremely candid right from the beginning, whether they believed him or not. And as far as Heloise was concerned, she believed she was the only woman in his life, which suited her just fine.

By the time Heloise was eight years old, she was the queen bee and mascot of the Hotel Vendôme. Her interests and pursuits were becoming a little more grown up. And although she still loved Ernesta and helping her push the turn-down cart at night, she had developed a strong friendship with their florist, Jan Livermore, whose flowers for the hotel were spectacular and artistic on a grand scale. Her gigantic arrangement in the lobby caught everyone's attention, and sometimes she let Heloise help her put it together. Heloise was spending more time with Jan now than with Mike the engineer, and becoming more of a young lady. And she loved watching Jan and her assistants do pieces for weddings, and bridal bouquets.

She had convinced Xenia the hairdresser to cut a few inches off her hair, and wore it in a long ponytail now instead of braids. Her new teeth had come in, and she was wearing braces, which only made her look more impish than ever when she smiled. She visited Mrs. Van Damme and Julius her Pekingese often, and loved walking him, for which the dowager paid her a dollar.

Heloise hung out with the phone operators, and still enjoyed pushing the trolley for the maids and checking out the new lotions and creams and shampoos. Her father's new assistant, Jennifer, pointed out to him discreetly that Heloise seemed to be craving female companionship, since she frequently sought out all the female employees and befriended them. He was aware of it too and felt badly about her mother's absence from her life. Miriam was always promising to send for her and never did. She had just had another baby with Greg Bones, this time a boy, and she was leaving Heloise more and more out of her life and rarely called. Heloise never complained about it, but he knew she was hurt. When her mother forgot her eighth birthday, she had looked crestfallen all day, and it made Hugues's heart ache just looking at her. He tried to be both mother and father to her, but it was hard to compensate for the failures of her mother.

Heloise's favorite pastime on the weekends that her father worked was slipping quietly into wedding receptions in the hotel's ballroom and mingling with the guests. She loved looking at the brides and watching them cut the cake. Hugues had caught her eye once as he walked past the ballroom himself and saw Heloise lined up with the single women to catch the bouquet. He had rapidly signaled to her and beckoned her out of the room.

'What are you doing in there?' he scolded her. 'You're not a guest!' She looked highly insulted when he said it.

'They were very nice to me. They let me have a piece of cake.' She had put on her best party dress, with a pale blue satin sash, and her shiny black patent-leather Mary Janes, and she looked crestfallen when he made her leave. 'I helped make the bouquet.' Her father shook his head, led her down the hall, and took her back to his office so she couldn't sneak back into the room. And Jennifer kept her busy after that and showed her how to use the Xerox machine. She liked Jennifer a lot, almost like an aunt.

Jennifer was a little older than Hugues. She was a widow and had two children in college, and she was very sweet to Heloise, and brought her small thoughtful gifts from time to time, like barrettes for her hair, or a game, or a pair of funny mittens with faces on them, or fluffy earmuffs. Her heart went out to her, and Hugues confided in her at times how painful it was that Miriam left Heloise out of her life now. His parents had been right, she wasn't a good wife, and she was an even worse mother, to Heloise anyway. She was far more interested in her two children with Greg Bones and her new rock star life with him. She was in the press incessantly as she followed him around. She had stopped modeling, and was constantly on tour with him, although she promised to have Heloise come to London for Christmas that year when they got back from a concert tour in Japan.

Heloise still hadn't heard from her by Thanksgiving. It was always a busy time at the hotel. The hotel was full, and several families were staying there. They had two weddings scheduled in the ballroom. A famous actress was staying at the hotel with her assistant, her hairdresser, her current boyfriend, her bodyguard, her two children and their nanny, and they had a block of suites on the tenth floor. And when she helped the maids turn down the room, Heloise had been excited when she caught a glimpse of the actress, Eva Adams. Heloise thought she was even prettier than her pictures. She had two Chihuahuas with her, and she had been very nice when Heloise asked if she could pet the dogs. She had wanted to ask for her autograph but knew that was against the rules, and that was one rule her father never permitted her to break. No one in the hotel was ever allowed to ask their celebrity guests for autographs, and he was intransigent about it. He wanted guests to feel at home and protected, not invaded by employees requesting autographs. And of course they weren't able to ask for photographs either. And no one ever broke those rules. It was one of the reasons why celebrities felt so comfortable at the hotel, because their privacy was respected, according to Hugues's orders to his staff.

'She's really pretty,' Heloise said happily as she chatted with Ernesta when they made the rounds.

'Yes, she is, and she's a lot smaller than she looks on screen.' The movie star in question looked tiny and delicate, and had a dazzling smile and enormous blue eyes. She had been lounging in the suite with her entourage when they came in, and she was very pleasant to the maids and thanked them for what they did, which wasn't always the case with movie stars. Heloise had heard many stories about how badly they behaved and how rude they were sometimes. But this one had been warm, friendly, and polite.

Heloise was still talking about her when she and Ernesta went down to the laundry with a rolling basket full of towels from the tenth floor. As Ernesta handed over the basket, Heloise noticed something sparkle in the heap of towels, and she reached in and grabbed it just before Ernesta dumped it into the big bin. Much to everyone's surprise, Heloise held up a diamond bracelet in her hand. It shimmered enticingly and looked very expensive. It was about an inch wide and was solid diamonds all the way around.

'Wow!' Heloise exclaimed as everyone stared at what she'd found.

'You'd better call security,' the head operator of the laundry told Ernesta, and she nodded and reached for the phone, but Heloise shook her head, still holding the bracelet.

'I think we should call my father.' It looked like a very fancy bracelet, even to her, and Ernesta didn't disagree. She wanted to get it into the right hands as quickly as possible. Someone was going to be reporting it as lost or stolen very soon. Guests often misplaced their valuables, and the maids were always the first to be accused. Ernesta wanted none of that. Heloise dialed her father's office, and Jennifer answered, and when she heard the story, she told them to come up. So far no one had called.

Hugues was in his office, signing some papers at his desk, when Ernesta and Heloise appeared, and his daughter held out the bracelet, and his eyes grew wide.

'Where did you find that?'

'In the towels,' Heloise said as she handed it across the desk to him, and he took a closer look at it. There was no question, it was real, and a valuable piece.

'I'll put it in the safe. Someone should be calling about

it very soon.' He smiled at Ernesta then and thanked her for her honesty, and she looked at Heloise.

'I didn't find it, sir. Your daughter did. She pulled it right out of the towels. I didn't even see it.'

'I'm glad she did,' he said, and handed it to Jennifer to put in the safe. 'Let's see what happens,' he said quietly, and much to everyone's surprise, no one called for two days. He had gone down the list of all the guests on the tenth floor, but none of them had reported the bracelet missing, and he had to wait for someone to call so it didn't wind up in the wrong hands. He wondered by then if it had been a visitor to the room and not a guest.

Then finally Eva Adams called, the movie star with the large entourage. And unlike most celebrities, she didn't report the bracelet stolen, she said that she had lost a bracelet somewhere in the last two days, and didn't know if it was in the street or at the hotel, and she wanted to let Hugues know in case someone found it. He said that a bracelet had been found and offered to come to her suite. He asked her to describe it, and it was clearly the one Heloise had found in the towels from her floor. He brought it to her room immediately, and she was thrilled. He didn't ask but guessed that it was worth half a million dollars or more. Maybe a million. The diamonds were large and the bracelet wide, it was a major piece of jewelry to lose, although he suspected it was probably insured. And she was ecstatic to get it back.

'Where did you find it?' she asked him as she put it back on her wrist with a look of gratitude and relief. He smiled, conscious of Eva's beauty. He had a weakness for women who looked like her, and for actresses and models in general, which had been his downfall once before.

'My daughter saw it in the towels in the laundry room. We knew it was from someone on this floor, but we had to wait for your call.'

'I had no idea where I'd lost it. I called everyplace I've been in the last two days. I didn't want to accuse anyone of taking it. I was pretty sure it must have fallen off my arm. What can I do for your daughter?' she asked, assuming that she was older than she was. She didn't make the connection with the little girl in braces who had come in with the maids two days before and asked if she could pet the Chihuahuas. She had assumed she was the maid's daughter, maybe following her mom at work over the holiday weekend. Eva hadn't paid much attention to her, although Heloise's impression was that she had been very nice. 'I'd like to give her a reward,' Eva Adams said immediately.

'That won't be necessary,' Hugues said, smiling at her. 'She's eight years old, and I wouldn't let her accept a reward. She was with one of the maids, if you'd like to give her something. But my daughter enjoys wandering around the hotel, she just likes meeting the guests and "helping" me out.' He laughed. He looked extremely handsome as he did, and Eva flirted with him a little. It was an occupational style for both of them and meant nothing.

Eva went to the desk in the room and signaled to her assistant, who rapidly brought her a checkbook. Eva sat down and wrote out a thousand-dollar check to cash for Ernesta, and handed it to Hugues. He accepted it gratefully for the maid.

'What's your daughter's name?' she asked him with interest.

'Heloise,' he said quietly, wondering what she had in mind, an autograph perhaps.

Eva Adams laughed. 'Like Eloise at the Plaza?'

'No.' He returned the smile. She seemed very human and very kind, and all of the employees who had dealt with her had said as much to him. She was a very nice woman and had caused no problem at the hotel. 'Heloise with an H. She's named for my great-grandmother, and she was born before I bought the hotel. But now she is Heloise at the Vendôme.'

'How sweet. I'd like to meet her before I leave so I can thank her myself.'

'She'd like that very much, and she's going to be very happy you got your bracelet back. She was concerned about it. We all were. It's beautiful and obviously a very special piece.'

'It's Van Cleef, and I was very upset when I thought I'd lost it. Heloise is pretty terrific to have found it. I'd like to see her before we go back to L.A. tomorrow, if you don't mind.'

'I'll be happy to arrange it,' he said discreetly, and left the room a few minutes later. He told Heloise about it that afternoon, and that Miss Adams wanted to see her the next day. Heloise was thrilled to hear it, and ran to find Ernesta to tell her the news that the bracelet had been claimed. The maid already had the check by then and was delighted with the reward.

'I should give it to you,' Ernesta said fairly, but Heloise smiled and shook her head.

'Papa wouldn't let me have it. I'm not allowed to take money from the guests, except from Mrs. Van Damme for walking Julius. He made an exception for that. So you get to keep the reward.'

Ernesta had a thousand uses for it and was smiling broadly as she went back to work turning down the rooms. Miss Adams and her entourage were out, or she would have thanked her herself. Instead she left a note on her pillow with an extra box of chocolates.

And the next morning Hugues reminded Heloise that she had to put on a nice dress and her party shoes because Miss Adams wanted to meet her to thank her before she checked out. And checkout was at one P.M.

Eva Adams called Hugues in his office at noon and asked him if he would bring Heloise to her suite. He called Heloise in their apartment and told her to get ready, and she was when he got there. She was wearing a pale blue smocked dress that she had worn several times to weddings and her Mary Janes with short white socks. She looked very pretty, and she had put a ribbon in her hair, and was excited to meet the movie star again.

Eva Adams opened the door to them herself and greeted Heloise with a broad smile and bent down to kiss her, with a quick glance at her father over her head. Heloise blushed nearly the color of her hair and looked at her in open adoration.

'You are one terrific kid, do you know that? You found my bracelet, Heloise. I thought it was gone forever.' As she smiled at her, she handed her a very large box and a small one, and Heloise stood staring at her in amazement.

'Thank you,' she said without opening either of them. All the people in Miss Adams's suite were rushing around getting ready to leave, the dogs were barking, and one of the children was crying. It didn't seem like the right time and place to open the gifts, and she didn't seem to expect it, so Heloise thanked her and kissed her on the cheek, and she and her father left and went back to their apartment, so she could open the gifts that Eva Adams had given her. She was a little overwhelmed by the experience of meeting her and being thanked so profusely. And she opened the big package first, while her father watched her. He was relieved that the bracelet had been found. They didn't need a scandal at the hotel, that a major piece of jewelry had disappeared at the Vendôme. Heloise had done not only Eva Adams a good turn but her father as well, and Ernesta with the reward.

Heloise tore off the paper and pulled open the box. There was tissue paper inside, and when she removed it, she saw the most beautiful doll she had ever seen. She had a delicate face and looked a little bit like Heloise. Miss Adams had inquired at the desk and been told that Heloise had red hair, and so did the doll. She was beautifully dressed and had several changes of clothes, and long silky real hair that Heloise could comb. She took the doll out of the box and stared at it in awe, and then she clutched it to her and looked at her father, and he smiled as he watched.

'She's very pretty. What are you going to call her?'

'Eva. I'm going to take her with me when I visit Mommy.' It was the prettiest doll she'd ever had. She couldn't wait to show all her friends in the hotel. It was a suitable reward for an eight-year-old girl. And then she remembered the much smaller box. It was a small velvet box, and she opened it and saw a small diamond heart on a chain inside it, and inside the heart was the letter H, for her name. She was even more stunned than by the doll, and her father put it around her neck. It was small enough not to be shocking on a child her age, but it was a beautiful and obviously expensive gift.

'Wow, Papa!' she said, bereft of words, as she looked at herself in the mirror, still holding the doll close to her.

'Why don't we go down to the lobby and say goodbye to Miss Adams when she leaves? You can thank her then for the gifts, and write her a thank-you letter for when she gets home.' Heloise nodded and followed him out of the apartment, holding the doll and wearing the necklace, and only minutes after they reached the lobby, Eva Adams and her entourage appeared, and Heloise stepped forward shyly to thank her, and Eva bent and kissed her again. She was wearing the bracelet, and had on an enormous sable coat and hat and diamond earrings on her ears. And she looked every bit the movie star as she swept through the door to the street. The paparazzi who'd been there all week went crazy outside, and hotel security helped Eva and her party into two limousines as rapidly as they could. Heloise and her father stood on the sidewalk and waved as they drove away, and he put an arm around his daughter as they walked back into the hotel. Heloise was beaming and knew she'd never forget her as she wandered into her father's office. Jennifer smiled at her.

'That was pretty exciting. What are you going to do for the rest of the day?' Jennifer said warmly after admiring Heloise's new necklace.

'Eva and I are going to a wedding in the ballroom at three.'

Her father looked up at her from his desk with a serious expression. 'I don't want either of you asking for cake or catching the bouquet. Is that understood?'

'Yes, Papa.' Heloise smiled broadly at him. 'We'll be good, I promise.' And with that she left his office, carrying the doll, to cruise the hotel and show her two rewards from Eva Adams to all her friends.

'That was sweet of her,' Hugues commented to Jennifer after his daughter left, thinking of how beautiful the actress was and how kind to his daughter.

'It was only fair,' Jennifer said. 'That was quite a piece of jewelry she almost lost, even if it was insured.' And she was happy too that Heloise had gotten such pretty gifts.

'I have to do something about her going to all the weddings,' Hugues commented with a worried look. 'One of these days someone will complain.'

'I think she's fine,' his assistant reassured him. 'She's very well behaved. She always dresses appropriately. And she's awfully cute.' He didn't disagree.

Miriam finally contacted Hugues at the last minute to set up Heloise's trip to London for Christmas. Heloise had been worried that her mother wouldn't call, but at last she did. She took the doll with her when Hugues put her on a plane to London the day before Christmas Eve. It was the first time she would be spending Christmas with her mother since she left four years before.

Hugues was nervous about her going, but he thought he should at least try to keep her mother in her life. She only had one mother, even if Miriam wasn't attentive to her. He hated it when Miriam upset or disappointed their daughter. She was thoughtless and selfish more than she was intentionally cruel. Heloise was going to be there for two weeks if all went well, and he hoped it would.

He hadn't laid eyes on his ex-wife since the divorce and didn't want to. In all fairness, she had demanded no money from him since she was still making a lot of money from modeling then, and she had married Greg almost immediately after the divorce. And she hadn't wanted custody of Heloise even then. All she wanted was Greg. She had been obsessed with him, and from what Hugues saw in the press, if it could be relied on, she still was. And now she had two children with him.

Poor Heloise had been abandoned by her mother and left out. And no matter what Hugues did or said to put a balm on it, inevitably it was still a wound for the child. But selfishly, in some ways, he knew it was easier for him to have Heloise to himself. Legally he had sole custody, and in reality it was as though she had no mother at all, except for the pain in Heloise's eyes when she talked about her, which cut through her father's heart like a knife every time he saw it.

When the plane landed in London, their driver was waiting for Heloise with a Bentley. He took charge of Heloise's luggage and chatted with her on the way to their house in Holland Park. Heloise had slept on the plane, and she was holding her doll on the ride to the house. It gave her comfort and made her feel less scared.

The driver walked her up the front steps, and a butler let them in, and he smiled as soon as he saw her and walked her upstairs to a sunny sitting room where

Miriam was nursing her infant son. Her eighteen-month-old daughter was careening wildly through a sea of toys.

Heloise hadn't seen her mother in a year but was used to her new look from pictures in magazines. Miriam was in *People* magazine all the time, and Heloise kept them all. Since leaving Hugues, she had dyed her hair white blond and cut it short. She had a row of diamonds in pierces up her ears, and she had tattoos on both arms. She was wearing a T-shirt and tight black leather jeans. She held an arm out to Heloise as she nursed the baby, whom Heloise had not seen before. She had met her half-sister Arielle the year before, and she squealed with delight when she saw Heloise's doll.

'What a pretty doll.' Miriam smiled at her as though she were someone else's child.

'Eva Adams gave her to me. I found her diamond bracelet that she'd lost in some towels,' Heloise explained almost shyly. Her mother became more of a stranger to her every time they met. Miriam had replaced her with two babies by a man she loved. Heloise was the reminder of a life and man she wanted to forget. And Heloise had no mother figure to replace her with, except the people who worked at the hotel. The only real parent she had now was her father. And she missed having a mom to cuddle up with, even though she loved her father.

Miriam leaned over and kissed her then, over the baby's head. He looked up at Heloise with interest, and then went back to nursing. He was a chubby, happy-looking baby. His older sister Arielle climbed into her mother's lap then, cuddling her mother and brother. There was no room for Heloise in her mother's arms, or her life. And a few minutes later Greg walked in and looked surprised to see Heloise as he glanced at his wife.

'I forgot you were coming,' he said to Heloise in a heavy cockney accent. He had far more tattoos than Miriam and 'sleeves' of them on both arms, and he was wearing jeans and a T-shirt and black cowboy boots. They were completely different from anyone in Heloise's world, certainly her father, although she occasionally saw rock stars at the hotel. But she couldn't even imagine her mother with her father now. She had no memory of the time when they'd been married, and they were totally different from each other. Miriam looked almost identical to Greg and in total harmony with him.

Greg was pleasant to Heloise, although she never felt totally at ease with him. He smoked heavily, used bad language, and had a drink in his hand most of the time. Hugues had warned Miriam that he didn't want any drugs around Heloise while she was with them, and she promised that there wouldn't be, although Greg usually smoked dope openly at home. She asked him not to during Heloise's visit, and he said he'd try to remember, although he had a joint in his hand most of the time.

They celebrated Christmas Eve together the next night, and her mother gave her a black leather jacket that was too big and a black Chanel watch with diamonds on the face that was unsuitable for a child her age and showed how little she knew her. Even a stranger like Eva Adams had chosen better gifts for her. Greg gave her a small guitar that she didn't know how to play, and they went to visit his parents in Wimbledon on Christmas Day.

And after that Heloise hardly saw them. Greg was recording, and Miriam sat in on the sessions with him and took the baby with her so she could nurse him, and they left Heloise at home with the nanny and Arielle. And after recording Greg and Miriam went out with his band almost every night. She made no effort to take Heloise anywhere, and when Hugues called to see how she was, Heloise said politely that she was having a nice time. She didn't know what else to say and didn't want to be disloyal to the mother she hardly ever saw and was afraid to lose entirely.

So she spent most of her time playing with Arielle, and with baby Joey when he was home. And the nanny was pleasant to her. She took Heloise to Harrods to shop for some clothes, and to Hyde Park, and to the stables of Buckingham Palace and the changing of the guard.

Heloise spent most of the week at the house, wishing she were home. She felt out of place and as though she were a guest and not part of the family. They made no effort to make her feel included, and sometimes they forgot that she was there, until the nanny reminded them. And on New Year's Day Heloise got in an argument with her mother, who was telling Greg how much she had hated living at the hotel, and what a bore it was, and even more so during the endless two years before that when Hugues had been renovating it, and what a drag it was, and so was Hugues.

'It's not a drag, and Papa isn't either,' Heloise shouted unexpectedly, as Miriam stared at her in surprise. She was normally so docile that Heloise even surprised herself with her own vehemence. 'The hotel is beautiful, and it's even prettier now, and Papa does a wonderful job,' she hotly defended it, and her father. He worked so hard to make everything perfect, and Heloise thought it was. It was her home, and she hated Miriam criticizing it to Greg, and even more so her father.

'I just didn't like living there,' Miriam explained. 'All those people around all the time, and your father was always too busy to spend time with me. Not like Greg,' she said.

Tears sprang to Heloise's eyes. She hated hearing her father criticized and compared to Greg. It had been a hard week for her, feeling like a stranger in their house and lives, with two babies who had taken her place in her mother's heart. Miriam made no secret of it, and it was obvious to everyone, including Heloise. The butler and nanny had talked about it quietly, that Heloise was always ignored or left out, but Greg and Miriam didn't seem to know or care. The servants all felt sorry for the little girl, and they thought she was a genuinely nice kid. She told them all kinds of funny stories about her father's hotel.

'I love living at the hotel,' Heloise said to her mother, in response to what she'd said to Greg. 'Everyone is really nice to me, and all kinds of important people stay at the hotel. Like Eva Adams, and other movie stars and senators, and the president even stayed there once. And the president of France.' She wanted to impress them, but she knew she couldn't. Nothing she or her father did mattered to them. They were only interested in each other, their babies and themselves.

She ran to her room in tears after that, and the nanny came to console her and brought her hot chocolate to make her feel better. Heloise told her about the English high tea they served at the hotel, and the nanny said it sounded wonderful to her, and that she was sure the hotel was beautiful. She felt sorry for the little girl.

Heloise had been there for ten days when Hugues called her again. Although he missed her fiercely, he had tried to refrain from calling so he didn't interfere, but he hated the forlorn way that Heloise sounded when she came to the phone. He asked if she was having fun, and she burst into tears and said she wanted to come home. She was lonely in her mother's house. He promised to work it out with her mother, and called Miriam that night. She said she thought it was a good idea for Heloise to leave too, she said she really didn't have time to spend with her, since Greg was recording his new album and she wanted to be with him. Hugues said politely that he was sure that Heloise would understand, and she needed to get ready for school. She didn't, and it was a weak excuse, but Miriam rapidly agreed and promised to put Heloise on a flight to New York the next day.

The visit had obviously been a bust, and Hugues was sad for his daughter and ached to hold her in his arms and give her a hug. She was so vastly loved and so essential in his life, and so superfluous and irrelevant in her mother's, and Heloise was well aware of it. She wasn't old enough to see it as a deficiency in Miriam and a fatal flaw in her character; she felt it only as a rejection, and all she wanted now was to go home. She didn't belong here, and they had made that clear to her.

Miriam kissed her the next morning after breakfast and told her to have a safe trip back, then left for the studio in the Bentley with baby Joey in her arms. And Greg forgot to say goodbye to her when he left. The butler and nanny took Heloise to the airport, and both gave her warm hugs. The butler gave her a sweater with a British flag on it in colored rhinestones, in the right size, which she loved. And the nanny gave her a pink sweatshirt. They waved as she went through security, and she smiled back at them and then disappeared with someone from the airline escorting her to the plane.

Hugues had upgraded her to first class as a special treat. She watched two movies on the flight and slept for a while, and then they landed in New York, and she was escorted through customs and taken to her father, who was waiting anxiously for her. And before he could say a word, she threw herself into his arms and clung to him. There were tears in his eyes when he saw her, and she squealed with delight and hugged him till he nearly choked.

She said nothing about her mother on the drive back from the airport. She didn't want to betray her or be disloyal to her. She knew it wouldn't have been right. But the moment they reached the hotel, she flew through the doors and stood smiling broadly as she looked around. She looked up at her father as though she had returned from another planet, and she was so happy she couldn't stop smiling as she saw the familiar faces in the world she knew and loved, and where everyone loved her. She was home.

Chapter 3

For the next four years Hugues continued to develop and improve the hotel, and to build on its success. It became everyone's favorite venue for fashionable weddings, a favorite destination of knowledgeable jet-set travelers, politicians, and heads of state. The president of France was one of their more frequent guests, as well as the British prime minister, and the American vice president, and numerous senators and congressmen. Hugues's staff handled the related security challenges flawlessly and made everything easy for the guests. Ten years after he bought the hotel, eight after he opened it, the Hotel Vendôme was an undeniable success and favorite haunt of the elite from all over the world.

His personal life didn't change during that time,

despite several brief affairs he managed to squeeze in between hotel association meetings, negotiations with labor unions, and overseeing improvements made to the hotel. And Heloise remained the bright star of his world.

At twelve, Heloise was still the princess of the Hotel Vendôme. She had started working for Jennifer in her father's office, doing small tasks, and organizing things for her, and she still loved helping Jan the florist and looking things up at the concierge desk when they were swamped, like the addresses of restaurants and obscure stores the guests asked for. She enjoyed spending most of her spare time at the hotel. She was in that no-man's-land between childhood and adolescence, when her interests were still focused at home and not yet fully directed at the outside world or consumed by boys. And in her case 'home' was a very interesting place. She stood next to her father sometimes in the lobby when he greeted important guests, and when she met the president of France she was a hero at the Lycée Français for several days.

Occasionally she invited girls from school to spend the night with her in the apartment upstairs, and her friends loved cruising the hotel and checking out the kitchens, visiting room service, getting their hair done when the hairdressers had free time, or stopping in at the spa, where they always got free samples of skin and hair products and now and then a five-minute massage. Spending a night at the Vendôme with Heloise was an exciting gift for her friends, and once in a while her father sent them downtown shopping in the Rolls. Her friends all thought it was very glamorous. And sometimes they peeked in at weddings and big parties too.

Her braces had come off by then, and she was beautiful and growing tall. She still had a child's body, had lost the curl in her long hair, and she looked like a young colt when she bounded down the halls. She was still close to Jennifer, her father's assistant, as a kind of surrogate aunt and older friend and Heloise confided in her on important matters, which gave Hugues a source of additional information about what was going on in her life and head. He was relieved that she wasn't interested in boys yet and still enjoyed childish pursuits, although her beautiful doll from Eva Adams had been gently placed on a shelf in her bedroom two years ago.

She hadn't been to London to see her mother since the last, unsuccessful visit, but whenever Miriam came through New York for a day or two with Greg, she would invite Heloise to spend a night at their hotel with them. She had seen her mother three times in four years. She fantasized about what life would have been like with her, if her parents had stayed married. She couldn't imagine it, although it would have been wonderful to have a mother. Miriam was completely absorbed into her rock star husband's life and didn't seem to care about Heloise or anything she did. Only Greg and their children mattered to her. Their two children were very cute, but whenever Heloise saw them, she thought they were wild and badly behaved. She said so to Jennifer but never to her father. She knew enough not to discuss Miriam with him. Even the mention of her name shot a look of pain into his eyes. And she knew he disapproved of her and was still hurt and angry. And Heloise had loyalties to them both, although more so to her father. Her mother became more of a stranger every year.

Heloise's world consisted of her father, a hotel full of people who loved her, and a mother who seemed not to and made rare cameo appearances, like a shooting star in a summer sky. Heloise had more of a relationship with Ernesta the maid, Jan the florist, and Jennifer her father's assistant who watched over her benevolently; they were all loving role models for her, better than her mother, Hugues knew. There had been a story in the tabloids about Miriam having a fling with a young cabana boy at a hotel in Mexico, and Greg had been arrested twice that year, once for possession of marijuana while on tour in the States and then for assault and battery when he got in a bar fight while severely inebriated. Videos of the fight and his subsequent arrest had appeared on YouTube, which Heloise admitted to Jennifer that she'd watched. She'd seen her mother in the crowd in the background at the bar, looking horrified when they dragged Greg out in handcuffs. Heloise had felt sorry for her mother, not for Greg. She told Jennifer he looked disgusting, and it seemed like he really hurt the man he hit with a vodka bottle. But apparently the man was his drummer, and the charges were dropped afterward. Hugues disliked the fact that Miriam lived in an unsavory world, but never commented on it to his daughter. He thought it would have been wrong to do so and never crossed that line with her. Jennifer was well aware of how much Miriam still upset him and what a terrible mother he thought she was, but she never mentioned it to Heloise either. She respected Hugues and Heloise too much to do so.

Hugues wanted his daughter to have good values and a wholesome, happy life. He was glad that she had no interest yet in boys, drugs, or alcohol. And although she lived in a fairly sophisticated setting at the hotel, he saw to it that she was well protected and only spent time with those he thought were good influences on her. He kept an eye on all she did, while appearing not to and seeming to be more casual and cool than he was. He was very Swiss about his child, with traditional and even conservative values and ideas for her, even if he was occasionally a little more playful himself, although always discreetly.

Heloise was completely unaware of any of the dalliances he had, and he kept it that way. He saw to it diligently that nothing of his personal life ever appeared on Page Six or anywhere else, no matter who he went out with. Jennifer teased him that he was the mystery man of the Vendôme. And his discretion always gave Heloise the impression that she was the only woman in his life. Hugues preferred it that way, since none of the women was important to him and he always knew his brief affairs wouldn't last. The only one who mattered to him was Heloise. And he thought she'd been through enough with her mother, without having to worry over the insignificant women he went out with too.

He had a penchant for women in their twenties and early thirties, always beautiful and somewhat striking, models, actresses, a few movie stars, an important heiress he met at the hotel. None of them would have been a good partner for the long haul, and he knew it, but they were fun for a night or two. And Heloise thought he hadn't dated since her mother. It was a myth he was careful to preserve, although Jennifer warned him he might regret it one day if he met someone he cared about, and

Heloise put up a strong resistance because she wasn't used to him dating and thought she was the only woman in his life. Hugues didn't agree with Jennifer's motherly or sisterly advice and said that would never happen since he couldn't even imagine being in a relationship again or falling in love.

'I'll deal with it if it happens,' he said vaguely, 'but don't hold your breath.'

'I'm not,' Jennifer said with a rueful grin. She knew him well. He was carefully defended against any woman getting past his protective armor to his heart again.

Among other solid values Hugues tried to instill in his daughter was a sense of responsibility for her fellow man, despite their comfortable surroundings. He didn't want her to think that life was only about luxury and people who lived well and were rich. And he pointed out that the wealthy had an obligation to help those less fortunate. The hotel had been donating a portion of its unused food to a local food bank since it opened. And Heloise was proud of her dad for that.

Hugues wanted her to realize how blessed she was and that there was more to life than just living in a fancy hotel. She lived in a rare and unusual world, but she had a social conscience as well. She volunteered in a soup kitchen through school, and collected toys for the fire department on her own at Christmas, asking hotel staff to donate old toys discarded by their children. She was acutely aware of how lucky she was and grateful to her father for the life they led. And she was generous with her allowance and collected money for UNICEF at school. World disasters, particularly those that affected children, went straight to her heart. More than anything, as difficult as it was in their surroundings and circumstances, Hugues wanted Heloise to have balance in her life and remain aware of those who needed help, and the suffering of mankind. She was a good girl, and more aware than many children her age.

She had been working in the florist shop all afternoon, helping Jan cut flowers and snapping thorns off stems, when she left finally and went upstairs to do her homework. She had a big assignment due at school. And there was a big wedding scheduled in the ballroom the next day that she wanted to attend. As usual, Heloise was planning to 'drop in' and check it out. Her father assumed that she had been watching the room being set up when she came in late for dinner with him that night. Everyone was talking about the wedding, which was going to cost a million dollars between flowers, catering, decor, and the bride's Chanel haute couture gown.

'Where were you?' he asked her casually as the room

service waiter brought their dinner in on a rolling tray. Hugues would have liked to cook for her himself, but he never had time. There was always some crisis he had to manage, or the constant overseeing of the hotel. The Vendôme was a huge success because he was always there himself, attending to every detail. And his staff knew that he was ever present, aware of everything that went on and everything they did. It kept them on their toes.

'I was with Jan all afternoon, working on the big wedding. She has a lot of work to do. She hired four assistants and she's still afraid she won't get it all done. I was lending her a hand,' Heloise said vaguely, as the room service waiter served them lamb chops and haricots verts. Hugues was careful about what they ate and spent an hour in the gym every morning before he went to work. At forty-five, he looked younger than his age and was in great shape.

'I went by there, and I didn't see you,' her father commented.

'I must have been up here doing homework by then,' she said innocently.

'A likely story,' he teased her with a grin. Her grades were decent even if they weren't great, and it was a difficult school. She was equally proficient in English and French, and her Spanish had remained fluent, due to her long conversations at the hotel. 'So what are you doing this weekend? Are you having friends over?' he asked warmly. He had four VIPs checking in that weekend and a foreign head of state on Saturday, which meant additional security and Secret Service in the lobby and all over the hotel. The foreign dignitary had booked an entire floor, save for Hugues's private apartment on that level, and they had to close off the floors above and below him, which was annoying since they couldn't use their two penthouse suites on the floor above, nor the presidential suite on the floor below. And those three suites alone were big revenue sources for them. They charged fourteen thousand dollars a night for the presidential and twelve thousand for each of the two penthouse suites. They had two dead floors on their hands for the weekend, although they were charging the foreign government a fortune for their occupancy, but the hotel's security costs would be high too, with their entire security staff working overtime all weekend.

'Yes, I think I'm having a friend over, maybe two,' Heloise said, staring at her plate. Hugues thought she was unusually quiet, but she'd had a cold and he assumed she was tired. They both had had busy weeks. It was January and bitter cold outside, and everyone was sick. Illness spread like wildfire through the hotel in flu season, with so many people working there. Signs everywhere reminded employees to wash their hands. 'I think Marie Louise is coming over tonight, and maybe Josephine. We're going to sleep downstairs.' It was a privilege he accorded her, particularly at this time of year when the hotel wasn't fully booked. There was a small room on the second floor that people used for their assistants or bodyguards.

'Just don't drive room service crazy with a lot of requests. No grilled cheese sandwiches at four in the morning, or banana splits. Order before midnight, please. The room service staff is too small after that to take care of you girls too.'

'Yes, Papa,' she said demurely, and smiled at him, which for a fraction of an instant made him wonder what she was up to. If he hadn't known her better, he would have thought she had a boy hidden somewhere up her sleeve, but Jennifer assured him she wasn't ready for that yet. But he knew that day would come, and he would mourn her childhood and total adoration of him when it did. He loved being at the hub of her world, just as she was at his.

They finished dinner quickly because he had to get downstairs for a security meeting in anticipation of the foreign president's arrival the next day. Heloise went to

Mrs. Van Damme's room then and offered to walk the dog for her. The elderly dowager was very pleased. She'd had a hip replaced recently and no longer walked Julius herself. And she liked it when Heloise took him out. She took him on long walks and came back with brilliant pink cheeks from the cold, and Julius had fun with her, more so than with the bellmen who walked him quickly around the block and brought him back.

Heloise left the hotel a few minutes later in a parka and jeans, with a wool cap on her head and a long knitted scarf and gloves. It was bitter cold, and she ran the old Pekingese quickly around the corner. She stopped in a doorway where a man was lying under a cardboard box in a sleeping bag. She tapped politely on the box as though it were a door, and a wizened old face peeked out and smiled when he saw her. He looked a little drunk, and he had a filthy blanket wrapped over the sleeping bag, which looked new. She had bought it for him with her allowance the week before. She had been checking on him for several weeks and brought him leftover food they gave her in the kitchen. No one ever questioned her requests or asked what they were for. They just assumed she had a healthy appetite or was taking it upstairs for a friend.

'Are you ready, Billy?' she asked the man lying on the

sidewalk, and he nodded. She looked like an angel fallen from the sky to him. She had promised him a room for that night. He didn't really think she'd do it, but he followed her anyway and was surprised she had shown up. He got slowly to his feet, and she helped him fold the blanket and the sleeping bag. He smelled awful, and she tried to hold her breath, as the Pekingese watched.

'Where are we going?' Billy asked her, and she pointed around the corner away from the main entrance of the hotel. There was a door that some of the employees used that led up a back staircase. It was kept locked, and she had taken a key from maintenance that day. And together they walked slowly toward the unmarked door that was on the back side of the hotel. She rapidly unlocked it and told him they had to walk up two flights of stairs.

The room she had blocked that afternoon herself on the computers was on the second floor. She knew the maids had already done their turn-down rounds, so the coast was clear, except for the security camera she hoped no one was watching too closely. She counted the half flights until they got to two, as Billy followed slowly and the dog panted on his way up. She had first met Billy two weeks before, when she stopped to talk to him one afternoon. He'd told her he'd been sick but hadn't been able to get into a shelter, and Heloise wanted to get him out of the cold and off the street. This was the only way she could think of to do it, and she'd been planning it for two weeks. This was the perfect night. They weren't fully booked, some of the security staff were out sick, and she was sure she could get Billy into a room, for the night at least. How to get him out again would be another problem, but she was sure she could figure out a way, so no one would ever know he'd been there. And she planned to put a Do Not Disturb sign on the door and clean the room herself after he left. But first she wanted to get him warm and fed and off the streets for the night. It was her gift to him.

'Are you okay?' She turned to smile at him, before she opened the door into the second-floor hall. Julius continued to watch them with interest, turning his head from side to side.

'I'm okay,' Billy reassured her. 'I like your dog,' he said politely as Heloise smiled.

'He's not my dog. I walk him for a friend.' And then she put a finger to her lips, opened the door, and led Billy to a door only a few steps away. She had the key in her hand and unlocked it rapidly and ushered him inside.

The homeless man looked around and began to cry. 'What are you doing?' he asked with a look of panic. 'I can't stay here. They'll put me in jail.'

'No, they won't. I won't let them. My father owns the hotel.'

'He's going to kill you for this,' Billy said, looking worried for her as well.

'No, he won't, he's a nice man.' She was turning on the lights in the room. It was one of their smaller rooms, which was how Heloise knew she'd get away with it. It would be one of the last rooms they gave out, and in the slow season like January they wouldn't need a room this size. Billy was looking around in amazement at the luxury and comfort she had brought him to. It looked like paradise to him. It had a king-size bed, an enormous TV, antiques all over, and a large immaculate bathroom. His eyes were huge in his ravaged face as he looked at the young girl who had brought him here.

'What about your mom? Won't she get mad at you?' He looked genuinely worried about her.

'She's married to someone else.' He stood there look-ing around him then, and Heloise gently suggested he sit down. 'I have to take the dog back. Why don't you watch TV or something? I'll come back in a few minutes and order you some food.' He nodded as he stared at her, genuinely bereft of speech, as she quietly left the room with Julius and took him back upstairs to Mrs. Van Damme.

'What a long walk you two had.' She had no way of knowing that Heloise had barely walked him more than a block, and he'd been back in the hotel the rest of the time. His owner took off his cashmere sweater, and Heloise kissed her on the cheek and hurried back out again. She was back in Billy's room on the second floor in less than five minutes and let herself back in with the key.

He was sitting on the edge of the bed with a stunned expression, afraid to lie down. He looked terrified and happy all at the same time and immensely relieved to see her again. She had already figured out that she would have to hide somewhere in the hotel that night, since she couldn't go back to her apartment if she was pretending to be with Marie Louise. And she obviously couldn't stay with Billy in this room, although she was sure he wasn't dangerous. She had spoken to him often in the last few weeks. He just looked cold and old and tired by his life on the streets. He had told her he was sixty-two years old, and this was something special she wanted to do for him, to show him someone cared.

'What would you like to eat?' she asked, handing him a menu, and he looked confused the moment she did. She wondered if he needed glasses and didn't own a pair. 'What's your favorite kind of food?'

'Steak,' he said with a big grin, although he was

missing a lot of teeth. 'Steak and mashed potatoes, and chocolate pudding for dessert.' Heloise picked up the phone and ordered it from room service, with a salad, and she translated the chocolate pudding into chocolate mousse, with a big glass of milk. And then she sat with him, while he turned on the TV with the remote, and she put the Do Not Disturb on the door. 'I've never seen a room like this in my life. I used to be a carpenter. I worked in a furniture factory when I was a kid, but we never made nothing like this.' She couldn't help wondering what had happened to him after that, but she didn't dare ask.

Half an hour later, room service arrived and knocked on the door. She answered immediately and spoke through the door, and the waiter delivering it recognized her voice.

'Thanks, Derek. We're not dressed. Just leave it outside. And thank you.'

'Sure thing. Have fun.'

She waited until she heard the elevator door close, then pulled the rolling table in as Billy's eyes grew wide. The food smelled delicious, and she pulled a chair up to the table for him. 'Have a nice dinner,' she said softly. She wrote down her cell phone number, and told him to call her if he had any problem, or wanted something else to eat. 'I'll get you breakfast tomorrow morning. You'll have to leave pretty early, before things get busy in the hotel. I can get you out the same door.'

'Thank you,' he said, his eyes filling with tears again, as he started to eat the delicious dinner. 'You must be an angel from Heaven, disguised as a little girl.'

'That's okay,' she said. 'Keep the door locked, and put the chain on and don't go out in the hall.' It never occurred to her that he might refuse to leave the next day. So far everything had gone according to plan. 'And don't answer the phone.' He nodded and devoured his steak as she let herself discreetly out of the room and went back down the stairs, happy with the way things had gone. The look on Billy's face was worth it all.

She checked things out in the ballroom, and the decorators and florists were setting things up for the wedding the next day. She hung around for a while, and then went down to the basement and visited the wine cellars. She stopped in the uniform room, where everything was hanging in dry cleaner bags. She knew it was going to be a long night, and all she had to do was avoid her father for the rest of it. No one was surprised to see her drifting from place to place. She let herself into the first aid station, knowing they had a bed and an exam table; with luck, she could spend the rest of the night there. It was after midnight when one of the room service cooks came in for some burn medicine and was surprised to see her there.

'What are you doing here?' she asked with a look of surprise to see Heloise lying on the exam table half asleep. She was listening to her iPod in the dark, and both of them were startled as she leaped to her feet.

'I'm playing hide and seek with a friend,' Heloise said nervously with a grin. 'She'll never find me here.'

'Are you up to mischief?' the cook asked her with a suspicious look.

'No. But please don't tell my dad.'

'You'd better go back upstairs.' The room service cook was not one of Heloise's closer friends and hadn't worked at the hotel for long. Heloise went back up to the ballroom then, and everyone had gone. There were voluminous billowing satin curtains, and Heloise concealed herself behind them and tucked in for the rest of the night. All she had to do now was wake up in time to get Billy out of the hotel. And by sheer luck, the morning cleaning crew started vacuuming at six A.M. and woke her up. She came out from behind the curtains and went back to the second floor and knocked on Billy's door. She could hear the TV on, and she spoke through the door and told him who she was.

He whispered through the door, 'Is that you?'

'Yes,' she whispered back, and he let her in. He looked as though he had bathed, and he was clean shaven. His hair was combed, and he looked happy to see her. 'Did you get some sleep?'

'Yeah, best night of my life.' There was an empty wine bottle next to the bed, from the minibar, but he didn't seem drunk, and he was wide awake. He was used to getting up early to clear out of the doorways where he lay.

'I'll order you breakfast. What would you like?'

'Fried, sunny side up?' he asked cautiously, and she ordered them, with muffins, a pastry basket, bacon, orange juice, and coffee. They were outside the door in twenty minutes, and Billy devoured the whole meal in ten. And then she told him they had to leave. He looked gratefully at her as he put on his ragged coat, but he looked infinitely better than he had the night before when he came in. And the night had passed without event. All she had to do now was get him out.

They went down the back stairs quietly after Heloise locked up the room. It was just two short flights, so not much time for the security cameras to spot them, and she hoped they wouldn't. She was going to come back and clean up after he left. Just before they reached the middle landing, she pulled the hood of her jacket up and turned her face, in case security was watching the video cameras. She didn't want them to recognize her. She opened the back door and followed Billy out. They were standing on the street outside the back door of the hotel. It was still dark. And he looked at her with so much gratitude that it brought tears to her eyes.

'I'll never forget what you did for me last night. You'll go to Heaven for that one day for sure,' he said, and gently touched her arm. 'I'll remember it forever.' Then pulling his coat around him, with his blanket and sleeping bag under his arm, he shuffled off. He turned the corner a minute later, as Heloise watched him, and then she went back upstairs to clean the room. She knew where the maids kept their carts, she had helped them a thousand times before. She knew just what to do. Half an hour later she had changed the bed and cleaned the bathroom, and no one would have suspected the room had been used. She put the cart away and headed back upstairs to their apartment. It was almost eight when she let herself in. Her father was reading the paper over breakfast and looked immaculate in a dark suit.

'You girls got up early,' he said, looking surprised. 'Where's Marie Louise?'

'She takes ballet on Saturday mornings, so she had to leave early. I serviced the room. Josephine didn't come, she was sick,' she said nonchalantly, picking at a blueberry muffin just like the ones she had ordered Billy two hours before.

'You didn't have to do that, but it was nice of you.' Her father smiled at her. He was expecting a busy day – several of their VIPs were coming in, and the foreign president.

As soon as he got to his office, Bruce Johnson, the head of security, came to see him. Hugues assumed it was to discuss their arrangements and coordinate with the Secret Service for their foreign dignitary. Bruce was a huge man and had worked for Hugues since they opened. He had a tape from one of the security cameras in his hands and a serious look on his face.

'There's something I want you to see,' he said quietly.

'Something wrong?' Hugues asked. Bruce looked more serious than usual, as he put the tape into a machine Hugues kept in his office. They had gone over tapes together many times when an employee was suspected of stealing, drinking, or taking drugs on the job, or had behaved inappropriately in some way.

'I'm not sure. You tell me. Back door, last night. I didn't catch it till this morning. I came in early and I ran the tapes from last night. I think entry was right after seven P.M. Exit was just before seven A.M. this morning. I think we had an unexpected guest last night. I checked all the other cameras after I saw this, and I don't pick him up anywhere. Whoever got him in and out of the hotel knows this place pretty well.'

Hugues's blood ran cold as Bruce said it and he wondered if Heloise had sneaked a boy in last night and not been with the innocent Marie Louise. If so, a new day had dawned, and it was not one he was going to like. Hugues braced himself for what he would see.

Bruce Johnson turned the tape on, and they watched a disheveled, dirty-looking homeless man come in through the back door. He was accompanied by a slight figure in a hooded jacket who had turned her face away, and they disappeared rapidly up the stairs. They turned up nowhere else. And then the same two people came down the stairs that morning. The homeless man looked some- what less untidy than he had the night before. He had a spring in his step; he was smiling, looked cleaner, and had combed his hair. And the person with him dodged the camera again. And that person came back into the hotel again a few minutes later and bounded up the stairs.

'What is that?' Hugues asked, looking upset. '*Who* is that? What the hell is going on? Am I running some kind of homeless shelter here? Do you think one of the kitchen people let him in?'

'Look again,' Bruce said softly with a slow smile. He was one of Heloise's biggest fans and had carried her around when she was two so she wouldn't get hurt while they were doing the renovations. 'Does anything look familiar to you?'

Hugues stared at the screen with wide eyes. He was relieved that Heloise hadn't sneaked a boy in instead of her friend, but she had done something far worse, and she could have gotten hurt in the process. Hugues shuddered as he looked at the man.

'Oh my God,' Hugues said with a horrified expression. 'Are you telling me she brought a homeless man in? Where did he sleep?'

'Probably in one of the rooms.' Bruce picked up the phone and called housekeeping then, but they had no knowledge of Heloise using a room. And then he called room service, and they told him Heloise had ordered breakfast and dinner for 202, but the DND sign had been on, so they left it outside. He turned to his employer then and gave him the news. 'She ordered a steak, mashed potatoes, chocolate mousse, and a hefty breakfast this morning of fried eggs and bacon and a pastry basket at six-fifteen.'

'I can't believe she'd do a thing like that,' her father said in amazement. He called her on her cell phone then and asked her to come downstairs. She was in his office five minutes later, and she tried to look nonchalant when she saw Bruce and gave him a big smile.

'This is very serious,' her father said without preamble, with a somber expression. 'Did you bring someone into the hotel last night? A homeless man?'

She could see the images on the screen herself. She hesitated for a moment and then nodded and jutted out her chin. 'Yes, I did. He's old and sick, and he was starving and it's too cold outside. He couldn't get into a shelter,' she said as though she knew him well.

'So you brought him here?' She nodded soundlessly as her father looked genuinely panicked. 'What if he had hurt you, or another guest? He could have hurt you . . . or worse. Do you have any idea how foolish and dangerous that was? Where were you all night? In the room with him?' He looked even more terrified by that. What if he had raped her?

'I slept in the first aid station till midnight. And then I slept behind the ballroom curtains till six. He's a good person, Papa. He didn't hurt the room. I cleaned everything up myself.' Listening to her, Bruce Johnson was trying not to smile. She looked so earnest and so serious. He was well aware that she had taken a terrible risk, but at least she hadn't gotten hurt. He was sure the Secret

Service wouldn't be comforted to know there were homeless people being sneaked in and sleeping in the rooms.

'I'm not going to let you have friends here anymore if you lie to me and do things like that,' her father said sternly.

'You always say that we have an obligation to poor people, and to remember that everyone isn't as lucky as we are. He might have died on the streets last night, Papa.' She wasn't apologizing for what she had done, and she was thrilled that it had gone off without a hitch. And if she was punished for it now, it was well worth it and she didn't care.

'We can fulfill our responsibilities in other ways,' her father said sternly. 'We give to the food bank. I don't want you ever doing that again. He could have been dangerous and hurt you or one of the guests or someone who works here.'

'He wouldn't do that. I know him,' she said softly. And as proof, everything had gone fine.

'You don't know that. He could be mentally deranged.' Hugues was trying not to shout at her, out of fear over what could have happened to her. She could have been dead in the room and no one would have known.

'Papa, letting him spend the night here may have changed his life or given him hope. He got to live like a human being for one whole night. That's not a lot to ask.'

'It's too dangerous,' her father insisted. 'I forbid you to ever do that again. And I want you to stay in the apartment and think about it today. You can go now,' he said solemnly as she left the room, and the two men looked at each other and shook their heads in amazement.

'You've got a little Mother Teresa on your hands. You'd better keep an eye on her,' his head of security warned him.

'I had no idea she'd ever do something like that. I wonder if she's done it before,' Hugues said, looking stunned.

'I doubt that. We'd have seen her on the screens. But she pulled it off pretty well last night. At least he got a good night's sleep and two good meals. Maybe she's right and it will change his life,' Bruce said quietly, touched by what she had done.

'Don't you start,' Hugues warned him. 'I am not turning this hotel into a homeless shelter.' He had an idea then and wanted to talk to Heloise about it later, but not just yet.

Bruce took the tape out of the machine. 'She's quite a gal, our little princess. And I think she's going to keep you busy for the next few years.' Hugues nodded and sat quietly in his office afterward, thinking about what his daughter had done and how brave and compassionate she had been, and then he went to see her upstairs. She was lying on the bed in her room with her iPod in her ears, and she sat up when he walked in.

'I'm sorry, Papa,' she said quietly.

'I just want to tell you something,' he said with tears in his eyes. 'It was crazy and dangerous and wrong in many ways, but I want you to know that I love you and admire you for what you did. I'm very proud of you, and you were very brave. But I still want you to promise that you won't do it again. I just want you to know that I respect you for it too. I wouldn't have had the courage to do what you did.'

'Thank you, Papa,' she said, beaming at him, and threw her arms around his neck. 'I love you so much.'

He nodded, choking back his emotions, which were overwhelming him. 'I love you too,' he whispered as he held her, and tears slid down his cheeks. And most of all, he was grateful that she hadn't gotten hurt. And then he turned to her with a slow smile.

'I have a job for you,' he said with a serious expression. 'I want you to work with the kitchen people who organize our food bank donations. I want you to learn everything about it, and when you're a little older, I'll put you in charge of that project. So that's your assignment from me.' She beamed at her father and hugged him again. And he had another idea too. 'And if you want to do more hands-on work, you can volunteer at a family shelter. But no more bringing them home to the hotel!'

'I promise, Papa,' she said solemnly. Bruce had come upstairs and given her a lecture too.

Hugues realized that she had a need to do some real philanthropy, and he was willing to help her do it. He was still stunned by what she had done and the sheer innocence and goodness of it. She was quite a girl! And he was a very proud father.

Chapter 4

Word of Heloise's escapade with Billy the homeless man had been whispered among the employees. No one discussed it with her openly. She started working on their food bank donations in the kitchen, and within a few weeks everyone knew about Billy, and thought it had been a brave and crazy thing to do. And she was tireless in her work on the food bank project, even carrying crates of food herself to the truck that picked them up. And her father found her a job at a family shelter downtown twice a week.

She had looked for Billy again when she walked Julius, but he had moved on and disappeared. She hoped he had gotten into a shelter by then. And she was still glad she had brought him into the hotel for a night. She wondered if she'd see him at the soup kitchen where she worked sometime, and hoped she would.

Two weeks later, with four February weddings scheduled, Sally Biend, the catering manager, fell off a ladder in the ballroom and broke her leg. She had been taking a closer look at the chandelier to see if it needed to be cleaned before the wedding the following week. Everyone was enormously relieved that it was only her leg.

Heloise visited her in the hospital. She was one of Heloise's favorite people and always let her sneak into the weddings. Her assistant was out on maternity leave, and they had to call an agency to find someone to take her place immediately. None of the candidates they sent over looked right for the Vendôme, until the final one, who came in looking like an angel, with excellent references from a hotel in Boston. She was a godsend. They hired her on a temporary basis for three months, until Sally could come back, hopefully in time for June, because they had so many weddings booked.

Hilary Cartwright had been catering manager at several hotels even before the one in Boston and seemed to know her stuff. And she looked more like a model than their usual hotel employees, with straight blond hair, long legs, and enormous blue eyes. And her references were excellent. She was attractive, well spoken, interviewed very well, and she said she was fully capable of handling the weddings they had on their books. She even mentioned to the head of human resources that she hoped to get a permanent job out of it in the long run. They had no openings now, but competent people were hard to find.

Heloise got a look at her the day before the first wedding she'd be handling, and announced to the florist that she thought Hilary was very pretty. Jan made no comment whatsoever, which was unlike her. Heloise was watching her and was startled when Jan, who was usually mellow, turned around with a tense expression.

'Little Miss Innocent Angel Face is a raving bitch.'

Heloise had never heard her say anything like that. 'She is?' Heloise looked stunned.

'She won't let me set up till tomorrow. She sent everything back down here and locked the ballroom. She told me the arrangements look pathetic, and she intimated to your father that I'm overcharging, padding the bill, and possibly cheating him and the client, and she can get better flowers and a better deal from a friend. Your father called me about it,' Jan said with tears in her eyes. She had never had a single problem in her eight years at the Vendôme. Till now. Thanks to Hilary

Cartwright. She started to cry then and blew her nose.

Heloise hugged her and tried to console her. 'Papa is probably just in a bad mood. I saw him with a ton of bills on his desk. He's always crabby when that happens.'

'No, he believed her,' Jan said, crying again, although she was one of the most respected florists in New York, and had won several awards for her work in the hotel.

Things got worse the next day. Hilary got in a full-scale battle with Jan before the wedding. She shouted at the waiters and had them reset the tables. She ran the ballroom with an iron fist. She got good results, but she had an aggressive confrontational style no one used at the Vendôme. Sally was always kind to everyone and got great work out of them. Hilary was hell on wheels and had people running and crying no matter how sweet she looked. Nothing she did or said was sweet.

But when Hugues came to check on things, she turned into a lamb and turned innocent eyes toward him, while the people she'd been brutalizing stood and stared at her in disbelief. Heloise couldn't imagine it of her father, but he fell for it like a ton of bricks and melted in a puddle at her feet. Heloise had never seen anyone do that to him, and she was shocked. He looked bewitched when he left the room.

'Did you see that?' Heloise whispered to Jan. 'He was

completely gaga. He believes all that stuff she says to him.' Heloise was horrified.

'It's going to be a long three months till Sally comes back,' Jan said sadly. Her boss seemed to be falling for the woman with the blond, blue-eyed looks of an angel and the behavior of a storm trooper.

Hilary turned her attention to Heloise then, after her father left the ballroom, and asked what she was doing there.

'Just visiting,' Heloise said politely. This was her fiefdom, not Hilary's, and she wasn't going to be chased off, no matter how tough she was.

'We don't want uninvited guests at a wedding, do we?' she said pointedly to Heloise, who was wearing a new dress for the occasion. It was a dark green velvet skirt with a velvet top, with a white lace collar and shiny flat black pumps and white tights. She looked like an ad for what girls her age should look like, but Hilary clearly didn't find it endearing. She told her to leave the ballroom before the wedding. Heloise flatly said she wouldn't, and that she had attended all the weddings at the hotel since she was six. There was a long pause between the two, and Hilary nodded.

Hilary had decided not to tackle Heloise just yet. She let her stay on the fringes of the wedding and watched her like a hawk, waiting for her to do something wrong. When Heloise ordered a Coca-Cola from a passing waiter, Hilary canceled it immediately and reminded Heloise that she was not a guest. But this was Heloise's world, not hers, and things were done differently here. The owner's daughter could do no wrong; they had all watched her grow up. Hilary clearly didn't find her charming, and her only interest was in Hugues.

'You don't order drinks here,' she told Heloise firmly. 'If you want to see the bride, that's fine. But if you want to eat or drink, go upstairs to your own apartment. And don't dance or talk to the guests.' Her tone was harsh and her blue eyes ice cold, as the other employees watched her.

'I always talk to the guests,' Heloise said firmly, without flinching. She was not going to be run off by a stranger. This was her home. 'I represent my father here,' she said with a tone that was braver than she felt. Hilary was scary.

'And I'm responsible for this wedding. You're not an invited guest, and I'm sure your father would agree.'

Heloise wasn't sure he wouldn't, so she didn't press the point. But two waiters who had heard the exchange went out to the kitchen and told the head chef that there was trouble in River City, and the new catering manager wouldn't let the boss's daughter order a Coke.

'She won't get far with that.' The cook laughed and rolled her eyes. They all agreed that Hilary wouldn't last three months if she was mean to Heloise. Her father wouldn't tolerate that.

The wedding went off perfectly. Heloise watched it for a long time and left before they cut the cake, which was unusual for her, but she felt unwelcome after what Hilary had said and could feel her eyes on her all the time. Heloise went upstairs and watched a movie, then came back downstairs after the wedding was over and walked into her father's office to say hi. She almost fell over in astonishment when she saw Hilary sitting there with her angel face on, laughing as Hugues poured them each a glass of champagne. Cristal, their best.

'What's she doing here?' Heloise blurted out as Hilary turned and gave her a victorious look.

'We're talking about the next few weddings, to bring Hilary up to speed,' he said calmly, looking unconcerned.

It amused him that whenever he wanted a private moment, his daughter never failed to show up. And he didn't know why, but he could sense the tension between the temporary catering manager and his daughter. It made no sense. He had invited Hilary to his office for a drink after the wedding. She had done a good job, said she wanted to talk to him, and he wanted to put her at ease. And she was a lovely-looking young woman. There was no harm in sharing a glass of champagne.

'Why don't you go upstairs, Heloise?' he suggested. 'I'll be up in time for dinner.' It was clear he wanted to be alone with Hilary. Heloise looked upset when she left the room and went back to their apartment.

'She's very possessive of you, and her turf,' Hilary commented with an innocent smile, and he looked at her ruefully and nodded.

'She's been the woman in my life since she was four, almost all her life, as she remembers it. She likes having me to herself.' He smiled apologetically.

'In a few years she'll be gone,' Hilary said thoughtfully, 'and you'll wind up alone.' She sounded sympathetic. 'You can't let her run your life. She's just a little girl.' And Hilary was a big girl who knew a golden opportunity when she saw it and planned to make the most of it while she was there. She would have liked nothing better than to become the girlfriend, or better yet the wife, of the owner of the hotel. She had read Hugues's bios in hotel magazines for years. The temporary job at the Vendôme was her dream, and so was he. She saw this as a long-term opportunity and had pounced on it when the agency offered to send her there. She had done her homework, and her plan was to seduce Hugues Martin, and she wasn't going to let a precocious twelve-year-old stand in her way.

They drank half the bottle of champagne together, and after that Hugues went to his apartment upstairs. He was attracted to Hilary, but it was against his better judgment to get involved with an employee. She was very seductive, and he told himself that at least she was a temp. Maybe he could go out with her after she left. He was very attracted to her; and Hilary was making the most of it and flirting with him.

When he got to the apartment, Heloise was watching a movie on TV, looking unhappy. She hardly spoke at dinner, and most of Hugues's efforts to engage her in conversation went ignored, until she finally turned to him, with tears in her eyes.

'That woman is after you, Papa. She's a liar, and she's mean to everyone. She yelled at Jan and made her cry.'

'She gets good results,' he defended Hilary quietly. 'We've never had a wedding as pretty. Everything went smoothly today. She runs a tight ship. And she's not after me,' he reassured her. It was more the reverse. He was after her. 'You have nothing to worry about. You're the only woman in my life.' He leaned over and kissed her on the cheek, and Heloise looked at him cautiously, wanting it to be true forever.

'Okay, I'm sorry,' she said, mollified, and they chatted till the end of dinner. But she hated Hilary more than ever. She could sense that she was after Hugues. And there was something insincere about her, although Heloise didn't know what it was.

For the next several weeks Hilary made enemies among the employees and put all her energy into charming Hugues. She was on a mission. She dropped by his office, used every excuse to talk to him, and constantly asked his advice about how 'things were done at the Vendôme.' It was a little oppressive, although he didn't seem to mind it, and it flattered him, and Jennifer noticed it too. Everyone did. By the time she'd been there a month, it was clear that she was determined to land the owner of the hotel, at the altar if possible, or at least in bed. She asked him to show up at every wedding, flirted with him shamelessly, and Hugues remained proper and discreet, but they could see he was attracted to her, and Jennifer caught them kissing once in his office. She'd never seen him do that before. Hilary was relentless in her pursuit.

Jennifer was uncomfortable about her. Hilary was obvious in all her games and ploys, but she was so convincing and seemed so innocent that Hugues appeared to be falling for it hook, line, and sinker, which was unusual for him. He was usually smarter than that but she was good at the game. She was twenty-seven years old, eighteen years younger than he, and she seemed like a dangerous woman to Jennifer. And Heloise had sensed the same thing about her. What everyone felt, except Hugues, was that Hilary was not sincere. And she was playing Hugues like a violin.

Hilary seemed to get a better grip on him every day. He looked completely besotted whenever she walked into a room. Heloise was beside herself over her and talking constantly to Jan and Jennifer about her. She wanted to protect her father but didn't know how, and then destiny intervened.

In Hilary's tenth week at the hotel, with everyone she worked with hating her and their boss in her back pocket, providence was on Heloise's side. She was working on a science project at school and didn't have time for lunch, and she was starving when she got home. Instead of ordering room service, as she often did, she went down to the kitchen to find something for herself. She walked into the cold room, not sure what she wanted, and found Hilary there, wrapped around one of the male sous chefs like a snake, with her skirt hiked up to her waist, and his hand between her legs.

Heloise had never seen anything quite so graphic, but she got the drift. She was too stunned to say a word, as he pushed Hilary against the wall and reached into his checkered pants. Heloise said nothing, but with impressive clarity of mind, she held up the cell phone in her hand and snapped a picture of them. The sous chef was Italian, unbelievably handsome, and about twenty-four years old. It was obvious even to Heloise what had been about to happen.

She ran out of the cold room, before they could stop her or grab the phone. She was halfway up the stairs before they came out of the cold room, looking embarrassed. Hilary tried to look dignified but only looked foolish as the young Italian grinned. The entire kitchen staff knew it had been going on for several weeks, when she wasn't pursuing Hugues. This was just a fling. Hugues was more of a long-term plan for her, an investment for her future, as everyone had figured out. She was a piece of work.

Breathless and with her hair flying, Heloise marched into her father's office and stared at him across the desk.

'Where have you been? You look like you've run a mile.' He was smiling at her.

She didn't say a word. She brought up the picture of Hilary and the Italian on her cell phone and laid it on her father's desk, right in front of him, and ran out of the room. It illustrated the old adage that one picture is worth a thousand words.

No one ever knew what happened between them after that. Hugues gave Heloise back her phone that night without a word. The photograph of Hilary and the sous chef had disappeared. Hugues said nothing to Jennifer or anyone else about it. Sally came back two days later, still on a cane, but happy to be back, a little earlier than planned. And Hilary disappeared without a trace the day after the photograph was taken of her with the Italian sous chef. No one dared to mention her, and the sous chef was smart enough to say nothing. It had just been a game for him.

Hugues looked slightly embarrassed when he glanced at Jennifer the day after the photo incident, as he sat down in his office. It had been a close call. He hadn't been fully involved with her yet, but he'd come close. And Hilary had had big plans for him in mind. Even he understood that now. Hilary had never been as innocent as she looked. By sheer luck, his daughter had spared him a dire fate.

'I guess it's never too early or too late to be a fool,' he said to Jennifer with a sheepish grin as she set his coffee down on his desk.

'She was good at what she did,' Jennifer said softly, and left the room. They were all grateful that Heloise had seen through her and exposed Hilary to her dad. Heloise had saved the day.

Chapter 5

At seventeen, the Hotel Vendôme was still all of Heloise's world. She finished her junior year of high school, or its equivalent, and passed her first baccalaureate at the Lycée, and her father planned a summer of work for her. She was working at the front desk, in a trim navy blue uniform suit, like the other women wore. She filled in at the concierge desk, and her father had arranged for an internship for her at a sleepy little hotel in Bordeaux. An old friend of his from hotel school ran it now, and Hugues thought it would be great experience for her as a summer job. He didn't expect her to go into the hotel business, and didn't think he wanted her to, but he wanted her to do more than just hang around the hotel. And she was going to spend part of August in St. Tropez with her mother and Greg. Hugues was a great believer in filling one's time. He wanted her to apply to college in the fall, preferably at Barnard or NYU so she could stay in New York, and he thought that two summer internships would look good on her application, one at their hotel and the other in Bordeaux. And Heloise liked the idea too. Like her father, she didn't like being idle.

At almost eighteen, the biggest change in her life in recent years, other than her looks, was the addition of boys to her life. She had had several flirtations at school, and Mrs. Van Damme had introduced Heloise to her grandson Clayton earlier that year, when he came to visit from St. Paul's. They had met when they were both thirteen and then forgot about each other. He had been in boarding school for four years of high school and graduated just as Heloise started her summer internship at the hotel. His grandmother had invited him to stay at the hotel with her in New York, and he was excited about it, and liked Heloise. They went to dinner and the movies several times and a concert in Central Park. He was going to Yale in the fall, and they enjoyed spending time together before Heloise was due to leave for France. It wasn't serious, and they both realized quickly they just wanted to be friends. There was no chemistry between them, but the makings of a real friendship. He was a year ahead of her in school, and they were both nervous about college, and talked about it. He was a sweet boy, and his grandmother loved seeing them together. She loved them both.

Heloise was a beautiful girl. She wore her red hair tied up in a bun when she worked at the desk, and Clayton loved to tease her when she was at work and he breezed through the lobby on his way out. The other desk clerks kidded her about him, but she didn't care. Everyone always asked her if she had a boyfriend, but she didn't.

Hugues had turned fifty that year and worked all the time, even harder. A little salt had appeared at his temples, woven into his dark hair. He was prouder of Heloise than ever. He loved that she had gotten the first part of her baccalaureate and would complete it at the end of senior year. And he wanted her to think about careers and what she wanted to do. His dream of having her work at the hotel had faded. He wanted more than that for her and was encouraging her to think about law school, which didn't appeal to her. He thought a career in law would open many doors to her, while the hotel would eat up her life. The one thing he didn't want was for her to go away to school, he would have missed her too much, and he said it to her often. And she didn't want to anyway. She had no desire whatsoever to leave the cocoon of the hotel and had never rebelled against it. Her life was still centered there.

She was particularly happy when a summer intern showed up at the front desk. He was a well-bred, intelligent boy from Milan who was attending hotel school in Europe and was going to intern at the Vendôme for three months. The chemistry was instant between them, and they often worked together at the front desk. His name was Roberto, he was twenty-one years old, and Hugues was very nervous when he saw them whispering one night behind the desk. He talked to Jennifer about it the next day. She was always his best resource for parental advice and female intuition.

'I don't want her to get involved with that boy,' he said to Jennifer unhappily, and she laughed at him.

'I don't think you're going to have much to say about it, or not for very long. One of these days she's going to fall head over heels for some guy, and there won't be a damn thing you can do about it, except pray he's a good guy.' Her own children had both married, and she was a grandmother now. What she worried about most for Hugues was that one day Heloise would find the man of her dreams and leave, and he would be heartbroken without her. She was an integral part of his daily life, even more so because she hardly ever saw or spoke to her mother. It created an unusually close bond between them. And Jennifer knew they were both going to suffer one day when the cord was cut.

Hugues was beginning to worry about the men who would pursue her. 'Roberto worries me. He'll break her heart.' He was four years older than Heloise, more sophisticated than she was, and flirted with all the women at the desk. Heloise was enthralled with him and told Jennifer she thought he was sexy and handsome, which was hard to deny.

'She's going away in a few weeks,' Jennifer reminded Hugues to reassure him about Roberto. 'But sooner or later there's going to be some guy. You'd better get used to it soon,' she warned him.

'I know, I know,' he said, looking worried. Jennifer was always a reality check for him. 'Just keep an eye on them, and let me know what you hear. He's too old for her right now, and a little too smooth for my taste.'

What they both heard in the ensuing weeks was that Heloise was smitten with Roberto, and he seemed to like her. But he was no fool. He wanted a good recommendation from Hugues and had no desire to anger him by toying with his daughter. So he was careful and respectful. He took her out to dinner a few times, she showed him the sights in New York on their days off, and they went for walks in the park on their breaks. But from what Hugues could tell, she hadn't slept with Roberto, and as far as he was concerned, she left for her internship in Bordeaux just in time. He wouldn't have trusted them together all summer. Roberto was just too handsome and appealing. Jennifer told Hugues that Heloise had told her she was still a virgin when she left. There had been a lot of kissing and fondling in the back room behind the front desk, but nothing dangerous. And when she came back from St. Tropez the end of August, Roberto would be gone. Hugues was relieved.

Heloise left for Paris on the first of July, and from there she was taking a train to Bordeaux. Hugues's friend at the château where she would be interning had promised that he would take good care of her. He and his wife had a daughter the same age. Heloise was going to work at the concierge desk and wherever they needed help in the hotel. It was a small, well-run family hotel, and people rarely stayed for more than a few nights as they toured the region. Heloise was excited about the trip, and the job, although she was a little disappointed when she got there. It was a sleepy hotel, and there was less for her to do than at her father's hotel in New York. The Château de Bastagne was tiny and quiet, but she liked their daughter, who drove her around the area and introduced her to her friends. Everyone they knew was in the wine business, and Heloise was learning about wine and how the grapes were grown. Everything was natural here, they didn't use irrigation, unlike California; one of the vineyard owners told her that the vines had to 'suffer' to make a great wine. She had a lot to report to her father when he called, and he was pleased.

'It will look good on your college applications,' he pointed out to her. And she liked the French kids her own age she was meeting in Bordeaux. She was sorry to leave when she had to go to St. Tropez on the first of August, particularly since she never knew what she'd encounter when she saw her mother. When she left Bordeaux, she felt she had made real friends there and promised to come back one day.

Her mother and Greg had bought a house in St. Tropez, and Heloise hadn't seen her mother in over a year. She wasn't sure what visiting them there would be like, but it was a fun place to visit, and she was looking forward to it.

She flew from Bordeaux to Nice, and her mother had her picked up by helicopter and flown to St. Tropez. And she arrived at the house at ten o'clock at night. Miriam acted as though she was thrilled to see her and exclaimed over how pretty she was, as though she were someone else's child. Heloise's half-brother and -sister were running around. Arielle was ten and Joey nine, and they were as unruly as they had always been, as an English nanny tried to keep track of them to no avail.

Miriam was wearing a see-through lace dress with nothing under it when she came to the door, and she was as beautiful as ever, at forty-two. Several major rock stars were there with assorted women. Greg waved hello to her from a set of drums he was playing, and Miriam showed her to her room with a glass in her hand. And when she opened the door, there was a couple making passionate love on the bed.

'Oops, wrong room!' she said, tittering. 'Silly of me. We have so many houseguests here, I don't know who's where. I think this is your room,' she said, moving on to the next one. It was a small, pretty room decorated in white lace and blue ribbons with a four-poster bed. No one was in it, and Heloise was rattled by the time she was alone and shut the door, while Miriam went back to their guests. It looked like a wild night. It was a beautiful house with an ocean view, and a pool where everyone swam naked. And when Heloise went to join the others, they were drinking heavily and doing drugs. A lot of coke seemed to be in evidence, and they were all passing joints around and doing lines. Heloise looked uncomfortable and turned all of it down and finally slipped away to her room, wishing she were back in Bordeaux with her friends there. This was a heavy scene with her mother and Greg's friends and more than she wanted to deal with. Her mother's world in St. Tropez scared her, but she wanted to try and stick it out. She saw so little of her, she wanted to give it a chance, and hoped things would settle down.

Heloise called her father in New York the next day. He hadn't had a vacation in two years and said he envied her a month in St. Tropez, although it wasn't his kind of place either. Most of Miriam and Greg's guests were English and from the music world, and sex and drugs seemed to be their main activities, which she didn't tell her father. She didn't want to upset him. By lunchtime everyone was drinking heavily again.

When her father asked her about it on the phone, he tried to sound casual and not concerned, and Heloise sounded equally so, to reassure him. He didn't want to keep her away from her mother; she saw little enough of her. But he also knew that Miriam's lifestyle was not entirely wholesome.

'It's a little weird,' Heloise admitted, but she didn't want to tell him that just about everyone except the kids was doing drugs. She had seen her mother snort a line of coke the night before. 'It's pretty loosey-goosey here.' It was who Miriam had become over the years, and maybe who she always had been.

'Are you okay? No one's bothering you?' He didn't want one of Greg's rock star friends coming on to her, although he trusted Heloise to handle it. But he was concerned that no one would protect her there. She led a very sheltered life at home. She had a hotel full of hotel employees to keep an eye on her.

'I'm fine. It's just the whole music rock star scene.' She had tried to talk to Arielle and Joey that morning, but she couldn't seem to connect with them either, although she made an effort. But they were so disjointed and used to such a different life than hers. She was very square compared to all of them.

'Are they doing drugs?' Hugues sounded worried. He didn't trust his ex-wife or her husband.

'I don't know,' Heloise lied to him. 'It's okay. I just haven't seen them in a while, and it's kind of a shock after Bordeaux.' It had been so easy and so much fun for her there, even more than she'd hoped.

'Well, if it gets too strange, just leave. You can tell your mother we had an emergency here and you had to come home. You can fly out from Nice.'

'Don't worry, Papa. I'm a big girl,' she reassured him.

'I'll see how it goes. I can always stay in Paris for a couple of days on the way home.' Two of her friends from school were there that summer, staying with relatives.

'I don't want you going to Paris alone. Maybe it'll be okay in St. Tropez. Give it a chance,' he said fairly, with no idea what was going on around her, and Heloise didn't tell him since she didn't want him to worry, and he would have.

By that night Heloise was more uncomfortable than ever. Everyone was drunk, doing coke, and having sex in every room available, including Greg and her mother with another couple, which they announced to everyone before the foursome went upstairs. It was more than she wanted to deal with, or know about her mother, and she was embarrassed to be there. She felt like she was in way over her head, although no one was trying to seduce her. Some of Greg's friends had come on to her, but they had realized she was too square. And she felt no connection with her half-brother and -sister, who were bratty and badly behaved, and sadly, she felt even less connection with her mother, who was a creature from another world. She was even less mature than Heloise, and the only person she seemed to care about was Greg. She appeared to have lost interest in her other children too and paid no attention to them.

Heloise stayed for two more days and then quietly decided to pull the plug on her stay in St. Tropez. It was just too awkward, and she was spending no time with her mother. And it was unnerving to be there, with everyone doing drugs. She felt sorry for her half-brother and -sister growing up in an atmosphere like that. Heloise didn't call to tell her father she was leaving, because she didn't want to worry him and didn't want him to make her come home. She wanted to go to Paris first. She told her mother that she had to get back earlier than planned, and Miriam didn't object or even ask her why. She could see how unhappy Heloise was, and as far as Miriam was concerned, she wasn't much fun to have around.

Heloise left the next morning, when everyone was still in bed, and left them a note thanking them. She took a taxi to Nice, which cost her two hundred dollars, and flew to Paris. She was in the city by four o'clock and looked up a youth hostel in an old convent in the Marais, in the fourth arrondissement. She took a taxi to get there. It wasn't fancy, but it was clean and seemed appropriate, with wholesome-looking young people hanging around outside with backpacks on. Some of them were American and said hello to her when she walked in. There were several British kids and Australians, a few Italians, and two boys from Japan. Heloise was able to get a bed in a double room for very little money.

It was the size of a closet, but she was immensely relieved to be there. She would have done just about anything at that point to get away from St. Tropez. Once again her mother had disappointed her, but Heloise was used to it by now, and she was thrilled to be in Paris and discover the city on her own. She had been there as a child with her father, but this time she wanted to explore it herself, go to museums, sit in the cafés, eat in little bistros, and she wanted to visit the hotels that had inspired her father when he put together his hotel.

The first stop on her list was the Hotel Ritz in the Place Vendôme. She had been warned not to wear blue jeans or they wouldn't let her in since she wasn't staying there, so she wore a pair of simple black slacks and a white blouse and put her long red hair in a bun, just as she did at the hotel, which made her look older than she was. And she was in awe of the elegant surroundings the moment she walked through the door: the long mirrored halls, the wood paneling. The chasseurs were her own age and wore almost the identical uniform to the bellmen at their hotel. She walked all through the lobby and looked into the elegant bar. Every inch of the hotel was beautiful, from the flowers to the chandeliers, and she could see why it had inspired her father to set up his own hotel in a similar style.

Using a map of the city, she went to the Crillon after that, which was another of the old elegant hotels, this one on the Place de la Concorde. She read in a guidebook she had bought that the guillotine had been located outside the hotel years before. The Crillon was beautiful as well. And from there she went to the Meurice on the rue Royale. It had been German headquarters during the Second World War and was another of the city's grand hotels.

She saved the Plaza Athénée and the George V, which was now a Four Seasons, until the next day and was equally impressed by them, for their elegance and beauty. But the hotel that had snagged her heart was the Ritz, and she went back to it again and again. She had tea in the garden, and brunch on Sunday morning in the Salon César, to see if she could borrow any ideas for the Vendôme.

And she took photographs of the flowers at the George V with her cell phone, so she could show them to Jan at home. The American designer Jeff Leatham had created a whole new style of flower arranging that was different from anything she had ever seen, with long stems sticking at odd angles out of tall transparent vases, creating a whole installation like a work of art. She wanted to try and imitate that for their lobby. For the first time she felt as though she were in partnership with her father, and was prouder than ever of the gem he had created with the Vendôme. Paris was like the mecca of the hotel industry, and she visited several smaller, elegant hotels as well, like the St. James in the sixteenth arrondissement, which combined the elegance of France with the atmosphere of a British men's club, with ancestral portraits, wood paneling, and deep leather couches in the bar.

She spent a week in Paris discovering every hotel she had ever heard of and even a few tiny ones on the Left Bank. And at night she would go back to the youth hostel and plan what sights she was going to see the next day. She had to switch youth hostels after a few days because she had stayed the limit of days they would allow. And she moved to one nearby, also in the Marais.

She didn't care about the national monuments nearly as much as she did about visiting the hotels. She took notes on what she saw, and photographs whenever she saw something that she thought they could imitate at home.

When she finally heard from her father, he was upset. He had tried her for several days at the house in St.

Tropez where no one answered, and finally Miriam told him that she had gone back to New York more than a week before. And when he tried her on her cell phone, it had taken another two days to reach her. He called their friends in Bordeaux, and their daughter knew she had gone to Paris, because Heloise had called her to say hello and report on her adventures.

'Where are you staying?' he asked, annoyed that she hadn't checked in. She had gotten much too independent over the summer, and he didn't like it. But she was on a quest, and her own personal mission, and she didn't want him to force her to come home, so she had stayed out of touch for as long as she could.

'I'm in Paris, visiting every hotel I've ever heard of and staying at a very nice youth hostel in the Marais. Papa, it almost makes me cry every time I see those hotels, they're so beautiful.' She spoke of them like shrines. 'The Ritz is the most beautiful hotel I've ever seen, after ours of course.' Although he was troubled by not hearing from her for so long, he laughed at what she said.

'I know all about those hotels. I worked there. Why didn't you call me when you left your mother in St. Tropez? How bad was it?'

'It wasn't great,' she said vaguely. He knew it must have been pretty bad if she left.

'I didn't want you to make me come home,' she said honestly. 'I wanted to see Paris anyway, on my own. I'm glad I came.' Things had gotten clearer to her since she'd been there, and she knew what she wanted to do now. She was going to discuss it with him when she got home, but not on the phone.

'Well, I'm telling you to come home now. Get your bottom on a plane. I don't want you floating around Paris alone. You've been there long enough.' But she wanted to stay forever.

'I'm fine, Papa. Can I have a few more days? I don't want to leave yet.' He grumbled when she said it and finally agreed to let her stay if she checked in with him twice a day. 'Okay, I promise.' But her father was secretly impressed that she had managed so well alone. She had definitely grown up.

'And don't go on the metro late at night. Take a cab. Do you need money?'

'No. I'm doing fine.' It shocked him to realize how self-reliant she had become. She had left her mother's house, for whatever reason, gotten herself to Paris, and seemed to be having a great time on her own. He couldn't wait to see her, but he knew that the experience was good for her. She'd had a job in Bordeaux, left St. Tropez, and was doing fine in Paris. It had been an interesting summer for her, and she had loved it. She thanked him profusely for letting her stay. She promised to come home in another week. And the week after that she was starting her senior year at the Lycée. The timing of this trip had been perfect for her, more than he knew.

She returned, as promised, eight days later, after several more visits to the Ritz and a drink on her last night at the Hemingway Bar. She had met up with her school friends once or twice. And several men had tried to pick her up, in bistros and bars, but she had fended for herself. She took a cab back to her youth hostel when she left the Ritz, and early the next morning she flew home. Her trip to Paris had been a total success.

She sat quiet and dreamy all the way back to New York on the flight and went through customs quickly. She had called her father before she left to tell him what flight she was on, and he was waiting for her at the airport, with the hotel driver and the Rolls. She jumped into his arms with an enormous grin, and he held her close, and was so grateful she was home. He had missed her more than he'd admitted to her or anyone else.

'You'd better get into Barnard or NYU,' he warned her on the drive back into the city. 'I'm not letting you go away for that long again.' She didn't answer him for a few minutes and was looking quietly out the window, and then she turned to him with a serious look of determination that he had never seen in her before. She looked into her father's eyes, and what he saw for the first time was a woman and not a child.

'I'm not going to NYU or Barnard, Papa. I'm going to apply to the École Hôtelière in Lausanne.' She said it in a quiet voice. It was the same school he had gone to, but the last thing he wanted for her now was a career in the hotel industry. She would have to sacrifice too much and have no other life. 'I looked them up online, and they have a two-year program that I qualify for, and one of those years is an internship in the industry. I want to run the hotel with you one day, and I have a lot of good ideas we can even try out right now.'

'I used to dream about your running the hotel with me,' he said sadly. 'But I want you to have a better life. You won't have a life. You'll never have time for a husband and children. Look at me, I work eighteen-hour days. I want more for you than that.'

'That's all I want and what I love,' Heloise said emphatically and looked like she meant it as she gazed intently at her father. 'I want to work with you, not just fooling around like I did as a kid. And I can take it over when you get old.' She had thought it all out and was completely sure that she wanted to work at the hotel, after what she'd seen that summer in Europe.

'I'm not that old yet, thank you very much,' he said, although he was touched. 'And I want a better life for you than working eighteen-hour days for the rest of your life. You just want that now because it's all you've ever known.' The hotel was familiar to her, but he wanted her to have a saner life than his own.

'No, I want it because I just saw every great hotel in Paris, and I love what you've done with the Vendôme. Maybe together we can make it even better. I love living at the hotel and working there. It's the only life I ever wanted.' As she said it, he felt acutely guilty for not getting her out of the hotel more often. He didn't want her adult world confined to a small hotel on the Upper East Side of Manhattan. He spent the rest of the drive into the city trying to convince her she was wrong.

'Why are you saying that?' she questioned him finally. 'Don't you like what you do, Papa?'

'I love it for myself but not for you. I want you to have so much more.' And then as he said it, he heard himself saying all the same things his parents had said to him thirty years before. He was giving her all the same reasons they had given him, wanting him to be a banker or a doctor or a lawyer. They had done everything to dissuade him from the École Hôtelière, just as he was doing to his own daughter now. He suddenly fell silent as he looked at her and realized that she had to make her own choices, and if this was what she loved and wanted to do with her life, he had no right to stand in her way and dissuade her.

'I don't want you giving up your life for a hotel,' he said sadly. 'I want you to have kids and a husband and a bigger life than mine.'

'Are you unhappy at the hotel?' she asked, as she watched him, and he shook his head.

'No, I love it,' he said honestly. He had found his niche early on, no matter what his parents thought about it.

'Then why won't you let me do what I love? I've loved being in the hotel all my life. There's nothing I could ever love doing more than that. It's what you taught me and what I want to teach my children one day, to pass it on.'

Hugues laughed softly as she said it. 'They'll probably want to be doctors and lawyers.'

She smiled at him. 'Well, I want to work with you till we both grow old.'

'And you're telling me you want to leave me and go to school in Switzerland for two years,' he said sadly.

'You can come over and visit. I'll come home for holidays and vacations, like Christmas and spring break.'

'You'd better,' he growled as he put an arm around her.

A page had turned for her while she was in Paris, and they both knew it. She had stepped out of her childhood into adulthood, and the adult life she wanted was at his side, running the Hotel Vendôme. 'I never should have let you go to Europe this summer,' he grumbled good-naturedly, looking at her and seeing how much she had matured in two months. She looked terrific and seemed very sure of herself and the future she wanted, more than ever before.

'It would have happened anyway. I don't want to go to NYU or Barnard. I want to go to hotel school. I'm proud of what we do, and I want to learn how to do it better so I can help you.'

'All right,' he sighed, as they pulled up in front of the hotel. He turned to his daughter with a resigned expression. 'All right, you win. And welcome home.'

He followed her out of the car and into the lobby as all the bellmen, desk clerks, and concierges ran to greet her and welcome her back. He could see that the child she had been had vanished forever, and the woman she was becoming had returned. Somewhere between Paris, Bordeaux, and St. Tropez, a butterfly had been born.

Chapter 6

Heloise began her senior year at the Lycée with more self-assurance than she'd ever had before. She knew what she wanted to do now, and had established clear goals. She sent her application to the École Hôtelière de Lausanne in October.

She told Mrs. Van Damme about it when she did. Her old dog Julius had died several years before and had been replaced with a white female Pekingese named Maude. Mrs. Van Damme emphatically approved of Heloise's idea of going to hotel school since it was what she loved. Her grandson Clayton was at Yale and wanted to study photography eventually, which Heloise knew from talking to him that summer, and his grandmother was encouraging him to pursue his dream too. She said that in the end it was all one had, and turning those dreams into reality was the only worthwhile path. Heloise liked hearing from Clayton but hadn't seen him for several months. She had been too busy since the summer, and he was enjoying his freshman year in college and seldom came to New York. But he called Heloise from time to time and said he liked Yale but was thinking of transfering to Brown, where he could study photography.

The elderly doyenne seemed to be failing in the past year. Heloise worried about her and always promised herself she'd visit her more often, but she was particularly busy with school-related activities, and it was her last year at home, if she got into the hotel school in Lausanne, as she hoped.

Over Thanksgiving Mrs. Van Damme got ill. She caught a nasty cold that turned into bronchitis, and to pneumonia after that. Hugues stopped in to check on her daily. And Heloise came in to see her religiously every day after school, and brought her little vases of flowers that Jan made for her. Her son came to visit her from Boston, and after consultation with her doctor, they put her in the hospital. She left the hotel by ambulance. And Heloise kissed her goodbye and promised to take care of her dog. Hugues and Heloise visited her and brought her a big bouquet of flowers. But Mrs. Van Damme seemed less and less interested as the days went by, and a week before Christmas, she quietly slipped away in the night. She was eighty-nine years old and the only grandmother figure that Heloise had ever had. All her real grandparents had died before she was born. And she mourned the loss of the elderly lady who had been kind to her all her life. And she was grateful when her son allowed her to keep Maude.

They went to her funeral at St. Thomas, and many of the hotel employees attended as well. Hugues asked Jennifer to arrange for a van to get them all there, there were so many. Even Mike the engineer went, wearing a dark suit. So did Ernesta, Bruce, Jan, several of the maids, an elevator man, two bellmen, Jennifer, Heloise, and Hugues.

Heloise saw Clayton there with his parents, but they barely had time to say hello as they left the church. He looked as bereft as she felt. And living in the same hotel with her, Heloise had had the chance to see her more often, and perhaps know her better, than her own grandson, who didn't see her often and rarely came to New York. It was a somber day for Hugues and Heloise, and put a damper on Christmas for them.

It was a busy season at the hotel, and Heloise had already tried to implement some of the things she had seen in Paris. Jan was trying to do their flowers for the lobby now like Jeff Leatham at the Georges V, from photographs Heloise had taken there. And she had added many things to their brunch menu that she had noticed at the Ritz. People were already commenting on how spectacular the flowers were, and how great the brunch. Hugues was proud of her and she was pleased. And she was applying what she had learned in Bordeaux to the wines she selected from their cellars. And as soon as she'd gotten back after the summer, she went back to work organizing their donations to the food bank, and working downtown at the soup kitchen and family shelter once or twice a week. Hugues was very impressed.

But the high point for Heloise came in January, when the École Hôtelière de Lausanne accepted her for the fall. She hadn't applied to a single other college. And she was ecstatic when she got their letter. It was exactly what she wanted, and it was her dream. She called all her friends at school to tell them, none of whom knew what colleges they were going to yet and wouldn't know till March. She was all set.

The months after that flew by, with the usual activities at the hotel, important guests, VIPs, foreign dignitaries, famous movie stars, and politicians. Her father narrowly averted a strike by the kitchen staff. Some employees quit or retired, and new ones were added. She rarely had time to stop and peek in at the wedding receptions. And she spent every weekend working at the front desk, for experience and practice. And everything he saw her do had a bittersweet quality for Hugues, knowing that she was leaving in a few months, even if it was only for a year or two. He was hoping that she would do her year of internship for her degree at their hotel, but Heloise wasn't sure. She was thinking of trying her wings at another hotel, possibly in Europe, before she came back to the Vendôme for good.

Hugues was sad about her leaving to go to school in Europe and said so to Jennifer, but she thought it would do him good. It was time for both of them to cut the cord. And she knew it would be hard because they were so extremely close.

Heloise went out with some of the boys from her class that spring, but she had no serious romance. Her whole focus now was on leaving and starting school in Lausanne. It was all she thought or talked about. And Hugues planned a trip around Europe with her for the month before he dropped her off at school in Lausanne. It was going to be the first real vacation he had taken in years. And Jennifer made all the arrangements for him. They were planning a few days at the Hotel du Cap/Eden

Roc at Cap d'Antibes. From there they were driving to the Splendido in Portofino, flying to Sardinia, and then to Rome. They were going to drive north then to Florence and Venice and eventually wind up in Lausanne. And they were both looking forward to it.

Jennifer could only imagine how lonely he would be when he came back alone. She had gone through it herself when her kids left for college. She wisely suggested he take on a new project for the fall. Heloise seconded the idea and convinced her father to redo some of the bigger suites, to keep them fresh and new, especially the presidential and penthouse suites. The hotel was now fourteen years old, and it was time. They had done small repairs on an ongoing basis to keep things in good condition, but Heloise suggested new colors, new fabrics, and a fresh decor in their big suites. They agreed that he'd need a decorator, and Jennifer got a list of names. There were four, three women and a man, and Hugues agreed to meet them when he came back at the end of August, after dropping Heloise off in Lausanne. She and Jennifer agreed that it was just what Hugues would need to keep him even busier and distracted without her.

The trip that they took in Italy and France was the most exciting of Heloise's life, and they had a wonderful time.

They stayed at the best hotels in each location, ate fabulous food, admired the virtues and details of each hotel, and decided to borrow a few. It was a terrific trip for both of them, and Hugues's heart was heavy when they got to Lausanne and checked into the Beau Rivage Palace, where he had done an internship himself when he was young. Being there was a trip back in time for him. It reminded him of his parents and how strenuously they had objected to his attending the venerable school that Heloise was about to start. And no matter how sad he was to see her leave, he had to smile in spite of himself when he saw how happy she was, how excited to be starting classes, and learn everything she could before coming to work at the hotel with him. It touched his heart.

The school itself was as beautiful as he remembered, with spacious modern buildings, neat walkways, handsome trees, and well-kept lawns. There were housekeeping services for the students, and phones in nearly every room, along with Internet access everywhere. The school was impeccably run. They even gave each student their own computer, which they would take with them when they left.

Heloise was required to take two of the eighteen sports they offered, and signed up for swimming and modern dance. They wanted to encourage healthy bodies and minds and expected them to work hard.

There was an excellent library, state-of-the-art kitchens, and several restaurants on campus, which the locals loved coming to. They offered courses in oenology, to learn about wine, which Heloise signed up for, after getting interested in it in Bordeaux. And there were two bars run by the students, which were full every night.

Heloise signed up for the Management of Hotel Operations Programme and would be taking classes in English and French. There were fifty students in her section, and another hundred and thirty in the longer program, representing eighty-five nationalities combined, equally divided between men and women. There was no question in Hugues's mind, or Heloise's, that she would have a wonderful time there, and learn everything she needed to know. But it made his heart ache to let her go.

The chill of fall was already in the air in late August, and the forests and mountains around the school were beautiful. It all reminded him so much of his youth. He had taken her to Geneva for a day as well. It was only an hour from the campus, and he had shown her where he and his parents lived when he was a child. This trip was a pilgrimage of sorts for him.

They both cried when he left her in her studio room. Heloise looked as sad as he did the day he left, but an hour later she was unpacking, and a flock of young people invited her out to dinner, and by that night she had half a dozen new friends. Hugues was on the plane to New York by then, looking out the window and wondering what he would do without her in New York. It made him miss her even more to see the dog when he got home. She looked at him expectantly, as though wondering where Heloise was. He unpacked that night and was in his office the next morning at six. Jennifer was surprised to see him there, with a stack of finished work piled up beside him, when she came in at eight.

'What are you doing here at this hour? Jet lag?' she asked, pouring him a cup of coffee and setting it on his desk.

'Probably,' he conceded. 'The apartment is so quiet without her, I couldn't stand it, so I came down here to work since I was awake.'

'Do you remember what we promised Heloise we'd do today?' she asked him in a maternal tone. He was suffering severely from empty-nest syndrome. Having been both mother and father to his only child, losing her to a school three thousand miles away was a big adjustment, and a hard one, just as they all had known it would be.

'What was I supposed to do today?' He looked blank.

'Pick a decorator, so you can start doing the remodel

on the suites on the ninth and tenth floors.' She handed him the list again, and he looked bored.

'Do I have to? I don't have time to think about it. The union is threatening a strike.'

'That's why you need a decorator, so you can take care of things like that.'

'Heloise and I can pick fabrics when she gets home. It's waited this long, it can wait another few months.' He tried to dodge her.

'No, it can't. You promised your daughter, and I promised her I'd see to it that you pick one of the decorators and get started before she comes home.' He growled but looked at the several photographs of apartments and hotels his assistant handed him. One was too modern and too stark; the rooms done by the man were too ornate. All four interior designers were the most successful in New York. The last two both did work that seemed in keeping with the hotel, elegant and sophisticated without being overdone. 'May I make appointments for you with both of them, so you can see which one you like? After that, they can submit designs and plans for the suites, and an estimate of cost.'

'Fine,' Hugues said, sounding irritated, and Jennifer was unimpressed. She and Heloise had agreed to follow it through whether he liked it or not. And for now, it was 'not.' The last thing he wanted was a decorator following him around, waving swatches in his face and color charts. The whole project sounded like a nuisance to him, but it needed to be done to keep the hotel elegant and fresh.

Jennifer left the room with the sample photographs, and he went back to the work on his desk and forgot about it. He had a text message from Heloise that afternoon. She said she was running between classes and didn't have time to talk, but everything was great. The obvious excitement in her text depressed him even more. He knew he was worrying unreasonably too. What if she found a job at another hotel, like the Ritz, and never came back? He was torturing himself with a thousand fears. He missed her terribly.

He was in a dark mood for several days and startled when Jennifer told him a week later that he had appointments with the two decorators back to back that afternoon.

'I don't have time,' he growled at her, which was unlike him. But he had been short with her and everyone else since his daughter left. He was in pain. Jennifer knew it well and had gone through the same phenomenon when both her children left for college within a year of each other. Her job at the hotel had distracted her and made the process less painful. And she was committed to helping Hugues get through it too. He had been a good employer and a good friend over the years, and if she was able to get him to adjust to Heloise's leaving for school in Switzerland, she was happy to help out. And the decorating project he had discussed with his daughter seemed like their best shot at it for now.

Despite a considerable amount of grousing and complaining, Hugues showed up in his office, five minutes before the first decorator was due to arrive, and shot his assistant a dark look. She had forced him to take the two meetings.

'Don't look at me like that,' she smiled at him. 'The suites on nine and ten will be even more gorgeous once you do it, and you can charge more for them. And if you don't hire someone to do it, Heloise will kill us both when she gets back.'

'I know, I know,' he said, looking exhausted, and ten minutes later the first of the two decorators arrived. Her credentials were excellent. She had decorated some of the most important homes in New York, a hotel in San Francisco, two in Chicago, and one in New York, and all were of similar size and feeling as the Vendôme. Hugues discussed the project with her for a few minutes and was instantly bored. She talked about fabrics, textures, window treatments, and paint tones in a way that put him to sleep. She was in her mid to late fifties, had a fleet of people working for her, and could easily have done the job, but nothing she said excited him. He had Jennifer take her upstairs to look at the four suites, and when she came back, she said he had to throw everything out. It was all dated and passé and yesterday's news. She wanted to give the suites a whole new look. What she said sounded too extreme to him, and he suspected that the bill she would present would be too. He asked her to give him an estimate, understanding that the fabrics and furniture he chose would be a variable, but he wanted a range, and told her he'd get back to her after that. But nothing about his meeting with her had inspired him to give her the job. And he looked bored when Jennifer walked back in.

'I have a feeling she could wind up costing you a fortune,' Jennifer commented, and Hugues agreed.

'She wore me out just listening to her. If her decorating is as boring as she is, the suites will look worse than they do now,' and they didn't look bad. Jennifer agreed with him, and twenty minutes later she escorted the second woman in. She was younger than the first one, looked quiet and conservative, and had a briefcase full of sketches, swatches, and suggestions for him. She had already looked at some of the suites online and had some interesting ideas that, much to his surprise, he actually liked. And she gave the project some energy and life.

Her name was Natalie Peterson, and she was best known for doing important homes in Southampton and Palm Beach, and a few in New York City, and she had done one small, elegant hotel in Washington, D.C. She was thirty-nine years old, so her list of accomplishments wasn't as long as the previous woman's, but she had won several awards for her design work. She was impressive in her presentation and delivery, and he liked her enthusiasm. She seemed vital and alive, and she had a twinkle in her eye.

'What made you want to undertake this project?' she asked him, which was an interesting question. 'What's your underlying goal? Keeping the hotel up to date, enhancing its reputation, charging more for the suites than you do now?'

'Keeping my daughter happy because she wants me to do it, and if I don't start it before she comes home for Christmas, she'll have my head.' Natalie laughed at the honest answer and smiled at him across the desk.

'She sounds like a young lady with a lot of influence on her father,' she said wisely.

'Absolutely. She's been the woman in my life since she

was four years old.' From what he said, Natalie wondered if he was widowed or divorced.

'She's away at college?'

He nodded with a proud expression. 'She's at the École Hôtelière, the school for hotelry in Lausanne. She just started a week ago. I was opposed to it, even though I went there myself.'

'You don't like the school?' Natalie asked with interest. She was curious about him. He looked like a serious, successful man, and he was obviously crazy about his child.

'I don't like having her so far away. And I didn't want her in the hotel business, but she's very determined. It's going to be a long two years, waiting for her to come home, unless she does her internship in hospitality experience here at home. I can't wait to have her back,' he said honestly with a wistful expression that touched her heart. He seemed very vulnerable when he said it. She had read his bio, and knew his experience and that he had just turned fifty-two. He looked younger than his years and was in great shape. 'Do you have children?' he asked her then, and she smiled.

'No, I don't. I've never been married. I've been too busy building my business, and now it feels a little late for that. And I won't be home with sick kids or dealing with teenage crises instead of doing your job.' He laughed at what she said, and she seemed comfortable with who she was. 'Your daughter seems like a good person to keep happy. Why don't we start work on one of the suites and see how it goes? We might even get it finished before she comes home for Christmas, if we get decent delivery dates on the fabrics. And I like the furniture you have. I'd like to incorporate it in the new designs.'

He liked the sound of that. It was far less expensive than the suggestion of the other decorator, who wanted to throw everything out. And they had beautiful things in the rooms now. They just needed some freshening up and new touches. He liked the way this woman thought. And he also liked the idea of trying her out on one suite instead of plunging ahead with four. And despite her reputation, because she was considerably younger than the first one, she was willing to make adjustments on fees and price, and she had more time, although she had a considerably smaller staff and did most of the work herself. She said she had two assistants and a design assistant, so she kept her overhead low. The other woman had a twelve-man office with three young designers working for her, and a color consultant on staff. When Hugues asked, Natalie said she did all the color work herself, and her clients had been happy with it so far. He had heard good things about the hotel she'd done in Washington, and he asked her to give him an estimate for the first suite if he decided to move ahead. She promised to have it on his desk within a week. She seemed hungry for the job, and he liked that about her too. She was matter of fact and down to earth and didn't put on airs. She stood up then and thanked him for the meeting, and said she didn't want to take more of his time. And they had already arranged for Jennifer to show her the suite before she left.

'I'll try to get the estimate to you this week. And if you decide to do the project with my office, I have some free time at the moment while another client is still building her house, and I think we could get off to a pretty rapid start, since there's no construction involved. But I work with a great architect if you ever decide to go in that direction.'

He had actually enjoyed the meeting and smiled as he shook her hand and then walked her to the door. Jennifer was waiting to take her upstairs and was back twenty minutes later, looking pleased.

'I like her,' Jennifer volunteered before he asked her, after the decorator left. 'She seems sensible, energetic, and young.' She was old enough to have experience, but young enough to be flexible and not too set in her ways.

'So do I,' Hugues admitted. 'I think Heloise would

love everything she said and would enjoy working with her. And she wants to use the furniture we've got. That's a big plus.'

'Did you hire her?' Jennifer was happy to see him smiling again and in a better mood. He was excited about doing something that would make his daughter happy when she got home.

'Not yet. She said she'd send me an estimate this week. But she came very well prepared.' He had been favorably impressed.

And true to her word, Natalie had the estimate on his desk in three days. Her price was reasonable for the design work and to oversee the project, and the costs were going to be even more reasonable since she had suggested they use the painters he had on staff at the hotel.

'What do you think?' Jennifer asked him after he'd read it, and he was smiling again.

'If she sticks to it, the estimate is great.' He was about to tell Jennifer to call her, and then decided to do it himself. Natalie was quick to come on the line. She sounded like an upbeat, happy person, and he liked that about her too.

'It's a deal,' he said simply. 'I like your estimate. When can you start?'

'How about next week?' It was going to be a scramble

for her, but she wanted to impress him so she'd get the other three suites to do after this. 'We'll get started. I'll work on fabric samples and color swatches this week.' She suggested doing the bedroom in pale yellows, and the living room in warm shades of beige and taupe, if that appealed to him. He liked that, and she suggested a meeting on Monday morning, unless he had time over the weekend.

'There are no weekends in my life anymore,' he explained, especially now that Heloise was gone. When she was at home, he would take breaks occasionally to spend time and do things with her, but now he worked seven days a week. There was always something for him to do in the hotel.

'There aren't in my life either,' Natalie said simply. 'That's the advantage of not having kids.' Or a husband, she almost added and then didn't. She had never married but had lived with a man for eight years, until he ran off with her best friend three years before. Since then she had done nothing but work, and she didn't regret it. Her business had been booming ever since, and she thought that getting a sample suite to decorate at the illustrious Hotel Vendôme was a major coup. 'How about Sunday afternoon? I just don't want to come too late. I'd like to show you the samples in the room, while it's still light. They have to work in electric light too without washing out, but you'll get a truer sense of the palette if we look at them in daylight first.' She was very professional with him.

'Why don't you come for brunch? We do a very decent brunch here. Particularly since my daughter changed the menu. We can go up to the room to look at the fabrics after we eat.' It sounded sensible to him and he liked talking to her. And Sundays were never as hectic for him as the rest of the week.

'That sounds great. Thanks very much. What time?'

'Meet me downstairs at eleven. I don't want to take up your whole afternoon,' Hugues said pleasantly.

'Thanks again.' They both hung up then, and Natalie let out a whoop of glee and shared the good news with her assistants. 'We got the job!' she shouted, and they echoed her delight. 'We're going to have to work our asses off to do this quickly. I really want to get the other three suites. And maybe the presidential suite after that. So let's not drag our feet on this one. I only want to show him fabrics that we can get quickly. No fourteen-week back-stock orders, and nothing that's been discontinued or has to be woven especially for us.'

'Got it,' Pam, her main assistant, said, and Natalie said she'd go to market herself to look for fabrics for the next two days. She wanted to see if she could find some new paintings for the rooms too, without destroying their budget. But she had some great resources for art and asked her second assistant, Ingrid, to check that out. She wanted to show him as much as she could on Sunday. And she wanted to get started soon.

The rest of the week was crazed for her. They had several other jobs they were working on, and she had Jim, her design assistant, tackle them, while she went out looking for fabrics and ideas for Hugues.

When Natalie arrived at the hotel at eleven o'clock on Sunday morning, she was carrying two enormous canvas bags of fabric samples, and several boards with paint samples that she had had mixed for him. Hugues came out of his office and suggested she leave them at the front desk, as they headed toward the dining room. A bellman took both bags from her. She was wearing a white Chanel jacket and jeans with sexy high heels. But everything about her shrieked 'respectable' and 'attractive.' She had long straight blond hair she wore pulled back and looked like a young Grace Kelly, and he noticed that she wore pearls at her neck and on her ears. There was nothing showy about her. She gave off an aura of competence and good taste. She was carrying a Kelly bag in a neutral cashew color, with an Hermès scarf tied to the handle. He liked walking into the restaurant with her, and she complimented him on the handsome decor of the room, which worked very well and was at the same time cozy and chic. It had long since become one of the most popular restaurants in New York, noted for its great food, fine wines, and casually elegant atmosphere.

They chatted about work and travel over brunch, which Natalie commented was excellent. She told him she had lived in London for four years, and then come back to New York.

'Do you miss living in Europe?' she asked him. He was still very European, in his manners and his dress, and the hotel had a decidedly European feeling to it, and in the way it was run. It was one of the things their guests loved most.

'Not really. This is home now. I've lived here for almost twenty years. I just hope my daughter doesn't decide she wants to live in Europe after going to school in Lausanne.'

'I doubt it. It would be hard to give up all this, and an adoring father. I'm sure she'll want to come back when she finishes school.' Natalie smiled at him warmly.

'You never know. She's only nineteen. She'll have fun there at her age.' She was already looking forward to skiing in the Alps and had been e-mailing him about it.

Natalie talked about some of her ideas for the rooms then, and she was anxious to show him what she'd brought. As soon as they finished lunch, she retrieved her bags from the front desk, and he grabbed a key and took her upstairs. She liked what she saw in the room. It was even prettier than she remembered, and the first thing she suggested was moving some of the furniture around, to give it a feeling of more space. She took one piece into the bedroom and suggested they get new lamps. He had never liked the ones they had, so he was pleased. She propped the paint samples against the walls then, and spread the fabrics around in groups and explained how she would use them.

Just looking at what she had chosen brought the room to life. There were warm taupes and dove grays, an ivory color, and a few dusty soft blues. It all worked together beautifully, and one by one they eliminated the fabrics he liked less. She suggested a new rug, and he agreed, and he liked her ideas for the window treatment, and the right wall color jumped out at both of them immediately, and she was going to trim some of the moldings in the living room in taupe. He loved what she suggested and how she did it.

She put what they had selected in one bag, and every-thing they had rejected in a stack on the couch, and then they walked into the bedroom and did it all again. The yellows she had selected were absolutely perfect in the room. In less than two hours they had made all the important decisions, and she promised to order everything in the coming week. And then they sat down in the living room, and she showed him photographs of the paintings that she liked. There were two that he approved immediately, and he was impressed by how reasonable they were. He thought she was a genius at what she did.

At three o'clock they were back in the lobby, and they were both excited by what they'd accomplished in a short time. One of her big bags was full of the samples of everything she was going to order, and the other was full of what he didn't want, although he had liked some of that too, but not as much as the rest. She had given him great choices, and he liked the prices of the fabrics she wanted to use. She had stayed away from expensive brocades and velvets and had stuck with sturdy fabrics that would hold up to constant use.

'It was great,' he said as he smiled at her. 'You made it fun. I wish my daughter were here.'

'We're going to knock her socks off with a fabulous new suite when she comes home,' Natalie promised, and she could hardly wait to start. She wanted to knock his socks off too, since he was paying the bill.

He thanked her again and walked her outside. The doorman hailed her a taxi and put her bags in it for her, as Natalie shook Hugues's hand and smiled at him.

'Thanks for brunch and a terrific afternoon,' she said warmly.

'Thank you for a beautiful new suite.' He returned the smile as she got into the cab, and he waved as they drove off, and then he walked back into the hotel with a happy expression on his face, and a spring in his step. He hadn't had this much fun since Heloise left for Lausanne. The concierge nodded at him as he walked by, wondering who the pretty woman was. He hadn't seen Hugues look that peaceful and relaxed in years.

Chapter 7

By Wednesday Natalie had ordered everything, fabric, paints, trim, the two paintings he liked, and she had found lamps and wall sconces that were perfect for the room. She dropped by the hotel on Thursday to show him rug samples, and he was impressed by how much she'd done. He hadn't said anything to Heloise about it when he spoke to her. He wanted to surprise her when she came home.

He had explained to Natalie that they needed to close the suite for as little time as possible. It was why he wasn't letting her do the high-revenue presidential and penthouse suites yet. He wanted to see how fast she worked. Natalie felt sure that if they began working on it at the end of October, once all the fabrics were in, she could have it up and running again by Thanksgiving. They had agreed to leave the bathroom as it was, the existing fixtures were good looking, and with a fresh coat of paint it would look bright and new. She assured him that she had everything under control. And he promised her that if the final result was as elegant as he thought it was going to be, he would give her the other three large suites to do and one day the presidential and penthouse suites as well. Natalie was thrilled, and so was he. He wanted her advice now about some of the other rooms, without redoing them all.

They met the following weekend to look at some other rooms, and she suggested simple fixes and adjustments that wouldn't cost a lot of money but would update their look. They had brunch in the restaurant again, and they seemed to find reasons to talk to each other every day. Jennifer smiled at him now whenever Natalie called, or Hugues mentioned her name. He seemed to be enjoying their new decorator a great deal. It made Jennifer happy to see him relaxed, interested, and enjoying a woman he was willing to spend time with, and not just the quick hit-and-run clandestine affairs he had had for years. The time he was sharing with Natalie contributed something to his life.

'Don't give me that look,' he said to Jennifer one day,

when she announced yet another call from Natalie. Her third of the day, and he called her just as often. 'It's just business. She's doing a great job. Heloise is going to be thrilled.' Jennifer was not so sure. If her father was as interested in Natalie as he appeared to be, not just as a decorator, Jennifer was concerned that Heloise might feel threatened by her. She was completely unaware of her father's quietly conducted dating life for the past fifteen years and had never shared him with anyone. It would be an entirely new experience for her.

He talked to Natalie about Heloise the second time they had brunch together, and went for a walk in Central Park afterward. It was a golden September afternoon. He told her how important his daughter was to him and what a special girl she was.

'I can't wait to meet her,' Natalie said, as they strolled along next to each other, enjoying the warm weather. He had left his suit jacket in his office, and she was wearing a T-shirt and jeans. 'It sounds from what I hear from everyone that she's part of the life force of the hotel.'

'I bought the hotel when Heloise was two. And her mother left two years later, when she was four. She's had free run of the hotel ever since, and she loves it as much as I do.'

'It must have been hard for both of you when her mom

left,' Natalie said gently, and he nodded, thinking about Miriam, which he seldom did. He hadn't cared about her in years. Heloise had filled a void for him. He didn't have a serious woman in his life, but he had a daughter he adored.

'Unfortunately, Heloise doesn't see much of her mother. She leads a very different life now. She's married to Greg Bones.' Natalie couldn't imagine the handsome Swiss hotel owner married to someone who would be married to Bones. 'That was a long time ago. It's been almost fifteen years. And she has two other children. She and Heloise don't have much in common when they get together. I guess she's too much like me.' He smiled at Natalie. He liked talking to her.

'That sounds like a good thing to me,' Natalie said, smiling at him. Greg Bones was well known for his cocaine and heroin addictions and his frequent stays in rehabs, and even visiting in their world didn't sound wholesome to Natalie.

'Thank God she didn't try to take Heloise with her. And I think she's been happy with me here at the hotel. Everybody loves her, and it's a safe, protected little world. Kind of like growing up on a ship.' It was a funny way to put it, but Natalie could see what he meant. The hotel was totally self-contained, almost like a town unto itself.

'She must miss it,' Natalie said sympathetically. Hugues sighed as they sat down on a bench in the park.

'Not enough, I'm afraid. She just started going out with a French boy at the hotel school, and she sounds like she's falling in love. My worst fear is that she'll stay over there.'

'She won't,' Natalie said confidently, 'not with all this to come home to. It sounds like she'll run the hotel with you one day.'

'I didn't want her to. I thought she should do something else. But once she decided to go to hotel school, that was it. She fought me like a cat about it when I tried to dissuade her. This isn't the life I wanted for her once she grows up. It doesn't leave room for much else.' She could see that that was true. Whenever Natalie called him, at any hour, he was at work.

'Were you never tempted to marry again?' She was curious about him. He was very reserved and a little bit aloof, except with her. Natalie made him feel comfortable and at ease, and he did the same for her.

'Not really. I'm happy the way things are. I'm too busy to be married, and I've had Heloise for all these years. That's been enough. What about you?' He turned to look at Natalie then. She was a beautiful woman, and she had never married. She lived for her work, as he did, and she had no children. In some ways, it seemed like a sad life to him, especially without a child.

'I lived with someone for eight years. It worked for a long time, and then one day it didn't. He never wanted to make a commitment, other than living together. Eventually we just led parallel lives with very little connection.'

'And then what happened?' Hugues could sense that there was more to the story, and she met his eyes squarely with her own.

'He left with my best friend. Three years ago. Things work out that way sometimes, like your wife and Greg Bones.'

'The funny thing is that if she'd stayed, I don't think we'd have been suited to each other. I was dazzled by her when we met, and fell madly in love with her. But I was young, and in the long run it takes a lot more than dazzle to make a marriage work.'

She smiled at what he said. And it was obvious that he didn't want marriage or even a serious relationship. He seemed content with his life the way it was. She wondered too if Miriam's betrayal had wounded him too badly to ever trust a woman fully again. She didn't inquire about his life in the ensuing years, and didn't think it was her place to do so.

'You're right. I'm beyond dazzle at this point too,' she said as he slipped an arm around her shoulders, and they sat there for a long time, peacefully, side by side. He liked the way he felt whenever he was with her. She was a kind, easy, open person, who worked hard, spoke honestly about herself and others, and seemed to accept life as it came. It was comfortable being with her, and she felt the same way about him. It was as if they had always been friends, and they worked well together. They had made quick decisions and seemed to have similar tastes and opinions about many things.

'How about an ice cream before I go back to work?' he suggested as a vendor pushed his cart past them, and she smiled at the idea. He bought two Eskimo bars, and they walked on for a little while watching families and children, and lovers kissing. The longer he stayed with her, the less he wanted to go back to the hotel. 'Would you have dinner with me one night?' he asked her, as they slowly wended their way back, and she nodded.

'Sure. But let's not do it at the hotel. People talk.' She said she could already tell that the hotel was a gossip mill. 'Neither of us needs the headache.' He appreciated her discretion. He wasn't sure what this was with Natalie, but he liked her, even if they just turned out to be friends. She would be a good friend to have. And without saying more about it, they walked back to the hotel, and she left him there, after thanking him for brunch again.

He called her at her office the next morning and invited her to dinner. He said he'd pick her up at her apartment and suggested a restaurant in the West Village. It sounded like a perfect evening to her as well. And she was in good spirits when he picked her up on Thursday night. They had a great time together and were the last to leave the restaurant. The night was warm, and they wandered down the street arm in arm before he hailed a cab.

'I had a great time with you, Natalie,' he said, smiling down at her.

'Me too.' It had been a long time since she'd spent such a pleasant evening with a man she barely knew and felt as though they were old friends. They exchanged ideas and talked about things they wanted to do and hadn't had time to do in their extremely busy lives. Most of all, the evening had been relaxed. It did them both good to get away from their desks and the pressure of their jobs. She ran a busy office too and was juggling many projects, not just his, although she loved working for him at the hotel, but she had other important clients.

'When am I going to see you again?' he asked as he stood facing her. He had an overwhelming urge to kiss her, but he thought it was too soon, and he didn't want to scare her off. She admitted to him that she hadn't dated in quite a while. If nothing else, he wanted to be her friend.

'Tomorrow afternoon,' she said, laughing in answer to his question. 'I want to check the final paint samples with you again.' He was beginning to think he should give her the whole hotel to redo so he had an excuse to keep her around. He loved spending time with her. He could smell the delicate scent of the perfume she wore, as he moved closer to her and touched her hair. He wondered if she thought he was too old for her; he was thirteen years older, and he was nervous that she might think there were too many years between them. Suddenly it was important to him what she thought.

'Maybe we should do something together this weekend. Would you like to go to a movie?' he asked cautiously.

'That sounds like fun,' she said softly, as he pulled her closer and looked into her eyes.

'Being with you is always fun,' he whispered, and then their lips came together and barely touched. And the kiss they shared after that seared them both. She looked at him in surprise afterward, wondering if it had been a mistake. He was a client after all, but for a delicious instant she forgot, and when he kissed her a second time, she forgot again. 'Is this okay with you?' he asked, and she nodded, and they kissed again. It was hard to stop, and then he just stood there holding her and smiling. He hadn't been this happy in a long time. He had forgotten what it was like to care about a woman and have her be important to him. 'I'd better get you home,' he said finally, and raised his arm to stop a passing cab. They both had to work the next day, and it was late.

They snuggled together in the taxi, and he kissed her again when he dropped her off.

'Thank you,' she said, looking at him with a smile. 'I had a wonderful time.'

'So did I,' he said, and then she turned and walked into her building as the doorman held the door open for her. She waved and went inside, and he closed his eyes and thought about her all the way uptown. It was two in the morning by then, and he wasn't even tired when he walked through the hotel, went to his apartment, and got undressed. He couldn't wait to see her again.

Chapter 8

Natalie moved into high gear in October on redecorating the suite. She found the hotel staff efficient, and with some supervision on her part, the painters mixed the paints in exactly the right shades. She kept a close eye on everything, which brought her to the hotel every day. Sometimes Hugues came up to see how things were going, or she stopped in to see him with questions or samples. She didn't want to disturb him, but they were both using every excuse they could to get to know each other better and spend a moment together in the midst of their busy days. And more than once he invited her upstairs to his apartment for lunch and ordered sandwiches from room service for both of them. He thoroughly enjoyed her company, and she felt the same way about him.

'I should really have you do some work up here too,' he said one day, looking around at his apartment, which hadn't been altered since they moved in. And Heloise still slept in her childhood room, which was filled with souvenirs from when she was a little girl. Her doll from Eva Adams was still sitting on a shelf. 'I wouldn't know where to start,' he admitted, 'and I guess this should be last on my list.' Right now, his focus and hers was on the suite she was doing, which was one of the largest and best in the hotel. And he was extremely happy with the minor adjustments she had made to several other rooms, just by adding or subtracting a few things, or trading furniture and objects between rooms. It gave each room she touched a whole new look. And she had suggested several new lamps and light fixtures, and some more art, to bring the hotel's appearance slightly more up to date, without changing the elegant flavor of the hotel. She had a great eye for detail.

'All you need here is a fresh coat of paint, a little more light, and maybe some new curtains. I'll see what we have left over after we finish the suite.' He loved that idea, as he smiled at her over their sandwiches. She was a practical, down-to-earth woman, who worked like a Trojan and had great taste. It was an excellent combination, and her philosophies about life and her work ethic were very similar to his. And one of the things he liked best about her was her obvious integrity. She was an honest woman, while never being unkind or blunt, and it was what she respected most in him as well. And beyond that, there was a chemistry between them that neither of them could put their finger on, which disregarded position, rank, or age. She was attracted to him, and he to her, and she loved how comfortable they were with each other. She stretched out her long legs as they finished lunch, and smiled at him. Her long, straight blond hair was pulled back, and he loved her looks; she managed to look both distinguished and sexy at the same time, just as he did in his white shirts and dark suits and handsome ties.

They'd been meeting quietly on weekends too, away from the hotel, for pizza and a movie, or a hamburger at restaurants downtown. Neither of them was sure if it was dating, but they were spending time together and always had a good time. And he had taken to calling her at night before he went to bed. She kept the same late hours he did, and they both worked often after midnight. It was a happy end to her day when her phone rang so he could say good night. And then they would somehow manage to run into each other the next day, by accident or design. It was hard for both of them now to imagine a time when they weren't part of each other's daily lives.

'So what's next after they finish painting?' Hugues asked. It had taken longer than he expected, although the painters were moving as quickly as they could under her meticulous direction, and they were just putting the additional touches on the moldings. It was looking even better than either of them had hoped, and the bathroom was already finished with a fresh paint job and a pretty new chandelier that she had found in the hotel's storage lockers downstairs. She was using as much of what they already had as she could, to keep expenses down, which he appreciated too.

'Everything's at the upholsterer now. I had some of the art reframed. The electricians are putting in the new fixtures next week. We can't put the carpet in for two more weeks, and after that we'll be ready for the installation. I promised you'd have the suite up and running again by Thanksgiving, and I think we're almost there.' She looked pleased and so did he. And they agreed that the two new paintings were going to add some real power to the room.

She could hardly wait for the guests who stayed there to comment on what they'd done, particularly those who had stayed in the suite before. They got so much return business that most of his best clients knew the suite well and were upset that it was unavailable right now. All of them said that they had loved it before, and the reservations manager assured them that they would like it even better once it was redone. Hugues and Natalie both hoped that would be true.

'There's an art show at the Armory this weekend,' Hugues commented as they finished lunch. As always, it was delicious, and even if just sandwiches, the hotel's kitchen and restaurant had added all the little flourishes and touches that they were famous for. 'Would you like to go?' he asked her. He was looking for every excuse now to spend time with her, even if it meant redecorating the entire hotel. He was totally smitten with her.

'That sounds like fun.' She smiled at him, finishing the last of their lunch. 'I'd love to find you a new painting for the lobby, something strong,' she said pensively, and explained to him exactly where, as he glanced at her with a pleased expression. He had the feeling that she was falling in love with the hotel, just as he had. She was, but she was falling in love with him as well.

'I can't wait till Heloise sees the new suite,' he said with a delighted expression.

'I can't wait to meet her,' Natalie added, 'although I have to admit I'm nervous about it. She's a legend in this hotel, much more than even Eloise at the Plaza.'

'Everybody here loves her,' Hugues admitted. 'They've seen her grow up since she was a baby, and they were wonderful to her when she was a little kid. They still are. She used to push the carts around with the maids, and she was always in the basement hanging out in the kitchen, or following the engineers. I used to worry that she'd want to be a plumber when she grew up. You have to be a jack of all trades in this business and wear a lot of different hats.' Natalie knew he did.

'How do you suppose she'll feel about our seeing each other, aside from just decorating the suite?' It had crossed Natalie's mind several times in the past month, since he had started asking her out. It hadn't gone further than dinner and some very enticing kisses so far, but his daughter was so much a part of his life, and so much of a central focus for him, that she knew whether or not his daughter liked her would matter to him a great deal. And Heloise had had her father to herself for a long time.

'I think we just need to let that develop over time. She's a big girl now, with her own life, and this French boyfriend I'm worried about. I think she's ready to let me have my own life.' Heloise had never stopped him. She just hadn't known about the women he went out with. But it would be different if he introduced Heloise and Natalie to each other. It was a big step for him.

'I don't think you have anything to worry about,' Natalie said as she leaned toward him, and he kissed her. She slipped into his arms then, and they kissed for a long time. The bond between them was slowly deepening and the attraction growing stronger, but they both wanted to let things happen naturally. Neither of them was rushing it, and both had been burned before, so they were cautious about who they got involved with. And she was a very different woman than the casual encounters he had had for many years. She was becoming important to him. And Natalie wanted to take her time and let things unfold, which was comfortable for Hugues as well. They were in no rush, and they both felt that if this were meant to be, and a relationship were to develop, it would blossom at the right time. She knew his resistance to marriage and commitment. They were having fun with each other and discovering new things about each other every day. She wasn't asking for anything more, and Hugues liked that about her too.

'I guess I'd better get back to work,' Hugues said regretfully as things started heating up between them. 'I'm having trouble with my head sommelier, and I don't want to lose him. I promised to meet with him to discuss it. Not to mention a disability claim one of the engineers is making, and threatening to sue me.' He looked unhappy about it. He had only been sued once by a guest in the past fourteen years, who had fallen in the bathtub and cut herself badly. She'd been drinking, and the fault was her own, but Hugues had settled to avoid bad publicity for the hotel, since the woman in question was well known.

It was a risk they ran daily with both guests and employees, not to mention with the unions, and the ordinary daily running of the hotel, with a constant flood of reservations and demanding guests. At times it was a heavy burden, and he still hated to have Heloise take all that on one day. He loved what he did, but the hotel's success and reputation didn't come easily and had to be constantly guarded and maintained. Natalie was becoming more and more aware of it as she got to know him better. It was not an easy business, and he did his job extremely well and had a gift for handling people, particularly those who were potentially trouble. He put balm on every situation and tended to every detail.

And he was kind to her as well. She thought he was a lovely person, and obviously a devoted father. She thought his ex-wife had been very foolish to have left him, particularly for the man she'd married. Greg Bones was no angel, and nothing Natalie would ever have wanted in a man.

They left his apartment together after kissing one last time, before stepping out into the hallway, and they looked professional and businesslike as they took the elevator downstairs. She got off on the floor of the suite she was working on, and he was going down to the lobby and back to his office. And a few minutes after Natalie checked on how the painters were doing, and was satisfied with their work, Jennifer came upstairs to see how things were going. Hugues had raved so much about the fancy paint job that she wanted to see how it looked for herself. And she was impressed with the artful job Natalie had gotten out of their ordinary hotel painters. It looked like a fancy first-class decorating job to her, and like everyone else, she could hardly wait to see it complete.

'The light in here is so good that it really helps,' Natalie said modestly, and Jennifer liked that about her too. She wasn't full of herself or a diva. Despite her obvious talent, she was a very unassuming person. Jennifer had brought a box of the hotel chocolates upstairs for her, and they sampled them together, commenting on how irresistible they were. 'If I worked here, I'd weigh six hundred pounds. The food is so good every time I eat here,' Natalie said as she ate a chocolate.

'Tell me about it,' Jennifer said with a woeful expression. And since they were alone, Natalie decided to ask her something that she was wondering about increasingly.

'What's Heloise really like? Everybody here talks about her like she's five years old in pigtails, and her father is so crazy about her, it's hard to get a reading on who she is.' Natalie wondered if she was horrifically spoiled or really a sweet kid.

'She's a lot like her father,' Jennifer said thoughtfully. 'She's very bright, and she loves this hotel as passionately as he does. It's the only home she's ever known, and the people who work here, and have for a long time, are her family. She has no one else except her father, and he thinks she walks on water.'

'I know.' Natalie smiled at her, helping herself to another chocolate. They really were impossible to resist. And they had little gold flecks on them for decoration, and a chocolate V. They were made exclusively for the hotel, yet another of the many touches that Hugues had insisted on from the beginning, even when he couldn't afford them. People bought them and sent them as gifts by the caseload from the shop downstairs, which was actually a lucrative part of the business.

'It sounds like they have a very special relationship, which is understandable since she grew up without a mother. I imagine she must be very possessive about him.

It sounds like there's been no woman in his life for a long time.' She was snooping, and Jennifer knew it, but she didn't mind. She would have done the same herself, and it was obvious to her that something romantic was happening between her employer and the interior designer he had hired to work on the hotel. She liked Natalie a lot, and thought she might be just the kind of person Hugues needed. And Natalie wasn't jealous about the hotel, she was coming to love it too, which Jennifer knew was important to him. But Heloise's approval would be more than important to him, it would be essential and a deal breaker for him. Natalie had correctly sensed that.

'Possessive?' Jennifer said, laughing. 'She *owns* him. She's had his heart in her pocket from the day she was born. And she was a mighty cute kid, with red hair, big green eyes, and freckles. She's a beautiful young woman now. And her father and this hotel are her whole life. It's pretty much the same with him. I'd be very careful with her, if I were you. If she feels you might take him away from her, she'll be your sworn enemy forever.'

'I'd never do that to her, or to him,' Natalie said quietly, and meant it. 'I respect the special relationship they have. I just wonder how she'd feel about his having anyone in his life, even without stepping on her toes.'

'It's hard to say,' Jennifer said honestly. 'It's never really happened before, not in a serious way.' And Natalie was beginning to think they were, or could be in time. 'I've always thought it would have been better for her if Hugues had had a woman in his life while she was growing up. She needed that, and it's a little late now. She's nineteen years old and pretty much an adult. But she's also never had to share him. I don't think she expects him to find someone now, and I don't think he expected that either. It's a new concept for both of them.' Jennifer looked pensive as she said it.

'I think it would be a big adjustment for Heloise if he had a serious relationship with a woman. It would be good for them both. But Heloise would have to get used to the idea, and it might take some time and a lot of diplomacy to get there.' It was good advice to Natalie and what she thought herself. 'She has a good heart, like her father,' Jennifer reassured her. 'She's just very much a daddy's girl, and this is her world. Any woman who falls in love with him will have to be mindful of that.' It was a clear warning, and Natalie was grateful for her wisdom and candor. She knew all the players involved and had for a long time.

'Thank you. That helps,' Natalie said, smiling at her, as they debated about a third chocolate. Jennifer decided to indulge herself, and this time Natalie resisted, which explained the difference of fifteen pounds between them. Jennifer always had a box of the delicious chocolates in her desk. 'It's pretty much what I thought. I'll bet it will be a big adjustment for him too if she has a man in her life eventually, which presumably she will. It must be hard for him to watch her grow up.'

'It's killing him,' Jennifer said honestly. 'He thought she'd be in pigtails forever, and this French kid she's involved with at school has him scared stiff. All he wants is for her to come home, as soon as possible, and not start a life over there. But we can't hang on to our kids forever, no matter how much we love them. I've got one in Florida and one in Texas, and they're all I've got. And this job. And I miss my kids like crazy.' She was in her fifties, and married to her job, and hadn't had a man in her life in years either. She'd had a crush on Hugues when she first started working there, but she had gotten over it very quickly when she saw how professional he was with his employees. He always said that she was the best assistant he had ever had, and that was enough for her now. She took pride in what she did and had a warm affection for him and his daughter, which showed in all she said about them. 'Try not to worry about Heloise,' she told Natalie, and patted her shoulder as she got ready to leave the suite and go back to her office. 'She's a good kid, and she loves her father. She's going to love you too. She'll want what's best for him in the end. Just give her a chance to get there. It may take a little longer than most. They've been through a lot together. Sometimes that makes it hard to add another person to the mix, but it's what they both need.' Natalie nodded, and went back to talking to the painters after Jennifer left. The wise woman who knew both of them so well had given her food for thought, and Natalie was smart enough to heed her words. What they all needed now was time. She wasn't plunging into anything blindly, and neither was Hugues. Natalie was proceeding slowly. And Jennifer's warnings about Heloise hadn't fallen on deaf ears.

Chapter 9

Just as Natalie had promised, the suite she'd been working on for almost two months was ready the week before Thanksgiving, and it was absolutely perfect. She'd been so sure they'd be finished on schedule that she had told Hugues they could safely book a reservation for Thanksgiving weekend, which worked out ideally for him. One of their regular guests, a senator from Illinois, had wanted to reserve it, and several other rooms, to spend Thanksgiving in New York with his children and grandchildren. And they were able to confirm the reservation.

Hugues stood in the suite with Natalie on the Monday before Thanksgiving and examined every detail with awe and admiration. She had created something warm and elegant that felt more like a home than a hotel room, which was exactly the effect they had both wanted to achieve. And the new paintings were spectacular in the room. She had worked on the installation all weekend and invited him up to see it when she hung the last painting on Monday afternoon. She had done a lot of the hanging and placing herself, as she always did, and she had been a taskmaster about the window treatments, which were beautifully made by a French woman she had used for years. The suite was exquisite. And she had had several pots of orchids placed in the rooms in key locations. Hugues looked at it with obvious delight, and then took Natalie into his arms and kissed her. The relationship they had been developing since she started working for him had been an unexpected bonus for them both, and not at all what he had intended when he hired her to do the job.

'You like it?' she asked happily, looking like a kid and wanting to clap her hands with glee when she saw his thrilled expression.

'I love it!' he confirmed. The final effect was even better than he had expected and she had hoped. He walked all through the suite, examining every detail, and then he turned to her as he held her hand. 'And more importantly, I love you . . . whether or not I like what you did here. But as it so happens, I do. You have an enormous talent.' And she had brought it in way under budget by using so many of the things the hotel already owned. 'The last two months have been the happiest in my life,' he said as he pulled her down on the couch next to him. 'I loved seeing you every day.'

'Me too,' she said, in awe of what he had just told her. She had fallen in love with him too. He kissed her again, and then called room service and ordered a bottle of champagne.

He opened the bottle of Cristal himself when it was delivered, and the waiter disappeared quickly, after commenting on how great the room looked. Hugues had a plan by then, and he spoke to her gently after they tasted the champagne.

'The general manager I worked for at the Ritz once told me that you never know how comfortable a room is unless you sleep in it yourself. I was thinking that maybe . . . if you agree . . . maybe we should try the suite tonight ourselves. I'd like us to be the first people who sleep here, while everything is brand new . . . How does that sound to you?' he asked her, and kissed her, and she smiled at him and put her arms around him. She had never been as happy with any man in her life. He was thoughtful and kind and considerate and such a loving person.

'I love that idea,' she said as they kissed, and then she looked at him with a worried expression. 'What about talk in the hotel?' That always concerned her.

'There's no reason why we can't have dinner here, quite respectably. What happens after that is our business. I own the place and have every right to sleep here if I choose. And I can spirit you out a back way in the morning, for the sake of your reputation. My daughter did that once very effectively with a homeless person. If she can do it, so can we.' Natalie smiled at the story.

'That must have been quite something.'

'It was. She has a very charitable side to her and was determined to prove that charity begins at home. He spent the night out of the cold and had two solid meals before she sneaked him out. It turned up on the security screens the next day, but our head of security will be very discreet in this case. I trust Bruce completely. So what do you think?' He looked hopeful and boyish as he asked her. They had been seeing each other and dating for two months, and they were both ready to move forward together.

'I think I love you, Hugues,' she said softly. In fact, she knew it and so did he.

They ordered dinner in the suite that night and had a feast. Hugues put music on, and they both relaxed and talked until nearly midnight. The room service waiter who had delivered their dinner and cleared the trays saw nothing unusual about their having dinner in the newly redecorated suite to celebrate its completion, and didn't even comment on it in the kitchen. And after that, with a Do Not Disturb sign on the door, the maids left them alone, and as the room was allegedly unoccupied, they had no reason to come in. He left his cell phone on, in case there was an emergency in the hotel, which was how the staff normally reached him since it was hard to know exactly where he was at any time. And if the owner wanted to try out the new suite, there was nothing surprising about that either. He had covered all the bases and finally turned the lights down low, kissed her, and led her into the bedroom when they were both ready.

He pulled the brand-new bedspread off the bed, and they put it on a chair together and then she fell into his arms and lost herself in his caresses and kisses. The bed enveloped them like a cloud, and all the pent-up longing of the last months and years and a lifetime without each other took them to a place that neither of them had ever dreamed of or ever hoped to find. She felt as though she had belonged to him forever as she lay in his arms after they made love, and he looked at her with the tenderness of a man who hadn't loved a woman in more than twenty years. He couldn't keep his eyes and hands and lips off her, and finally around four A.M. they wound up in the enormous bathtub, and when they got back to bed, they fell asleep instantly in each other's arms like happy children.

The sun was streaming into the room when they woke up the next day, and he couldn't resist making love to her again, even though it was later than they had planned, but he still thought he could get her out of the hotel without causing comment or having anyone notice. And they both forgot about that as they made love again, and then they showered together. He couldn't stop watching her as she dressed. He was in love with her mind, her heart, and her body.

'Have I told you yet this morning how much I love you?' he whispered into her hair, as he kissed her again once they were dressed, sorry that he had to leave her and go to his office. He wanted to stay with her forever.

'I love you too,' she whispered back. They could hardly tear themselves away from each other as they kissed for a last time and finally left the room. He put the tag on the door for maid service and led her down the back fire stairs, just as Heloise had done with Billy. He knew they would appear on the security screens, but he knew that Bruce Johnson would never comment on it if he saw them; nor would the others. The security staff dealt constantly with indiscretions committed by their guests, in the course of their illicit affairs, and their security men were like tombs. The guests of the Hotel Vendôme counted on its discretion, and so did Hugues. He pushed open the outer door downstairs and led Natalie out into the chill November morning.

'Do you want to come to my place tonight?' she asked him, and he nodded. They both knew they would never forget their first night in the brand-new suite. It had felt so right that they should be the first ones to stay there. And the adventure they had just embarked on, after two months of preparing for it, felt right to them both. 'I love you,' she whispered when he kissed her, and then hailed a cab for her at the corner.

'See you tonight,' he promised and waved as she drove away, and he felt as though a piece of him were going with her, the best part, his heart. And there was room in it, he knew now, for both Natalie and his daughter. There was no conflict there. He loved them both, it was just that simple.

He walked around the corner to the front entrance then and said good morning to the doorman, who looked mildly surprised to see him since he hadn't seen Hugues go out, but he was too busy to think about why that was. And a moment later Hugues strode into his office with a peaceful, happy expression and smiled at his assistant.

'Good morning, Jennifer,' he said, and walked into his private office. She picked up the phone immediately and ordered his usual cappuccino, and she brought it in to him when it arrived five minutes later.

'Did you sleep well?' It was a question she asked him often at the start of their day.

'Actually, I did. I tried out the new suite last night, just to make sure it's all in order for the senator on Wednesday.'

'How was it?' Jennifer asked with interest.

'Absolutely perfect. You should go up and look at it later.' He knew she hadn't had time to the day before, after the final installation. 'Natalie did a fantastic job. By the way, I want her to start on the three other suites we discussed, right after Christmas. Just wait till Heloise sees this one.' It had a younger feel to it than the previous decor, although the changes were very subtle and in no way shocking. And Jennifer wasn't surprised by his decision to let Natalie redo the other suites. She had expected that, for a variety of reasons. And just for a flash of an instant, she wondered if he had spent the night in it alone or with the woman who had decorated for him.

She almost hoped that was the case but rapidly decided it was none of her business. All she hoped was that he was happy, and he looked it, more than he normally did on a Tuesday morning.

He called Natalie after he checked his messages and drank his coffee. He was sitting at his desk, thinking about her, and decided to call her. She sounded as happy as he was when she answered and saw his number appear on her phone.

'I'm crazy about you, Natalie,' he confirmed to her, and the best part was that loving her was not crazy at all. It made perfect sense to them both.

'Me too. I can't wait to see you tonight.'

'We can always sneak back upstairs this afternoon if you want to. The senator isn't arriving till tomorrow.' They both laughed at the suggestion and knew that for now they were safer at her place, until they were ready to share their secret with the world. But he wanted to tell Heloise before he did that. It was a respect he felt he owed her, and Natalie agreed. They had talked about it the night before in the bathtub. Hugues said he was going to tell her about them over Christmas, which sounded right to her too, and not over the phone. She was coming home in four weeks, and they could be discreet for that long. And it was kind of fun keeping their relationship a secret. 'By the way, I want you to do the other three big suites. We can talk about it when you have time.'

'Thank you,' she said, smiling. She was happy about doing the other rooms, but she was much more excited about him and everything that had happened the night before.

'See you later.' After that, his day took off. He was busy until nine o'clock that night, and as soon as he could get away, he took a cab downtown to Natalie's apartment. She was wearing a pretty sweater and jeans, and before he could even open the champagne, they were in bed, exploring everything they had started to learn about each other the night before. They couldn't get enough of each other. And it was nice to be away from the hotel where they didn't have to worry about being discovered.

He lay in bed afterward and looked at her with love and wonder. 'How did I get lucky enough to finally find you?' he said, and meant it.

'I feel exactly the same way. I feel like I wasted all those stupid years before you came along.' She kissed him, and he smiled at her.

'They weren't wasted. They were the price we both had to pay to deserve each other. And I don't care how long it took, or how solitary it was, you were worth the wait, Natalie. I'd have crawled around the world on my knees to find you.' She smiled at the romantic words and put her lips to his again.

'Welcome home, Hugues,' she said softly, and he held her close and knew he was.

Chapter 10

The day of Heloise's return from Switzerland for Christmas vacation, the whole hotel was buzzing with excitement. The pastry chef baked her favorite chocolate cake for her, Ernesta made sure the maids thoroughly cleaned her room, Jan sent up flowers just the way she liked them, and all the Christmas decorations were set up in the lobby. Hugues was so pleased that she was coming home. He could hardly wait to see her. It had been almost four months, the longest he had ever been away from her in her lifetime. And he went to the airport in the Rolls to meet her.

He and Natalie had talked about it the night before, and she admitted that she was nervous about meeting his daughter. What if Heloise didn't like her? Hugues said that was absurd, of course she would, although he didn't want to tell her the night she arrived, but wanted to give her a few days to settle in. So much had happened. He and Natalie had spent every night together for the past four weeks, and they were going to miss each other for the two weeks that Heloise was home. She had three weeks' vacation, and Hugues had been upset to hear that she was planning to spend the third week skiing in Gstaad with her French boyfriend. His parents had a house there. Hugues had tried to object, and Heloise had brushed him off and said that all her friends were going. But he was grateful for every moment of the two weeks he was going to spend with her. He expected it to be just like old times when she was home. And somewhere in those two weeks, he was going to tell her about Natalie and his plans for them to meet each other.

Her plane arrived from Switzerland half an hour early, but Hugues was already there, and she hugged him so tight he could hardly breathe. She looked different to him, more grown up, suddenly more subtly European, and she had cut her hair a little shorter, which made her look more sophisticated too. Her first big romance with the French boy had somehow altered her. She had left a girl and returned a woman.

She chattered excitedly about hotel school all the way

to the city, and an astonishingly large number of the hotel's employees were waiting for them in the lobby when they arrived. It looked like a family scene, with the Christmas decorations around them. They hugged her and smiled at her, pounded her back and spun her around. Jan was there with an armload of long-stem pink roses for her. Jennifer came out of the office just to hug her. No VIP had ever gotten as warm or lavish a reception from the hotel. Three bellmen rode the elevator upstairs with them to assist with her single bag. And she looked ecstatic when she walked into their apartment and hugged her father again. And he looked every bit as happy as she did.

'Everything looks so wonderful!' she said, as she looked around and saw flowers everywhere, and the rooms were immaculately clean. 'And so do you,' she said, beaming at him. He had never looked better to her in her life. 'I missed you sooooo *much*!'

'Don't even talk to me about that,' he said with an exaggerated, pained expression to cover his feelings. 'I felt like part of me was missing, like my liver and my heart and both legs, for four months.' And then he remembered. 'And wait till you see nine-twelve. It's been completely redone.' He had told her it was in progress but wanted to save its completion as a surprise.

'Does it look great?' She seemed excited, and he took the key out of his pocket and grinned at her.

'Come and look. Someone's checking in tonight, but it's empty right now.' He took her by the hand, and they ran down the service stairway to the ninth floor, and he let her in. Hugues let Heloise go first, and he heard her literally gasp as she saw what had been done.

'Ohmigod, Papa! It's fabulous! It's soooo terrific, and just what we needed. It looks young and happy and elegant, and the new paintings are fantastic. And I like the lamps and the rugs.' She ran from the living room into the bedroom and liked it even more. 'The decorator must be amazing. She did a gorgeous job.' He had mentioned Natalie to her in the past four months but had been careful not to do so too much, so he didn't arouse her suspicions that there was something going on between them. And he had been artful about it, because he saw no hint of a question in her eyes. All she saw was the decor. 'I love it, I just love it,' she said as she sat down on the couch and looked around some more. And as he did, she loved all the little touches and accessories Natalie had added, and the things she had brought from other rooms that suddenly looked so much better here.

'And she came in under budget. I just gave her the

other three big suites to do. And she's been tweaking some of the other rooms.'

'She's very, very good,' Heloise said admiringly. 'I'd like to meet her sometime. Is she young? There's a really nice fresh feeling to what she does, while staying in the whole tone of the hotel,' which was old-world elegance with a new touch.

'She's young to me. Not to you,' Hugues said, referring to Natalie's age. 'I think she's thirty-nine.' He knew exactly how old she was but didn't want to look too sure, or appear to know too much. It would have been the perfect opportunity to tell her he was dating Natalie, and in love with her, but he didn't want to tell her so soon and risk upsetting her on her first night home. He wasn't sure. So he didn't say a word, except about Natalie's decorating and her age.

'I'll bet she's cool,' Heloise volunteered.

'She is,' he said quietly, and then Heloise wanted to go back upstairs. They had room service in their apartment that night, and she told him everything about the school, and François, the boy she was going out with.

'Are you in love with him?' her father asked her nervously, afraid of what he'd hear.

'Maybe. I don't know. I don't want to get distracted from school and screw it up. It's pretty hard. But we're both applying for internships next summer for our hospitality year. We're applying to the Ritz, the George V, and the Plaza Athénée.' Hugues looked crestfallen the moment she said it.

'I thought you were going to do your internship year here with me,' he reminded her.

'I can do both,' Heloise said sensibly. 'I can do six months in Paris, and the rest with you. That way I'd be home by Christmas next year.' But he had been expecting her return six months earlier, in June. It meant she would be gone for another year, and the last four months had already felt like an eternity to him. But not to her. It was obvious that she was having a ball in Lausanne, with François, the school, and all her new friends there. She said there were going to be ten of them staying at François's parents' chalet in Gstaad over New Year's. They were very successful and owned a hotel in the South of France. So they had that in common and a lot more. It was her first affair, and whether she admitted it or not, her father could see that she was in love.

She went downstairs after that to visit her old friends all over the hotel. She knew all of the night staff, stopped to visit the phone operators and the front desk, and kissed the concierge on duty before she came back upstairs again. Hugues was talking to Natalie when she came in.

And once Heloise was in the room, he said good night and hung up.

'Who was that?' Heloise asked with a smile. To her father, she was still a child, whether or not she really was. And it was difficult to explain to a child that he was in love with Natalie. Saying it made him feel uncomfortable and disloyal to her somehow. He knew that that was foolish, but that was how it felt.

'Actually, it was Natalie Peterson, the interior designer who did nine-twelve. I told her how much you love what she did. She says she'd love to meet you. Maybe in a couple of days.'

'Sure.' Although she'd noticed it, Heloise didn't comment on the fact that he had called her at ten o'clock at night. Heloise assumed they'd probably gotten to be friends while she did the work. 'That would be fun,' Heloise said with a smile, and went to their kitchen to help herself to some wine. Her father noticed it and was surprised. That seemed grown-up to him too, although he had always let her drink wine at table if she wanted to, which she rarely did. He hoped she wasn't drinking to excess with her friends at school. There was so little he could control now, or even influence, from so far away, which was the plight of all parents in his shoes. Once they grew up, they were on their own, with all their good and bad decisions and consequences thereof. All you could do was hope that what they did wasn't too high risk and the consequences weren't dire.

'What are we doing tomorrow?' she asked him, as she sat cross-legged on the couch, sipping the wine, while he tried to get used to the idea.

'Whatever you like. I'm at your full disposal for the next two weeks.' He still had to work, but he had let everyone know that he would be in and out of the office while his daughter was in town. And he had warned Natalie that he would see very little of her too. She was going to Philadelphia on Christmas Eve for a few days, to stay with her brother and his family. She was going by train with her older nephew, who had just started law school at Columbia.

'I have to do my Christmas shopping tomorrow,' Heloise explained. 'I didn't have time to do it in Lausanne. I had exams till yesterday.'

'How did you do?' he asked with a look of concern. He was afraid that François might be distracting her.

'Okay, I think. I know a lot of the stuff we're studying, from being here,' she said, looking relaxed.

They chatted for a little while, about school, Switzerland, and what the school had been like when Hugues had gone there, and eventually Heloise yawned and went to bed. On Swiss time for her, it was very late. And just as he had for nineteen years before she left, he kissed her and tucked her in.

'Night, Papa . . . it's so good to be home,' she said sleepily. She blew a kiss in the air, turned on her side, and was almost asleep by the time he left the room.

He went to his own room then, sat pensively for a minute, thinking about her and how good it was to have her home, and then called Natalie again. She was still awake and wondering how it had gone.

'How is she?'

'In love with that boy, I think. But she seems happy to be home. Now she says she wants to do an internship at a hotel in Paris next year before she comes back. That means she'll be gone for another year from now.' He sounded disappointed as he said it, and Natalie felt sorry for him. He was having a difficult time letting her go.

'It will go by very quickly,' Natalie reassured him, 'and you can go over and visit her anytime.'

'It's hard to get away from here.' She knew that was true too. He was so attentive to the hotel and on duty and available almost all the time. He always left his cell phone on when he was with her, even at night. And it was rare for him to let it go to voice mail, except when they were making love. Any other time, he answered.

'So when am I going to meet her?' Natalie sounded excited at the prospect, and she wanted to get the ice-breaking over with so she could get to know her.

'How about coming for a drink tomorrow? After work.'

'That sounds perfect,' Natalie said happily. 'I can't wait. This is like meeting a celebrity or a movie star,' she said, laughing.

'She is to me,' he confirmed, but she knew that. 'How about seven? If it goes well, maybe we can all go to dinner.'

'Great!'

'I miss you,' he said in a whisper. He didn't want Heloise to hear him, although he knew she was sound asleep, but just in case.

'So do I. I love you, Hugues.' And she hoped that one day she would love his daughter too. She wanted that for all of them. She wanted to be Heloise's friend, not stand in for her mother, which wouldn't have felt right. More like a favorite, very close aunt.

'I love you too, Natalie,' he said gently, and a moment later they hung up. He went to stand in Heloise's bedroom doorway for a moment. She was sleeping peacefully with a small smile on her face. He closed the door softly and walked to his bedroom with a feeling of peace he hadn't had since she left. He knew where she was tonight, that she was safe and that he would see her at breakfast in the morning. All was well in his world.

The next morning Hugues and Heloise ordered room service for breakfast. Two waiters came upstairs to serve it instead of one, and both kissed her excitedly when they saw her and told her that the hotel wasn't the same without her and she'd better hurry up and finish school and come back.

And after that she went out Christmas shopping, and her father insisted she take an SUV from the limo service since it was snowing, and he knew she wouldn't find a cab.

She shopped all day, met an old school friend from the Lycée for lunch, and was back looking happy and tired at five o'clock. She bounded into her father's office, and Jennifer looked up at her with a smile.

'It sure is nice to have you back,' Jennifer said as Heloise kissed her on the cheek on the way past her into her father's inner office. He was signing checks at his desk, and looked up with delight when he heard her come in.

'Do I have any money left, or did you spend it all today?' he asked with a grin.

'I spent most of it. But I left you enough so you can

buy me a Christmas present.' She cackled at her own joke, and he laughed.

'Oh really? What did you have in mind?'

'I don't know, something I can use at school. Like a tiara maybe, or a full-length sable coat.' Her face grew serious then. 'Actually, I was going to ask you if I can have new skis. My old ones are all beaten up, and I'd love to have new ones for Gstaad.' It was a reasonable request, and one he liked.

'I was thinking of that myself.' He had also bought her a shearling parka at Bergdorf that he thought she could wear to school, and a gold bangle bracelet with her name engraved on it, and 'Love, Papa' engraved inside. He had had a much harder time shopping for Natalie, who was simple and chic and appeared to have everything, and he wanted to give her something sentimental that she would wear. He had settled on an antique locket with a diamond heart on it, on a long gold chain, at Fred Leighton, and he hoped that she would like it. 'Do you want to go out to dinner tonight, or just eat here?' Heloise looked embarrassed the minute he asked. She didn't want to hurt his feelings, and she wanted to spend time with him, but she wanted to see her friends too. She had made dinner plans with two of them, and they were going to a party afterward in Tribeca.

'I'm sorry, Papa, I'm going out with friends. How about tomorrow night? I won't make other plans.'

'Don't be silly. That's fine. Of course you want to see your pals.' He tried not to look disappointed and had to remind himself that he was not the only thing in her life, and she was young. 'By the way, Natalie Peterson, the decorator, is coming over to have drinks with us at seven. She wants to meet you.'

'I'd like to meet her too, but I don't know if I have time. We have a dinner reservation downtown at eight.'

'You don't have to stay long. She's thrilled you like the suite.' Heloise smiled, gathered up her packages a few minutes later, and went upstairs to get organized for that night. And Hugues tried to look calmer than he felt. He didn't want to insist on her meeting Natalie, but it was important to him, and he was trying to act nonchalant.

When he went upstairs himself at six-thirty, Heloise was racing around the apartment wrapped in a towel, talking to a friend on her cell phone, making additional plans for that night. She waved to her father and disappeared into her own room. And the desk called him promptly at seven to tell him that Miss Peterson was downstairs. He told them to send her up.

He opened the door to her himself and didn't dare kiss

her in case Heloise ran back into the room. He whispered to Natalie instead.

'It's a little crazy around here. She's going out. I told her you were coming for a drink because she liked the suite so much.'

'That's fine,' Natalie said, looking relaxed. She was used to young people Heloise's age from her nephews and nieces. Her brother in Philadelphia had four, among them twins Heloise's age.

He poured her a glass of champagne, and half an hour later Heloise appeared in black leggings, a black leather tunic, and toweringly high-heeled black sandals, and her hair was still wet. Hugues had never seen her wear an outfit like that before, and hecouldn't tell if the tunic was a dress or a top. She had always been much more conservative, and in the sexy outfit she looked frighteningly sophisticated and adult. A very fashionable adult, like the women in the halls of the hotel and the bar.

'This is Natalie, the interior designer who worked magic in nine-twelve,' he said as he introduced the two women, and Heloise smiled at her. She thought Natalie looked like a nice person. She had a warm, easy manner and a sincere smile.

'I really love what you did,' Heloise said truthfully as her father handed his daughter a glass of champagne and invited her to sit down. 'I can only stay five minutes. I have to pick everyone up at quarter to eight, and we have to get downtown.' It had stopped snowing, but at this time of year, before Christmas, it would be hard to find a cab. She accepted the champagne anyway, sat down on the couch, and took a sip. 'My father said he's giving you more suites to do. I bet they'll be gorgeous,' Heloise said politely, with a cool smile.

'Maybe you can help me pick the fabrics this time,' Natalie said easily, watching her. She was a very pretty girl and looked more sophisticated than she'd expected or than Hugues had described.

'That would be fun. But I'm leaving pretty soon. I'm sure you and my father will do a good job.' She glanced at her watch then with a look of panic and stood up. 'I've gotta go,' she said to her father, kissed him on the cheek, and looked at Natalie, oblivious to anything that was going on between them. 'Nice to meet you,' she said, and two seconds later they heard the front door close.

'I'm sorry,' Hugues said, looking disappointed. 'I wanted you two to have a chance to talk. She wants to see her friends while she's here. I forgot to take that into account.' Most of all, Natalie realized, he had forgotten to take into account that she had her own life now.

'It's fine,' she said easily. 'Kids don't want to waste their time with old farts like us.'

'I may be an old fart,' he said with a smile, 'but you very definitely are not.' She looked anything but in a short skirt, high heels, and a pretty blouse.

'I am to her,' Natalie said realistically. 'To her we're practically dead, and she only has two weeks here, so it makes sense that she wants to see her friends. Does she suspect anything about us?'

'Not at all,' he said firmly. He had been very careful that she didn't. 'I haven't said anything except about your design work in the hotel. I wanted her to meet you first. And she just got back last night.' Natalie nodded and kissed him as he poured them each another glass of champagne. 'She's grown up a lot since she left,' he said, looking slightly unnerved. 'I think it's the boy.'

'I think it's her age. And going away to school. The same thing happened to my nieces when they went to Stanford. Going away matures them.'

'And makes me feel old,' he added. He was still sorry that Heloise hadn't had more time to get to know Natalie. He desperately wanted Heloise to like her, and they had barely met.

They went out to dinner at La Goulue on Madison Avenue that night and had a relaxed dinner in a setting they both enjoyed, and then they walked back to the hotel. He didn't want to go to Natalie's in case Heloise came home early. They had a nightcap upstairs, and Natalie left before midnight. Heloise came in long after he was asleep, at four.

She looked a little tired the next morning at breakfast, and he didn't dare bring up Natalie's name again. He didn't want to tip his hand by looking too determined about it.

'What are you up to today?' he asked her offhandedly.

'I'm going skating with friends in Central Park. And another party downtown tonight. Everybody's home from college for Christmas,' she said reasonably, and he was beginning to realize he was going to have to stand in line for her time. The chances of spending an evening with her and Natalie, getting to know each other, were less than slim. There were too many other things she wanted to do in her limited amount of time.

By Christmas Eve there had been not a single break in Heloise's busy schedule for them to meet again. He was meeting Natalie for lunch to exchange presents, and she was leaving for Philadelphia that night. She was coming to the hotel to see him, and then they were having lunch downstairs. And Natalie arrived at the apartment promptly at noon. Heloise was just about to go out to meet friends again.

'Oh, hi,' she said as she saw the interior designer at the door to the apartment and didn't know what she was doing there. She looked at Natalie with a blank expression. She clearly suspected nothing between her and Hugues.

'Merry Christmas,' Natalie said, smiling at her. 'I'm having lunch with your father.'

'I think he's downstairs, in his office.' As she said it, Hugues walked in. He was both pleased and nervous to see the two women in his life together and wondered what had been said. He gave Natalie a friendly peck on the cheek as he would have to any friend. 'Hi, Papa. I'm going out,' Heloise said, putting on her coat.

'So I see. No parties tonight, I hope. Let's spend a quiet evening together, like old times. And midnight mass.'

'Of course,' she said, as though she wouldn't have considered doing otherwise, but so far she had been out every night. And she was leaving in six days. The visit had been crowded and rushed, but he was grateful that she was there. Just living in the same apartment with her again and seeing her every morning warmed his heart. She opened the door then, smiled at them both, said 'Bye' to Natalie, and was gone.

Hugues looked unhappy after she left. 'I've hardly seen her since she's been back,' he complained to Natalie, who still had spent no time with Natalie at all. The hope that they would get to know each other had vanished into thin air.

'You think you'll have time to tell her about us before she goes back?' Natalie asked, looking somewhat concerned. 'I feel a little dishonest not having her know. She's such an important part of your life, she deserves that respect.' *And so do I*, Natalie thought but didn't say it. She felt as though they were sneaking around and not being open with his daughter, and she was uncomfortable about it.

'I know she deserves to know,' he agreed with her, and he still had no idea how Heloise would take it. As far as she was concerned, Natalie was just someone who had done work for the hotel and nothing more. How she'd feel about Natalie being important to her father now was impossible to assess. 'I have to have enough time with her to tell her about us, and I can't tell her on Christmas Eve. And she's leaving in less than a week after that.' That also didn't give him enough time to calm her down and let her adjust to the idea if she was upset. It was a mess. 'I'll do the best I can,' he said, and put his arms around Natalie, but he could see that she was disappointed too.

'I guess it's hard in a situation like this when she's away at school. But it also doesn't feel right to me to be involved with each other, and say nothing to her.' They had started sleeping together around Thanksgiving, but in effect they had been dating since September, and it was already Christmas Eve. 'There's a sneaky feel to all this that I don't like. Maybe you just need to tell her, and let her get used to the idea when she goes back to school.'

'I don't want to do that,' Hugues said firmly. 'It would be different if I'd ever been serious with another woman before, but I haven't. This is a first, and it's liable to be a big deal to her.' It was to him.

'It's a big deal to me too,' Natalie said sadly, 'and I'm a firm believer in truth in packaging. We're in love with each other. That's not a crime.' But they both knew it might be to Heloise. Natalie hoped not, but as tight as Hugues's relationship had been with his daughter, this was an unusual situation and harder to predict.

'Just let me find the right time to tell her before she leaves. I promise I will,' he assured her, and after that they both made an effort to speak of other things. He had lunch sent up for them, instead of going downstairs, so they could be alone, and after they finished, he kissed her and gave her his gift. Natalie loved the locket, thanked him profusely, and put it on immediately. She was sorry she had made such a fuss about telling Heloise about them, but it was unnerving for her to remain a secret from his daughter. She wanted to be open about it, and make friends with her, and that hadn't happened yet. And then she gave him her gift. She had bought him a very good-looking set of leather-bound books that were all first editions of the French classics that he referred to so often. There were twenty of them, and they were a beautiful collection that he was proud to own.

They sat and cuddled after that, and he was aching to make love to her, but on the off chance that Heloise might come home, they didn't dare. Natalie had to leave at three o'clock to catch the train to Philadelphia and was coming back in two days. There would still be time for her to have lunch or dinner with Heloise, if Hugues could find an opportune moment to explain the situation to her.

He kissed her tenderly when she left, and they wished each other a merry Christmas, and then he went back to his office. He didn't see Heloise again until six o'clock that night, and she was true to her word and spent a quiet evening with him. They had dinner in the dining room, went back upstairs after that, and went to midnight mass at St. Patrick's, and when they got back from church, she had a call from her mother in London. Miriam said she was up early getting things ready for the children, and she wanted to wish Heloise and her father a merry Christmas.

'Thanks, Mom,' Heloise said pleasantly. Her mother knew she had been in Lausanne since September but hadn't invited her to London and said she was too busy. Greg and his band were cutting a new album. The conversation was brief, and Heloise sat quietly for a moment after she hung up. Talking to her mother always left her feeling empty. She tried to explain it to her father, and he felt sad for her. Miriam never failed to disappoint her. She was the classic narcissist and a totally inadequate mother. 'I guess we were lucky that we were alone together for all these years.' She smiled sadly at her father. 'I can't imagine what life would have been like with her. I don't even remember when you two were married.' She had been too young to still remember it now. 'And I guess it was lucky too that you never remarried,' she said, and smiled at him, as a tremor went through him, knowing what he did now, although he and Natalie had no plans to marry. It was all too new, but he could already imagine spending the rest of his life with her, with Heloise's approval. It was a big leap for him, in contrast to his past fifteen years of refusing to commit or get seriously involved. 'I like having you to myself,' Heloise said honestly. 'I don't think I'd have wanted to share you.' It was a big statement for her to make now, and it unnerved Hugues a little.

'And now?' he asked her quietly, watching her eyes.

She laughed at the question since it wasn't an issue. 'I don't want to share you now either. I like being the only woman in your life, Papa.'

'And what happens when you fall in love and get married one day?' It was an honest question.

'Then we'll all live here together, and live happily ever after. But I like it this way for now.' She had no plans to marry François. They were both too young. The thought hadn't even crossed her mind.

Hugues sighed as he listened to her, and she didn't notice the sadness in his eyes. There was no way he could tell her about Natalie now, after what she had just said. He suspected it would cause a real explosion and a rift between them he didn't want. He didn't want to hurt his daughter. Her mother had given her enough pain for a lifetime.

'Then you'd better come home and be the woman in my life,' he teased her to lighten the moment. 'If you stay in Paris with François, I'm coming to get you.' Heloise laughed when he said it, and she reassured him a moment later.

'Don't worry, Papa. I'm coming home for good next Christmas. I promise.' She moved closer to him then on the couch and put an arm around him. 'I'm going to be your girl forever.' She had been all her life, and in her mind nothing had changed. It was inconceivable to her that there was any other woman in his life. There was no sign of it. 'I love you, Papa,' she said softly as she leaned her head on her father's shoulder. Unlike her mother, in her entire life he had never let her down.

'I love you too,' he whispered, and pulled her closer, feeling as though he had betrayed Natalie by not telling his daughter about her. But his first allegiance was to Heloise, always had been and always would be. It was the old saying that blood was thicker than water. And the bond they shared was more powerful than any other.

Chapter 11

When Natalie came back to New York the day after Christmas, Hugues said he was taking Heloise to the theater that night. It was the most successful new play of the season, and they both wanted to see it. He would have loved to invite Natalie, but he didn't dare. He had realized on Christmas Eve that there was no way he could tell Heloise about his romance with Natalie before she left. Not after what she had said that night, about wanting to be the only woman in his life. In light of that, Natalie was not likely to be a good surprise. And he didn't want to risk it.

He didn't see Natalie again until the night Heloise left, which had been a sorrowful parting for them. He had promised to come to Europe for her Easter vacation and take her to Rome. It was almost four months away, which was a long time for them both, but it would have been hard for him to get away before that, and she was busy with school in Lausanne.

Her eyes filled with tears when he left her at the airport, and he choked up, and he had the car stop at Natalie's apartment on the way back. She was surprised to see him. She had tried not to be upset about how busy and unavailable he had been while Heloise was there. The last time she had seen him was for lunch on Christmas Eve, six days before, which was a long span for them to be apart.

'Do you hate me?' he asked, as he followed her into the apartment when she let him in.

'Don't be silly. Why would I hate you?' She smiled at him, but she seemed cooler to him than the last time he'd seen her, when they exchanged their gifts. He was happy to observe that she was wearing the locket he had given her.

'Because I didn't tell my daughter about us?' he answered her question. He felt guilty about it, and a little bit dishonest with Heloise. 'After church on Christmas Eve, she told me that she loves being the only woman in my life. It was tough trying to tell her about you after that. I think she'll need more time to adjust to it than a few days before she leaves. You're going to be a big surprise to her.'

'I was hoping to be a good one,' Natalie said, still looking disappointed, 'not a major trauma.' It was an unpleasant situation to be in and not the role she wanted. She wanted to make friends with Heloise, not destroy her life. 'When are you seeing her again?'

'Not till Easter. I'm taking her to Rome for her school vacation. Maybe I can tell her then.'

'And not before?'

'I don't think I should say something like that over the phone or by e-mail. And by then we'll have spent more time together, which isn't such a bad thing,' he rationalized. If the relationship had fallen apart by then, then he wouldn't have to tell her at all and would never have upset her. Natalie understood the implication.

'Why? So I can audition?' She was starting to look angry then and seriously upset. She had no intention of auditioning for him. She loved him and believed that he loved her.

'You don't have to audition for me,' he said, looking upset. 'You have to understand, my daughter virtually never had a mother. I'm all she has in terms of family. Anyone entering that inner circle is bound to be a threat to her. You know how kids are.' He was struggling to justify a most unusual situation, and although Natalie was sensitive to it, not all the component parts made sense to her.

'She's not a kid, Hugues,' Natalie said quietly. 'She's nineteen. Some people have their own children by then. My mother did. And I am trying to understand it, but it's a weird situation for me. I don't like being a secret. We're not doing anything wrong, and it puts a huge burden on us. We can't even move around the hotel freely, in case someone tells her. That's not how I live. I'm an honest woman, and I love you. I'm willing to make allowances for this, but I want you to know that I'm not going to stay hidden forever.' She was being totally clear with him.

'And I don't want you to,' he insisted. 'Just give me till Easter. I'll tell her when I'm in Europe with her. I promise.' She smiled at him slowly then. It was a bit of a crazy situation, but sometimes life was crazy. 'Do you still love me?' he asked as he moved closer to her, and she smiled at him.

'Yes, I do. If I didn't, all this wouldn't be a problem. I love you very much, and I want to lead a normal, open life with you, so I can show off and be your woman. I'm very proud to be with you.' She had told her family about him over Christmas, and her older brother was pleased for her. He had never liked the man she'd lived with and thought he was a jerk. Hugues sounded like a good guy to him. Her brother, James, was a banker in Philadelphia, and his wife, Jean, was a lawyer, and they had four really great kids. They were a close-knit family, and they were happy to know that she was no longer alone.

Hugues sent the car and driver back to the hotel then and spent the rest of the evening trying to make it up to her for how inattentive he had been for the past two weeks, and not telling Heloise about them, and an hour later they were in her bed, making love. He spent the night with her and was planning to spend New Year's Eve with her. He wanted to see the new year in with her and start it off right. They had already agreed to spend it at her place after he got their New Year's festivities organized at the hotel. They always had revelers in the bar that night, a formal dinner in the restaurant, and later guests who'd had too much to drink weaving as they crossed the lobby. Some of them had to be helped to their rooms. And as long as Heloise didn't know about them, Hugues and Natalie were trying to be discreet, which she didn't like. Hiding their romance seemed like a lot of trouble to both of them and dishonest, but they agreed that it was the wisest course if they didn't want hotel employees to let the cat out of the bag.

He left her and went back to his office the next

morning. Hers was closed for the week between Christmas and New Year's, but his office was never closed. And they always doubled their security on New Year's Eve in case too many of their guests got drunk, or someone got out of control. He would have preferred to be at the hotel that night, but he wanted to be with her, so he had agreed to spend the night at her place. He came back at nine o'clock that night and brought caviar, lobsters, and champagne with him in an ice chest. They lay on the couch, eating a feast, and made love at the stroke of midnight. It was the perfect way to see in the new year.

Chapter 12

After the holidays Natalie got to work on the suites Hugues had hired her to redo. She put as much energy and creativity into it as she had the first one, and by the end of March the results were just as spectacular, and they had four new suites that everybody loved. Guests who had been there before were clamoring for reservations in those rooms, and Hugues was thrilled. They even raised the rates for those rooms and several others where Natalie had worked her magic. Working for him at the Vendôme was becoming a lucrative business venture for her as well. He had become her best client. He had put off redoing the presidential and penthouse suites for a few months, out of budget concerns, not because of her decorating. He promised to give her the project in the next year.

Natalie became a familiar sight at the hotel, talking to painters, installing drapes, trying out paintings that she dragged down the halls herself. Ernesta told her how much she liked the new art in the rooms, and Jan was so excited when she saw the new suites that she put special orchids in them. And Bruce, the head of security, complimented her too. She found several beautiful new pieces of art for Hugues, and with her gentle touch and great taste, she added new spice to the hotel, and everybody loved her. Hugues mentioned her to Heloise every chance he got, but never in such a way that she guessed they were involved. It felt wrong to him to tell her on the phone, so he was waiting for her Easter vacation, when he was picking her up in Lausanne, spending a night in Geneva with her, and taking her to Rome.

Natalie was still uncomfortable about being a secret to his daughter. They had been romantically involved for six months, and it just didn't feel right to be clandestine. Most of the hotel employees had figured out by then that there was more happening than just decorating, but no one asked, and no one ever dared comment on it to Hugues. It was kind of an open secret in the hotel as time went on. And he finally admitted it to Jennifer, but she knew anyway. Natalie had told her months before. Jennifer was her biggest fan and happy for both of them.

He deserved more of a life than he'd had for years, and Jennifer was thrilled that he had found a woman to love, other than his daughter, and the flash-in-the-pan women who drifted through his life for two dinner reservations or a night somewhere else. Jennifer had always taken care of the dinner reservations for him. He took care of the nights himself.

Natalie had confided to Jennifer several times how upset she was that Hugues hadn't told Heloise about them yet, and Jennifer understood better than she did how potentially delicate that situation was, given how close they were, and she urged Natalie to be patient. She was, but she was more anxious than ever for him to tell Heloise about them over Easter. It was almost as though their relationship didn't exist in reality, until Heloise knew. Natalie told him that she was beginning to feel like the Other Woman, and a dark secret. He insisted that wasn't true. She was the woman he loved. But so was his daughter. It was beginning to seem extremely neurotic to Natalie, and she hoped that the veil of secrecy still surrounding them would drop soon. She was ready to be out in the open with him and had been for a long time.

In spite of the tension of Heloise not knowing, romantically things were going well. They were more in love than ever. And she would have loved to go to Europe with him over Easter, but there was no question of it with Heloise still unaware of her existence, other than as the designer who was redoing four suites at the hotel. She had even suggested meeting him in Paris, after he dropped Heloise back at school, but he said he had to get back, as they had several important guests arriving in late April, and even more in May and June. It was a busy spring for him too.

He flew to Geneva on the Wednesday before Easter, landed on Thursday morning, picked Heloise up at school in Lausanne, and spent the night with her at the Hotel d'Angleterre in Geneva, which was a gem. It was an exquisite small hotel with beautiful rooms, and was a great beginning for their trip. And on the morning of Good Friday they flew to Rome and strolled down the Via Veneto, tossing coins into the Trevi Fountain, eating gelato, and standing in the Sistine Chapel gazing at the ceiling in rapture that afternoon. It was exciting just being there, and they were going to stand in the square with millions of others on Easter Sunday, to receive the Pope's blessing. It was the perfect place to be.

They were staying at the Excelsior, which had been a favorite of his since his boyhood, when he had gone there with his parents, and he loved sharing his memories there with his daughter. They loved traveling together and always had fun. And this time he was determined to tell her about Natalie. He had promised, and he had every intention of following through. They were going to be spending a whole week together, and there would be plenty of time for her to absorb the news that he was in love with a good woman who wanted to get to know Heloise too.

They were sitting in a café that afternoon, enjoying the spring sunshine, when he asked her how things were going with François. She was always a little vague about him, and he was never sure if that meant he wasn't a big deal or was a Very Big Deal. She was surprisingly evasive about him, which wasn't like her.

'He's fine,' she said, staring into space, as her father watched her for telltale signs that might alarm him. He was always on the lookout for warning signs of her not coming home. So far, much to his relief, there had been none.

'What kind of fine? Fine as in you're so nuts about him you can't see straight, or fine, he's an okay boyfriend but no big deal?' She laughed at her father's description. She was wearing jeans and running shoes and a sweater and had put her hair in pigtails for the first time in years. She looked even younger than she was.

'Somewhere between the two. Fine, as in I love him,

but I'm still coming home, if that's what you're asking me. We got our internships in Paris for our hospitality year,' she announced, and Hugues's eyebrows shot up. This was the first time she had confirmed it, and that made him a little nervous too, although it would be good experience for her.

'Where?' His heart was racing as he asked her.

'The George V. It's one of the best hotels in Paris now and would give us a leg up with the Four Seasons, who own it, if we ever want to work at one of their other hotels.'

'What does that mean? You don't need a leg up with the Four Seasons if you're coming back to work with me. Has any of that plan changed?'

'No. I told you, I'm still coming home, at Christmastime this year. I start at the George V on June first. François and I are going to try and find a studio together, he's staying for the whole year. I'll only be there for six months.' He knew the plan, but it was all too real now, and living with François in Paris was new.

'You're going to live with him?' She nodded. 'Isn't that a big commitment?'

'Not for six months,' she said practically, 'and I don't want to live alone. I'm twenty years old, Papa, or I will be by then, or almost. People do that these days. It makes a lot of sense.'

'To whom?' he asked, looking annoyed. 'I would pay for an apartment for you. You don't have to live with him.'

'I want to,' she said, smiling at him.

'What if I did something like that?' he asked her bluntly, trying to open the door he'd been attempting to open for six months.

'Don't be silly. You wouldn't live with someone. And if you did, I wouldn't like it. That's not respectable at your age. I'm just a student. It's not the same thing.'

'Why not? What if I fell in love?' he said, trying to introduce the hypothetical before the real to test the waters and see what she'd say.

'I'd probably have a fit and have to kill her,' she said with a smile as his heart sank. 'You belong to me,' she said without hesitating for a beat, with the confidence that came from a father who had never loved anyone but her and she liked it that way and wasn't afraid to say so.

'I could belong to you *and* a woman I love, other than you, like a partner of some kind.' He was skirting all around it but didn't have the guts to spit it out, particularly given her responses to him. She looked totally unembarrassed to be so blunt.

'No, you couldn't,' she said, drinking lemon soda through a straw. 'I wouldn't let you. Besides, she'd probably be after your money, or mess everything up at the hotel. You don't need a woman, Papa, you have me.' She beamed at him and sat back in her chair, and he didn't have the heart to ruin the rest of the week, telling her he was in love with Natalie. A week, or even two, never seemed like enough time to deliver that kind of news, especially given her resistance, which was openly declared. He knew from the way she was looking at him that he was going to be no braver at Easter than he had been at Christmas. How could he ruin the week with her, when he only saw her once every three or four months? He couldn't risk it. She meant too much to him. And if he lost her, Natalie would never be enough. He wanted them both in his life, not either or.

'Tell me about your internship and what it entails,' he said, looking somber, and she seemed oblivious to the sad look in his eyes. He knew that he had already failed Natalie and broken his promise to her, and the trip had just begun. He'd have to explain it to her when he went home, if he even could. He hoped she'd be reasonable about it. He was beginning to wonder if it would be smarter not to tell Heloise anything about Natalie at all until she came home for good in December. If he told her before that, she might decide to stay in France. There was no telling how betrayed she would feel, or how angry, no way to measure the vehemence of her reaction until the words had been said and the news delivered. She was the only child he had, the love of his life, and he wasn't willing to take the chance. It was cowardly perhaps, but he didn't want to lose his child. He loved Natalie very much, but even she wasn't worth that to him.

For the rest of the trip, they went to museums and churches and had delicious dinners, mostly small, informal restaurants in Trastevere, on the other side of the Tiber River. They received the papal blessing on Easter morning, went to the Colosseum, and had a wonderful time together as father and daughter. She spent an enormous amount of time talking on her cell phone to François and texted him everywhere they went, but in spite of that, Hugues couldn't bring himself to tell her that there was a woman in New York that he was in love with and spending time with, and that there was room for both of them in his life. By the time they got back to Lausanne a week after they'd arrived in Rome, she still knew nothing about Natalie's importance in his life. François was waiting for her at the school when they returned, and she beamed the moment she saw him, and François kissed her. It angered Hugues that she was allowed to have that intimacy and he wasn't, but the one he was angry at was himself for being too cowardly to tell her, and unwilling to take the chance that she'd be furious with him. Natalie said she'd get over it. But what if she didn't?

He took Heloise and François to dinner on the last night, at La Grappe d'Or on rue Cheneau-de-Bourg. It was the best restaurant in Lausanne. And François was a nice boy, although a little full of himself because his parents owned a well-known hotel and he thought he knew everything there was to know about the business. But he wasn't a bad kid, and Heloise looked besotted with him. With any luck at all, she'd be ready to leave him by the end of the year. And in the meantime Hugues realized that he and Natalie would have to continue to be discreet for as long as it took. Maybe in a few months Heloise would be ready to hear it and would have matured. He hoped so, but now he had to go back to New York and tell Natalie he had broken his promise, and Heloise still didn't know.

He hugged her tight when he left her that night, and the next morning he took the early flight back to New York, which arrived at Kennedy at nine A.M. local time, so he could get to work. He had spoken to Natalie several times while he was gone. She didn't want to push him, so she hadn't asked if he had told Heloise yet, and now he had to tell her that he hadn't. He felt as though his heart were dragging on the runway when they landed, and now he had to face her.

He was in his office by ten-thirty and tackled his desk first. He took a quick walk around the hotel to see that everything was in order, and he was heading back to his office when one of the concierges mentioned that Natalie was upstairs installing another painting in one of the suites. He thanked him and took the elevator to the seventh floor and let himself into the suite. She was alone, wrestling with a big painting. She got it on the hook with a grunt of victory as he walked into the room, and she turned to smile at him, and he strode across the room to hug her. He held her tight and closed his eyes, wishing he hadn't failed her, but he felt he had no other choice.

'You're back!' She looked thrilled to see him, and he kissed her with all the tenderness of apology and regret of a man who knew he had betrayed her. She pulled away to look at him. She could feel in the way he held her that something was wrong. 'What happened?' She looked worried, and he blurted it out immediately. He didn't want to lie to her too.

'I didn't tell her. I couldn't. She said some things in Rome on the first day that told me it would be a huge deal to her. I was afraid she wouldn't come back here if I told her. I'm sorry. I wanted to, Natalie, but I just couldn't.' There was a pounding silence in the room after he said it, and she looked angry for an instant and then sad, and then she nodded. She was a sensible woman. She loved him and didn't want to lose him either, just as he was afraid to lose his daughter.

'Okay.' Her shoulders were drooping then, and so were his. They both felt defeated. For now Heloise had them on the run without even knowing it. 'It'll happen sooner or later. It can't stay a secret forever.' Their relationship was good and kept getting better, except for this one issue, which was a big one. His loyalties were divided between her and his daughter, and sooner or later he'd have to make it clear to everyone that he could handle both. 'Did you have fun?' she asked him generously, and he loved her more than ever, for how kind and reasonable she was and loving to him.

'I did.' He pulled her close to him. 'But I missed you.' Not being able to talk about her had made the longing worse. And all he wanted to do now was hold her and kiss her and caress her and make love to her, and make up to her for what he hadn't done and said he would. He was starving for her as he put the Do Not Disturb sign on the door of the empty suite and the chain on, and pulled her into the bedroom with him. Their clothes were off instantly, and she was just as hungry for him. She had worried about what would happen all week, and now she no longer cared. She just wanted to be with him again, and whether or not his daughter knew no longer mattered. All they cared about as they made love was how much they loved each other, and everything else disappeared. And by the time it was over, she had forgiven him for not telling Heloise. They were both breathless as they lay there, and he smiled at her and pulled her back into his arms. If anything, he loved her even more.

Chapter 13

For the next two months, their life seemed totally normal. Natalie's brother James and his wife came to town, and she and Hugues had dinner with them, and the two men got along famously. James thought he was a great guy and perfect for his sister. The two men talked business all night, and Natalie talked to her sister-in-law about the kids and the cases she was working on.

Natalie's business was booming, and she was still doing some things for Hugues at the hotel. In some ways it was almost as though he didn't have a daughter, because she wasn't part of Natalie's life and she had no idea when she would be, if ever. She had stopped worrying about wanting to make friends with her. She was in a separate part of Hugues's life, and they were building their relationship without her. It felt solid and strong, and their lives were blending nicely. They couldn't move in together because he lived at the hotel, and Heloise would be coming back in December. But in every other way, their relationship was going well and the bond they shared strengthened every day.

Hugues was busy at the hotel, and he enjoyed talking to Natalie about it. She was an intelligent woman, was interested in it, and always gave him good advice. They went to the Hamptons for Memorial Day weekend, and while they were having dinner at Nick & Toni's, she said something about an art exhibit she wanted to see at the Museum of Modern Art, and he told her he was going to Paris the following week.

'On business?' She looked surprised. It was the first time he had mentioned it, and she knew it must have come up suddenly for him not to have told her about it.

'No, to see Heloise. She's starting her internship at the George V on the first of June. I told her I'd come over and see her before she starts work.' Natalie was quiet for a minute and then nodded. There were occasional reminders that he had a whole other part of his life that she couldn't share. It hurt her feelings, but she tried not to think about it. It was almost as if he had a wife tucked away somewhere and she was his mistress, the woman that he loved and hid with. She would have liked to go to Paris with him, and she had the time, but there was no way that she could. Not until he told his daughter about them, and he was no longer saying that he would. They had taken the path of least resistance and were enjoying what they shared.

'That feels a little weird,' she admitted to him, and she didn't ask him if he was going to tell her this time. She knew there would be some excuse when he didn't, about how much it would upset her and how he couldn't risk it. And she didn't want to be disappointed again, and knew she would be. 'I'd like to go to Paris too.'

'Maybe next year,' he said softly, feeling like a heel. Sometimes she wondered if he was going to break up with her when Heloise came back in December, just so he wouldn't have to tell her. It was beginning to remind her of the relationship she'd had for eight years, with the man who had refused to commit. Hugues appeared to be committed, but as long as he hadn't told Heloise about them, Natalie knew he really wasn't. She was a phantom in his life that he was in love with, but only Heloise was real.

'What happens when she comes back in December?' Natalie asked him sadly.

'I'll have to tell her then.' But they both knew he

didn't. He could play this game forever, as long as Natalie let him. She felt as though someone had let the air out of her tires hearing that he was going to Paris to see her, and he wasn't even promising to tell her this time. He knew he couldn't, and so did she. He was too frightened to upset her, alienate her, or lose her and was still unwilling to take the risk, even for a woman he loved.

Natalie was very quiet on the ride back to the hotel, and Hugues could feel the tension in the car and said nothing. He didn't want to confront the subject again. It made him feel too guilty about her and anxious about his daughter. She took a walk on the beach alone the next morning, and Hugues knew she was still upset. There was nothing he could say to her, unless he agreed to tell Heloise when he saw her. And he didn't want to promise that again and not deliver. He felt like a jerk.

Natalie said nothing more about it for the rest of the weekend. There was nothing left to say. When he dropped her off at her apartment Sunday night, she didn't ask him to come up, which had never happened before, and he went back to the hotel. He was leaving in four days. He called her the next day and asked if he could come over. She was loving to him when he did, and cooked him dinner, but he could feel that a wall had come up between them. He had disappointed her too many times about telling Heloise, and suddenly it had become an even bigger deal, and neither of them was sure why.

'Look, I know it sounds crazy,' he said to her at the end of dinner. 'I know this isn't right to keep it from her, but it gives us time to get our relationship solid and squared away. Of course I'm going to tell her when she comes home. I just don't want to risk it before that. She has too many other options, particularly this boy in Paris. She's young, she's not as understanding as we are. She may overreact. Once she's home, I'll deal with it. I promise.' She looked at him for a long moment and shook her head.

'I'm not understanding about it either. And I'm not young. It's insulting. I've become the woman in the closet. You're happy to have a relationship with me, you just won't tell your kid. What does that mean? That you're ashamed of me? That I'm not good enough? How am I supposed to feel? To be honest, I feel like shit.'

'I know you do, and I'm sorry. It's just a very strange situation. We were alone for almost sixteen years. She's had me to herself. We've been over this a thousand times. You know why I won't tell her yet.' He looked as upset as she did, but she felt worse.

'Maybe you never will. How do I know what you'll do

when she comes home? We've been sleeping with each other for six months now, and you still haven't told her. And maybe you never will.' She didn't know what to believe now.

'Look, I'm going over to see her for a week. That's all. I haven't seen her since Easter. And I may go over once in the fall, and then she'll be home.'

'And then what? What if she tells you to break up with me and she pressures you until you do? How do I know what kind of power this kid has over you? She seems to be winning so far. And I could wind up the big loser here. I've been there before.'

'That was different. He ran off with your best friend.'

'No different. He couldn't make a commitment. Neither can you, to tell your daughter. No balls.' It was the harshest thing she had ever said to him, but he knew he deserved it, so he didn't object. He wasn't going to tell Heloise in Paris or even promise it this time, no matter what she said. He loved Natalie, but his relationship with his daughter meant too much to him to take that risk. And he didn't know what he'd do if she begged him to let Natalie go when she came home. It was a horrifying thought, for both of them.

He went back to the hotel that night and didn't stay with her. And she wouldn't see him again before he left.

He knew it was a bad sign. And he was troubled about it on the flight to Paris. He called her on her cell phone when he arrived in Paris, and she wouldn't answer. He was afraid that it had been too much for her this time, but there was nothing he could do. He couldn't get out of his mind Heloise saying to him that she wanted to be the only woman in his life when they were in Rome. It was unreasonable, he knew.

But how far was she willing to go to prove the point and demonstrate that to him? What if he lost her for years? And it wasn't fair of Natalie to expect him to take that risk when Heloise was living three thousand miles away and he only saw her for a few days. He told himself that Natalie didn't understand, she didn't have kids. But somewhere in his heart of hearts he knew how unfair he was being to her and hated himself for it. And for now, it looked like Natalie hated him too. She had shut off all communication with him and didn't even answer his texts of abject apology and undying love for her. As long as he kept her a secret, she no longer believed a word he said or wanted anything to do with him for now. He hoped that she'd calm down by the time he got back.

He tried to have a good time with Heloise in Paris anyway, but the time was short and stressed. She was trying to organize the tiny apartment they had found, and he helped her furnish it at IKEA in a day. She and François were nervous about their internships, so they were tense and argued constantly. And there was a general transport strike halfway through his trip, which meant no buses, no subways, no taxis, no trains, and the airport was closed. The city was a tangled nightmare of private cars and bicycles so people could get to work.

In spite of that, the Ritz was as pleasant as ever, and he took the kids out for several meals, when they weren't squabbling with each other. But he got very little time alone with his daughter, and his worries about Natalie weighed heavily on him during the entire trip. And once again, this would have been totally the wrong time to tell Heloise about her. Heloise was much too nervous about her job at the George V and would have reacted badly. It was almost a relief to leave the day before she was to report for work. She promised to call him and let him know how it was going, and he wished both of them good luck.

It was strange leaving her with François. Heloise was moving on to her own life, but she hadn't released her father to have one of his own. He thought both of the women in his life were unreasonable, and he was exhausted when he got back on the plane to New York. The transport strike had ended the day before. And his plane was crowded to the gills with people whose flights had been canceled during the strike. And the final blow was that his luggage never made the flight.

The car picked him up, and he rode to the hotel, happy to be back. It hadn't been an easy trip. He tried calling Natalie from the car on the way in. Just as he had for the past week, he got her voice mail and nothing else. He called her office, and they said that she was out. She was nowhere. And wherever she was, she still wasn't talking to him. And when he got to his office, he discovered why. Jennifer handed him a letter that she said that Natalie had dropped off for him earlier in the week. It was marked personal so she hadn't opened it, and the envelope was thick. He strode into his office and closed the door behind him so he could read it in peace. He had hardly said a word to Jennifer when he walked in except that he had lost his bags. He had asked the concierge to call the airline to try and find them.

The letter told him everything he didn't want to hear. That she loved him passionately, with her entire being, and would have been happy to spend the rest of her life with him, but she was an honest woman, not a dirty little secret to be hidden from a nineteen-year-old. If he didn't love her enough to tell his daughter about her, after seven months, then there was clearly no place in his life for her.

She was not going to allow him to humiliate her any longer by hiding her existence and denying his relationship with her. She said she sympathized with his problem and his fears about his daughter, but if the sixteen years he had devoted to her exclusively were worth anything at all, then his daughter would forgive him damn near anything, surely the fact that he was in love with a woman who loved him and who would have been kind to his daughter too. At the end of the letter, Natalie said she wished him well, told him it was over, and asked him not to call her again. She signed it simply, 'I love you. Natalie.' And that was it. Over and out.

He sat at his desk feeling as though a bomb had exploded in the room. He knew he deserved it, but he hadn't wanted this to happen. And he knew that the only thing that could change it was if he was willing to tell Heloise about her, and he wasn't. Not for another six months. And maybe she was right. Maybe not even then. He was appalled at his own lack of courage, but the reality was that his relationship with his daughter was more important to him than the one with Natalie. She knew it, and so did he. All he could do now was let her go and accept her decision, out of respect for her. He loved her, but as she had said so poignantly in her letter, not enough. Not enough to respect her and treat her right. And he agreed with her. She deserved better than this. She wasn't a dirty little secret. She was a woman who deserved everything she wanted. He just couldn't give it to her. There were tears in his eyes when he folded the letter, put it back in the envelope, and put it in a locked drawer in his desk. He put his face in his hands and sat there for a few minutes, and then he got up and walked out of the room. He looked grim.

'Is everything all right?' Jennifer asked him softly. He hesitated and then nodded and walked out to the lobby to catch up on things at the front desk. Jennifer didn't know what was in the letter, but she could guess. Natalie hadn't called her either, but she knew how upset she was about Hugues never telling Heloise about her. And sooner or later she knew that Natalie would have enough of it and jump ship. The look on Hugues's face told Jennifer that Natalie just had. She hoped not. But seven months was a long time to wait for a man to tell his kid. And she was sorry for them both. It was obvious that he loved her, but he loved his daughter more. And Jennifer knew it wouldn't have been easy either if he told her. Heloise was never going to like having another woman in his life, no matter who that woman was. And she thought Natalie was terrific, and she deserved better than this. Apparently, Natalie thought so too.

Jennifer didn't see Hugues again for the rest of the day. He was all over the hotel, catching up, and eventually he went upstairs to his apartment, locked the door, put the Do Not Disturb sign on, lay down on his bed, and cried himself to sleep.

Chapter 14

It was a long, hot, lonely summer for both Natalie and Hugues. Natalie took on several new decorating jobs, none of which she enjoyed as much as the suites she had redone at the Hotel Vendôme. She agreed to do a beachhouse in Southampton, another in Palm Beach, and two apartments in New York. All of her new clients were very nice and loved her work, but she had never felt as uninspired and depressed as for those three months over the summer.

Natalie felt like she had to drag herself to work every day, and she felt physically sick for the first few weeks after leaving Hugues. She'd been there before, and she knew that there was no way around it. She just had to live through it. She genuinely loved him, and losing him was agony for her.

All three of her assistants were worried about her, and she had them doing most of the work. She couldn't concentrate on anything. And then finally she got back into her work again and took refuge in it. She flew to Palm Beach twice to meet with the client and architect on the project. And another new client called while she was away, to have her do an enormous house in Greenwich. Business was booming, but she felt awful.

By September, she was still in a funk, but getting used to it and working hard. She pushed herself through the days and was sleepless for most of the nights. She thought of Hugues constantly, but she had nothing to say to him, and after he got her letter that she had left at the hotel for him, he stopped calling her. She wanted to get over him, but she had no idea how long it would take. Every day felt like a lifetime, and every month like a century.

By Labor Day weekend, she felt as though she had been moving underwater with a cement block on her head for three months. She had never been so depressed in her life, even when the man she had lived with had gone off with her best friend. Hugues was a major loss for her, and she felt that he had never given her a decent chance. He had sent her a brief note in response to her letter telling her how much he loved her and how sorry he was. He admitted that he hadn't done the right thing but was too afraid to, under the circumstances. He told her again that he loved her and wished her well. He knew she was right to end it, but he felt just as bad as she did all summer. And all he could do to dull the pain was work constantly and never take a moment off. Those who had been there when his wife left him said he hadn't looked as bad as this.

No one knew exactly what had happened, but Natalie's sudden absence was conspicuous, and people suspected that it wasn't because she had finished the job. And they were sorry to see her vanish from their lives. She had been a sunny presence and a nice woman whom everyone had liked. But Hugues was the sorriest of all.

He started taking long walks alone in the park and worked till after midnight every night. His temper was short, which was rare for him, and he tolerated no nonsense from anyone. As best they could, his employees tried not to cross his path and hoped he'd be back to himself soon. Jennifer tried not to annoy him, and he barked at her several times, which was most unusual. By September he still looked terrible, and Jennifer was worried about him. She had never dared mention Natalie to him again, and when he'd gotten back from Paris in June, he told Jennifer to pay her final bill, which she did.

As far as she knew, there had been no communication between them since.

The temperatures were over the hundred-degree mark on the Labor Day weekend, and they had trouble with the air conditioners on the fifth and sixth floors. The engineers were going crazy trying to get them working again while guests complained. Hugues told the front desk to discount the rooms, but the guests in them were unhappy anyway. The heat was unbearable all over the city. It was too hot to go anywhere or do anything. In spite of that, Hugues decided to take a break and headed toward Central Park when the weather started to cool down a little, which meant in the nineties, but there was a breeze at least. He had thought about taking Heloise's dog with him, but it was too hot for her too, so he left her at the florist, where she had spent most of her time in recent months in Heloise's absence, since Jan loved her more than Hugues did.

He was walking around the reservoir in his suit trousers and his shirt sleeves, and he had taken off his tie. Then the sky opened up, there was a clap of thunder, a bolt of lightning, and a sudden downpour. It was the only thing that could help the city in the blistering heat. He was instantly drenched, and his shirt was glued to his body, but the weather was so warm, he didn't mind it. He kept walking, he was thinking back to June and Natalie's letter and the things he should have done differently. But it was too late now. And he still missed her.

He kept walking around the reservoir in the thunderstorm, which continued, and he had almost come full circle to where he had started when he saw a woman who looked like her in gym shorts and a T-shirt. She was as soaked as he was, and she was splashing through the mud on the dirt track. He told himself that she only looked like Natalie because he'd been thinking about her. She had long blond hair in a ponytail that was wet and plastered to her back. He could tell that she didn't mind the rain either. She turned and changed direction then, and when she did, he saw that it wasn't an illusion, it was Natalie walking toward him. She looked as surprised as he did, and neither of them knew where to look or where to go. They kept walking toward each other, and he didn't know if he should say hello. She looked down at the path then and was about to walk past him, when a force stronger than he was made him step forward and block her path. She looked up at him, and the expression in her eyes nearly killed him. She looked as miserable as he was.

'I'm sorry I was so stupid,' he said as they stood there in the pouring rain.

'It's okay.' She smiled sadly at him, making no effort to

walk around him. 'I loved you anyway. Maybe I should have waited, but I couldn't take it anymore.'

'I don't blame you. I was afraid to lose her. And instead I lost you.' He looked devastated as the rain poured down their faces.

'It was probably a better choice. She's your kid.'

'I love you,' he said, without reaching out to touch her. He was afraid to. He didn't want to offend her.

'Me too. It won't get us far, though. She probably would have made you give me up anyway.' His daughter had a death grip on him. Natalie knew that now.

'I won't let that happen ... if ... if you give me another chance. I don't know if I'd tell her before she comes home. She'll be home in three months. And I'd fight like a dog for us then.' Natalie smiled at what he said, but she didn't believe him. 'Can I call you?'

They were both so soaked they looked like they had no clothes on, and he wished they didn't. He remembered too well what her body looked like. He had dreamed of it night after night, and her face and her eyes. And he could see most of her body now through the soaked T-shirt and gym shorts.

'I don't know,' she said honestly. 'I don't want to go back to where we were, with me in the closet and you hiding me from her.' He nodded.

'And if I tell her in December when she gets home?'

'She'd probably kill you.' Natalie smiled at him, and he nearly melted. 'Maybe it's a good thing I never had kids.'

'It's worth it,' he said gently. 'So are you. I'd love to see you.' She didn't answer. She would have loved it too, but too much, and then they'd just be in the same mess again, and even more so, if Heloise had a fit once she knew. Natalie didn't want to go there. But he was willing to now, more than he had been in June. He knew just how much he loved her now. The last three months had told him. Enough to fight for her with his daughter.

'I don't want to screw up your life,' she said kindly. She looked like she wanted to move on. It had shaken her up seeing him, and she didn't have the answers he wanted, just as he hadn't for her before.

'Take care of yourself,' he said sadly, and moved aside. He had to let her go. He knew he had no other choice. She walked away, and then turned back to look at him, and he was standing there, watching her, in the rain. It was still pouring, and she stopped walking again and just stood there and started crying. He walked toward her then and put his arms around her. There was nothing that either of them could say. They knew the whole story, and how it had ended. And then he kissed her, he couldn't help himself, he had to. She put her arms around his neck and kissed him back, and they stood there kissing in the rain, their bodies pressed together.

'I don't want to lose you,' she whispered as they pulled away and looked at each other.

'You won't. I promise. I won't be that stupid again.'

'You weren't stupid. You were scared.'

'I'm braver now,' he said, and she smiled. 'Do you want to come to the hotel and get dry?' She nodded. They walked back into the hotel in silence and stood dripping in the lobby. They made a dash for the elevator, and the elevator man smiled at her. He was happy to see her again. He didn't say anything, but he noticed that Mr. Martin was smiling for the first time in months.

Hugues let her into his apartment and went to get them both towels. She took off her shoes and left them in the entry hall and dried her hair first.

'We can have your clothes dried if you want.'

'Thank you,' she said politely. She walked into the second bathroom and came out wearing one of the hotel's thick terrycloth robes. He was wearing one by then too, and he rang for the maid and handed Natalie's mound of wet clothes to her and asked her to dry them. When the maid left, Natalie smiled at him. She was barefoot and naked under the robe, but he didn't dare approach her.

'Tea?' he suggested.

'Thank you.' She had never expected to be here again, at the hotel, with him, in his rooms. She had tried to close the door on everything she felt for him, and so had he, and neither of them had succeeded.

When the tea came up, he handed her a cup of Earl Grey just the way she liked it, and she sat down and looked at him. She didn't know what to do now. Was this a moment or a lifetime? Neither of them knew, and providence had brought them back together. She had been jogging in Central Park, and then it had started raining, and there he was. He didn't say a word to her, he just reached out and touched her hand.

'I meant what I said to you in the park. I'll fight for us, if you let me.' She didn't answer, she just looked at him and set her cup down. She held out her arms to him, and he took her in his own. Her robe fell away, and then his did, and he carried her into his bedroom and laid her down on the bed and just looked at her.

'You don't have to fight for me,' she said softly. 'I don't want a war. I just want to be a family so we can love each other.' He nodded. It was what he wanted too. He knew that now, and how precious she was to him and always had been. He didn't say anything else to her then; he made love to her as he had wanted to for three months, and she gave herself to him with all the love and longing that had refused to die. And when it was over, they lay there together, shaken by what they'd almost lost and found again. And this time they both knew that whatever it took, they wouldn't let it go.

Chapter 15

Hugues went to see Heloise in Paris again in October. The weather was beautiful, and he was happy to see her, and she was excited about coming home. He never mentioned Natalie, but Heloise could sense that something was different. She questioned him about it over dinner.

'You're all grown up now,' he said quietly. 'Maybe we both are. I think I needed to grow up too. It'll probably feel strange when you come home. You've been gone for a long time, living your own life, even living with a man.' He smiled at her. And she was loving her internship at the George V. 'You've gotten very independent.' She looked worried at the idea of things changing. He was trying to prepare her for what was coming. But they had a good time anyway. He only stayed for four days this time. He had a lot to do at home. And when he got back, he made a suggestion to Natalie.

He asked her to redecorate a lovely small suite of rooms on the fifth floor for his daughter. He knew it would be a shock to Heloise to be moved out of his apartment, but she needed that too. And he needed a place to be with Natalie. He was paving the way for the life he wanted to share with her, and Natalie realized immediately that that was what he was doing. Things were different this time, in a good way. She felt loved and respected.

'How do you think she'll feel about it?'

'Upset, scared, angry, happy maybe. All the things people feel when they're growing up.' He asked Natalie to make the rooms beautiful, as only she could, and to spare no expense. He wanted it to be a surprise for Heloise when she came home, so Natalie had two months to do it. It wasn't a lot of time, but he knew how capable she was.

She got started immediately, and by Thanksgiving it was almost ready. She promised him the suite would be finished in two more weeks. It was young and stylish and very chic and just the right place for a young woman who had lived in Paris for six months. Hugues had decided not to disturb her old room for the moment, and he would let her move into her new apartment when she felt ready, which seemed wise to Natalie too.

She put the last touches on it three days before Heloise was due home. He wasn't sure what kind of shape she'd be in when she got there. She had called him in tears two weeks before; she and François had broken up. She said they had been fighting for months, and he was angry that she was leaving, and she had discovered that he was cheating on her with another intern at the hotel. It was over, and she was staying with a friend. She was leaving her IKEA furniture in the apartment, and she was upset about the break-up. Hugues was sorry for her, but in some ways he was relieved. It was a tie she no longer had to keep her there.

And he had been working on a homecoming party for her in the ballroom. Jennifer was organizing most of it, and Sally the catering manager was doing the rest. They were having the party the day after she got home. And she was planning to go skiing with friends the day after Christmas. She was going to start working for him officially after New Year's. She wanted to have some fun first. She had worked hard at the George V.

Everyone in the hotel was busy before she arrived. Her new apartment was ready. The party for her was all planned. The hotel was full. Natalie was incredibly busy, and Hugues was fielding the usual problems. A drunken guest had fallen down a small flight of stairs and was threatening to sue them. There had been some food theft in the kitchen, and they had to fire three key employees at a busy time of year. And in spite of how busy they were, Hugues and Natalie were happy and peaceful. She was nervous about Heloise's return, but she had the sense now that Hugues was going to handle it in the best way possible for all of them. She had waited a long time for this, and she trusted him now to finally do it. They'd been happy again since September, after their agonizing summer. And Jennifer was happy to see them back together. Hugues was a different man, and a better one, once Natalie came back. And a lot nicer to deal with than he had been all summer. He was himself again, only better. And Natalie was totally at home in the hotel and stayed in his apartment on most nights.

When Hugues picked Heloise up at the airport, he took the hotel's van with him for her bags. She had been gone for sixteen months, and it looked more like sixteen years when he saw how much she had brought home with her. She had eight suitcases and several boxes, full of things she had bought at the flea market in Paris. And she threw herself into his arms the moment she saw him. She looked very sophisticated in a black Balenciaga coat she had bought just before she left, with his permission, and high-heeled boots, and her long red hair was tucked into a knitted cap. She looked very stylish, and she chatted animatedly all the way to the hotel. She didn't mention François, and her father could see that she felt better. She'd obviously been ready to give that up, and they had talked anyway about breaking up when she left. But he had chosen an unpleasant way to do it.

As they had the year before when she came home for Christmas, many of the employees were waiting for her in the lobby, which looked beautiful with the tree and decorations. She hadn't been home for a year, and the party in the ballroom the next day was going to be a surprise for her, as was the apartment. But Hugues wasn't ready to tell her about that. He didn't want to rush her and thought he'd give her a few days to settle in before he showed it to her. He didn't want her to feel like he was pushing her out of the familiar apartment where she'd grown up. And Natalie was going to stay at her own place for a few days until Hugues had a chance to talk to Heloise about them. And Natalie knew he would this time. He wanted their time together now as much as she did, even if it meant upsetting his daughter. She had her own life, and he needed one too. But it was going to be a major change for Heloise, and possibly not one she was going to like. He hoped she would understand, but he also realized she might not. He was braced for an explosion.

As she had the year before, Heloise went out with friends the night she got back, after having dinner with her father. She was dying to see everyone, but she seemed more settled now and more mature. The internship at the George V had taught her a lot. She had worked at the concierge desk for the past two months, which was always hectic, and she had proven herself to be calm under fire.

Hugues was planning to put her at the reception desk, at least for the first month, to hone her skills handling guests. And he was even thinking of having her spend a month in accounting. She had to learn all aspects of the business now. And a few weeks at the room service desk would do her good too, and the concierge desk for several months. He wanted to round out her experience by June, and then she had to go back to Lausanne for graduation, which he was going to attend with her, and maybe even Natalie by then, if all went well. He was guardedly optimistic, and Natalie hoped he was right.

The morning after she returned, Hugues and Heloise had breakfast together, and then she went all over the hotel dropping off little gifts she'd bought in Paris for special people like Jan, Ernesta, a box of Belgian chocolates for the telephone operators, Jennifer, and Bruce, the head of security. She stopped to chat with each of them, and then she went out to finish her Christmas shopping.

She had told her father that she might go out with friends that night again, and he told her that he needed her in the hotel to help him. She looked a little startled that he expected her to get to work so quickly, but she didn't argue with him and said she'd be there, and asked him what time. She seemed far more mature about everything after her job in Paris. They had trained her well.

'If you're back by seven-thirty, that should work. I'll meet you here. We have some important guests coming in,' he said to get her to her surprise party in the ballroom. He had invited Natalie too. He wanted her there. Heloise promised to be on time, and then left for the day.

She was dressed and ready as promised, at seven-thirty, and Hugues looked formal and official as they went down in the elevator. He had told her to wear a cocktail dress, since they had to stop by a function in the ballroom too. And she was wearing a pretty black lace dress she had bought in Paris, with high heels, and her hair in a bun. He loved the way she looked, and he smiled as they rode the elevator to the second floor. He told her they would stop at the ballroom first, and then greet the VIPs in the lobby after, as they came in. She didn't ask who they were but followed him blindly to the ballroom. There was music playing and balloons everywhere, and as soon as they walked in, she saw everyone she knew and most of the employees waiting for her, as everyone shouted 'Surprise!' and she looked genuinely stunned for a moment as she turned to her father.

'Is this for me?' She was amazed. Even her friends from the Lycée were there, and everyone was smiling at her, while she fought back tears. She was so touched by what her father had done for her and that everyone was there.

'Yes, it is. Welcome home!' There were over a hundred people there. She couldn't believe they'd given her such a big party, and in the ballroom. It took her a few minutes to absorb it, recover, and start moving around the room to talk to everyone there.

Hugues walked over to Natalie as Heloise made her way through the crowd, and eventually Heloise came back to where they were standing and thanked him again. She was touched by how beautiful the party was. Her father and Natalie were standing together when Heloise came up to them.

'I'm sure you remember Natalie,' he said, introducing

her again and trying to sound casual about it. 'She's done several more suites for us since you were home last year. And one I think you'll particularly like,' he said cryptically but offered no further details. Heloise was too excited to pay close attention to what he'd said. She said a few words to Natalie, and then drifted away.

Eventually Hugues and Natalie left the party, as did most of the adults and older employees, and the young people danced till two A.M. He and Natalie sat in the bar for a long time afterward, and he sent her home with the driver and Rolls. He was sorry he couldn't spend the night with her. But she knew it was too soon for him to disappear. It was only Heloise's second night home.

And in the morning, Heloise thanked her father again for the fantastic party. She hadn't suspected a thing, and actually thought he was going to make her work with him that night. And then she looked at him with mischief in her eye.

'Were you flirting with the decorator last night? Or did I imagine it? She's very pretty, and I think she likes you.' Heloise looked amused and not worried as he smiled. Her father was handsome, and women always tried to get his attention. He bantered a bit, and Heloise believed he never pursued it and was a confirmed bachelor.

'I hope she likes me,' Hugues said quietly over their

breakfast. 'We've been seeing each other for a year now. She's a very special person, and I hope you get to know her.' He had finally opened the door that had terrified him for a year. It was like a breath of fresh air for him. He wasn't going to lie to her anymore.

But Heloise looked as though he had dumped a bucket of ice on her as she stared at him. She couldn't believe what he'd just said.

'What do you mean "seeing each other"? You mean sleeping with her?' She was looking at him in disbelief. She was not ready for this announcement, and she wanted him to say he was joking or they were just friends. But he didn't say that to her. The gloves were off. And it was time to grow up. He had promised this to Natalie, and it was long overdue, for all of them, Heloise too, whether she liked it or not. And for the moment it looked like it was 'not.' 'Is she your girlfriend?' She glared at him, waiting for an answer she didn't really want.

He answered very calmly, 'Yes, Heloise, she is.'

'Why didn't you tell me before?' She looked outraged and hurt at the same time and probably felt both.

'I wanted to, but it never seemed like the right time. You were so far away. And we stopped dating for a while too.' Heloise didn't know what to say. She stood up and walked away to stand at the window, thinking. And then she turned to her father with a heartbroken look that ripped his heart out. 'Why? Why do you need a girl-friend? You never had one before.' She was wondering if it was because she'd been gone. 'Were you lonely?' she asked, looking sorry for him. Natalie seemed like a decent, respectable woman, but Heloise wished he'd gotten a dog instead. 'You never had a girlfriend before. Why now?'

'I've gone out with a few women over the years,' he said to her honestly. He didn't want to go on lying to her, and she was old enough now to know. It felt much better to be truthful. 'But none of them meant anything to me,' he went on, 'so I didn't introduce them to you. But Natalie is different.'

'How?' Heloise looked panicked as she met her father's eyes. She didn't want to give up her place to someone else. 'We have something special together. Why ruin it?'

'Natalie can't ruin it,' Hugues said gently. He wanted to cross the room to hug her, but he didn't. She looked like she wanted space and distance, so he respected it. 'Besides, you just lived with François in Paris. Why can't I have someone in my life?'

She looked even more panicked then. Natalie was even young enough to have a baby, although Heloise hoped she wouldn't. She didn't point out that he was fifty-three years old and Natalie was thirteen years younger. Heloise looked devastated but remained polite. She seemed shell-shocked.

Her father spoke quietly to her then. 'We had some wonderful years together alone, and I wouldn't trade them for anything in the world. But you've grown up. You just lived with a man for six months, and I didn't complain about it, although it worried me. I thought you had a right to make your own decisions. Please respect mine. Natalie and I have a very nice relationship and she's not going to take anything away from you.'

But she already had. Heloise knew that she had lost a part of her father to her. Things weren't the same. She was no longer the only woman in his life. She wanted to crawl back into the womb.

He spoke to her very clearly then, seeing all that she felt in her eyes. 'You're not going to lose me. You never could. No one is ever going to replace you. There is room for all of us here.' He said it with enormous love for her in his eyes.

'No, there isn't!' she said with tears in hers. It was the worst shock she'd ever had, since she didn't remember her mother leaving. 'I'm going back to France,' she said, pacing around the room, and although he didn't feel it, Hugues tried to appear calm.

'No, you're not. You have an internship to do here. You won't get your diploma without it. And besides, this is your home.'

'Well, it's not hers. I don't want to see her around here.'

'I'm not going to hide her from you, Heloise. I respect you both too much. I should have told you a year ago, and I didn't. It was a big mistake, and I'm not going to do that again. I hope you'll get used to the idea, and to Natalie. She wants to be your friend.'

'I have enough friends. I don't need her. She's twice my age.' He didn't say anything and waited for her to calm down, and instead she grabbed her coat, turned to look at him, and said, 'Thank you for ruining my life.' With tears running down her face, she ran out of the apartment and slammed the door. He was sure she was going to one of her friends to complain about him, but at least he had finally told her. Now she had to make the adjustment to Natalie being in his life. And he knew it might take her a while. He wasn't shocked by what she said, just sad for her.

He called Natalie later that morning and repeated the conversation to her, without the comment about ruining her life. He had been true to his word. He had told Heloise at last and got the reaction he had expected. She was grateful it wasn't worse.

'How is she?' Natalie asked, sounding worried. She hoped it hadn't been too bad, for either of them.

'She's very angry at the moment. And probably scared, and hurt. She'll get over it. She just needs a little time.' He sounded confident and calm now that he had done it.

Heloise slept at a friend's that night, and on Christmas she was still not speaking to him. Natalie was at her brother's in Philadelphia, as she was every year for Christmas, so he didn't ask her to join them, which was just as well. It was a very tense Christmas. Heloise refused to have dinner with him and worked at the front desk instead.

And the day after Christmas, Natalie came over when she got back to town. They were having dinner quietly in the apartment, when Heloise came in, saw her, stomped into her room, and slammed the door, without saying a word. The fear and hurt she felt had turned to rage. She looked like a tornado tearing through the suite, and she was acting like a child.

'Wow!' Natalie said softly. She could see why he hadn't told her before. She was being anything but gracious about it. Heloise had spoken to several of her favorite people around the hotel, including Jennifer, and they had all said that Natalie was a kind person and good for her father, which made Heloise even more upset. She wanted them to hate her as much as she did, but no one would sign on. She was alone in the fight, and they all thought that it was time he had a serious woman in his life again. Heloise thought they were all traitors and hated them too. But she hated her father most of all, for the ultimate betrayal of replacing her. She had no intention of sharing him with Natalie or anyone else. He was hers.

'She'll be all right,' Hugues tried to reassure Natalie, but she was upset too. She hadn't wanted to destroy his family, or the relationship he had with his only child. But there was nothing they could do now except wait out the storm. And it looked like it was going to be a long wait.

The next day Heloise left to go skiing in Vermont with friends. And she said not a word to him when she left. In a way it was easier that she had gone away for a few days. Natalie could stay with him, and they could spend New Year's Eve together in peace. They had no particular plans other than being together, and Natalie was worried now that she might be ruining his life.

'Do you want me to get out of your life again?' she asked him, feeling guilty for the trouble she'd caused.

'No, I don't!' he said sternly. 'I did this for us, and it's the right thing to do. Now help me see it through. You can't just bail out of the boat the first time we hit a wave.'

She nodded and didn't know what to do to calm things down, other than support him and wait it out.

'Do you suppose she'll ever give me a chance?' Natalie asked him, looking anxious.

'Not for a while. She was always a very stubborn child, and she hasn't changed. The storm will have to blow itself out. And I'm sure it'll be pretty unpleasant for a time.' He put an arm around her and kissed her. And as much as he had feared Heloise's reaction for the last year, he was ready for it now and willing to endure it. It was Natalie who looked scared.

When they went to bed, she tossed and turned for most of the night, and she looked tired the next morning.

'Try to stop worrying about it. We just need to give it time,' he said firmly.

Natalie finally relaxed on New Year's Eve, and they spent a wonderful evening together, watching old movies and drinking champagne. Hugues had tried to call Heloise to wish her a happy new year, as he always did, but she didn't answer her phone. He left her a voice mail and sent a text message. Natalie was amazed at how calm he was. Now that he had finally told her, he was fine. And he refused to talk about it that night. The evening was theirs.

Much to everyone's amazement, Heloise was still angry

when she came back. More so than ever. He had betrayed her, in her eyes, and betrayal was something she couldn't forgive. She started her job at the front desk two days after New Year's, and she scowled at her father whenever she saw him. He gave her plenty of space and didn't force the issue. She had the information she needed, that Natalie was part of his life now. She had to get used to it, whether she liked it or not.

She didn't relent for all of January and barely said two words to him in five weeks and ignored Natalie entirely. Hugues was a little discouraged by then. He wondered how long she could continue the vendetta. Apparently a very long time. Jennifer tried to talk to her too, to no avail. Heloise didn't want to hear it, from her or anyone else. She said she hated Natalie and that was it. But Jennifer dared to disagree.

'This isn't the temporary catering manager flirting with your father and sleeping with the sous chef in the freezer,' she reminded her. The reference actually made Heloise smile. She had forgotten about Hilary. 'Natalie is a decent woman. She won't give you a hard time. And she's not trying to take him away from you. You should give her a chance.'

'Why? I don't need a mother. I have one. And I don't want to share my father with her.' It was honest at least, although she sounded about five years old, which was part of the problem. In some ways she still was. She was acting immature and spoiled. And Jennifer told her so, which made her even more furious. Jennifer told her she wasn't being reasonable, and that she was better than that. Heloise stormed off in a huff and went back to the desk, where she was doing a very good job. Her father was pleased to hear it and giving her a wide berth. Natalie was staying away from the hotel when Heloise was there.

At the beginning of February, Heloise was still angry and upset, Natalie was a nervous wreck, and Hugues was getting a little tired of it all. Natalie kept offering to leave him, Heloise would have loved it if she did, and he wanted them both to calm down. He reported to Jennifer about it every morning, and she kept telling him to hang in and be patient. He said he was.

'Why don't you just marry her then?' Jennifer said one morning. 'You might as well be hung for a sheep as a lamb. If Heloise is this mad, she'll just get mad all over again if the two of you ever get married. Why not get it over with all at once? And then Natalie can just move in.' He hadn't shown Heloise her new apartment. He didn't want to spoil it by doing it when she was so angry. He wanted her to enjoy it and was waiting for her to settle down, and she hadn't yet. And it was beginning to look like she never would. But he liked Jennifer's idea and thought about it for a few days. Maybe she had a point. Heloise was already mad and had been for nearly two months. What difference would it make? And he loved the idea of spending the rest of his life with Natalie. They had talked about it a few times, before the furor began when Heloise got home.

He didn't say anything to anyone, and he bought Heloise a beautiful red Givenchy coat for Valentine's Day and gave it to her at breakfast. He could tell that she was tempted to give it back to him, but instead she opened it with a surly expression that melted when she saw the coat.

'Papa, I love it!' she said, and looked like her old self for about five minutes. He hugged her, and she put it on, and then she went back to her bedroom and slammed the door again. At least it had been a break in the clouds, which gave him hope. Maybe one day the hurricane would pass. Her relentless fury was getting old.

And that night he took Natalie to dinner at La Grenouille, which was her favorite restaurant, and then they went back to her place to talk, relax, and eventually make love. It had been a stressful two months for both of them. They were both working hard, and Heloise was making life miserable for them. He loved getting away from the hotel now, whenever he could, to be with Natalie and enjoy their time together in peace.

They were lying in bed afterward at her apartment, talking about Heloise again, and Hugues changed the subject. He didn't want Natalie to get upset again. It was all they talked about now, most of the time, while they tried to guess how long it would take Heloise to relent about them. Maybe never, at the rate she was going. It had been a very long two months.

He was trying to tease Natalie to distract her, and kissed her, and then he looked at her with a worried expression, as though he saw something he didn't like. 'What's that in your ear?' he asked her, and she looked scared for a minute.

'In my ear? Is there something in my ear?' She brushed her hand past it as though it might be a bug of some kind.

'There's something in your ear,' he insisted, still frowning. 'Let me have a look.' He peered into it, and she giggled. He was tickling her.

'What are you doing?'

'I think it's stuck. Maybe I should get a pair of pliers or something.'

'Don't be silly,' she said as she turned around and kissed him, which distracted him for a minute. He wanted to make love to her again, but there was something else he wanted to do first.

'Do you have a pair of pliers?'

'No, I don't. And you're not going to put a pair of pliers in my ear!'

'Oh, here it is! I got it! I knew there was something in there!' He handed something to her, and she didn't know what it was at first, and she looked at it and stared in disbelief. It was a beautiful diamond solitaire. He had followed Jennifer's suggestion and gone to Cartier that day. It was much larger than any engagement ring Natalie had ever dreamed of, and she looked at Hugues in amazement.

'Are you serious?'

'That looks like a very serious ring to me,' he said, laughing. 'It's a good thing I got it out. We might have had to cut off your ear to get to it.' And then he grew serious too. 'Will you marry me, Natalie?' He slipped the ring on her finger as he asked her and then kissed her.

'Yes, I will,' she said when they came up for air. 'I would even without the ring. I never expected anything like that.' That made it even more fun for him. He loved spoiling her. And she had earned it. She had waited a long time for him to do the right thing. And now he was doing more.

'When shall we get married?' he asked her, looking happy and relaxed as he lay next to her, and she was flashing the handsome diamond on her finger and grinning from ear to ear.

'I don't know. Is tomorrow too soon? What if you change your mind?'

'I won't.' He got quiet again for a minute. 'I have to go to Heloise's graduation in Lausanne in June, and by then I hope you'll come with us. I'd like to give her a party when we get back and combine it with her twenty-first birthday. I don't want to steal her thunder. What about July? How does that sound to you?'

'Perfect,' she said, as she turned and kissed him. The whole evening had been perfect. Their lovemaking, the proposal, the gorgeous ring. And a life with him forever. And then she looked worried again. 'What are we going to tell Heloise?'

'That we're getting married,' he said simply. 'She hates me right now anyway. How much madder can she get?'

'Maybe a lot,' Natalie said, looking nervous.

'She'll get over it.' He still believed that. And he had told Natalie when she came back to him that it was for good. And he was true to his word. 'When she calms down, I'm going to ask her to be my witness.'

'I'll ask my brother to give me away,' Natalie said

happily. 'Actually, Heloise might like my nephew. He's awfully cute. We can introduce them at the wedding.' She loved the sound of it as the words rolled off her tongue . . . 'at the wedding' . . . It was sheer bliss.

'That might help,' Hugues said, looking equally happy. 'I assume we'll have the reception in the ballroom?' he asked her.

'Of course. We could have a minister do it there.' She wasn't particularly religious, and he was divorced, so it sounded right to both of them. It all did. The wedding. And the life that would come afterward. He had a life again. And he was going to have a wife who loved him. And one of these days, he might even have a daughter again too.

Chapter 16

Hugues decided to speak to Heloise the next morning. After leaving Natalie at her apartment, he walked back to the hotel, saw Heloise at the front desk, and asked her to come into his office. He looked very official as he said it. She was standing at the desk in the navy suit that was the uniform for female desk clerks, and she came in to see him a few minutes later.

'Am I in trouble?' she asked, looking nervous, forgetting for a moment that she was angry at him. She wondered if she had done something wrong while working at the desk, or a guest had complained about her, but he shook his head and asked her to sit down.

'No, I probably am. But you're already angry at me. I want to make it clear to you again that I love you, that no one ever could or will take your place. You're my daughter. And there's room for you *and* Natalie in my life. Those are two very different roles. We had a crazy life for a long time, and we both loved it, with only the two of us. But you're not going to stay alone forever, and I shouldn't have to either. That's not fair.' She was squirming in her seat as he said it. He looked at her quietly then and went on. 'But since you're so mad at me anyway, I figure I don't have much to lose. I want you to be the first to know that I asked Natalie to marry me last night, and she accepted. I'd like you to be part of it. I want you to be my witness, instead of a best man. And no matter how mad at me you are, I love you. And I hope you give Natalie a chance and get to know her one day. We're going to do it in July, after your graduation, which is a very big deal to me too.'

Heloise stared at him then, with a look of silent pain as tears rolled down her cheeks. 'How can you do something like that? You always said you'd never get married again.' She couldn't believe what he had just said and what he was planning to do. It was the worst news she'd ever had. And then she wanted to hurt him too.

'She'll probably just walk out on you like Mom did,' she said with an angry look. Hugues made an effort not to react to what she said. He spoke to her quietly from across his desk.

'She's a very different woman than your mother. I hope our marriage works, but if it doesn't, it'll probably be because I screw it up, not because she runs off with a rock star or anyone else. She's a serious woman. Give her a chance. You might even get to like her too.'

Listening to him, Heloise looked sad. She was losing her father to a woman she hardly knew. She was sorry now that she had gone away to school. She was sure that if she had stayed it never would have happened. She looked heartbroken at his exciting news.

He stood up and came around the desk then, with a loving look at her. He could see how upset she was and spoke to her in a quiet tone. He had just had an idea and hoped the timing was right and that it might help. 'Please go to the front desk and get the key to five-oh-two.' They walked out of his office together, and he waited for her at the elevator while she got the key from the front desk. She hadn't asked him why. She was too upset. The assistant manager smiled when she took it. He had been wondering when her father was going to give it to her. It had been sitting empty for two months.

They rode up in the elevator together in silence and got out on five, and he took the key from her as they walked down the hall. She had no idea why he wanted her there. He unlocked it, pushed open the door, switched on a light, and waved her inside. She walked in and glanced around the room. She could tell that it had been recently decorated. The living room was all done in oatmeal and sand colors. And the bedroom was a delicate shade of pale pink. The fabrics were beautiful. She liked the paintings, and the rooms still smelled of paint. It had an open airy feel to it, and the sun was streaming through the windows.

'It's very nice,' she said in a flat tone, 'and I like the paintings. Am I supposed to be admiring Natalie's decorating, or is there something you want me to do?' As she asked him, he handed her the key.

'I've been waiting to show this to you for two months.'

'Why?'

'Because I had it done for you. It's yours, whenever you want it. You can stay upstairs in the apartment if you like, but I thought you might like some privacy too. You led a pretty independent life in Paris, and if you want to do the same here, I thought you might like your own place. I'm not pushing you out of the apartment, but whenever you want this, it's yours. Keep the key.' He could see her face slowly come to life and the excitement in her eyes when he said it, and she didn't know what to say, and then a worried look crossed her eyes.

'Is this a bribe because you're getting married?'

'No, Natalie started working on this for you in October. I only decided to marry her two weeks ago.'

'I wish you hadn't,' she said sadly, and he pulled her into his arms and gave her a hug.

'I promise you, it will be all right. And you're never going to lose me, no matter what.' He stood there holding her, as tears slid down her cheeks. He hated causing her pain, but he knew that marrying Natalie was right. 'You can move into this apartment whenever you want. Or if you prefer, you can stay upstairs with us. And maybe you just want to entertain your friends here. But if you stay upstairs, I expect you to be polite to Natalie.' He was making it very clear to her. She didn't say a word for a long moment and then she stopped crying and smiled at him. She was touched by what he'd done for her.

'Thank you, Papa. It's a beautiful apartment, and I love it.' She gave him a hug then and a kiss on the cheek. She was obviously torn between being devastated and being excited about her new apartment. Her emotions had been on a roller coaster since she got home. She couldn't wait to invite her friends over to see her new rooms, and she hated to leave now and go back to work. She walked around again and loved everything she saw. She was trying to forget that he was going to marry Natalie and to enjoy the gift. 'I really like the paintings,' she said finally. They were great: contemporary, bright, and young.

'I picked them all for you,' he said gently. 'I'm glad you like it. I would have been really disappointed if you didn't,' he told her honestly.

'I'm still mad at you for marrying Natalie,' she said, equally honest with him, but the fire had gone out of her. She was in shock. She had never expected him to marry again.

'I know you are. I hope you get over it one day. Will you be my witness?' he asked her with a serious look.

'Maybe.' She looked sad again then, glancing around her new apartment. 'She's a very good decorator. But you don't need a wife. You have me.'

'And I always will. A daughter can't be replaced. But you're not going to stick around forever. It's nice for me to have companionship in my old age. And I love her. But I love you too and always will.' Heloise nodded as she listened and slipped the key to her apartment in her uniform pocket, as though she were afraid he would take it away because she had been so angry at him for the past many weeks.

'Thank you. I love the apartment.'

'Good,' her father said as he put an arm around her

shoulders. 'And I love you. Now get back to work.' She smiled as he said it, and they went back downstairs. Everyone at the desk was smiling. They knew where they had been, from the moment she took the key.

'What do you think?' the assistant manager asked Heloise, and she smiled broadly.

'It's very cool.' She glanced at her father, and he smiled as he walked away. And he called Natalie to tell her all about it after that.

'Did she like it?'

'Are you kidding? She loved it. I told her we're getting married, and I wanted her to know that she doesn't have to live with us if she doesn't want to. She can move downstairs to her own place if she prefers. And she won't feel as displaced. She can do whatever she wants.'

'Was she furious that we're getting married?' Natalie asked, still sounding nervous. She didn't want the stepdaughter from hell living with her for the rest of her life, or even the next six months.

'I think she was more shocked. She'll adjust,' he said confidently. 'I think seeing her own apartment was a good distraction. She loved it. She also told me that sooner or later you'll get smart and leave me for a rock star too.' He was smiling as he said it. It had been a childish thing to say.

'How awful,' Natalie said. 'I'd never do that to you.'

'I know you wouldn't.' It had been quite a morning, and he felt drained. He hoped that Heloise would start to calm down now and get to know Natalie. It would be good for her to have a stable woman in her life too, not just him. Natalie was going to be a blessing for them both.

'I asked her to be my witness,' he told her then.

'What did she say?'

'She said maybe. That's the best we can hope for right now. By July she'll have calmed down.'

'I called my brother and he said he'd give me away. Now I have to find a dress.' Their wedding was only five months away, and there was a lot to plan.

'You should talk to the catering manager as soon as possible,' he told her. 'She's a great girl. And we have to set a date. Fortunately, in July, the ballroom isn't usually too booked. Everyone wants to get married in May and June, on Valentine's Day, or at Christmas.' But they both liked the idea of July. 'Where do you want to go on our honeymoon, by the way?' Having told Heloise, now they could make plans.

'Someplace pretty,' she said innocently. 'You decide.' And as she said it, he knew just the place. The One & Only Palmilla in Baja, California. He sent guests there all the time, and everyone loved it. It was the height of luxury and a perfect place for a honeymoon. Either that or the Hotel du Cap in Cap d'Antibes. But he thought Baja sounded like more fun.

'Thank you for doing such a nice job on Heloise's apartment. One day she'll thank you, but maybe not just yet.'

'She doesn't need to thank me. It was your idea, and you paid me to do it. She should thank you.'

'She did,' he said, smiling, as he sat at his desk. They talked for a few more minutes and hung up, and Jennifer walked in a few minutes later with papers for him to sign and a cappuccino, and he smiled at her.

'Thank you for the excellent suggestion,' he said to her. 'I asked Natalie to marry me last night. It was all your idea, and it worked out very well. She said yes, and we're getting married in July. If we can get a date for the ballroom.'

'I think I have connections, and maybe I can help you,' she teased him. 'And congratulations to both of you. Or best wishes to the bride. Have you told Heloise yet?' she asked, trying not to look worried.

'I just did.'

'Was she all right with it?'

'No. But she will be. It was a shock.' Jennifer wasn't

surprised to hear it, but she was glad Hugues had followed her advice.

Jennifer smiled as he signed the papers, and she left the room with them. She was happy for him. And she was absolutely certain that Natalie was the perfect woman for him. And once they got Heloise on board, it would be smooth sailing for them after that. She was excited about their plans. And hopefully Heloise would get used to the idea soon. Jennifer was happy too that Heloise was getting the mother figure she had needed for so long. Natalie was what they both needed, whether Heloise knew it or not.

Chapter 17

The months leading up to Hugues and Natalie's wedding, and Heloise's graduation, were hectic for all of them. Natalie was trying to run a business, plan a wedding, have a relationship, and make peace with a stepdaughter who continued to wage a cold war against her and ignored her anytime she was in the same room. It was stressful to say the least. Hugues was trying to be patient and reassure both of them, but nothing he said or did changed Heloise's refusal to acknowledge Natalie or accept her as her father's future wife. She ignored her pointedly. She refused to have anything to do with the wedding, which left Natalie to handle it with the catering manager, the florist, and a wedding consultant on her own.

Heloise was using her new apartment to entertain

friends regularly and admitted that she loved it. But she was continuing to live upstairs with her father in her old room, which meant that she and Natalie ran into each other frequently whenever Natalie came over to have dinner with him, or they were in the apartment going over wedding plans. He spent the night at Natalie's whenever he could. And all he could do with Heloise was keep her as busy as possible in her internship at the hotel to distract her from the wedding. He frequently had her working double shifts, long hours, and late nights, and he moved her from department to department, so she would learn different aspects of the business. It was what the École Hôtelière expected him to do, and he had assured them, when they agreed to let her do her internship with him, that he would make no allowances for her because she was his daughter.

Heloise had a tendency to assume that she knew everything because she had grown up in the hotel, and she still had much to learn about the business. But everyone agreed that she was a hard worker, willing to do anything she was asked, and diligent about her work.

Her father was proud of her, but the one area where Heloise would not relent was Natalie. She had told him finally that she wasn't coming to the wedding, neither as witness nor as guest, and Hugues didn't insist. He didn't want to make it worse by pushing her and was hoping she would calm down by July. He still wanted her as his witness.

By the time Heloise was due to go back to Lausanne for her graduation, it was obvious that Natalie wasn't welcome there, and she said she didn't mind, as she had too much to do at home. The wedding was scheduled on the Saturday of the July 4 weekend, on July 7, which was the only day the ballroom had been free. Heloise's only comment about it was that it was fine with her, since everyone they invited would be away for the long weekend and she hoped no one would come.

Her graduation and twenty-first birthday party was to be held in the same room three weeks before, on June 15. She was looking forward to it, as was everyone in the hotel, and it wasn't a surprise this time. Heloise was planning it herself, working closely with Sally, the catering manager who was also handling the wedding. Heloise refused to hear their plans and refused to speak to Sally or Jan about it.

Heloise's evaluations from her internship were excellent. Her style, her dedication, her judgment, and her way of dealing with guests and co-workers had all been highly praised. And her meticulous attention to detail and innate sense for the hotel business had been noted by all of her supervisors. Her years of following her father around the hotel had served her well. The only consistent criticism was that she was a little too independent and inclined to make decisions on her own. They felt she was less of a team player than destined for management one day, which was where she was headed anyway. And she would be joining the hotel's regular internship program, working in reception and filling in with the concierge, as soon as she got back from Lausanne. And most of the guests who had already seen her at the desk had no idea that she was the owner's daughter. She followed the same rules and guidelines about dealing with the guests as all the other employees, and she wore the same sober uniform, which was a dark blue suit for women that Hugues had had designed for them, and morning coat and striped trousers for the men. And there were rigorous standards for the appearance of the employees. She always wore her bright red hair pulled back in a neat bun on duty, and very little makeup, which was typical of her anyway.

Heloise was flying to Geneva a week before graduation, and her father was planning to arrive four days later. She wanted a little time with her classmates in Lausanne before he got there, and she stopped in at his office the morning she left. As usual, he was signing checks.

'You're leaving?' He looked up when he heard her come in, and she nodded. In spite of their differences, he was proud of her for the degree she had just earned. He had been opposed to it in the beginning, but he could see now that there was no denying that she was a natural for the hotel business. She had lived, slept, and breathed it since she was two years old, and just as it was for him, it was what she loved most and the only job she wanted. Particularly working for him at their hotel. 'Do you need money?' he asked, like any other father. He asked her the question every time she walked out the door, even for pizza with friends.

'I'm fine,' she said, smiling at him. 'I got some from accounting.' They always sent him the cash reports. And she would be paid a tiny salary for the internship program when she returned. Her schedule before had been set to meet the requirements of the École Hôtelière, and her father had already told everyone that she was to be given no favors or preferential treatment when she joined their regular internship program. She was to be treated like everyone else. 'I'll see you on Friday when you get there,' she said warmly to her father. 'There's a dinner for the parents that night, and a reception after graduation.' He smiled as he walked over to give her a hug, and it reminded her of how happy she was that Natalie wasn't coming. She was around all the time now. And for once, perhaps for a last time, she would have him to herself. Their life was about to change forever and, in her eyes, already had. Her answer to it was to act as though Natalie didn't exist. She hadn't invited her to her graduation, nor apologized for not doing so. She wasn't overtly rude to her in what she said. She just totally ignored her, which was rude enough.

'Have a safe trip.' Hugues's eyes were full of all the love he felt for her, no matter how difficult she had been for the past six months. 'I'm looking forward to graduation, and your party when we get home.' He didn't mention the wedding, since it was such a sore subject with her. And this week and the following one were all hers. And as usual, her mother wasn't coming to her graduation. Heloise had invited her, but she was on vacation in Vietnam with Greg, and despite a year's notice, Miriam said she had been unable to change her plans. It was always the same story with her. Heloise didn't care as long as her father was there. And he walked her out of the hotel, where a car and driver were waiting for her to take her to the airport.

'Thank you, Papa,' she said quietly. She had seemed to calm down in the last few days. She was excited about her graduation and felt very adult suddenly. Working in the hotel, even for her father, had taught her a multitude of new skills. It was different than just running around as a kid. She had real responsibilities now, occasionally challenging situations to handle, and supervisors to satisfy, who were sometimes stern with her and always demanding, even if they'd known her for years. She had to meet the Vendôme standards now, not just those of the École Hôtelière. 'See you Friday,' she said, slipping into the car, carrying her graduation dress in a garment bag, and she waved as they pulled away from the curb. He looked pensive as he watched the car drive away, thinking of all the years they had shared and the strange life they had led, safe in the cocoon of the hotel. He knew how hard it was for her to include someone else in that life, which made him more tolerant than he might have been otherwise with her behavior of the past many months. He knew that underneath her anger and upset over Natalie, she loved him, just as he loved her. It was hard for him to believe that she was grown up now and almost twenty-one, and about to be a graduate of the same school he had gone to. He smiled thinking about it as he walked back into the hotel.

When Heloise got to Lausanne, she met up with her classmates of the year before. All of them were equally excited to be graduating, and full of stories about their internships around the world. Heloise's had been quieter than most, in her own familiar world, which made her happy that she had had six months before that at the George V. And she saw François for the first time in six months. He had a new girlfriend with him, which ruffled Heloise's feathers. Several of them had brought significant others along. She hadn't been dating anyone since her return to New York. Working double shifts at the hotel, she hadn't had time.

They all went out to dinner at local restaurants every night, including the ones on campus and the two student-run bars, and attended final seminars and a rehearsal for graduation. It was an emotional time. Some of them had signed up for an additional two years in the International Hospitality Management Programme, and still others were planning to go on for a master's degree at the school after that. But Heloise was ready to go home and get the rest of her training at the Vendôme.

And on Friday her father arrived and checked into the hotel attached to the school, which it ran as a learning experience for its students. It was a treat for any visitor to stay there, and Hugues had worked there himself for a few months as a young man. It was always fun for him to come back here and see how things had changed. His own time at the École Hôtelière had been among the best years of his life before his career began. He couldn't help wondering as he walked around the familiar, immaculate campus if one of his grandchildren might even come here one day. It was hard to imagine, but with Heloise's deep love for the business, he could almost see that happening sometime in the distant future. He suddenly felt like the head of a dynasty as he thought about it, and not just the proprietor of a small hotel.

'What were you thinking about, Papa?' Heloise asked him as she caught up to him. She had seen him walking along alone when she went looking for him. She had put her nuclear weapons away for these few days, particularly since Natalie wasn't there. It was almost like old times.

He looked up and smiled when he saw Heloise and put an arm around her. 'It sounds silly, but I was thinking that maybe your children will come to school here one day.' He had never expected her to do so, and suddenly it had become a tradition as she followed in his footsteps. He wondered what his parents would say. This had never been their dream for him, but it had been a good life and a career he still loved.

'I don't think I want children,' she said pensively, as they walked along arm in arm, and he was surprised to hear it. He had always expected her to marry and have babies, even now that she would be working at the hotel.

'Why not?' he asked, watching her eyes.

'They're too much work,' she said, brushing the idea away, and he laughed.

'So is a hotel. And let me tell you that no matter how much work children are, they're worth it. My life would be nothing without you.' The emotion he felt for her was strong in his voice.

'Even now, with Natalie?' Heloise was haunted by her. Her eyes were sad when she looked at him, and he nodded emphatically.

'Even with Natalie. That's not the same thing. I loved your mother very much, and I love Natalie. But the love you feel for a woman, or a man, is not the same as what you feel for a child. It doesn't even compare. My love for you is forever. Love for a partner is there for as long as it lasts, sometimes it lasts a lifetime, sometimes not. My love for you is to my grave.' It was a serious thing to say, and she was quiet for a long moment as they stopped walking, and she looked into his eyes.

'I thought that had changed,' she said quietly, and he shook his head.

'It will never change. Never. In my entire lifetime.' She nodded then and looked relieved. It was hard for him to imagine that even as grown up as she seemed to be, she was only a child who thought she would lose her father to someone else, or already had. It explained her rejection of Natalie. And it wasn't so surprising since at the age of four she really had lost her mother to a man. But in Miriam's case, Heloise had never had her. Her mother had only been on loan for a brief time. The defection and abandonment of her mother had been the ultimate betrayal, which had made her fears about Natalie, and her resulting anger at him, so much worse. He understood that better now. And he was glad he had come alone. He held her tightly in his arms for a moment, stroking her long silky hair, and then they walked back to his hotel arm in arm with a feeling of peace. He had said everything she needed to hear. It hadn't been enough to know it, or assume it, or hope it; she had needed the words, and she had needed to hear them from him.

The eve-of-graduation dinner that night at the school-run hotel was a festive event. It was held in an auditorium that had been festooned and decorated, and a number of the students as well as the director of the school gave speeches, some of them very emotional. And afterward most of the students went to small nightclubs and bars around Lausanne, and the bars on campus, for a last time. Heloise went out with her friends, and she was genuinely sad to leave them. After this they would all be scattered around the world, although two of them said they were doing internships in New York, but neither of them were people she knew well. And she heard that François had secured a job in Paris at the Plaza Athénée, which he preferred to working at his family's hotel in the South of France. From now on they would all be crawling their way up the corporate ladder in the hotel business, satisfying their supervisors and serving their clients' needs. It wasn't an easy business, they all knew by now, but it was the path they had chosen, and they couldn't wait to get started. Only two people had dropped out, one because of family illness and the other due to pregnancy and a shotgun wedding, but even she had promised to return. There were a hundred and seventy-eight students graduating in Heloise's class, and fewer than two thousand in the school, including graduate students. It was acknowledged to be the finest hotel school in the world and a major coup to graduate from there.

And the graduation ceremony was very moving the next day. It followed all the school's venerable traditions and hadn't changed a bit since Hugues had graduated more than thirty years before at her age. Prizes were given, and Heloise got two honorable mentions. The crowd in the auditorium stood up and applauded them at the end of the ceremony as an orchestra played, and then a huge cheer rose from the students and the crowd, and they were distinguished graduates of the illustrious École Hôtelière de Lausanne. There were tears streaming down Heloise's cheeks and in her father's eyes as she found him and they embraced.

'I'm so proud of you,' he said in a choked voice, and there was no one in the room for her, or in the world, except the two of them at that moment. And he was glad once again that he had come alone. He had needed to share this with her, and to confirm his dedication to her and his love. He was deeply sad for her that Miriam hadn't come. She was such a fool and had missed the boat with Heloise all her life. She had absented herself from every major occasion, just as she had this time. She cared about no one but herself. He was sorry he had given Heloise such an inadequate mother, and he hoped that she and Natalie would be friends one day. It was too late to act as her mother, but it would be good for her to have a staunch, mature female friend, other than Jennifer, Ernesta, and Jan, all of whom had been good to her. But Natalie would be family now. He had tried to be everything to her, mother, father, mentor, adviser, but he still felt she needed a woman in her life, and he was sorry he hadn't provided one before this. In some ways he had waited too long, and now instead of welcoming it,

Heloise resented it and had declared war on Natalie. He hoped there would be a truce one of these days, but he didn't mention it to her in Lausanne.

The graduation dinner that night was a grand affair, with excellent food and a very decent band. He danced with his daughter, and she danced with her friends for the last time. After all their hard work for two years, this was a night of celebration and saluting their accomplishments. And the next morning they congregated for the last time, after being out the night before till six A.M. Heloise hadn't even bothered to go to bed. After hugging all her friends and exchanging contact information, she got in the car with her father, went to the airport in Geneva, and fell sound asleep as soon as they boarded the plane. He covered her gently with a blanket and smiled as he looked at her. She looked like a little girl again with her bright red hair and her freckles. She was a woman now, with a life and career ahead of her, but she would always be his baby, in spite of her accomplishments. He leaned over and kissed her and watched her while she slept as the plane headed to New York.

afternoon a week later, with more of her decorating accessories and belongings, when Natalie got into the elevator and found herself looking at Heloise and Brad. They were on their way up to her apartment. Brad kissed his aunt and looked surprisingly comfortable, as though both the hotel and Heloise were familiar to him now. It was Heloise's day off. Now that her father was back, she had a little more time to herself.

'What have you two been up to?' Natalie asked, intrigued to see them so happy together. They'd been holding hands when she got in.

'We just went to a street fair downtown,' Heloise said, looking radiant. Brad put an arm around her shoulders, and a minute later they got out on the fifth floor. Natalie asked if they wanted to come up later for dinner, but Heloise was quick to say that they were going out again. And she didn't know why, but after they got out, Natalie didn't think she believed her. Obviously they wanted to be alone. She smiled to herself as she got off on her floor and let herself into their apartment. Hugues was working out at the gym as she put her things away, and she mentioned to him later that she had seen Heloise and Brad.

'Do you suppose that's serious?' he asked, glancing up at her, and she smiled as she shrugged.

Chapter 18

They both hit the ground running when they got to New York. Hugues was handling the usual dicey situations at the hotel, employee disputes, threatened lawsuits, labor unions, arriving important guests. And Heloise was on duty at the front desk the night they got home. Her diploma was still in her suitcase, but it made no difference here. She had to help an arriving guest with lost luggage deal with the airline, find a change of rooms for a complaining guest who hated the suite she had, which was hard to believe since it was one of the new ones, but the guest in question said that the color green made her anxious and gave her migraines and there were green tassels on the drapes. And miraculously Heloise was able to switch suites with a guest who hadn't arrived yet. She had to call a doctor after midnight for a guest whose five-year-old had a high fever, and she had to get security to deal with a domestic argument between two drunks on the fourth floor, without calling the police if at all possible so they didn't wind up on Page Six of the *New York Post*. And she had to scold room service several times at two A.M. for not answering their phone, and explain to another guest why the concierge desk was not open at five A.M. She finished work at seven, and was dead on her feet when she got to her father's apartment and saw that Natalie was there. She hadn't seen her since she got home the day before, and she was so tired she didn't care. They were having breakfast as Heloise walked past them to her room with a cursory hello. She hated the look in her father's eyes when he looked at Natalie. He looked like he was about to melt into a puddle on the floor. Heloise thought it looked ridiculous for a man his age to be so lovesick, but she tried not to notice as she headed to her room.

'How'd it go last night?' he asked as she went by.

'Okay. We had a nasty situation on the fourth floor. The Morettis got into a fight, and both rooms on either side wanted to call the police.'

'What did you do?' He looked concerned, and she seemed mildly sheepish as she answered.

'I sent Dom Perignon to all the people who complained. Bruce spent about an hour with the Morettis. Apparently he had made insulting comments about her mother, and Bruce sat with them until they were so tired and so drunk that Mr. Moretti went to bed, and we gave Mrs. Moretti a complimentary room on another floor. I didn't know what else to do. And I got a doctor for six-nineteen at two A.M. Her kid had strep, and an ear infection.'

'You did all the right things,' her father praised her. She had learned more than ever in the past two years that hotelry was as much about diplomacy and ingenuity as about service, and you had to think on your feet. She was good at it and had the correct instincts.

'The Morettis need a shrink,' she said with a grin, as she took off her uniform jacket and threw it on a chair. She had kicked off her shoes at the front door. She glanced at Natalie then. The wedding was in less than four weeks and her own party in a few days. 'How's the wedding coming?'

Natalie grinned and then sighed. 'My sister-in-law broke her ankle Rollerblading last week. Both my nieces have mono and may not be able to come. There's a threatened air strike in Holland so we're not sure about the flowers. We haven't set the menu yet, and your father doesn't want a wedding cake. And three of my clients want their installations that week while they're away. Other than that, it's fine.' Heloise couldn't help laughing at what she'd said. She seemed a little mellower now that she had her degree and had spent three days alone with her father in Lausanne. Natalie was glad she hadn't gone, and with all she had to do, she couldn't have anyway. And she knew that Heloise would have viewed her as an intruder if she had.

'That sounds about right for three weeks to D-day. Most of that stuff usually happens a few days before. You're ahead of the game,' Heloise said, as she spoke to her more pleasantly than she had in months, and her father smiled. Their time together at the graduation in Lausanne had done her good.

'I'm not sure that reassures me.' Natalie looked nervous and as though she had lost weight, but she seemed happy when she gazed at Hugues. Her future stepdaughter still scared her, but she was being friendlier than she had all year. Maybe she was just tired from a long night and the flight the day before and didn't have the energy to be nasty to her. Natalie wasn't sure. She didn't trust her yet after her fury of the previous months.

'Sally will help you work it all out. She's great. She can pull anything off!' Heloise said easily. 'She found a rabbi once in half an hour when the one they had didn't show up. He was on his honeymoon in the hotel, and she got him out of bed to do the wedding, and she called a cantor that she knew. It went off perfectly. And why don't you want a cake?' she asked, looking at her father disapprovingly.

'I feel silly. Maybe I've seen too many weddings. Besides I never like them. I want a decent dessert,' he complained.

'You have to have a wedding cake. You can order dessert from room service, but you should have a cake,' she scolded him as she grabbed a muffin off their breakfast table and ate it as she headed to her bedroom. She was so tired, she could hardly think. 'I have to be back on duty at three o'clock. The front desk schedule sucks,' she said over her shoulder as she walked into her room and closed the door, but at least she didn't slam it this time. Natalie looked at Hugues with a surprised expression once the door was closed.

'Better?' she asked him. It certainly looked that way.

'Maybe,' he said softly, so Heloise didn't hear him. He was wondering if she was going to move to her new apartment after the wedding. He would have liked more time alone with Natalie, especially if Heloise was going to be difficult about her, but so far she showed no sign of moving out, maybe just to annoy her. 'I think she's afraid to lose me,' he whispered. 'I told her that couldn't happen. You can't steal me from her, and I know you don't want to. Thanks to her mother, I'm all she has, for now anyway, and for the past seventeen years. It makes you a much bigger threat than you would be otherwise.' Natalie nodded. They had talked about it before, and she understood better than Heloise realized, which was why she had tried to be understanding, although Heloise's behavior had been beyond the pale for six months. She hoped she was calming down and was happy that it looked that way now. She had lost hope of their ever being friends.

'Her mother wasn't at the graduation?'

'Of course not. She was on vacation with Greg in Vietnam, although she had a year's notice of the date. She would have missed it for a hair appointment or a new tattoo,' he said angrily.

'That's hard for Heloise. You can't explain to yourself why your parents aren't there when they could be. If they're dead, at least you can understand. If they're alive and don't show up, all it tells you is that they don't give a damn. It's hard to feel loved by anyone after that. Your parents can really do a job on you,' she said with a knowing look.

'I tried to make up for it for all these years, and I was always there for her. But Miriam never has been. Sometimes I think the absentee parent does more harm than the present parent can do good.' Natalie nodded, and then she mentioned the wedding cake again and reminded him of what his daughter had said.

'All right, all right. Wedding cake. You pick it. I'll order something else. I think they're tacky and embarrassing. And I won't do that ridiculous thing where you shove it in my mouth and smear it all over my face.' He was too European for that, and it was a custom he detested and had never understood. 'You can feed it to me with a fork.'

'I promise,' she said, looking pleased. She wanted all the customs and traditions and little superstitions. Something borrowed, something blue. She had a garter trimmed in blue lace, and even a penny for her shoe. She had waited forty-one years for this and given up all hope of getting married and had stopped caring until he came along. Now she was going to enjoy it to the hilt. He knew that and was touched, and had humored her in all of it except the cake.

'Just don't ask me to sample fourteen of them in the kitchen like every other bride. You order what you want.' She already knew she wanted a chocolate mousse interior with ivory-colored buttercream icing, marzipan ribbons decorating it, and fresh flowers. She had shown the baker a photograph of exactly what she wanted. This was her dream wedding, and she planned to have only one in her lifetime, so she was going all out. And she loved her dress. It didn't look ridiculous for someone her age. It was simple and elegant, and she wanted Hugues to be swept off his feet. She knew he had seen a lot of weddings and brides at the hotel. She wanted to be the most beautiful one he had ever seen.

An hour later they both left for their day. Natalie was seeing new clients. She had promised to look at one of the hotel rooms that had had a leak, which was a good opportunity to redo it. And Hugues had a dozen meetings back to back, and a meeting of the Hotel Association to attend. He had been the chairperson several times over the years. And it was always a useful way to maintain good relations with the owners and managers of other hotels. Heloise was back at the front desk at three and had promised to cover for one of the concierges for two hours.

The days afterward were equally insane. Heloise barely had time to get ready for her party, and Sally handled all the details, although Heloise had gone over everything with her again the day before. It was going to be a grand celebration of her birthday and graduation. The room was all decorated in white and gold with white flowers on every table and gold balloons hanging from the ceiling. And her father had hired a fantastic band, and let her friends stay till four A.M. After that they served breakfast in a smaller room. Heloise said it was the best party she'd ever been to, and she had a ball. Her father wanted to reward her for her work at the École Hôtelière, and he had also wanted her to feel special and not pushed out of place by their wedding.

Hugues and Natalie disappeared discreetly around eleven and left the young people to have their fun. As it turned out, it was a happy prelude to their wedding, Natalie enjoyed it, and Heloise had definitely been nicer to her since they came back from her graduation. She was being more mature about it and was clearly less angry at her father and even his future wife. It was as though she had finally understood that she wouldn't lose him. She wasn't happy about his marriage to Natalie, but she was no longer on a mission to make her life a living hell. And she was a little embarrassed now by how angry she had been. She had admitted it to Jennifer when she got back from Lausanne.

Natalie was spending the weeks before the wedding struggling with the seating at the reception, and in spite of the holiday weekend, they were expecting just over two hundred guests. But so far everything was going according to plan, although Natalie was visibly nervous about it and had never organized such a major event in her life. She found it much harder to keep track of than designing an apartment or a house, or keeping all the orders straight. This wasn't her thing at all, and she was relying on the hotel staff to guide her and give her advice, and trying not to disturb Hugues about it. He had enough to do running the hotel, and she wanted him to be surprised.

They were having a rehearsal dinner the night before the wedding, for family and people from out of town. The only family she had were her brother, his wife, and their children, and Hugues had none at all except Heloise. But they were still expecting sixty guests at the rehearsal dinner and holding it in a room they used as a private dining room upstairs. There would be no music and no dancing, so it was a simpler event to plan. But they still needed flowers, and had to decide about the menus and the wines, and the calligrapher had to do place cards and seating charts. Natalie felt as though she were running a war, with charts and lists everywhere, and she carried a radio so Sally could communicate with her at all times. Natalie had left Heloise out of the arrangements in deference to her, but she had invited her to her bachelorette dinner, which Heloise declined, saying she had to work, which was true. But she also didn't want to celebrate the fact that her father was marrying her. It would have been hypocritical and sounded embarrassing to her to watch middle-aged women give her sexy underwear to seduce her father. Natalie was doing fine as it was.

The male employees of the hotel had given Hugues a surprise bachelor dinner the month before, with Moroccan food and belly dancers, but in spite of that it was a pretty tame event. They had also invited his few friends, all of whom worked or ran other hotels. Given the amount of time he spent working, it was hard for him to maintain friendships with anyone, which was the nature of the business. The hotel and the people in it became your life and left you time for no one else. But the bachelor party had been fun, and Hugues had danced with several of the girls, but no one had done anything embarrassing or gotten out of line, which wasn't always the case with other bachelor dinners they'd had at the hotel, where hookers were often involved and paid for by one of the guests. No one would have dared do that to Hugues, he wasn't that kind of man, and it was all good fun.

By the day before the wedding, Natalie was a nervous wreck. She had taken a room on another floor to hang her wedding dress and where she would get her hair and makeup done the day of the wedding. And her brother and sister-in-law were staying at the hotel. Only their two boys had come; their twin sisters were still too sick with mono. And the day before the wedding, Natalie had booked a massage and a manicure and pedicure. Heloise saw her at the hairdresser that afternoon, wearing a masque. She stopped in to say hello, and Natalie opened her eyes when she heard her voice. She had hardly seen her in days.

'How's it going?' Heloise asked politely.

'Terrible,' Natalie said, trying not to move her mouth too much so she didn't crack the masque, which looked like green clay. She felt like the witch in *The Wizard of Oz*. 'My face is breaking out. My stomach is upset. The singer for the band is stuck in Las Vegas and isn't coming. And I wish we'd eloped.' She looked like she was about to cry.

'It'll be fine,' Heloise reassured her. 'Just try to relax.' And then, with a sigh, she conceded silently. She knew a lot more about these things than her future stepmother, and she had done nothing to help so far. 'Do you want me to talk to Sally?' she asked softly. Natalie stared at her and nodded.

'Would you mind? I have no idea what I'm doing, and

I'm so nervous I feel nuts.' And she was taking medication that made her feel more so, but she didn't tell Heloise that. Hugues was aware of it and trying to do all he could to calm her down. But the medication, coupled with the normal stresses of planning a wedding, was overwhelming her, and she looked it.

'I'll go up to her office in a few minutes when I have a break,' Heloise promised with a smile. 'Just concentrate on your hair and nails. Leave the rest to us. And take a nap.' Natalie nodded and watched her leave the hair salon. She had the feeling the war might finally be over. She wasn't sure that it had ended, but she hadn't heard gunfire since Heloise and Hugues had returned from Lausanne.

Half an hour later Heloise was upstairs with Sally, going over the details of the wedding. Most of it was under control, and she and the very competent catering manager discussed what wasn't and made a few changes that no one would notice, about placement of tables, and the size of tabletops. Someone had ordered the wrong chairs, and Heloise asked for the best ones. The flow of guests, the timing, seating charts, where to place the ceremony so everyone could see it – they were subtle changes, but they made a difference. Together she and Sally corrected it all. And Sally said it was nice of her to do it.

There was supposed to be a rehearsal, but it had been canceled because her relatives were coming in too late and there was no time before the rehearsal dinner. And Heloise told Sally to have all the flowers for Natalie and her sister-in-law, for Natalie's hair and both bouquets, sent up to the suite that Natalie was using for her dress. And the sprig of lily of the valley for Hugues's lapel should go to his room, not hers. Suddenly it no longer made Heloise feel sick to think about the wedding. She had made her peace with it and wanted to help.

'What about you?' Sally asked her cautiously. There had been no flowers ordered for her. 'Are you carrying a bouquet?' She hadn't dared ask Heloise anything about the wedding until then. Now she seemed to be on board.

'I'm not in the wedding,' Heloise said quietly, looking a little sheepish.

'You're not?' Sally looked surprised, and realized she had never discussed it with the bride. She didn't ask Heloise why. She knew. And so did everyone in the hotel. Heloise had made no secret of how much she disapproved of the marriage since it was announced.

'My father asked me to be his witness, instead of a best man.' It was more of a European tradition, but she had never confirmed it to him, and he hadn't pressed the point. He was just going to be grateful if she came to the wedding, without expecting more. And even that hadn't been sure. She had threatened not to many times. She thought about it then as she looked at Sally, and they were old friends, since she'd been a child. 'You'd better make a sprig of lily of the valley for me, and I'll pin it to my dress.' It identified her with the groom, not the bride, and was what a best man would have worn in her place, or a small white rose, but she preferred lily of the valley, which had been her favorite flower all her life. She loved it when brides used it in their bouquets. Natalie was carrying white *Phalaenopsis* orchids, which she said would work well with her dress and were more sophisticated.

Heloise finished up the details with Sally then, and both of them were satisfied. They had tied up a lot of loose ends that Natalie had been unsure of, and Sally didn't want to make the decisions for her. Now Heloise had it all in good control and had made excellent choices. She loved weddings and was great at details.

And then she went upstairs to their apartment. She was on her lunch break from the desk. Natalie had just walked in and was lying on the couch, looking sick.

'Are you okay?' Heloise asked solicitously, happy with the subtle improvements she and Sally had made to the wedding.

'No. I'm a wreck. Did you see Sally?' She looked panicked, as Heloise smiled.

'Everything is under control. Don't even think about it now. Just coast from here to tomorrow. What are you wearing tonight?' Heloise hadn't even thought about it yet herself. She had never gone shopping for the wedding since she wasn't sure she would go.

'A blue satin dress,' Natalie answered. 'The flowers on the tables are blue too.'

'I know. I just reviewed everything.' She smiled. 'Do you want a cup of tea?'

Natalie nodded, looking anxious, and smiled gratefully when Heloise handed her a cup of Earl Grey a few minutes later. Heloise was like a different person now and Natalie was impressed. Hugues had been right. Heloise had calmed down.

'I think this is what mothers are for,' Natalie said, after sipping the tea, which seemed to help. 'Although mine never was. I had one of those uptight Main Line mothers who acted like we were strangers and had never taken her clothes off long enough to have sex or give birth. She was ice cold.' Heloise smiled at the description and thought of her own with her rock star life. 'My father died when I was twelve. She put me in boarding school then, and I hardly ever saw her again. She moved to Europe, and had me over for a couple of weeks a year with my brother, whom I never got to see either. And she died when I was in college. It was like going to a stranger's funeral. I never really knew her, and she had no interest in knowing me. I barely knew my brother till I was out of college, and now we're good friends. He's ten years older than I am, so he was older when my father died, but our mother was a total mystery to both of us. She should never have had children, but did because it was the right thing to do. And as soon as my father died, she got rid of me, and my brother had already been in boarding school for years, and I hardly saw him when he was in college. I have no idea what her life was like after my father died. I always wondered if she had a boyfriend. I hope so for her sake. All we ever talked about were the weather and good manners, and she played a lot of bridge. I was never on her radar screen except for a few weeks a year. So she wouldn't be helping me do this wedding either, if she were still alive. Thanks for talking to Sally,' she said to Heloise, who looked pensive and was smiling at her. She was touched by what Natalie had shared.

'My mom is pretty weird too. She's married to a rock star, I guess Dad told you. He does a lot of drugs and has a lot of crazy people hanging around. She loves it. She left my dad for him when I was four, had two new kids pretty quickly, and I was history after that. It's kind of the same deal as your mother. She acts like I'm someone else's kid and talks to me like a stranger when I see her. I hate going there. I see her about once a year, if it's convenient for her, which it never is. I feel like she divorced me when she divorced my dad.' What she said was honest, and Natalie could see that it was painful for her, by the look in her eyes.

'That must hurt,' Natalie said sympathetically. It was the first time they had spoken to each other like human beings, and they shared an unexpected bond. The Crazy Mothers Club, as Natalie called it to her friends. Or maybe it should have been called the Lousy Mothers Club. There seemed to be a lot of those in the world. And they inflicted scars on every child they touched. Natalie had invested years in therapy to get over hers.

'It does hurt,' Heloise admitted to her, and, more important, to herself.

'I used to cry for weeks after I saw mine,' Natalie confessed. 'It's horrible to say, but it was easier for me after she died. She couldn't disappoint me anymore. It's worse when they're alive and don't want to see you, or do and act like they don't remember who you are. I hated that.'

'I hate seeing mine too,' Heloise said. It was a relief to talk about it and admit the truth. She didn't like talking about it with her father. Just hearing Miriam's name upset him, and she felt disloyal to her mother when she told him how bad it was, so she rarely did. 'It always hurts. And I always feel like the forgotten person when I'm there. Like I'm a houseguest or a stranger or someone she never knew. I don't know how she could just walk away like that, but she did. She's not so great with her other two kids either, they're both brats,' she said with a smile.

'It's all about who she is as a person,' Natalie explained to her, 'not about something you did wrong or don't have. It took me years to understand it, but people like that don't have anything to give. To anyone. It's only about them.'

'Yeah,' Heloise said as though a lightbulb had gone on while they were talking. Natalie understood it perfectly.

'I've always been afraid to have kids because I was afraid I'd be like her. And I don't want to do to anyone what she did to me,' Natalie said honestly.

'I feel that way too,' Heloise said softly. 'My dad was great, but it's weird having only one parent when the other one is out there somewhere and doesn't want you. I hated explaining that to my friends, although for a while they were impressed because of Greg. But he's a jerk.'

'At least you had your dad,' Natalie reminded her, and Heloise nodded. And now she had to share him with her. But it didn't seem quite so bad now. She could see why her father loved her. She was honest, sincere, and caring, and she tried hard. And Heloise also realized that Natalie had never lost her temper once in the past six months, no matter how badly Heloise behaved. It said something about her. 'I hardly ever saw my father, and he was even colder than my mother,' Natalie added. 'I think they both hated kids.'

'My dad is great,' Heloise confirmed. The two women looked at each other for a long moment and exchanged a smile.

'Thank you for helping me with the wedding. I'm really scared,' Natalie confessed. It made her seem so young and vulnerable that Heloise felt sorry for her. She didn't seem like an ominous opponent anymore, just a lonely woman of very human scale who had mean parents and was grateful to have found Hugues. It was something Heloise could cope with, and not the Mata Hari she had feared.

'The wedding will be fine,' Heloise reassured her. 'I promise. And if anything happens, I'll take care of it.' And she was fully capable of doing so, with or without Sally's help. She felt a bond with Natalie now after what they had shared. 'You just relax and have fun. It's your special day.'

'I had no idea weddings were so complicated and stressful to organize when I planned this. I've been in way over my head,' she admitted with a grin. 'I never planned to have one, so I don't know anything about all the details.'

'Weddings are not that hard,' Heloise said easily. 'Decorating is much harder, and you're great at that. This is just a lot of silly details. I love my apartment, by the way. You did a great job. All my friends are jealous of me.' She smiled, and Natalie looked pleased. They were getting a lot of housekeeping done that afternoon, throwing out the garbage, opening the shades, and letting the sunlight in.

'It was fun to do.' She got off the couch then and looked better than she had before. She would have liked to hug Heloise but didn't want to overstep any boundaries. They had come far in the last two hours, and they both knew it. And she didn't want to spoil it now by rushing Heloise or crowding her.

'I've got to go back to work. See you at the dinner tonight,' Heloise said as she put her uniform jacket back on and her shoes. 'And remember, all you have to do is look pretty and have fun. Leave the rest to us. You don't need to be scared, or worry about a thing.'

'Thank you.' Natalie smiled and looked touched, and a minute later Heloise left to go back to the front desk. Five minutes after that Hugues walked into the apartment and had missed Heloise completely.

'What are you doing here?' he asked, surprised to see Natalie there at that hour, looking a little dazed.

'Trying to catch my breath,' she said honestly. 'I just had a really nice talk with Heloise,' she reported, and looked happy about it.

'What about?' He looked surprised and pleased as he sat down on the couch with his future wife. He loved the idea that she was going to be his wife and could hardly wait.

'Our mothers. Mine ?wasn't such a sweetheart either. I told her about it. And she talked about hers. Different look and lifestyle, but same kind of people. Narcissists. Women who should never have had kids.' Hugues agreed. He had been making up for it ever since, and he was sure her other two children would turn out to be disasters, or on drugs like their father. 'It was nice talking to her. She's a really sweet kid. She's helping me with the wedding,' Natalie said gratefully. 'She was wonderful to me.' Tears sprang to her eyes as she said it. It was a huge relief. The past six months of being the object of Heloise's hatred had been hard. She had gone back to her therapist about it.

'I'm glad she came around,' Hugues said, looking relieved too, and then he leaned over and kissed his bride. 'You look gorgeous, by the way. What are you doing now?' he asked as he took off his jacket.

'Nothing. Why? I was going to have a nap before tonight. And I'm having a massage at five.'

'Perfect. My three o'clock just canceled. I have a haircut at six. And I need a nap too.' He looked at her mischievously, and she grinned. And they rushed into the bedroom like children. The Do Not Disturb was already on the door. Their clothes were off within seconds, and he slid into bed with her and they made love like two wild happy kids. And she loved knowing that in one more day she would be his forever.

Chapter 19

The rehearsal dinner went off without a hitch, and Natalie looked lovely. She wore a short ice-blue-satin strapless dress with the diamond earrings Hugues had given her as a wedding present, which looked spectacular with her ring, and her mother's string of pearls.

Heloise found a simple black cocktail dress in her closet and was sorry now that she hadn't gone shopping, but it was Natalie's night anyway, not hers. And she liked Natalie's brother and wife, who was hobbling around in a cast with her broken ankle, and she liked both their boys. The younger was seventeen and just finishing high school and going to Princeton in the fall, and the older, Brad, was at Columbia Law School, twenty-five years old, and a strikingly handsome young man. They were seated at separate tables so they didn't get much opportunity to talk, but Heloise remembered that he was seated at her table the following day at the wedding, and he had looked somewhat intrigued by her.

Both Natalie's brother and Hugues made speeches, and her sister-in-law read a clever poem she had written about the bride and groom that came to the conclusion that they were the perfect couple, and instead of hating it as Heloise would have before, knowing what she did about her now, and her lonely childhood, she was touched and thought the poem was sweet and funny. And it was obvious that Natalie enjoyed it. She was loving every minute of all the festivities around the wedding, and afterward she went upstairs to sleep in the separate room where her wedding gown was, because she didn't want to see Hugues from the rehearsal dinner till the wedding. He kissed her outside the suite, and then went upstairs to his own apartment, and Heloise went with him.

'Nervous, Papa?' she asked him as they walked into the apartment together. Normally, she would have liked it, but for the first time, it felt strange not to have Natalie around, and she almost missed her, after their exchange that afternoon.

'Yeah, I guess so,' he admitted. 'It's a big step for anyone, even an old man like me.' He had never in a million years expected to marry again, and now he was.

'You're not an old man, Papa.' He looked young and handsome to her.

'Will you be my best man tomorrow?' he asked her, and she nodded. He really wanted her to be, and he was grateful that she was warming up to Natalie at last.

'Of course.' She still hadn't figured out what to wear, but she had remembered a dress that she had worn to a New Year's Eve party three years before. It was short and kind of a pale dusty gold. It looked serious and dressy, wasn't too low cut, and it had a short bolero jacket that she could wear during the ceremony, and the dress underneath was strapless, which would be sexier when the dancing got going. She was planning to pull it out later and try it on.

They chatted for a few more minutes, and then Hugues decided to go to bed, and Heloise wandered around the apartment. She didn't feel as though she belonged here anymore, not because Natalie had displaced her but she seemed to have outgrown it. She was thinking about moving downstairs to her own place when they were on their honeymoon, and it would be nicer for them too. She didn't need to prove her point or defend her turf anymore. She was beginning to think that there was room for all three of them in her world. Natalie hadn't stolen anything from her, she had come to join them, and there was a place for her.

Heloise got up at six o'clock the next morning, just as she had in the past when there were important weddings scheduled at the hotel. She put on jeans, a T-shirt, and sandals and went downstairs to check on all the activity in the ballroom. The flowers were being set up, the tables, the stage, Sally's two assistants were there, and Jan. Jennifer had come in to help them and check the seating. Bruce was in evidence. Heloise chatted with them for a few minutes and checked on all the details. Everything was going well. She left the ballroom at seven, checked with room service to see if Natalie had ordered breakfast, and they said she just had, so Heloise stopped in to see her on the way up. Natalie looked unbelievably nervous when she opened the door.

'Everything is fine,' Heloise reassured her. 'I've just been to watch them set up. Everyone's down there. It's looking gorgeous.' Heloise sat down and chatted with her until her breakfast came, kept her company while she ate it, and then went back upstairs. Her father was still asleep, and there was nothing for her to do. She had promised to go back down in two hours to help Natalie get dressed, and the hairdresser was coming to do her hair. They had several new ones who were very good, and Xenia, who had done her braids as a little girl, had retired the year before.

Heloise got ready herself in that time and had decided the gold dress would be a good choice. It still fit her perfectly. She put on very little makeup, did her hair in a sleek simple bun, and wore high-heeled gold sandals to go with the dress. At ten-thirty she was back at Natalie's door, and her sister-in-law, Jean, let her in.

'How's the bride?' Heloise asked her conspiratorially. Suddenly she was fully part of the wedding that she had avoided assiduously for five months.

'Glued to the ceiling,' Jean confirmed as Heloise walked in. But she already looked beautiful as the hairdresser swept her long blond hair into an elegant French twist that made her look like a model or a movie star.

Natalie was almost too nervous to talk, but she listened while Jean and Heloise chatted, and Heloise got her a cup of tea and a digestive biscuit, as Natalie thanked her gratefully.

And at noon they were ready to get her into her dress. Both women put it carefully over her head and slid it down over her slim figure. It was high-necked, long-sleeved, floor-length ivory lace, with a little round lace cap to match, and a full veil, and there was a long lace train. The dress molded her figure, and she looked absolutely exquisite. Both women took a step back to look at her, and she took their breath away. She had wanted a real wedding gown, because this was her dream wedding, but it wasn't too much or vulgar or overdone for the time of day. It was in perfect taste, and the orchids she was going to carry with it were perfect. She looked like a bride from another era, and just looking at her, both women felt a lump in their throats. She was what every bride should look like and few ever did. Heloise couldn't even imagine what her father would say. Even he wasn't prepared for something as spectacular as this.

'I've never seen a more beautiful bride in my whole life, and I've seen a lot of them,' Heloise said honestly, and Jean nodded. She was wearing a simple navy blue silk dress with a beaded jacket and navy satin heels. It was very proper and looked a little bit mother-of-the-bride, which had felt right to her.

And as soon as Natalie was dressed, Jennifer appeared to check on them and started crying as soon as she saw Natalie. She only stayed for a few minutes and then left for the ballroom to see Sally. This was a big day for them all.

Both women took her down in a back elevator, and Heloise had had them line it with sheets and hang muslin drapes. She didn't want anything touching the dress and had thought of everything. They folded the train into the elevator, and Heloise had used her radio to check with Sally that they were ready for them. All the key players in the wedding were carrying two-way radios. Everything was being handled with the precision of a bank robbery or a war. It was the boss's wedding, after all.

Sally told Heloise on the radio that her father was front and center, waiting for Natalie at the altar, and the minister was there. All the guests were seated. They were ready to rock and roll, Sally said with a chuckle. And the music started as soon as they got out of the elevator, smoothed out Natalie's dress, straightened her train and veil, and waited in a back hall, and then Sally came to get them. She beamed when she saw the exquisite bride.

'Ready when you are, Mrs. Martin,' she said to Natalie as tears filled the bride's eyes.

'Don't you dare cry and screw up your makeup!' Heloise warned her. The makeup artist had come up with the hairdresser that morning and done a beautiful job with very light makeup. You could hardly tell she was wearing any at all, which was just the right look for her.

'I'm so excited and so scared!' Natalie said, torn between giggles and tears.

'You're okay!' Heloise reassured her, and left her with

Sally. In the ballroom Jean's oldest son Brad escorted both Heloise and Jean down the aisle. Jean took her place next to her youngest boy, and Brad slipped in next to her. Their father had gone to find his sister and walk her down the aisle to give her away, and Heloise took her place beside her father at the altar. They were wearing matching sprigs of lily of the valley, and he looked nervous, kissed her, and squeezed his daughter's hand. He looked as anxious as Natalie had, waiting in the hallway. The music was playing softly, and then suddenly, the orchestra began to play Debussy's water music, and the vision that was Natalie appeared in the doorway on her brother's arm and proceeded sedately down the aisle. She looked absolutely gorgeous and deceptively calm, and when Heloise turned to glance at her father, she saw that there were tears rolling down his cheeks as he looked at his bride.

The bride and groom both cried through the ceremony, and then finally the minister declared them man and wife and told Hugues he could kiss her. And as soon as he had, in a single swift gesture, he turned to kiss Heloise as well, and he had an arm around each of their waists. It was the most powerful message he could have given her that she would never be left out, and they were a threesome now. And then Natalie and Heloise kissed each other and both of them were crying, and there wasn't a dry eye in the house.

The music picked up as they formed a receiving line to greet two hundred and fourteen guests, and the wedding was under way. Sally came over to check with Heloise several times, but everything was going smoothly. There were no problems, everyone was having a good time, and the orchestra was very good.

Hugues and Natalie did the first dance, and then he danced with Heloise, and Natalie with her brother, and eventually people found their seats for the late lunch that Natalie and Sally had planned. And all the most important long-term staff members were there. Heloise was too excited to eat. When she finally sat down, she found herself sitting next to Brad, and they struck up a conversation about law school and the École Hôtelière in Lausanne. He seemed fascinated by what she did, but mostly he was entranced with her. He asked her to dance shortly after she had danced with her father. And they hardly left the floor all afternoon. Natalie noticed them with a smile, and said something to Hugues. He glanced over casually and observed his daughter deeply engrossed in conversation with the tall handsome young man who looked totally mesmerized by her.

And then finally the moment came to cut the cake. As

promised, they cut it, and Natalie fed him a forkful of it discreetly, and the waiters took it away to serve it after that. It had been a painless procedure for Hugues, who was having a ball at his own wedding. He danced with his wife, kissed her every chance he got, and told everyone he had never seen such a beautiful woman in his life. He wanted to dance with Heloise again too, but every time he looked for her, she was on the dance floor with Brad, and he didn't want to interrupt or cut in, so he danced with Natalie again.

And at last it was time for Natalie to toss the bouquet. A small staircase had been set up to make it easier for her to do it and a prettier shot for the photographers and video camera. She stood at the top of the short staircase covered in white satin and flowers, as all the single women gathered round, and just as she had so often wanted to as a little girl, and occasionally managed when no one was looking, Heloise stood in the middle of the crowd and waited for the bouquet to fly over her head. There were easily two dozen women standing there, watching Natalie in rapt anticipation, and she took careful aim. Her eyes met Heloise's for a knowing moment, and almost in slow motion, she reached up and tossed in precisely the right direction, and the tossing bouquet landed squarely in her stepdaughter's outstretched hand.

Everyone in the room cheered, and Heloise held it aloft like a trophy and smiled widely at Natalie and mouthed 'Thank you!' It made up for all the times she hadn't been allowed to reach for it as a little girl, and Hugues's smile, watching her, was just as wide. It was an additional gift for him. The two women he loved had made friends.

Brad came back to find her again just after she caught the bouquet, and the music was starting up. It was getting livelier and younger as the afternoon wore on. 'If that's an omen that you're the next bride in the room, then you're a dangerous woman to dance with,' he teased her. 'But I'll brave it anyway. Care to dance?' She set the prized bouquet down at her table and headed back to the dance floor with him. They were there for ages until Sally came to tell her that Natalie had gone upstairs to change. Her sister-in-law had gone with her, and Sally said Heloise could stay at the party, and she'd let her know when they were ready to leave. Her father had disappeared too. And they had already posed for photographs earlier in the day, right after the receiving line, in a small room adjacent to the ballroom.

The bridal couple were flying to Los Angeles that night, staying at the Bel Air, and then flying on to the Palmilla in Baja the next day. They had thought of spending their wedding night here at the hotel, but Hugues knew that if he did, he'd be called on for every crisis, and he wanted to leave town immediately after the wedding, which was why they had decided on a daytime ceremony and reception.

Heloise continued dancing with Brad until Sally came to get her, and then they both went outside with a crowd of people to watch them leave the hotel. Jennifer and Bruce were there with other wedding guests. The Rolls was waiting for them, and bellmen were handing out rose petals, and a few minutes later Hugues and Natalie appeared. He wore a beige linen suit with a white shirt and an immaculate yellow Hermès tie, and Natalie was wearing a white Chanel suit and her new diamond earrings. They looked like a magazine cover as Hugues pulled his daughter into his arms and hugged her tight.

'I love you,' he said, holding her for a minute, and then Natalie hugged her, everyone threw rose petals, and a moment later they got into the car, and they all waved as they drove away. Heloise stood watching them for a long minute, fighting back tears, and feeling unexpectedly abandoned as Brad touched her arm and was looking down at her.

'Are you okay?'

'Yes, I'm fine. They'll be back in two weeks,' she

reminded herself, and then went back to the party with him.

It had been hard watching her father leave, but Brad was a good distraction when they went back to the wedding, and she smiled when she saw Jennifer and Bruce dancing a fast dance together. They were pretty good. And Brad and Heloise got back on the dance floor too as the band played on.

They were among the last guests to leave, and it was the best party she had ever been to. And as the party ended, Heloise invited some of the young people, and both of Natalie's nephews, to her new rooms. They ordered beer and hamburgers and pizza much later, and the room was full of laughing, and talking until after midnight, and Brad looked as though he hated to leave her. He said he was spending the next day with his parents before they went back to Philadelphia with his brother, but he asked if she'd like to have dinner with him sometime next week. And she smiled at him and nodded. She liked that idea very much, and it was interesting that he was at Columbia Law School and not somewhere far away. He promised to call her and set it up, and she stayed in her own apartment that night. It would have been too lonely upstairs without Natalie and her father. She had already decided to move her things down the next day.

And as she climbed into her new bed, thinking about everything that had happened that day, the ceremony, the dancing, all the people she had met, dancing with her father, catching the bouquet, and meeting Brad, she decided that it had been a very special day, and a turning point for her as well as them.

And on a plane headed for Los Angeles, the bride and groom toasted each other with champagne and kissed as they sailed through a star-filled sky and held hands. And the captain announced over the PA system that there were honeymooners on the plane. 'Good luck to Hugh and Natalie,' he said, shortening Hugues's name, and everyone on board cheered, as the newlyweds beamed.

Chapter 20

While Hugues and Natalie relaxed in the lap of luxury at the fabulous Palmilla Hotel in Baja, Heloise worked seven days a week at the hotel and kept an eye on everything for her father. Two assistant managers were in charge in his absence, but Heloise was an excellent additional pair of eyes to see that all was going smoothly and people were behaving. She was working double shifts at the front desk in his absence, but she managed to take time off to have dinner with Brad Peterson the week after the wedding. He was taking summer classes so he could finish law school sooner. At the moment he was torn between becoming a tax attorney or an entertainment lawyer. Both fields interested him. But Heloise intrigued him even more when he had dinner with her. They went to a Chinese restaurant near Columbia that was full of students, and they talked about her experiences at hotel school and the George V again. And he was fascinated hearing her stories about their hotel. It sounded like an exciting place to grow up.

'Do you think you'll take over for your father one day?' he asked with interest. He got the feeling that she was capable of it, or would be in time.

'I don't know. I want him to run it forever. I'd rather be number two under him. I can't imagine the Vendôme without him. He put it all together himself, and it's just a perfect little hotel. We offer all the same services the big hotels do, just to better clients and with fewer rooms.' He could see how proud she was of her father's hotel, and how loyal she was to him. She talked about her mother a little bit, but only superficially. She said her parents had divorced when she was four, and her mother was married to Greg Bones, the rock star, which sounded interesting to Brad. Everything about her interested him, and he was powerfully attracted to her. She was American, but she looked very European, and he liked the way she dressed. She managed to look young, sexy, and chic all at the same time. She was much more exciting than any of the girls he'd met.

He invited her out again the following weekend. He

took her downtown to the Café Cluny, and she invited him to watch movies and have room service in her new apartment on Sunday night. They saw each other again twice the following week, and by then he kissed her, and they were falling all over each other like two puppies.

By the time Hugues and Natalie came home from their two-week honeymoon at Palmilla, Brad and Heloise were definitely an item, and he was becoming a familiar sight at the hotel. Everyone thought they looked cute together, and they liked Brad a lot. And so did Heloise.

She was thrilled to see her father and Natalie when they got home, suntanned, happy, and rested, and she mentioned Brad casually when she had dinner with them on their first night back. Her father noticed that she had moved most of her things downstairs.

'It would have been too lonely up here without you,' she said simply. 'Besides, you guys need some privacy, and so do I.' He thought it was a powerful statement and wondered what she'd been up to while they were gone, other than working. And then she mentioned Brad in an offhanded way, and her stepmother smiled.

'So is this a big deal?' Natalie asked her, and Heloise shrugged with a mysterious smile. Her father was startled to see it. They had been gone for two weeks, and suddenly she had a new romance. But she was twenty-one after all, and Natalie had told him before that her nephew was a great guy and she wanted him to meet her. Heloise hadn't dated anyone seriously since François, in nearly a year.

'I don't know. It's too soon to tell. It might be,' she said cryptically. She hadn't slept with him yet and wasn't ready to. But Natalie had the feeling it wasn't far off.

'Well, that sounds interesting.' Natalie smiled at her and was happy for her. She needed more than just work in her life, and she was so dedicated to the hotel. Everyone had told Hugues that she'd done a great job while he was away, and did much more than just her internship duties at the front desk. She had been all over the hotel checking on things a dozen times a day. And he was pleased by how responsible and diligent she was.

And the honeymooners looked happy and rested and more in love than ever. They were planning to spend August settling into married life. Natalie was giving up her apartment, and moving in the rest of her things, and putting some of it in the hotel storerooms. And in September she was planning to tackle new projects, and a few more rooms to renovate in the hotel. And he still wanted to give her the presidential suite to do when there was room for it in their budget.

She was coming back from her apartment one

'As much as it can be at that age. But it's sweet anyway. They're both good kids with good values and their eyes on serious careers. She could do a lot worse.'

'Okay,' he nodded, reassured. He trusted her judgment, even about his daughter. He missed having Heloise in the apartment, but he knew it had been the right time for her to move downstairs. And he liked being alone with his wife. It gave them a lot of privacy and freedom they wouldn't have had otherwise.

September was extremely hectic at the hotel. It was always a busy month as people got back after the summer or came to New York on business or for social events. And most of their regular guests showed up in September. And to complicate matters, they had a terrorist threat that forced them to empty the hotel. Hotel management had been told that a bomb would go off within the hour. Hugues assessed the threat with the police, and they had called for the bomb squad and evacuated the hotel immediately. The police suspected that it was a false threat, but they couldn't take the chance.

Employees knocked on doors on every floor, security manned the stairways, and Heloise was racing from floor to floor with her father, to check that all was orderly and to reassure people as they left their rooms with some concern. Jennifer, Bruce, and the doorman were directing people outside, and in twenty minutes they had everyone out and corralled safely two blocks away behind police lines, while hotel employees handed out coffee and tea from rolling carts. It happened in the early evening, when many people had come back from their day and hadn't yet gone out to dinner. Natalie arrived from her office just as the guests were pouring out of the hotel. And once they got them all out and at a safe distance, Heloise called Brad on her cell phone and told him all about it. They talked to each other constantly now, and sent texts all day.

'Do you want me to come and help?' he offered, and she liked that idea.

'Sure, if you want to.' He arrived half an hour later, having come down from Columbia by subway. He was amazed at the huge crowd of hotel guests standing in the street. It looked very orderly, although some of them were visibly upset. And they all wanted to know how soon they could go back to their rooms. Bruce and his security men were walking among them, reassuring people, while room service waiters served tea, coffee, and bottled water. Many of the guests had evening plans and were standing there in bathrobes. And SWAT teams were sweeping the hotel for bombs, floor by floor.

Vans brought food out for all the guests, and Brad

helped Heloise and the room service waiters hand out sandwiches and cookies. He was extremely pleasant to everyone, and very helpful, calming people down when he could. No one appeared to be angry, but many were justifiably concerned. And Hugues was extremely grateful that it had happened in good weather and not in the dead of winter, which had happened once before. All hotels were vulnerable to that kind of threat these days.

And three hours later, the police declared the hotel safe and let everyone back in. Much to everyone's relief and annoyance, it had been a false alarm. And once they were all back inside and had gone up to their rooms, Brad went up to Heloise's apartment with her. They were among the last to leave the street. Brad had been impressed by how well she handled herself, how poised she was, and how cool in a crisis. She was definitely in the right business. And she had thought the same thing about him. He had been calm and helpful throughout and handled the guests well.

'That was fun,' he admitted sheepishly. He liked the excitement and helping her. He had chatted quite a bit with the police.

'Don't say that to my father,' she said with a grin. 'He hates that stuff. It upsets people. It takes a lot of effort to make it up to them later. He probably won't charge for any of the rooms tonight. You pretty much have to do that, even though it's not our fault.' She had finally collapsed on the couch next to him and looked tired as she took her shoes off. She'd been out there in her navy suit and high heels all night, looking very competent and official and older than her years. It was hard for Brad to believe sometimes that she was only twenty-one, but she looked it now with her jacket off, as she loosened her long hair from the bun, and it cascaded past her shoulders. And suddenly the dusting of freckles on her face looked more apparent too. She had gone from woman to kid in two minutes. And as he smiled at her, he leaned over and kissed her, and she melted into his arms.

'You look so sexy when you let your hair down,' he whispered, and suddenly after all they'd done that night, they were both overcome with desire for each other. It had been a busy evening, and instead of tired, both of them were wound up, and it found expression in a suddenly insatiable hunger and passion, more than ever before. Their excitement had been building for two months. And before either of them could stop or wanted to, they were making love on the floor. They had waited a long time for this, by mutual agreement, and now nothing could stop it. They were breathless and spent afterward and laughed as they held each other.

'Ohmygod, what happened?' he said as he looked at her. He had been hit with a tidal wave of longing for her so powerful that nothing could have stopped it. And he felt it mounting in him again.

'I've been wanting you so much,' she admitted to him, as they both got up, and then laughing again, he raced her to the bedroom, where they both dove into the bed, still giggling. Being with him was fun. It had none of the intensity and eventual boredom and dishonesty she had experienced with François in Paris. This felt so right, and they seemed so well matched. She liked hearing about his experiences at law school. And he was fascinated by the hotel and most of all by her.

They made love twice more that night, and he spent the night with her for the first time. He had to get up early the next morning for a class, and she ordered break-fast for him, and then put on running clothes, and walked him to the subway when he left. She was on her way back when she ran into her father and Natalie coming out of the elevator, dressed to leave the hotel in comfortable clothes. It was seven A.M.

'What are you two doing going out at this hour?' Heloise asked them without thinking, as her father avoided her eyes, and Natalie looked vague.

'I have an early morning meeting,' she said after a

strange pause, but she wasn't dressed for it. She always dressed impeccably for her meetings, and she was wearing jeans and a sweatshirt and sandals, which was totally unlike her. And they were obviously in a hurry to leave. Natalie said she'd call her later, Hugues was already outside, and Heloise went upstairs to take a shower. She'd had an incredible night with Brad. He texted her from his class a little while later and told her that he loved her and she was the sexiest woman in the world. It wasn't the first time he had told her he loved her, but it was the first time they had made love. And it had been unbelievable. All she wanted now was more.

When Natalie got into the taxi, she looked nervously at Hugues. 'Do you think she knew something?'

'No,' he said, putting an arm around her to calm her. 'I don't think she'd ever imagine it. And we're not doing anything wrong.' She had waited a lifetime for this, without even knowing that she had. Hugues had been giving her hormone shots for three months, which were making her seriously jumpy, and they were on their way to the fertility clinic they'd been going to, for the implantation of four fertilized embryos. They had retrieved her eggs and were putting them back, fertilized by Hugues's sperm, today. The egg retrieval had been a painful process, today was going to be much easier for her. And then they'd have to wait to see what happened, and if the fertilized embryos would stay. They had wanted to try and get pregnant naturally, but at her age, with weak hormone levels, they'd discovered, her doctor had recommended IVF.

She was so anxious, all she wanted to do was cry, which she did the moment she got to the clinic. As soon as they led her into the room, she burst into tears, not because she was frightened but because she wanted so much for this to work. At her age, statistically they had a six to ten percent chance of success, which wasn't high. But it was worth a try. They had discussed it for several months after Hugues proposed, and he had agreed since it meant so much to her. She had never wanted babies before, but now that she was in love with him, and married, it was all she could think about. He would have been perfectly happy not to have children with her, but he felt an obligation to her, since she had never had any of her own. He had Heloise, and that was enough for him. And it was a little odd now thinking about starting over again, with a baby or even several of them if she had a multiple birth. He was fifty-four, she was almost forty-two, and they were implanting four embryos that morning. They had decided that four embryos were the right number.

More than that would have been dangerous for her and the eventual babies. She didn't want a litter, and she would have been satisfied with one baby, as long as it was Hugues's. They had agreed to say nothing to Heloise, not to upset her again. It had taken her six months to adjust to their marriage, and they didn't want to rock the boat again so soon, and particularly if their efforts never worked. They were going to tell her only if it did.

Natalie had been praying for this and had even lit candles at church.

They implanted the embryos using an embryo transfer catheter, and Hugues was at her side. An hour later they were on their way back to the hotel. They told her to stay in bed that day and take it easy for a few days, no exercise, heavy lifting, or hot tubs. She had to continue taking progesterone to aid with implantation. And she could take a pregnancy test in two weeks. After that they would do a sonogram to see how many embryos had stayed. It was going to seem like an endless wait, and they had already told them that it might take several attempts. Many people didn't succeed until the third or fourth, if they could afford it, which at leastwasn't a problem for them. It was a costly procedure, but their greatest fear was that it wouldn't work. Natalie was obsessed with having Hugues's child.

He brought her home from the clinic and tucked her into bed, just as he had Heloise every night for all those years. And he bent down and kissed her.

'Now you and our babies stay here,' he said gently. 'Don't get out of bed.'

'I won't,' she promised, holding his hand. He had been so sweet to her about it, which made her feel even closer to him now, and she knew he was only doing it for her. She was terrified to move and lose them, so she stayed in bed all day. She was watching old sitcom reruns on TV and having room service when Heloise called her on her cell phone.

'Where were you and Dad rushing off to this morning?' she asked, sounding curious.

'I had a meeting with a client at dawn in a weird neighborhood, and your dad offered to take me. I didn't want to take the car or get stuck there without a cab.' At least it was a good story, and Heloise believed it.

'Where are you now? In your office?'

'No. I came back after the meeting. I'm in bed upstairs. I think I have the flu.'

'Oh, that's too bad. Did you order stuff from room service?'

'Yeah, chicken soup. I feel a little better. It's probably nothing. I probably got up too early.' She sounded all right, but she was determined to do what she was told and take it easy for the day. She was directing projects in her office by phone.

'Do you want me to send something else up?' Heloise offered, but Natalie said she was fine with what she had upstairs.

'What were you doing out so early, by the way?' Natalie asked her. 'I hope you're not running in the park at that hour, it's extremely dangerous,' she warned her, and she'd noticed the running clothes. But Heloise giggled.

'No, I walked Brad to the subway.' She felt comfortable with Natalie now and liked having a woman to share her secrets. She was even more open with her than she had been with Jennifer over the years, but she was older now, and Natalie was closer to her age. 'He spent the night,' Heloise confessed. She sounded almost proud as she said it and very much in love.

'Was that the first time?' Natalie was touched that she had told her, and thought it was great news. She loved the idea of the two of them together and thought it would be a nice relationship for them both.

'Yes, we held out till last night. The bomb threat did us in. We came upstairs, and that was it.' Natalie smiled as she listened. It had been quite an evening.

'Well, if it makes any difference, I approve.'

'Thank you. Just don't tell my father. I don't tell him stuff like that. He might be upset.' He hadn't been thrilled with François, although he had accepted it. She was still his little girl.

'It's just between us,' Natalie assured her, wishing she could tell her about the in vitro fertilization that morning, but it was too soon. 'Have you seen him around today?' Natalie was missing him, alone in their apartment.

'Yes, he was in his office writing letters to the guests, apologizing for last night. And he's been in the lobby a lot today, reassuring people and telling them how sorry he is. People have been pretty nice about it. But they still don't like it. You don't want them to think there will be bomb threats whenever they stay here. But I think most people were pleased that we evacuated and didn't take the chance. Better inconvenience them than risk blowing them up,' she said bluntly, and Natalie smiled.

'Yeah, I'll say.' She was glad it wasn't today. She didn't want to move.

'I'll call you later and see how you feel,' Heloise promised, and then she went back to work.

Hugues came up later than usual that night; he'd been busy all day smoothing ruffled feathers about the bomb threat. And he was concerned about her when he came in.

'How do you feel?' He looked worried, and he knew that if she got pregnant, particularly with several babies, he'd be even more so. This was a big deal, particularly at their age.

'Fine. Nothing weird. Just a little cramping.' But they had warned her that might happen, so she wasn't worried. She smiled at him, and he bent down to kiss her. In his spare moments he had thought about it all day, imagining what it would be like to have a baby with her, and a little one running around, or more than one. He was beginning to like the idea, and it made him feel young.

Two days later Natalie went back to work, and life went back to normal. The hotel settled down. She went to her office every day. It seemed like an endless two weeks waiting to take the test. They told her she could do it at home, and then she'd have to come in for a blood test and a sonogram. And once a pregnancy was confirmed, she would have to switch to an obstetrician. Their job was to get her pregnant, not to follow her once she was.

She had bought a pregnancy test and had it in a drawer in her bathroom, waiting for the big day. She was so nervous about it that after she peed on the test stick, she just sat in her bathroom and cried in anticipation of the news. She was going to be so disappointed if it hadn't worked, and so stunned if it had. She had hardly dared to hope for the past two weeks, but it was all that she could think of. And she tried not to talk about it too much with Hugues, but it was on his mind too. After she did a pregnancy test at home, she was going to have a blood test to confirm her HCG levels.

She was holding the stick in her trembling hand and looking at her watch. It was time. In fact, it was a minute longer, and she hadn't looked yet. And then finally, holding her breath, she did. She stared at it in utter amazement and burst into sobs. There were two pink lines just where they were supposed to be. Two strong bright pink lines, just the way the instructions said. She was pregnant!

Chapter 21

When Hugues came up from work the evening Natalie took the test, he saw that she'd been crying. She'd been crying on and off all afternoon, totally overwhelmed by what had happened and thrilled beyond belief. The moment he walked in, she burst into tears again, feeling stupid, and he rushed toward her. He knew immediately what the result was or thought he did. He assumed she had taken the test, since he knew this was the day, it had been negative, and she was bitterly disappointed. He rushed to the couch where she was lying and took her in his arms immediately and held her as he consoled her.

'Darling, we'll do it again. I promise. Remember what they told us. Some people have to try three or four times. The next one will be the right one,' he said, saying

anything he could think of to comfort her, and she kept
shaking her head, which he thought meant she didn't
believe him. And then suddenly she was laughing through
her tears. She looked hysterical to him, and he was getting
worried. 'Natalie? Are you all right?' And then she nodded.

'Yes, I am. I'm *pregnant*!' She squealed with delight and
hugged him, as he looked stunned.

'You are. I thought . . .'

'I don't know why. I've been crying all afternoon. I'm
so happy, I think I'm crazy.' She had never been so
emotional in her life, and he was shaking when he held
her and kissed her. He hadn't thought it would mean that
much to him, but suddenly it did.

'My God, it worked the first time. When do we go for
the sonogram?' He wanted to know how many babies
there were and how careful she had to be. He was going
to guard her and their babies with his life.

'Next week. We won't see much. Just the number of
embryos and sacs.' It would show them how many babies
had held.

He held her in his arms like blown glass, and they
dreamed and talked late into the night, as he ran a gentle
hand across her still-flat belly. All they could talk about
were the babies they were going to have. And they had
never loved each other more.

*   *   *

The blood test she had confirmed that she was pregnant. And the sonogram showed them what they wanted to know: three embryos in three sacs. She was pregnant with triplets. Hugues looked shell-shocked when they left the clinic. Three babies. He was going to be the father of four children. And Natalie looked equally stunned. They still couldn't believe it had worked so easily and so quickly, but they'd been working on it for months. She had started taking the hormones in June. And their babies were due on the first of June, if they held that long. With triplets, it was almost a given that they would come early, or she could lose them long before that. The doctor had warned her that if she remained pregnant, she would probably be on bedrest. The next three months would be telling. And they had offered to reduce the number to twins or a single child, and she and Hugues had refused. It was all or nothing.

They both looked thunderstruck on the way home in the cab, and they had already agreed that they weren't going to tell anyone until they knew the pregnancy was solid at the end of the first trimester. So they weren't going to tell Heloise about it until December. Hugues hoped that she would be happy for them, now that she had accepted Natalie, but she would undoubtedly be stunned too, just as they were.

For the next three months, Hugues was busy averting a threatened strike of his kitchen staff, which took most of his attention and energy and some serious diplomacy to handle it, with advice from his lawyers. He dealt with other more ordinary employee problems too, and the occasional guest crisis. Heloise was busy at the front desk and wherever she was needed, and her romance with Brad was thriving. The hotel was extremely busy between September and Christmas, and they were fully sold out for Thanksgiving. And in their quiet moments, Hugues and Natalie talked about their triplets. So far, the pregnancy was holding. They had gone to the sonograms together, and seen all three babies and three heartbeats. She had the photographs they'd given her in a little folder on her desk, and she looked at them often, telling them to stay in there. And two weeks before Christmas, she had reached the magical three-month mark. Officially the babies were safe, but because there were three of them it was delicate, and whether or not she had them prematurely, and how much so, would be key. She was trying to work less and less at her office and relying more on her assistants, and she had wound up as many projects as she could and refused to take on new ones. All she cared about now were their babies.

Natalie didn't want to wait another minute to tell

Heloise and wanted to share the news with her. She'd been wearing loose shirts and tunics for the past month, but with triplets she was already starting to show.

They invited Heloise upstairs to dinner Saturday night, but she was seeing Brad that night, so she came up for lunch instead. He was studying for finals that day. And after talking to Hugues, he was getting interested in labor law.

Heloise looked great in tight black pants, tall black riding boots, and a soft white cashmere turtleneck sweater. She hugged her father and Natalie when she got there. She had noticed recently that Natalie was putting on weight, but she looked pretty anyway. She assumed it was due to the great hotel food and too much room service at night.

They talked about hotel business for a minute, and then Natalie couldn't stand it any longer and broke into the conversation. Hugues was smiling proudly as Natalie told her.

'Hang on to your hat,' she said to Heloise with a big smile. 'I'm pregnant. It's triplets.' She got it all out in few words as Heloise stared at them in disbelief. She stood up as though she wanted to get away from them, and she looked horrified by the news.

'Are you kidding? *Triplets?* How did that happen?

What were you thinking? Don't you know enough to use birth control at your age?' She looked stunned. They had had three months to get used to it. She had had three minutes and felt like she'd been hit on the head with a hammer.

'We want them,' Natalie said, looking disappointed. 'This wasn't a mistake.'

'Why?' Heloise asked, as she paced nervously around the room. 'Why would you want to have babies at your age?' She looked from Natalie to her father and included them both in the question.

'Because I've never had them. And I wanted at least one before I was too old,' Natalie said honestly.

'You *are* too old,' Heloise said harshly. They had just turned her life upside down again with their shocking news. 'You'll be sixty years old when your kids go to college, and you'll be seventy,' she said, looking at her father. Natalie answered her gently but firmly.

'A lot of parents are these days. Women older than I am are having babies.'

Heloise collapsed on the couch and stared at them miserably. She made no comment. She had just gotten used to their being married, and now they were hitting her with three babies. 'I don't know what to say.'

'How about "Congratulations"?' her father said quietly. 'This is going to be hard enough, particularly on Natalie, without having you beating us up too. Could you be happy for us? They're going to be part of your life too.' He spoke to her very gently. He wanted her as an ally this time, not an enemy again.

'I don't know what to think,' she said honestly. She didn't know if she was jealous, angry, hurt, or just shocked. It seemed like a crazy idea to her.

'Neither did we at first. Three babies is a lot to wrap your mind around,' Natalie said, looking at her, 'and I have to have them. If anyone should be freaked out, it's me.'

'Are you?' Heloise looked at her curiously, as though she had suddenly grown two heads.

'Sometimes. I'm happy, sad, scared, thrilled, terrified, the happiest woman in the world, and all of the above. But bottom line I'm really excited, and I want this more than anything in life.' She reached out and touched Hugues's hand as she said it, and Heloise felt shoved aside again. First by his wife, and now by their three babies. It was a lot to take in.

'Did this just happen, or is it something you planned?' Heloise asked her.

'We had them by IVF, in vitro fertilization. We worked hard at this. It didn't just happen. It was our dream.'

Heloise looked at her father as Natalie said it. She couldn't imagine this being his dream too. It was obviously her idea. Her father had never said he wanted more children, quite the reverse. He always said that he was happy with the one he had and that was enough for him. And now they were having three of their own. It reminded her of her mother having two babies with Greg, after she abandoned her. It made Heloise feel a little sick. She stood up then and looked at them both.

'I think I need to think about this. Give me a little while to absorb it. I can't deal with it right now.' It was better than her reaction the year before, when they told her they were in love. It was beginning to feel like every Christmas they hit her with another atom bomb. And this one was really big. She left their apartment quietly and went downstairs to her own. And then she called Brad. He could hear instantly that she was upset.

'What's up?'

'Umm . . . it's complicated to explain. I'm feeling kind of weird.'

He sounded instantly worried. 'Are you sick?'

'No. I just need to talk to you. Can you come down as soon as you finish studying?'

'Sure. I should be done in half an hour. I can come

now if you want, and finish later. Is something really wrong?'

'Yes . . . no . . . I don't know . . . I'm just upset. I'm probably being stupid.'

'Did I do something wrong?'

'No, of course not.' And then she started crying. She was very upset, and she needed a reality check from him. Maybe she was crazy. But she wasn't happy about their babies. And her mother's two children had never made her happy either. She didn't even like them. And why would she like these any better?

'I'll be there as soon as I can,' he said seriously. He wasn't going to be able to study now anyway, while he was worrying about her.

He was at the door to her apartment in twenty minutes, and she was sitting on the couch crying. She folded silently into his arms the moment he walked in, and it took her another five minutes to regain her composure. He was staring at her intently then.

'Tell me what happened.'

She blew her nose in a tissue she'd been holding and looked at him. 'This probably sounds stupid to you. But Natalie is pregnant. She's having triplets. They knocked themselves out to have them by IVF.' She started crying again then as he listened. 'So now they have each other.

They're madly in love and they have three babies. They're suddenly the perfect family overnight. And I have a mother who hates me and never remembers I'm alive, and she had two new kids too, after she dumped me. So where am I now in all this? Who am I to all of them? Where do I fit in? I feel like I've been fired. I'm the old model. Now they have three new ones.' He didn't say a word to her at first, he just held her as tightly as he could and listened to her as he stroked her hair. He was just glad that she could articulate what she was feeling. And he could see how painful it was for her and why it would be. Her mother had abandoned her, and now her father was in love and having three more children. It would have hurt anyone's feelings.

'First of all –' he pulled away to look at her as tears slid down her cheeks and she hiccupped – 'I don't think you're stupid. I would feel exactly the same way. It's gotta be a strange feeling. But I don't think you've been replaced. They can't replace you. You're you. And your father loves you. And I know Natalie really likes you. She's never had kids, and she's probably desperate for them before it's too late, so they did the science project thing and had three test-tube babies, which probably feels a little crazy to all of you. But I don't think in a million years your father thinks they're going to replace you.'

'What if he likes them better than he does me? Old guys like having babies. It makes them feel young. Half our sixty-five-year-old hotel guests have twenty-year-old wives and two-year-old children.' It was only a slight exaggeration and a phenomenon of modern times. Just this year one of their fifty-year-old female clients had had a baby, and an eighty-six-year-old retired diplomat from Europe had married a twenty-two-year-old and had twins.

'He's still not going to forget you. You have twenty-one years of history, just the two of you. No one can ever take that away,' Brad said, and put his arms around her again and held her. 'To tell you the truth, I feel sorry for them. That's a hell of a lot to take on at their age. It would freak me out too.'

'Yeah, and I'm not going to babysit for three screaming babies. I've got enough to do in this hotel without that.' Brad laughed at the image.

'I'll help you. Or better yet, we could really freak them out and have one of our own, and we wouldn't need a test tube to do it.' She smiled at him. She almost liked the idea, but not to annoy her father. But she also didn't want a baby. She was just head over heels in love with him and not with the idea of babies yet. She sighed as she looked at him and snuggled into his arms.

'Thank you for understanding. I'm sorry I got so crazy. I just feel like I have no place in their family, not if they have three new kids.' It made her sad to say it to him. But she'd already had that experience with her mother and Greg.

'Yes, you do have a place, and one day you'll have a family of your own. It's just weird with all these old people now who decide they want kids when they're in their forties and fifties.' She nodded.

'Thanks for coming over and talking to me.' They went for a walk, and he said to her that if his parents divorced and remarried, he'd be pissed if they had more kids too. He remembered how furious he had been when his brother was born when he was eight, and his twin sisters when he was four, and he'd like it even less now. Afterward she called Natalie and apologized for getting upset. There was no war this time. There was no point. It wouldn't change anything. And Brad had helped a lot.

Natalie was relieved to hear from her and thanked her for her call. Heloise told her Brad was there, and she invited them to come up, but Heloise said they were both tired. She needed some space. Her father came down to see her later on; he was worried about her. He had seen the shock and hurt on her face when she heard the news, and it made his heart ache for her. He chatted with Brad and her for a little while, and then he hugged his daughter and went back upstairs. Brad had brought his books with him and did some studying, and he spent the night, which was comforting for her. He was staying with her more and more often, and they were comfortable with each other. Everything worked better and made more sense when they were together.

It was a strange Christmas for Heloise after Natalie's announcement. Everything felt surreal. She watched the big Christmas tree go up in the lobby and supervised the installation of it, and everyone commented on how exciting it was that her father and Natalie were having triplets. Jennifer was already planning a shower. It made Heloise feel left out again, but she forced herself to ignore it and not react. Her father had a new wife and family, and all she could hope was that he still loved her. Time would tell.

And she had Brad now. They went out whenever they had time, or he came over. But privately she was down about the triplets. It was hard to know where she fit in now. She was part of history for her father. The triplets were his future. And if she wanted to be part of a family, she knew she'd have to make her own one day, and she wasn't ready to yet.

Brad went home to his family in Philadelphia for

Christmas, and Natalie convinced Hugues to go to Philadelphia with her for two days, while she could still travel. But Heloise didn't want to go. She told her father she'd keep an eye on the hotel, and he felt badly about it, but Natalie was insistent that she wanted to go home, and he felt torn. Heloise was staying in New York. And Natalie was so emotional now that she was pregnant and she cried about everything constantly. In the end he agreed to go, and Heloise signed up for all the Christmas shifts. Her father called her as soon as they got there, and first thing on Christmas morning. She was already at the front desk by then. And for the first time, but not surprisingly, her mother didn't call her at all.

Chapter 22

A group of Dutch businessmen checked into the hotel in January and took four of the big suites, on the ninth and tenth floors. They apparently represented a European consortium, and Heloise saw her father with them several times. It wasn't unusual for him to spend time with important guests. They had taken over the big conference room, and she saw two of them in her father's office one afternoon, chatting with him, and two others walking around the hotel with Bruce Johnson, the head of security, and Mike, the head engineer, which she thought was strange. But the hotel was so full that she didn't have time to think about it, and it was only after they left that Mike said something to her.

'That'll be strange, won't it, if your father sells the

place? I hear they're willing to offer him a fortune for it!'

'Who is?' She looked at him as though he had grown a tree out of his head or were a creature from outer space.

'Those Dutch guys. The ones who were here last week. Your father had us show them everything. I hear they're going to make an offer that's impossible to refuse, or maybe they already did. The rumor is that he's going to sell.' She felt dizzy when she heard his words. The ground rolled under her feet and she felt sick.

'Don't believe everything you hear,' she said, wanting to squelch the rumor immediately, and she was shaking when she walked into her father's office. He was alone at his desk, and Jennifer was out to lunch. She wanted to hear it from him, if he was going to sell. And if it was true, he should have told her long before this. She knew that he worried about their overhead, but the hotel was a huge success.

'Something wrong?' She looked as though she had seen a ghost, and he assumed she'd had a problem with a guest. So far, she was handling even the most delicate situations extremely well. She had a wonderful way with people and was learning a lot about the business.

She didn't beat around the bush. She never did with him. 'Mike says you're selling the hotel.' She didn't know what to think. First he got his wife pregnant with three babies, intentionally, and now he was selling her home. 'Is that true?' She was still shaking as she stood on the other side of his desk.

He hesitated for a long moment. Too long. And he answered her with a look of pain. But he knew he had to tell her the truth, or she'd hear it from someone else. 'I wasn't trying to. But if they offer me enough, I might. I haven't decided yet. It depends on what they offer. It fell from the sky. I didn't look for the offer. It found me.' He looked guilty as he said it.

'How can you do that?' she blazed at him. 'This hotel is our home. It was your dream. Now it's mine. You can't sell our dream.' Her voice was shaking with fear and rage.

'I'm fifty-three years old. In a few months I'll have four kids, not just one. And I have to think of all of you, your future, Natalie's, and mine. If someone is crazy enough to offer me an insane amount of money, I'd be even more insane not to take it.' It was a concept she was too upset to understand. She had a lifetime ahead of her. He didn't. And he had a lot more people to worry about now. His family was about to double in size and he suddenly felt old, and a little scared.

'You have no loyalty to anyone or anything,' she accused him, so furious with him that she could hardly speak. 'I'll never respect you again if you sell,' she said vehemently, and he nodded. He suspected that would be the case. But if the offer was big enough, he had no choice but to sell. She didn't want the money, she wanted the hotel. 'I'll never forgive you if you sell the hotel, Papa,' she said, looking him squarely in the eye, and then she turned around and walked out of the room.

She didn't talk to him for the next three days, and when she saw him in the elevator, she said not a word. The rumors were flying all over the hotel. She told Brad about it, and he knew how upsetting that was for her. She wanted to work there for the rest of her life and take over from her father one day. It was why she had gone to the École Hôtelière, and now he had made a mockery of her career and all she'd learned.

It was a tense, unhappy time for her, and the only comfort in her life was Brad. Her father knew how upset she was and was staying away from her. And once again she blamed Natalie. She understood nothing of the hotel or their business, and she had no idea what it meant to both of them. Heloise could easily imagine her encouraging Hugues to sell just in order to make a lot of money. But the Hotel Vendôme was not about money to Heloise. It was about love and dedication, the people who worked there, and her father's vision, and dreams, and now her own. You couldn't pay for that with money. Her father had promised to tell her what his decision was as soon as he got the offer.

She was at war with her father and Natalie again, and this time she wasn't relenting. She had meant what she said about never forgiving him if he sold the hotel. And Brad had never seen her so determined. She didn't talk to anyone but Brad about it, but he understood what it meant to her. Her father no longer did. And she refused to discuss it with anyone else. She was too upset.

She was in her room after work one afternoon, and she and her father were living now on separate floors like strangers. She hadn't spoken to him or Natalie since the day Mike had told her the news that her father might be selling. And she had no desire to speak to either of them again until she knew what he was going to do. Which made it surprising when she got a call from Natalie that afternoon, on her cell phone. She sounded like she was being strangled.

'What's wrong with you? Are you sick?' Heloise asked her coldly. 'You sound terrible.'

'Can you come up? Are you in the hotel?'

'I'm in my apartment.' Heloise's tone was as cold as she felt. Once again they had betrayed her. Or they were hoping to, if the consortium paid them enough money. She didn't want the money. She wanted to live and work at the Vendôme forever. 'Is something wrong?' Heloise asked Natalie, and she made a terrible groaning sound in answer.

'I'm in a lot of pain . . . I'm bleeding . . . I can't reach your father.'

'Oh shit,' Heloise said as she ran out the door of the apartment and tore up the back stairs with her phone still in her hand. She didn't want to waste time waiting for the elevator. And luckily, she had her passkey in her pocket. She let herself into the apartment and ran into the bedroom and found Natalie lying on the bed, writhing in pain. 'Should I call an ambulance? How much are you bleeding?' She had taken advanced first aid as part of her training. She approached Natalie and could see there was blood on the bed where she was lying, and she didn't want to frighten her. 'I think you'll be more comfortable going to the hospital in an ambulance, Nat,' she said gently, their battle over the sale of the hotel instantly forgotten.

She went into the other room and dialed 911 from the landline. She explained to them clearly and precisely that one of the guests was hemorrhaging, and she was four months pregnant with triplets. They promised to send paramedics and an ambulance immediately. She gave them the room number, and then she called the front desk and told them, and told them to find her father. They called her back immediately and told her that her father was out of the hotel at a meeting, and his phone was still on voice mail.

'Keep trying him, and get the paramedics up here immediately when they get here.' She went back to Natalie then, sat down on the bed next to her, and stroked her hair.

'I don't want to lose my babies,' she was crying, and then Heloise remembered to get the name of her doctor and called her. She said she would meet them at the hospital as soon as they arrived. Natalie was sobbing; she knew that at four months they couldn't save them, while Heloise did all she could to reassure her.

The paramedics were there in less than ten minutes, and they asked if her husband was around or if someone would go with her. Without hesitating for an instant, Heloise said she was her daughter. And as soon as they put her on a gurney and covered her with a blanket, Heloise followed them into the freight elevator, holding tightly to her stepmother's hand.

'It's going to be okay, Nat. I promise,' she told her blindly, with no idea what would happen. They took her out the service entrance so as not to frighten people in the lobby, and Natalie was sobbing loudly, while one of the paramedics asked her questions. And they started an IV as soon as they got in the ambulance, turned the sirens on, and took off for the hospital at full speed. There was an obstetrical team already waiting for her, and her own obstetrician arrived twenty minutes later. They wouldn't let Heloise stay with her. And it was a full hour before they found Hugues, and he called Heloise on her cell phone.

'What happened?' he asked, sounding panicked. He was already in a cab and had come straight from the meeting.

'I don't know. She called me in my room, she said she was in pain and that she was bleeding. I called nine-one-one immediately, and they're working on her now.'

His voice was hoarse when he asked, 'Did she lose the babies?'

'I don't know,' Heloise told him honestly, 'they haven't told me anything, but she was bleeding pretty heavily when we left.' It didn't look hopeful to her. 'Her doctor is with her.'

'I'll be there in ten minutes.'

'I'm in the waiting room outside obstetrics.' They had moved her up from the emergency room in case she delivered. But at eighteen weeks there was very little chance the babies would survive, and if they did, not in decent condition.

Five minutes later she saw her father fly past her and disappear into the treatment area beyond where she was sitting. He waved as he went by but didn't stop to talk to her, and for the next two hours Heloise had no idea what had happened. She didn't know who to ask, and it was six o'clock when her father came to find her.

'How is she?' She didn't dare ask him if she'd lost the triplets. He looked worse than Natalie had when she came in, and Heloise could see then how much they mattered to him, and even more how much Natalie did, and she felt sorry for him.

'She's okay. And so are the triplets for now. They did a sonogram, and she didn't lose them. She may have placenta previa or some other condition. But she's hanging on to the babies. They're going to keep her overnight, and if nothing else happens, they're going to send her home with a monitor and keep her on bedrest. She'll probably be in bed for the rest of the pregnancy, but if she can keep them for another month or two, they might make it.' It sounded like it was the most important thing in the world to him, and Heloise reached out and hugged him. 'Do you want to come in and see her?' Heloise nodded and followed him through two sets of double doors, down more hallways, and finally to her room, where there were monitors all over her, and Natalie looked terrified and traumatized by everything that had happened.

'How do you feel?' Heloise asked her gently.

'Scared shitless,' she said honestly with a weak smile. 'I just don't want to lose them.'

'I hope you don't,' Heloise said and leaned over to kiss her hand. 'You're going to have to take it very easy.' Natalie nodded. It was worth it to her. She was willing to do anything to save their babies.

Heloise didn't want to wear her out, and she left a few minutes later. Her father was going to stay with Natalie, and he promised to call her if anything happened. And Heloise thought about it on the way uptown, that no matter how angry she got at him about the sale, or Natalie, or the triplets, in the end they were a family, and the only thing that mattered was being there for each other and being loving and forgiving. She really did hope that Natalie didn't lose the babies.

And miraculously, she didn't. Natalie came back to the hotel the following day, in an ambulance. They put her straight to bed. She was on full bedrest for the rest of the pregnancy, with a bedpan. She couldn't even get up to go to the bathroom. Her feet weren't allowed to touch the floor, and she looked terrified as she lay there. Hugues was with her, and he told her to ring for the maid or call him on his cell phone if she needed anything. And Heloise told her to call her or anyone at the front desk as well. Natalie promised not to move, and she looked pale and frightened when Heloise went back to the front desk and Hugues to his office.

They rode down in the elevator together. He didn't tell her that he had had the offer from the Dutch the day before and had been meeting with their bankers. The offer was a good one and would be hard to refuse. He didn't know if he would ever get an offer like that for the hotel again. He had told them he would get back to them in a few days. And then Jennifer had called, and he had rushed to the hospital. He thanked Heloise again for her help as they parted in the lobby. Things were still tense between them, and he knew they would be until he made his decision.

For the next several days Natalie managed not to lose the babies. Heloise checked on her, Jennifer came up to see her, the maids visited her. Ernesta brought her little treats and chocolates. The concierge sent up all the newest magazines. Room service brought her anything she wanted. And Natalie lay there, still panicked that she would lose them. She had delegated all of her projects at the office. Her life was on hold. And the day after she came home from the hospital, the unions that controlled their maintenance men provided a new distraction. They had given Hugues notice of a strike that morning. It was a rogue strike and was supposed to serve him as a warning. He had notified them that he was going to let go two employees, without replacing them, and they had told him that he couldn't. He had followed all the appropriate procedures, and they had put a picket line in front of the hotel to annoy the guests. And the men on the picket line were pounding on pots and pans with soup ladles and causing a terrible racket to disturb the guests. You could hear it for blocks.

Heloise went into her father's office to talk to him, and he was talking to his labor lawyer on the phone. The union wanted him to reinstate the two men, even though he had followed all the proper procedures. He called the union office then and told them to get their goddamn picket line away from the front of his hotel. And the man he spoke to said that if he didn't rehire the two men, there would be trouble. Hugues hung up in a fury and looked up at his daughter.

'There isn't a damn thing I can do,' he said unhappily. 'And I want you to be careful. That jerk was threatening me on the phone, and you never know what those guys will do.' They both knew that the responsible people at the unions dealt with them sensibly, but there were always one or two hotheads who preferred violence to negotiation. 'I don't want you floating around alone, either at the doors to the hotel, or in the basement.' And he was worried that they would harass the other employees when they left after their shifts. Bruce brought in all their security, and all the employees were warned.

The picket line finally disbanded at six o'clock, much to everyone's relief, and Heloise was working a double shift on the desk that night that would keep her there until morning. There were two men on duty with her, and by ten o'clock the hotel seemed to have settled down for the night. And the security men were cruising through the lobby often. Hugues had gone up at eight o'clock to keep Natalie company, and eventually Heloise sat down to chat with her two co-workers. They were talking about what a nuisance rogue strikes were, and how annoying the picket line had been all afternoon. And by midnight only a few guests were drifting through the lobby on their way in. Hugues called down to check on them before he went to bed, and Heloise told him everything was fine.

At one o'clock a fire alarm went off in the basement. They had a control panel at the desk, and it indicated a fire just outside the kitchen. It probably had nothing to do with the strike and was more likely a warming oven someone had left on with something in it. Heloise was alert immediately, and without stopping to think, she told the junior man at the desk to call the fire department immediately, and security. She ran to the service stairs to see if there was anything she could do downstairs; and when she got there, a small blaze was devouring a couch and several rolling trays right outside the kitchen. It was around the corner from room service, so no one saw it until they heard the alarm.

One of the security guards was spraying the contents of a fire extinguisher on the couch and the trays when the fire department arrived with full alarms, bringing hoses with them. They had the fires out in less than ten minutes. There was a nasty, acrid smell of smoke, and two inches of water on the basement floor, but the fire was out. The kitchen and surrounding areas were swarming with firefighters, checking everything. They wanted to make sure that nothing else had caught fire. And Heloise stood watching them and thanking them for what they'd done. They had come very quickly. Hotel fires were always taken seriously, and they often started in the kitchen. Her father had taught her to have a deep respect for fire and for every safety practice they could think of.

She was still talking to two of the firefighters, when another fireman came up to her with an oil-soaked rag that reeked of smoke. It lay in an oily heap when he dropped it on the floor.

'There's your igniter,' he said, looking at Heloise and two of the security men. 'Somebody set that on fire. There's another one under the couch. I'd say somebody is playing games with you.' It probably wouldn't have caused a big enough fire to burn down the hotel, since their alarm system was up to date and very efficient, but it could have caused some damage if the fire department hadn't been as quick. And as she was talking to them, she saw one of the room service dishwashers grinning. He hadn't worked at the hotel for long, and while he was watching Heloise talk to the firemen about the rag, he looked amused. She saw the look of defiance in his eyes, and she slowly walked toward him.

'Did you see somebody do this?' she asked him directly, and he laughed at her.

'You think I'd tell you if I did?' he jeered at her. He knew who she was, but he didn't care.

'What do you know about this?' she persisted. She wasn't afraid of him at all.

'I know your daddy fired two guys, and the union is gonna kick your ass if you don't take them back,' he said defiantly, as the security men moved closer to them both. Bruce was off for the night. 'They told you there was gonna be trouble, so maybe someone lit a little fire tonight to show you what they mean. You can't fire anyone just like that. The union won't let you do it,' he said, he was standing inches away from her, and the way he looked at her would have frightened anyone else, but it didn't frighten her. He was threatening her hotel.

'Did you do this?' she asked him, moving an inch closer to him. She was a slim woman, and twenty-one years old, but she was as brave as any man in the room.

'What if I did?' he said, and laughed at her again, and as he did, one of the firemen got on his radio and called the police. There was going to be trouble. He could smell it, and the security men from the hotel knew it too.

And then before they could stop him, he reached out and grabbed Heloise by the neck and slammed her against the wall. 'Bitch,' he spat at her, 'don't tell me what I can do.' Heloise never took her eyes off him and remained completely calm. None of the men around them wanted to make any fast moves, in case he had a gun or a knife. They were waiting for the police. And with that, without saying a word, she landed her high heel squarely on his instep with her full strength, and as he doubled over, cursing her and shouting in pain, she took a nice clean swing at him with a fist and punched him in the nose, and as he wheeled a step backward, she raised her leg sharply and kneed him in the groin. She had taken self-defense in high school, and it served her well.

She took a step away from him as the police came through the door. His nose was bleeding, and he was spitting at her. The cops put him in handcuffs as one of the security men explained what had happened, and Heloise hardly looked ruffled, although she had ripped her skirt to the thigh when she kneed him in the groin.

'Thank you, gentlemen,' she said pleasantly. One of the patrolmen asked for a statement from her, and she was in the middle of it when her father came rushing downstairs. He had woken up to the sound of fire engines, saw them outside, and dressed quickly. The elevators had been stopped for safety so he took the service stairs. He took one look at the situation and turned to his security men. 'What's going on here?' Smiling, one of the firefighters described the scene to him. She had put them all to shame.

'Are you all right?' he asked his daughter, and she looked at him. She wasn't even unnerved, although she'd been mad as hell at the man who'd set the fire.

'I'm fine. I think some asshole at the union paid the guy to set a fire in the basement tonight. We lost a couch and some rolling trays. But it could have been a lot worse.'

'Are you crazy?' her father said to her. 'To hell with the couch. They just told me you punched the guy. He could have stabbed you. Did that ever occur to you?' He looked at her like she was insane.

'He set the fire. Someone paid him to do that. I'm not going to let a jerk like that burn down our hotel and destroy everything we've built.' Her eyes were rock hard as she looked at her father. She wasn't going to let him destroy it either. The message was clear.

'Did the alarm go off?'

'Yes, it did. That's why I came down here. The security boys were putting out the fire, and the fire department got here at the same time I did,' she told her father. 'They found the rag he used to light it.'

'How do you know it was him?'

'He pretty much said so, or he implied it, and then he grabbed me by the throat.'

'And then you hit him?' Her father looked stunned by both the stupidity and the courage of what she'd done.

'She broke his nose, sir,' the young patrolman filled in.

'You broke his nose?' Hugues stared at his daughter as though seeing her for the first time.

'It was actually a very sweet move,' one of the fire-fighters commented. 'Instep with her stiletto, punch in the nose with a fist, and then she kneed him in the groin.' Hugues turned to look at all of them then.

'And what were the rest of you doing? Taking pictures? Why did *she* break his nose and not you?'

'Because this is our hotel,' she said with a small smile. 'And I love it more than you do,' referring to the pending sale.

The patrolman took the rest of her statement then. He said they were going to book the dishwasher for arson, and he doubted they could ever pin it on the union, unless he talked. But since they were pressing charges and he was in custody, he might.

They told Heloise then that she was free to go, and that there would be no charges for assault since it had been self-defense with a dozen witnesses to prove it. Her father shuddered at the words, as the security men called for the maintenance crew to get rid of the trays and the remains of the charred couch.

Heloise headed for the service elevator and said she had to change her skirt before she went back to the desk.

'I'll ride up with you,' her father said somberly, and for the first few minutes after they got in, he didn't say a word. He was still trying to sort out what he'd just heard. 'Do you realize you could have been killed?'

'Do you realize he could have burned down our hotel?' He was trying not to smile, thinking of what she'd done to the arsonist. But this was nothing to smile about.

'You can't do things like that. You can't risk your life.'

'I'd rather die here, defending what we love, than somewhere else,' she said calmly.

'I don't want you dying anywhere, or taking chances like that.' And then he smiled. 'I can't believe you broke his nose.'

'It was a pretty cool move,' she said with a grin, as the elevator stopped at her floor. 'It worked. They called it ING at school. Instep, nose, groin. It works every time.'

'You're dangerous,' he teased her. 'Why don't you take the rest of the night off? I'm afraid you might injure someone else.' He followed her to her apartment door.

'I'm fine. They'll be short-handed if I don't go back.' She was standing in the doorway of her apartment, with her skirt slit nearly to her waist, from raising her knee high enough to kick the arsonist in the groin. And she had packed a hell of a punch. 'How's Natalie?'

'Okay, I guess. Time will tell. She hates being stuck in bed. And her office is going crazy without her. But she's too scared to argue about it. It's going to be a long five months, or however much she has left.' She had planned to take the last few months off but not be on bedrest this soon.

'I'll come up and see her tomorrow,' she promised, and

then went inside to change. She was back at the front desk ten minutes later in a fresh skirt, with her hair neatly combed and brushed. She spent the rest of the night talking to the men she worked with, and she was about to go upstairs at seven when she went off duty, when her father came down to the lobby and asked her to come into his office. She wondered if he was going to reprimand her for assaulting the arsonist when he asked her to sit down. He obviously had something to say to her, and he looked as though he hadn't slept the night before. She'd been up all night and she looked better than he did as he spoke to her. When he did, his voice was gruff.

'I'm not selling the hotel. I'm probably crazy. It's an insane amount of money to turn down. We'll never have an offer like it again, and we may be sorry one day. But I can't have you willing to risk your life for what I built, while I sell out for the money. You reminded me last night of what this hotel means to me, to us. I don't ever want you taking chances like that again, no matter how brave you are. But I'm not going to sell something that you love that much. I'm turning down the offer.' Heloise sat and smiled at him, and he smiled at her too. The hotel was something very special that they shared, and she wasn't willing to give that up, or let anyone hurt it or take it from them. And now he wasn't either.

'I'm proud of you, Papa,' she said softly, coming around his desk to hug him.

'Don't be,' he said quietly. 'I'm proud of you. I almost sold us out. You were the one who risked your life to defend the hotel.'

They walked out of his office together, arm in arm. He called his lawyers later that morning to turn down the offer, and they called the labor union after that. Their attorney told the union they were not taking back the two maintenance men, and they would bring charges of arson if they ever pulled a stunt like that again. The union representative told the attorney that they had no idea what he meant. But the message was clear. The dishwasher was in jail. And the picket line did not come back again. And he made equally clear to the Dutch that the Hotel Vendôme was not for sale. Now or ever.

Chapter 23

By March, Brad was staying at the hotel with Heloise every night. They weren't officially living together, but it was working out that way, and her father didn't object. He was a very nice young man. Heloise's life was mature beyond her years, but it always had been, growing up in the hotel. She had seen more of life than most girls her age. And she and Brad were a good match. He didn't complain about her long hours and double shifts. And he was interested in the hotel. He was getting increasingly interested in labor law. Neither of them was afraid of hard work. He studied when she worked, and he was graduating from law school in June. And then he had to pass the bar. He was starting to look for a job.

They went to dinner at the Waverly Inn downtown on

a rainy night in March, to take a break from his studies and her work. Natalie was still on bedrest, and Heloise had seen her that afternoon. She tried to drop in as often as possible and brought her all the latest magazines and DVDs. She'd been on bedrest for two months. She was six months pregnant and the babies could survive if they were born now, although they were still very small. Every added week was a help. She was trying to direct her office from her bed, and her assistants were coming to see her every day. It was frustrating for her. But the babies came first.

Heloise was talking to Brad about his job search as their cab approached the hotel, and as soon as it did, she saw a fire department rescue truck parked right outside. She immediately wondered if a guest had had a heart attack, and they both thought of Natalie instantly, as Brad paid the driver and they both jumped out and ran inside. No one had called her on her cell during dinner, so she assumed it was a guest, and as she flew into the lobby, she saw her father going past her on a gurney, surrounded by paramedics with a defibrillator on his chest. She was totally shocked and ran after them and followed them outside. The front desk manager, Bruce, and two security men were following them with a terrified expression, and guests were watching around the lobby. 'What happened?' she asked the manager, as the paramedics slid the gurney into the truck.

'I don't know. He clutched his chest and fell down at the front desk. They just got here. I think he had a heart attack.'

'Whydidn't you call me?' she said with a look of panic as the paramedics talked to her father, and Brad stood next to her.

'We didn't have time. I was just about to.'

'Does Natalie know?' she asked quickly. He shook his head. 'Don't tell her,' Heloise said firmly, and then jumped into the rescue truck with a last look at Brad before they closed the doors. An instant later, the siren was on and they were speeding to the hospital. Two paramedics were next to Hugues and watching him closely. He was conscious by then and looking at Heloise with a dazed expression.

'What happened?' he asked in a hoarse voice. 'I have a terrible pain in my chest.' There were IVs in his arms, and the paramedics told him not to talk. It looked like too much effort, and he was holding Heloise's hand while she fought back tears and prayed he would be all right.

They rushed him to Coronary ICU and made her wait outside while they examined him, and then they let her come in. They said he had had a mild heart attack. They had done an EKG and were talking about doing an angiogram that night. Heloise gave them his history, and her father looked at her with frightened eyes.

'Don't tell Natalie,' he whispered. 'She'll lose the babies.'

'I didn't, and you're going to be fine,' she said, holding his hand and willing it to be true. She couldn't imagine her life without him. She needed him too much. She stayed with him until they took him to do the angiogram. And then she called Brad and told him where she was. He had waited in her apartment, and he came immediately, and they sat in the waiting room together for hours.

It was two in the morning when they brought her father back. They had done an angioplasty, and they put him back in ICU so he could be monitored, while she and Brad sat in the waiting room, and she called the front desk at the hotel.

'What did you tell Natalie?' She was worried about that, if he didn't come up to bed.

'We told her that one of the guests had an accident, and your father went to the hospital with him, and he told her not to wait up,' the assistant manager said.

'Perfect.' Heloise was relieved.

'How is he?' Everyone was worried about him. He had gone down like a rock behind the desk.

'They did an angioplasty, and they said he should be

fine. I don't know how long he'll be here. He's still sedated now.'

'Keep us posted.'

'I will.' She turned back to Brad then and nestled into his arms, as they spent the night in the drafty waiting room. She could go in and see her father for ten minutes every hour, but he was sleeping from the sedation and didn't see her all night. It was morning before he woke up, and Heloise and Brad were there. Bruce had brought them sandwiches at six A.M. and a Thermos of hot coffee that room service had prepared. Heloise couldn't eat, but Brad was starving and devoured two sandwiches with a sheepish expression by the time Bruce left again.

When Heloise saw her father early that morning, he was groggy and looked like he had aged a decade overnight. There were still monitors all over him, beeping loudly in the frenzied activity of the ICU. They were waiting for the doctor to come, and she went back to wait with Brad, after she kissed her father and told him she'd be back. He was asleep again before she left. And he didn't look good.

The doctor came to talk to her finally at eight o'clock. He was smiling when he came out of the ICU, which relieved Heloise's mind enormously as she squeezed Brad's hand.

'You can go home and get some rest. He's doing fine. We're going to keep him for a few days just to keep an eye on him, and then he can go home. I'd like him to rest for a few weeks before he goes back to work, maybe a month. Exercise, diet, he needs to monitor all that. This was a warning shot across his bow, but I think we patched him up pretty well last night. With a few weeks' rest, he'll be as good as new.' Heloise smiled at the thought. That would have been hard to believe a few hours ago.

'His wife is having triplets, and she's on bedrest. I guess we'll have to keep them in bed together.' She smiled at the doctor, and he laughed.

'As long as he doesn't get frisky with her, that would be fine. But if she's on bedrest with triplets, I guess there's no risk of that.' All three of them laughed at what he said.

'Can I see him again?' she asked.

'He was asleep a few minutes ago,' the doctor said, 'but you can check.'

She went in to see her father again then, and he stirred and looked at her and apologized for the trouble he had caused.

'You didn't cause any trouble, Papa,' she said softly, holding his hand. 'But you have to be careful now. You and Natalie are both on bedrest. You have to take it easy, but you can keep her company until the triplets come, and the doctor said you can go for a walk every day. We'll take care of the hotel.'

'This is so stupid,' he complained. 'I don't know what happened. I'm fine. I must have just been tired or something.'

He looked more awake but still very beaten up, and Heloise didn't look great either. It had been a long night for both of them. 'I can't let you do all the work,' her father said, looking agitated.

'You're not coming back to work until the doctor says you can,' Heloise said sternly. 'The rest of us can handle whatever comes up. We need you, Papa,' she said softly. 'I need you. I'd be lost without you. You're all I have.' There were tears in her eyes as she said it, and he gently stroked her hair with his hand.

'I'm not going anywhere. Tell Natalie I'm fine, and not to have the babies till I get back.' He smiled at her.

'You'll be home in a few days. I'll come back later. Brad is here with me, and he sends his love.'

'I'm glad he's here with you. Tell Natalie I love her, and I love you too,' he said, smiling weakly at his daughter, and then he turned his head on the pillow and closed his eyes. He drifted off to sleep then, and she quietly left the ICU and went back to Brad in the waiting room, and they walked out in the morning sunshine. She felt like they'd been in the waiting room for a week as Brad hailed a cab and they went back to the hotel. They talked quietly in the back of the cab about what had happened. It had been the most frightening night of her life.

Everyone had a thousand questions when they saw her walk into the lobby. She looked exhausted, but not devastated, and everyone was relieved to hear that her father was doing well and would be home in a few days.

Brad went to her room to shower and change. He had class that morning, and Heloise went straight upstairs to see Natalie in her father's apartment. She walked into the bedroom, and Natalie was wide awake, watching the morning news on TV. She had the TV on constantly now. She had nothing else to do except eat, watch TV, call her office, and watch her belly grow. And she was huge now with three babies inside her.

'Where's your father?' she asked immediately with a worried expression. Heloise hadn't planned to tell her, but there was no way she was going to be able to hide it from her for several days. And Natalie's radar was telling her that something had happened to her husband.

Heloise sat down on the edge of the bed and smiled at her. 'He's fine. He's really fine, and he'll be home in a few days. He gave us a scare last night. He's at New York Hospital, he had a mild heart attack, they did an angioplasty, and they said he's going to be good as new. And I'm making him take four weeks off. He can keep you company till the babies are born.' She had told her everything in one fell swoop, and strangely, Natalie looked relieved. She knew something had happened, and she'd been panicked about what it was all night.

'Thank you for telling me the truth,' she said, clinging to Heloise's hands. 'Is he really okay?'

'Yes, he is. I promise.'

'Can I talk to him?'

'He just went back to sleep. He had a long night. You can call him in a couple of hours when he wakes up.' She jotted down the number for her and put it on the pad next to her bed. 'I'll stay here with you while he's gone,' Heloise offered, and Natalie was relieved. She didn't want to be alone at night in case she went into labor and couldn't move, or had the babies right in her bed with no warning. She was terrified that would happen, although it was unlikely to happen that fast. They were planning to do a cesarean when they were ready to be born.

'Thank you,' she said softly. 'I wish I could go see him instead of being stuck here like this.' She felt completely helpless and useless lying in bed, unable to do anything, but the stakes were too high. She couldn't get up, even for Hugues now.

'He'll be home soon,' Heloise reminded her. And then she went into the living room and lay down on the couch. She woke up two hours later when the phone rang. It was her father calling for his wife. Natalie picked it up and burst into tears when she heard him, she was so relieved. And they talked for a long time.

Heloise ordered lunch for her, and then went down to change into her uniform. She was on duty at three o'clock, but she went back to see her father first. He was out of ICU and in a private room by then, with a nurse, and happy to see his daughter as soon as she walked into the room. He thanked her again for everything she'd done the night before, and for taking care of Natalie while he was gone. Natalie had told him that Heloise was being very sweet.

She spent an hour with her father and then went back to the hotel to take her shift. She was right on time and stayed there until eleven o'clock that night. It was too late to see her father then, and she practically crawled back to her room to get her nightgown and see Brad.

'You look exhausted. Get to bed.' He was worried about her, as she shook her head and picked up her nightgown from the back of the bathroom door.

'I can't. I have to sleep with Natalie tonight.' He looked genuinely sorry for her, and walked her upstairs to her father's apartment, and spent a few minutes talking to Natalie before he left and went back downstairs. He was talking about giving up his apartment near Columbia because he was never there anymore. He was always at the hotel with her.

After Brad left, Heloise changed into her nightgown and got into bed with Natalie. They chatted for a few minutes, and Heloise was so tired she was about to drift off to sleep when Natalie took her hand and put it on her belly. There were arms and legs and hands and feet kicking all over the place. It felt like a war going on in a cartoon.

'How do you sleep with all that happening?' Heloise looked at her in amazement, and Natalie smiled at her.

'I don't. They jump around most of the time.'

'It must feel so weird,' Heloise said sleepily, but she couldn't keep her eyes open any longer. She had to go to sleep, and a few minutes later she was out like a light, while Natalie stayed up late and watched TV. The days and nights were long, and if she was lucky and they stayed in there, she had three more months to go.

Two days later Heloise's father came home from the hospital. They brought him home in a wheelchair, but he insisted on walking into the hotel on his own. He looked pale and tired but infinitely better than when he'd left, and he went upstairs to his apartment rapidly, to see his wife. She burst into tears when she saw him, and clung to him when he sat down on the bed. He put his hands on her enormous belly and felt their babies kicking and smiled at her. This was all he had wanted, to stay alive and come home to her. He had too much to live for now to let anything happen to him. He swore she had gotten bigger in the few days he'd been gone, and he got into bed with her a little while later and lay there beside her, grateful to be home.

Heloise visited them as often as possible, but she had taken on extra work while he was gone. She came up to ask his advice and called him frequently on his cell phone, and he was happy to feel connected to the activities and decisions of the hotel. Natalie didn't like it and was on a vendetta against the hotel now. She thought his work was too stressful, it had almost killed him, and now she wanted him to sell the Vendôme. She wanted him to call the Dutch consortium and accept their offer. It was all she talked about. And when he was in the shower, she called Heloise and told her sternly not to call him so often. It made Heloise worry about him more.

'It's out of the question,' he said firmly to Natalie

about selling. 'I can't do that to Heloise. She loves this place too much.'

'She loves you more,' Natalie insisted. 'If we lose you, it will destroy us all. You have to live for her and our babies, and this place will kill you if you don't slow down.' He didn't know how to slow down so she wanted him to sell. He was constantly on the phone to Bruce, Jennifer, and the front desk to find out what was going on.

'I'm taking a month off,' he reminded Natalie, hoping to mollify her, but Natalie's only mantra now was for him to sell the hotel. She didn't say anything to Heloise about it, but she said it to Hugues constantly, and he told her he wouldn't, in no uncertain terms. She was stressing him more than the hotel. It was the only argument they had. The rest of the time they enjoyed being together. She loved having him home with her.

He went out for a walk around the reservoir every day, and came back with little treats for her. Four weeks after his heart attack, he looked better than ever, and by then Natalie looked like a woman lying under a mountain. He smiled every time he looked at her. She could hardly move.

The doctor came to visit her on a regular basis, and an OB nurse came to check her every day. It was April by then, and she was having contractions. The obstetrician thought it would be soon, but she was seven months pregnant, and the babies were growing nicely. They could survive if they were born now.

They were watching an old *I Love Lucy* rerun and eating popcorn one night, when Natalie suddenly made an odd expression and then looked at Hugues, as though she didn't understand what was happening. She was suddenly lying in a pool of water, which rapidly spread to his side of the bed. He was afraid that she was bleeding, but when he looked at the sheets, he saw it was just water, and then they both realized what had just happened.

'Oh my God, my water just broke,' she said to him with a look of panic. But at seven months the triplets were in much less danger, even though they were small, and all three would almost certainly survive. Hugues called the doctor, and she said to bring Natalie in as quickly as possible. She had no idea how rapidly labor would happen, and she didn't want to have the babies born at the hotel or in a taxi. Hugues called security and asked them to bring up a wheelchair. They had several of them in the hotel, one of which he'd used to come home from the hospital himself a month before. He was fully recovered, and after his long daily walks, he felt better than ever, and he had been planning to go back to work that week.

Bruce brought the wheelchair up to them in a few minutes, and Hugues helped Natalie get dressed. It was two o'clock in the morning. And he was wondering if their babies would be born that night. It was very exciting. And if so, they knew the babies would have to stay at the hospital for a while, in incubators, depending on how big they were. But in her belly they looked enormous to them.

Once she was dressed, Hugues helped her from the bed to the wheelchair, and she smiled up at him once she sat down.

'It looks like this is showtime,' she said softly. They had waited so long for this. The hormone treatments the previous summer, the IVF, and now seven months of being pregnant, and she had been in bed for nearly four months. She felt ready to face what was coming. She just hoped that their babies were too.

Hugues and Bruce took Natalie down the elevator in the wheelchair. If it had been earlier, he would have called Heloise, but he didn't want to disturb her and assumed that she was sleeping.

None of the drivers were around at that hour to drive them to the hospital. And it was simpler to take a taxi. The doorman hailed one for them, and Natalie held Hugues's hand in the cab. It felt so good to be out in the warm spring air and see the city again. She felt like she had been in prison for months.

The doctor was waiting for them at the hospital, and they got Natalie to Labor and Delivery just as the first serious pains started, and she was surprised by how strong they were. But once her water broke, the doctor had told her that she might go into hard labor very quickly, which seemed to be what was happening now. And she was clinging tightly to Hugues's hand. He was quietly reassuring her and helped her into the bed, where they examined her and she immediately cried out in pain.

'You're already dilated to eight centimeters,' the doctor explained to her. 'You must have been having contractions all night.' They wanted her to have some contractions before the C-section, to get the babies ready to breathe when they were born.

'I've had so many lately, and they kick so much, it's hard to tell,' Natalie said as another pain hit, and the doctor checked her again, and this time she screamed, as Hugues winced, watching her. It looked excruciating to him. Miriam hadn't let him be there when Heloise was born, so this was the first delivery he'd seen.

'We're not going to be able to stop it now,' the doctor said to Hugues and Natalie. 'With the water broken, there's a risk of infection, and she dilated too quickly. I'd like to see if we could slow it down a little, so we can get some medicine into you.' They wanted to give her an IV, to protect the babies' lungs, as they weren't fully mature. 'Let's see if we can buy a little time.' They wanted to get two bags of IV fluid into her, and the medication for the babies' lungs. And the doctor explained to Hugues and Natalie that the best way to slow her labor a little bit would be to give her an epidural, if it wasn't already too late. They would need it for the C-section anyway, since they weren't going to let her deliver naturally. And if it was too late for the epidural, they'd have to put her out completely, which they didn't want to do.

They got an anesthesiologist into the room and had him administer the epidural, through a needle in her spine. It was painful for Natalie, but once it was in place, she stopped feeling the contractions, and eventually they slowed down. It was giving them the time they needed to get the babies ready to enter the world.

Natalie was lying on her side, looking exhausted and worried. She had been poked and prodded and examined, and she was worried for their babies. A fetal monitor was reporting all three heartbeats, and Natalie lay quietly, holding Hugues's hand, as tears slid down her cheeks.

'I'm scared,' she whispered to him, 'for them, not for me.'

'It's going to be fine.' She wanted to believe him, but she didn't. There was so much that could still go wrong. And by eight in the morning they had gotten everything into her that she and the babies needed, and they lightened up on the epidural, and as soon as they did, Natalie was immediately in pain. There seemed to be no way to get through this easily, and Hugues hated that for her. But the doctor still wanted her to have some more contractions to get the babies' lungs ready to breathe. She assured them that she wasn't going to leave her in labor for long, and they would do the C-section soon. Hugues thought it looked like the worst of both worlds, a painful labor and then a cesarean section, which meant major surgery. They examined her again then, which only made it all worse.

'I want to go home,' she said to Hugues as she burst into tears. He wanted to take her home too, but with their babies in their arms, safe and sound. And for now they needed to be here.

Two more doctors entered the room shortly after, and half a dozen nurses. The epidural was stepped up, and things started to move very quickly, as they rolled Natalie onto a gurney between contractions and rolled her down to surgery, with Hugues holding her hand and the whole team following. Because she was having triplets, there was a lot more going on than usual. With hormone treatments and IVF, they were seeing many more multiple births, and three was still a reasonable number. They had delivered quadruplets the day before.

Once they were in the surgical suite, everything moved quickly, too quickly for Natalie to even know what was going on. They turned the epidural up and numbed her completely. Her stomach was being swabbed, three pediatricians came in, three incubators appeared out of nowhere, and a sheet was put up just past her shoulders so she couldn't see what was going on, and they asked Hugues to stand near her head. Both her arms were strapped onto boards with IVs into them, so he could no longer hold her hand, but he bent to kiss her face, and she smiled up at him through her tears. And then things started moving even faster. One of the heartbeats had become irregular on the monitor, and the doctor in charge of the team told her they were starting the procedure.

Hugues sat down on a stool next to her, and the monitors kept bleeping, and he wasn't sure, but he thought he could only hear two heartbeats now instead of three, but he didn't want to ask, and he didn't want to frighten Natalie, who was terrified enough as it was.

There was a constant exchange between the fleet of

doctors, and then suddenly as he pressed his face next to Natalie's, they both heard a tiny wail coming from the other side of the sheet.

'You have a little boy,' the doctor announced proudly as both Hugues and Natalie burst into a sob at the same time, and a pediatrician whisked him away to examine him and put him in the incubator. And then within seconds there was another tiny wail. This one sounded stronger. 'And a baby girl.' Hugues and Natalie were beaming through their tears. Neither of them could hear the monitor then, and Hugues was wondering if they had turned it down, but for a long time there was no third wail. And then there was a rhythmic slapping sound, and stern exchanges between the doctors.

'What's happening?' Natalie asked in a choked voice. And none of them answered. But without being told, they sensed what was happening. There was still no third wail, and they could hear both of their other babies crying. The doctor came around the sheet then and looked at them both, and the moment they saw her face, they knew.

'We tried to save your second little girl. Her heart gave out. She was just under two pounds. We've been trying to revive her . . . I'm sorry,' she said, looking genuinely distressed, as Natalie broke into wracking sobs, and

Hugues gently stroked her face, as his own tears fell onto her cheeks. They had two healthy babies, but they had lost the third. The bittersweetness of life, to receive two enormous gifts and have another taken away.

The team was sewing Natalie up, and the doctor came back to speak to them. 'The little girl you lost is beautiful. She's all cleaned up. Would you like to see her and hold her for a few minutes?' She knew from experience that sometimes people that didn't imagined all kinds of things, that the baby had been stolen or switched or hideously deformed. Natalie nodded her head in answer to the question, and a few minutes later they freed her arms and brought her the baby that had been stillborn. She had a sweet little face, and black hair like Hugues, and she looked like she was sleeping in her mother's arms, as Natalie sobbed and Hugues touched the tiny face. And then a nurse gently took her away. And as Natalie lay crying, they brought both of the others and held them up for her to see. Their son was crying lustily with a fuzz of blond hair and looked like his mother, and their little girl had the face of an angel and curly dark hair. Both babies were just over three pounds. And the one that hadn't made it had been half their size. But even having two was a victory, and the one they lost was a baby who had never been meant to be. The doctor tried to focus their attention on the ones that had lived. They were put in incubators, but the doctor said they could go home when they reached four pounds.

And by then Natalie had been all sewn up. They covered her with a warm blanket, and she had a violent case of the shakes, from the shock, the emotion, and the surgery. She was shaking like a leaf. And Hugues felt as though they had gone over Niagara Falls. He was happy and sad, excited and victorious and heartbroken over the baby they had lost, all at once, and so was Natalie. They kept Natalie in the operating room for an hour and then wheeled her into a room. And the baby that had died had been taken away. The other two were in the neonatal ICU because they had been premature, but both were doing well.

When they got to Natalie's room, Hugues took her in his arms and told her how proud of her he was, how brave she had been, and how beautiful their babies were, and like the doctor, he tried to remind her how lucky they were to have the two they did. Natalie couldn't forget the face of the tiny baby girl they'd lost as Hugues spoke to her quietly.

And as soon as she calmed down a little, they called Heloise and told her the news, that she had a brother and a sister, and then she waited, and her father told her that they had lost a little girl. It saddened her too, but she was relieved to hear that Natalie and the other two were okay, especially with the risks involved. She would be coming back to the hotel in four days, and the twins in a few weeks.

'How is Natalie taking it?' she asked her father soberly. Natalie was still shaking too hard to talk.

'She's fine, and she was very brave. We're both sad, but we're very grateful to have the two . . . and you,' he added with a smile.

'Can I see her?' Heloise asked him, but Natalie was in no shape for visitors yet, especially given what had happened.

'Maybe a little later. I think they want her to sleep for a while.' She was totally overwrought, and completely worn out, and she couldn't stop crying. One moment they were tears of joy, and the next they were tears of grief. And he felt as though he had been on a roller coaster too.

'Are you okay, Papa?' Heloise worried about him too, especially since his heart attack. This was hard on him as well.

'I'm fine.' But he was worried about his wife. She had been through so much.

'I'll tell everyone at the hotel.' Jennifer put up pink and

blue balloons, and Heloise discreetly told them that they had lost one of the triplets, but the other two were fine, a boy and a girl, and Natalie was doing well.

She worked all day with the concierges, and then she and Brad went to see them that night. They saw the two babies in their incubators, and Heloise said they were gorgeous. And her father told her quietly in the hallway that as soon as Natalie left the hospital, there would be a burial service for the third baby. It made Heloise infinitely sad for them and put a damper on the moment, especially since they couldn't bring the other two home yet, and she wished they didn't have to go through it, but as her father said, it was part of life.

Natalie looked so exhausted and was in pain from the cesarean, so they didn't stay long, and afterward Heloise and Brad went back to the hotel and talked about it. It sounded like she had gone through so much, and her father had too.

'It seems so complicated,' Brad said sadly. He never wanted Heloise to go through anything like it. And they talked about the future now, even though they were both young. It was one of those relationships that happened early and seemed to stay on a straight path. They knew they wanted to be together for a long, long time. And Brad pointed out that his aunt had waited a long time to have babies, and he agreed with Heloise that they were lucky to have the two that had survived. She could have had them earlier in the pregnancy and lost them all. It put it back into perspective, but Brad held her close that night, grateful that they had found each other nine months before. All he wanted was to protect her and take care of her, and he hoped they survived whatever bumps life provided them in the years to come.

Hugues wanted that for his wife as well. He was staying at the hospital with her, and taking care of her through the night, which made Heloise grateful too, that he was well enough to do that. They'd both been through a lot in the past two months, between the heart attack and the babies.

It was a hectic week while Natalie was in the hospital. Everyone wanted to see her and the babies, but she wasn't up to it yet. And she was still mourning the baby girl that died. And it was a tragic day when they buried the baby girl after Natalie got home. Only she, Hugues, Heloise, and Brad attended the small service, and it tore Heloise's heart out to see a casket so small. It was white with pink flowers on it, and Natalie sobbed uncontrollably, and then at Hugues's insistence they stopped at the hospital to see the others, to remind them of what they had. They had named them Stephanie and Julien. And Julien made funny faces at them as they looked at him in the incubator. Stephanie just lay there and looked peaceful and dozed off to sleep as they watched her. They looked like little angels. Brad and Heloise were mesmerized by them, they were so small, and Heloise had forgotten all about feeling displaced. They were part of her family now and had won her heart when they were born. She'd been buying little presents for them all week, and Brad teased her about it.

All four of them went home to the hotel and they had dinner together in Hugues and Natalie's apartment. It had been another exhausting day, with the burial and all the emotions of that. Natalie went to bed before they finished dinner.

Once Natalie was home from the hospital and settled in, Hugues went back to work in his office for the first time in over a month, and it felt wonderful to him. And they went to the hospital together when Natalie went to feed the twins. Her milk had come in, and she was nursing, and leaving breast milk at the hospital for them. And she was worried about Hugues working too hard. She still wished he'd sell the hotel before it killed him. They were talking about it one night as they lay in bed together.

Natalie shook her head as she looked at him lying next

to her. He seemed more content now that he'd gone back to work. 'I'm not going to convince you to sell this place, am I?' She felt closer to him than she ever had, after all they'd just been through, and he felt the same way about her.

'Never.' He answered her question with a smile. 'I almost made that mistake once. I won't do it again. One day Heloise will run it, and maybe even Julien and Stephanie. And then you and I will travel the world and have fun.' He made it sound like it was just around the corner, but Natalie knew now that it was years away. She couldn't even imagine him turning over the reins of the Vendôme. Sharing it with Heloise perhaps, but he wasn't ready to retire, and she wondered if he ever would be. The hotel he had devoted his life to for twenty years was still his passion, and now so was she.

'All right,' she said with a sigh of resignation. 'I concede. You're all crazy. Heloise works as hard as you do. She was doing double shifts the whole time you were sick.' And she had done it again that week. 'Just don't kill yourself doing it,' she warned him. 'I need you for a long, long time, Hugues Martin.'

'I need you too,' he said as he pulled her close to him to kiss her. 'You're the woman I love, and the mother of my children. And one day, I promise you, we'll get out of here, when Heloise is ready to take it on.' It was a promise she didn't intend to hold him to, but she had finally understood that he was never going to sell and probably shouldn't. The Hotel Vendôme was his life.

Chapter 24

In May they all attended Brad's law school graduation. His parents and siblings came up for it, and everyone was excited for him, Heloise most of all. She had watched him study every night and knew how hard he had worked. She was proud of him, and really thrilled. His parents had given him a trip to Europe, and he was taking Heloise with him in August. They were going to Spain and Greece and winding up in Paris. They could hardly wait. He was going to take the bar in July and was already preparing for it.

He had been interviewing for jobs at law firms for three months and finally realized that both antitrust and tax law bored him. He had gone through a brief phase of thinking that he wanted to do criminal defense work, but he didn't want to work in the public defender's office. What he really wanted to do was labor law. He found it fascinating and talked to Hugues about it, who arranged an interview with the law firm that handled all their labor disputes at the hotel. And the week before graduation they had offered him a job. He was starting at the end of August, when he and Heloise got back from Paris, and he was really excited about it. He knew it was the right line of work for him, and he teased Heloise that maybe one day he would be the labor lawyer for the hotel. She hoped he would be.

He was giving up his apartment near Columbia before they left for Europe, and Hugues had given his blessing for him to move into the hotel with Heloise. He stayed there every night anyway, and her schedule was so intense that they saw more of each other that way. And they'd been dating for a year. They complemented each other well. And Brad's parents were pleased too. They were too young to decide on their future, but they seemed to be heading that way. They were just starting out on their careers, had much to learn and a long way to go. She was about to turn twenty-two by then, and he had just turned twenty-six. Still babies, as their parents said.

Hugues hosted a beautiful graduation dinner for him that night at the restaurant at the hotel, for both families and a few of Brad's friends. It was a beautiful celebration. Heloise had worked on the menu with the chef and picked all the wines, and everyone loved the selections she'd made.

The twins were home by then, and thriving. Natalie had taken a three-month maternity leave to be with them full time. And she was loving every minute of it, and nursing them both. They still remembered and often thought of the baby they had lost, but they were enjoying the ones they had. And she was trying to figure out how to work part time and take fewer projects when she went back to work.

Natalie took the babies out in a double stroller every day, while Hugues went for his walk in the park. He was giving Heloise more and more responsibility, and he was taking Natalie and the twins away for their anniversary in July. They had rented a house in Southampton for the week. He had just given Heloise the title of Assistant Manager. She had completed her internship for him, in addition to the one she had done for the École Hôtelière, and she had earned her stripes. At twenty-two, she was a supremely competent young woman, and her father was very proud.

Brad and Heloise stood on the sidewalk and waved when her father and Natalie left for the Fourth of July weekend to celebrate their first anniversary. They had their babies with them, and a mountain of equipment. And Brad reminded her that it was their anniversary too, they had met exactly a year before at Hugues and Natalie's wedding, and so much had happened since then. Their lives had grown and changed, she looked very official in her navy uniform as they walked back into the hotel and he went upstairs to finish unpacking. He had just moved in. And their trip to Europe was a few weeks away. They could hardly wait.

Chapter 25

Heloise looked at her watch and decided to run by the ballroom for five minutes. Sally had stunned them all by taking a job at a hotel in Miami and had left a few months before. The salary had been irresistible, and they had a new catering manager that Heloise wasn't sure of yet. Everyone had been heartbroken when Sally left, and she said she might come back one day. So now Heloise was diligently overseeing all their catering events. And this was an important event. It was her father's sixtieth birthday party, and they were expecting over a hundred guests for dinner and dancing. He and Natalie had been married for seven years, and the twins had just turned six.

When she got there, the ballroom looked just the way she wanted it to, with topiary trees, and flower arrangements on every table, and the ceiling was covered with balloons. The new catering manager loved balloons, a little too much for Heloise's taste, and worst of all, Jan had left too. She had opened her own florist shop in Greenwich, but she came to visit often, and she and Heloise had lunch every few weeks. So they had a new florist, Franco, too. He had trained with Jeff Leatham in Paris at the George V, and he was very good. His topiary trees and large arrangements were exquisite, and already causing comment at the hotel.

She checked everything, and once she was satisfied, she went upstairs to dress. Brad had just come home from his office. He'd been working on a strike all week for one of his clients, and he kissed her as she flew through the door, took off her uniform jacket, and pulled out the dress she was planning to wear. They had just updated the uniforms that year, and she'd picked the design. It looked younger, and fresh.

'How does it look?' Brad asked her, knowing she must have just checked the ballroom. She was as attentive as ever to detail, and he knew her well after seven years.

'Perfect.' She beamed at him, and then hopped into the shower, and a minute later popped her head out again. 'I meant to call you. I have a guest who slipped in the shower and is threatening to sue.' He still worked for the hotel's law firm, and he did more and more work for the hotel.

'Your father called me about it,' he reassured her. 'I already contacted the guest. They're coming back for Thanksgiving with their kids. They want three suites and a free stay for four days. It's cheaper than litigation or a settlement.' Heloise nodded, relieved. The woman had broken her collarbone and arm, and it could have been expensive. Brad had handled it well. He always did. He was terrific with all their labor issues. He was a partner of the firm now.

Brad and Heloise arrived at the ballroom just before her father, Natalie, and their children, and Stephanie looked up at her with a toothless grin. She looked surprisingly like Heloise, except that her hair was blond instead of red. And she said that she wanted to work at the hotel one day. She wanted to be the hairdresser or the florist, and Heloise had told her that there were even more fun things to do if you ran it. Stephanie said she didn't want to wear a uniform. She wanted to wear pretty dresses to work and sparkly shoes. Julien wanted to be a baseball player and had no interest whatsoever in the hotel. And they both went to the Lycée, just like Heloise. Natalie was working as hard as ever at her design business, although only three days a week, and Jim, her design assistant, had become her partner, which took the pressure off her. She had just redone all their suites at the hotel, and given them a whole new look, although this time Hugues had grumbled at the expense and was constantly looking to cut costs. And she had redone the presidential and penthouse suites too.

Hugues's birthday coincided with the hotel's twenty-fifth anniversary, and it was a double celebration for the hotel and for him. And Franco had ordered all silver balloons. And within half an hour the celebration was under way. The band was playing, people were dancing, and everyone was gathered around the buffet. All the familiar faces were there, even Jan who had come in from Greenwich. Hugues looked ecstatic as his dedicated employees circled around him. And the pastry chef had made him an enormous cake. Heloise smiled at Brad across the table when her father stood up to make a speech. He rapped a knife on his champagne glass and held it high as he looked around the room at his wife, his three children, his employees, his favorite guests, and his friends. Everyone he cared about was in that room.

'I'd like to thank all of you for your loyalty to me, to this hotel, to my family, and for making the last twenty-five years here a joy for me in every way. If I named you all, we'd be here all night.' He smiled. Heloise rolled her eyes as she listened. It sounded like a retirement speech instead of an anniversary speech, and she saw that Brad was thinking the same thing. Her father had been very emotional about the anniversary and this birthday. 'I've had fun here,' he went on, 'I've had headaches here, I've had children here. Twenty-five years ago Heloise was almost three years old when I started to renovate this hotel. And when we opened she was almost five. She's been terrorizing most of you for the last twenty-five years, and I've had the pleasure of watching her grow into the lovely and extremely competent woman she is, and as some of you know, she keeps me in line. I was almost foolish enough to sell the hotel a few years ago, and she stopped me, because she loved this hotel so much. She was right, of course, and it would have been a terrible mistake.

'So, my friends, I won't bore you any longer. I am here to thank you for these extraordinary twenty-five years, to celebrate my birthday, and to make an important announcement. I will be retiring later this year, and I have the pleasure of introducing you to our new general manager tonight, and I ask you to raise your glasses to congratulate her and wish her well. I give you Miss Heloise Martin, the general manager of the Hotel Vendôme.' He stood there holding his glass up to her, as

Heloise stared at him in disbelief, and tears rolled down her cheeks. She had had no idea that he would do that, and as she glanced around the table she could see that Natalie hadn't known about it either. She looked just as shocked, and so did Brad. Jennifer didn't look as surprised and had a wistful expression as she sat next to Bruce. And Heloise realized that she knew and hadn't said a word.

And as she looked at her father, everyone had risen to their feet and was toasting her. Heloise walked across the room and kissed him then.

'What are you doing, Papa?' she whispered.

'It's your turn, darling. You've earned it. I always knew you would one day. And after you, maybe someday one of the twins.' Heloise knew that it would be Stephanie, and not Julien.

She raised her glass to her father then and toasted him. 'I have to tell all of you, I'm quite stunned. My father didn't warn me that he was going to do this tonight, or ever. I always wanted to run the hotel with him, not after him,' she said, fighting back tears. 'I will never be able to live up to the legend he has been here, nor to be the general manager he has been. But I promise you, Papa, solemnly, and all of you whom I've known for most of my life, that I will do my best, and I will try. Happy birthday,

Papa! Here's to you!' She kissed him, and there rose a cheer in the room as she went back to her seat. There was a huge clamor everywhere as people exclaimed over what he'd done.

'You didn't know?' she said to Natalie across the table, who looked as surprised as she did.

'I had no idea.' She was stunned. She wondered what he was going to do now. She couldn't imagine him doing nothing.

'Neither did I,' Brad said as he joined in, but he thought it was a great idea. Heloise was twenty-seven years old; she had prepared and trained for almost ten years and grown up in the business. At Stephanie's age the hotel had been her playground, and in the years since, it had become her life. And in subtle ways she had improved and modernized it and enhanced her father's original vision. It was an exceptional hotel and a legend in New York.

Hugues took his wife out on the dance floor then, while he told her about the travel plans he had for them, the things they were going to do, the year in Paris he wanted to spend with her and the children, if she was willing to let Jim run her business for that long, and he hoped she might. He was full of excitement and ideas, as Natalie spun around the floor with him, dizzy with what he said, but excited by it too. His enthusiasm was contagious, and she loved the idea of spending a year in Europe with the twins. The best part of his retiring was that he was still young enough to enjoy it, and so was she. She had just turned forty-eight, and Hugues was a handsome, sexy, youthful sixty. She and the children had kept him young.

'What did Papa just say?' Stephanie asked as she came up to Heloise with a puzzled expression. Her hair was in long blond pigtails with ribbons.

'He said that I'm going to run the hotel and Papa will have more time to play with you.' Heloise smiled at her. She was crazy about them both.

Stephanie looked annoyed when her older sister explained it to her. 'I want to run the hotel too.'

'Then you have to work very hard and spend a lot of time here, and one day you can work with me.' Stephanie looked satisfied with the suggestion, and Brad took Heloise out on the dance floor and smiled as he looked down at her.

'Well, that was certainly a big surprise. Do you think he'll actually be able to relax?' He couldn't imagine Heloise doing that either. They lived for the hotel. But Brad enjoyed his work too, and what he did for her and the hotel, among other clients.

'Natalie and the twins will keep him busy,' she said as Jennifer and Bruce danced past them and waved.

Heloise was still having trouble absorbing what her father had just done as she and Brad talked and danced. He was smiling down at her proudly.

'He did a smart thing,' Brad complimented her. 'You'll be a wonderful general manager, if you don't let it kill you.' It was a family trait, they both worked too hard. But she loved it, just as Hugues did. And she was tireless. She worked all the time, except when Brad could get her out for an evening, or away for a few days, which was rare.

They were still talking about her father's big announcement when they ran into Jennifer and Bruce at the buffet a little while later. Julien was hiding behind it, throwing bread balls at his twin, and Heloise discreetly signaled to him to stop. He was full of mischief and more naive than Stephanie, who seemed much more grown up. She was more like Heloise's twin than his. He was more easygoing, and Stephanie loved knowing everything that went on in the hotel. She had loved following Ernesta around with the turn-down cart, until Ernesta had retired the year before. But she was there that night for Hugues's birthday, and Heloise had given her a big hug. She was one of the treasures of her childhood, and Ernesta's eyes always lit up when she saw her, and she had cried when

Hugues announced her as the new general manager.

'So, Madame Manager, what do you think?' Jennifer asked her with a warm smile, as Brad and Bruce chatted and helped themselves to lobster that the chef had prepared the way Hugues liked it. Heloise had ordered it for him.

'You knew, didn't you?' Heloise accused her with a warm smile. She had seen it on Jennifer's face earlier. She hadn't been nearly as surprised as everyone else in the room. She knew everything Hugues did, and thought, even more sometimes than his eldest daughter and wife.

'He didn't tell me exactly, but I had an idea. I'm glad he's doing it. He needs to get out and have some fun while he's still young. I think it would be great if they go to Paris for a year. And you can go over and visit.' But she also knew that Heloise would be busier than ever, taking over the reins of the hotel, with all that entailed. But she was the right age to do it. Bruce and Brad moved closer to them then, and Heloise saw Bruce and Jennifer exchange a warm smile. She had known for years that they were quietly seeing each other. It had happened sometime along the way, and they made a nice couple. As Heloise was thinking that, Jennifer turned to her with a shy smile.

'We have an announcement too,' she said, and blushed

as the big security man laughed. 'We're getting married. And I'll probably retire next year.' She looked like a giddy young girl as she said it, and Heloise hugged her, and then wagged a finger at her.

'You can get married. But you can't retire till I take over this hotel and know what I'm doing. You probably know more than I do about running it. You're not going anywhere!' Jennifer laughed in answer, and suddenly Heloise realized that she'd be sitting in her father's office, at his desk, and it was a strange feeling. She didn't see how she could ever step into his shoes and do the job he had. She still had so much to learn. It was humbling thinking about taking his place, and it made her sad. She was having so much fun working with him that she didn't want him to leave, but she realized that it was probably better for him, and he felt ready. She wasn't sure she did. She needed to get used to the idea.

Jennifer and Bruce surprised them then and said they were getting married on Thanksgiving when her children could be there. And Bruce had three children too. Heloise was happy for them, although she was upset when Jennifer said she would retire in the next few months too. And Heloise managed to say hello to everyone before the party ended. It was a beautiful night for her father and she enjoyed it too. And they were talking about it when she and Brad went upstairs after the party. She was tired and still overwhelmed by her father making her general manager and passing her the baton. He was the master of surprises. He had done it to her with his marriage to Natalie, then the twins, and now this.

'What if I can't do it, or I screw up, or I destroy the hotel in some way?' she said to Brad with a look of panic as they undressed. Her father had always been there with her. She had never run it alone, except briefly when he was sick.

'You'll do it even better than he did,' Brad said confidently as he pulled her onto the bed and into his arms. 'You already run this place, you just don't know it yet. Your father would never have passed it on to you, if he didn't think you could do it. He loves this hotel too much to take that risk. He knows you can do it, and so do I.' She was the only one who wasn't sure. It was a big responsibility for her at her age. Being general manager of one of the most successful hotels in New York at twenty-seven was a major feat. And he had no doubt that she would do it brilliantly.

'Will you help me when I screw up?' she asked, as she leaned against him and he held her close.

'Yes, but you won't. You're not going to need a lawyer to help you run it, just the good people you already have.'

They had been in business long enough for some of the staff to retire and move on in the past few years, like Ernesta, and now Jennifer, and even her father, although he wasn't very old, only sixty. She hadn't expected him to retire for another ten or fifteen years and figured she'd be ready by then. But having young children and a younger wife made him want to enjoy his life and not just work till he dropped. 'I've been thinking lately, by the way, that we need to make some changes ourselves.' Brad looked serious as he said it, and Heloise looked puzzled. Her father had said that night that when they came back from their year in Europe, he wanted to buy an apartment, and Natalie could decorate it, and they would move out of the hotel. He was going to give Heloise their apartment when they went away. She was ready to move into a bigger space. She had been in the same small suite for years with Brad, and they liked it. It was home to them now. Everything was suddenly changing so fast. She told Brad about her father's apartment then, and he seemed pleased. Living at the hotel was convenient for both of them, although it meant that she was on call all the time. But he was used to that too. It was her style, and Hugues's. And maybe Stephanie's one day too.

'Those aren't really the changes I had in mind, although it'll be nice to have more space. I was thinking of something else,' he said quietly, as she looked into his eyes.

'Like what?' She hoped he didn't want them to move out of the hotel. She would never do that, especially now, even though she knew it was intrusive sometimes living where she worked.

'I think you'll be much more efficient as a general manager,' he said pensively as though pondering it, 'if you have a stable home life.'

'I do,' she said, smiling at him and realizing that he was teasing her. 'We've been together for seven years. How much more stable can it get?'

'Quite a bit,' he said, laughing, as he held her close. 'I think what I mean is a respectable home life. You can't have an important job like general manager and live with a guy.' He grew serious then and stunned her for the second time that night. 'Heloise, will you marry me? I've been meaning to ask you that for months. I think this might be the right time.' He took her breath away with the question. She had never worried about marrying him, she knew they would one day. She just didn't know when. She thought they might do it in their thirties if they wanted kids. They weren't ready for that yet. She hadn't even thought about marrying him now.

'Are you serious?' she asked him with a solemn expression, and he nodded with a smile.

'Very much so. And if your father is retiring, I think we should do it before your life becomes completely crazy when you take over from him. Let's do it soon.' She looked shocked, and then he kissed her, and she lay in his arms and smiled. 'You haven't answered me,' he reminded her with a slightly worried look. Maybe she was going to turn him down.

'I'm enjoying the moment,' she said happily. She had gotten a husband that night, and a hotel. It had been a very big night for her, and she smiled happily at Brad. 'Yes. Of course I'll marry you,' she said, beaming at him, 'I never realized till right now how much I wanted you to ask.' He grinned broadly at her then and kissed her again. It had been a perfect night for her. Especially now, with Brad.

Chapter 26

Heloise and Brad picked a date in September. It was a gorgeous sunny afternoon. Natalie was her matron of honor, and her bridesmaids were three of her friends from the Lycée, and Jan. Stephanie was the flower girl, and Julien was the ring bearer, although he kept misplacing the rings, and his mother was holding on to them for him.

Her father was going to give her away, and Miriam and Greg Bones had come, which accounted for an army of paparazzi outside. Everyone who had ever mattered in her life was there, the employees she had worked with, the ones she'd grown up with, Ernesta, Jennifer, and Bruce, the friends she'd had in high school, and even one of her friends from the École Hôtelière. And all of Brad's family and friends were there too.

Heloise had taken care of all the wedding plans and details herself. And this time Natalie helped her. She had gone with her to shop for the dress and helped her pick out the bridesmaids' dresses. And Heloise had very definite ideas about how the wedding should look, the flowers, the tables, the decorations in the room. She worked closely with Franco the florist, and had Jan come in to consult with him to get exactly the look Heloise wanted, with garlands and topiary trees, and Jan was making her bouquet of lily of the valley. She and Brad picked the music and the band, and she ordered new tablecloths for the ballroom. Just as Natalie had, and all the brides who had come to the hotel, she wanted her wedding to be perfect for her and Brad.

She had invited her mother and admitted to Natalie that she didn't know if she'd come, and wasn't sure she cared. It was too late for them by then. Her mother had let her down too often. But it felt rude not to ask her, and her father said she should, and at least give her a chance to show up for once.

'Do you want her to come?' Natalie had asked her honestly. Heloise thought about it for a long moment, sighed, and then nodded.

'I feel stupid saying it. But I think I do.'

'Don't feel stupid. No matter how inadequate and

disappointing they are, they're still our mothers. I actually missed my mother on my wedding day, and she probably would have been mean to me if she was there. She always was.' It was a bond that Natalie and Heloise shared, and had been their first, when Natalie told her about her mother, the day before she married Hugues. It had been the end of Heloise's campaign against her, and they had been close ever since. And Heloise knew that if her mother didn't come, Natalie would be enough.

And much to her amazement, Miriam had accepted, and said she'd be delighted to come, with Greg, Arielle, and Joey, and she asked for two large suites at the hotel, complimentary of course, since she was the mother of the bride. She asked for the presidential suite, but it was occupied, and Hugues wouldn't move the important guest in it for her. So they gave her two very nice suites on the ninth floor. And the paparazzi went nuts outside because of Greg.

It had been an insane week, but everything had gotten done, everyone had helped her, especially Jan, Jennifer, and Natalie, and Heloise had worked till the last minute.

And then finally they had the rehearsal dinner and closed the restaurant to do it there, and the big day came faster than Heloise expected. And the next thing she knew, Natalie and her mother were helping her dress.

Predictably, Miriam was wearing an almost-see-through sexy white gown, totally oblivious that she wasn't supposed to wear white to a wedding, and even less if her daughter was the bride. And Heloise's half-brother and -sister by her mother were there, Arielle and Joey. They were nineteen and twenty, were wearing jeans and sneakers, and had as many tattoos as Greg and her mother, and Stephanie said they were very rude. Joey had even arrived carrying his own beer bottle into the rehearsal dinner, but Heloise didn't care.

She had selected a simple white organdy gown with a huge skirt and full sleeves you could see her arms through that made her look like she was floating in a cloud, with her red hair in a neat bun under her veil. And her father's eyes filled with tears when he saw her. All he could think of now was what she had looked like at seven as she ran around the hotel. And he looked proud as he walked her down the aisle, to the steps where Brad was waiting. He looked at her as though he had waited for this moment all his life. They both had, and the moment was perfect.

The ceremony was short and simple, and Julien handed them the rings and didn't lose them. The minister pronounced them man and wife, and when Brad kissed her, she knew she was in the right place with the right man at the right time. They danced all night and had a terrific time at their wedding.

Brad looked down at her with a blissful expression as he danced with her and thought he had never seen a more beautiful woman in his life, and Heloise had never been happier. She loved knowing that she was his wife.

'Was it everything you wanted it to be?' he asked about their wedding, and she nodded, looking peaceful and totally happy.

'Everything and more. And I feel like a guest at the hotel.' She was trying not to play assistant manager that night and not worry about anything.

And even her mother had behaved. Her father had danced with her once, and after years of being happily married to Natalie, he realized that he wasn't angry at Miriam anymore. It was a relief. And she said the hotel was even more beautiful than before. Greg was polite too, and both their children got so drunk, they had to go back to their suite before dinner.

Julien and Stephanie behaved like angels and took turns dancing with their parents and each other.

Her whole wedding night felt like a dream to Heloise. It was perfect. And the ballroom had never looked lovelier, with Franco and Jan working on the flowers together.

They stopped dancing at eleven so the bride and groom could catch the one A.M. flight to Paris. They were going to stay at the Ritz, and then fly on to Nice to stay at the Hotel du Cap in Cap d'Antibes, which was perfect for a honeymoon.

When Heloise tossed the bouquet Jan had made her for that purpose so she could keep her own, she aimed it straight at her sister Stephanie, who caught it and screamed with glee, as Julien rolled his eyes and wondered how she could be so silly. It was a legacy, for all the bouquets Heloise had wanted to catch as a little girl and hadn't been allowed to, and in memory of the one Natalie had tossed her seven years before, on the day she met Brad at their wedding. And Stephanie held the bouquet high like a prize. Her father and Natalie and all their friends watched as they got into the Rolls outside the hotel, and Heloise stopped long enough to kiss her father, and then with a last wave they got into the car.

And as they drove away from the hotel in a flurry of rose petals, her cell phone rang. She glanced at the number and saw that it was the hotel. Her father was babysitting the hotel for her, and when they came back, he was retiring and leaving for Paris. They had just rented an apartment on the Left Bank. These were going to be his last weeks of running the Hotel Vendôme, and after that Heloise would take over. She started to answer her phone, and Brad took it from her hand and kissed her.

'You're not on duty,' he reminded her. 'You're all mine for the next two weeks.' But more than that, she was his for the rest of time. And the hotel would be there when they got back. It was hers now. He kissed her again, and she turned her cell phone off and put it in her pocket. For now the hotel could wait. It would all be there when she got back, just as it had been all her life.

Every woman makes choices – but
what if those choices risk her family?

Turn the page for a sneak preview of Danielle
Steel's thought-provoking new novel,

The Sins of the Mother

Chapter 1

Olivia Grayson sat in the chairman's seat at the board meeting, listening intently to the presentations, her intense blue eyes taking in each member of the board. Her eyes were quick and sharp. She was totally still, wearing a well-cut navy blue pantsuit, and a string of pearls around her neck. Her hair was a sleek bob, cut to the level of her jawbone just below her ears. It was the same snow-white color it had been since her early thirties. She was one of those striking women you would notice in any room. She was timeless, ageless, with high cheekbones and an angular face, and elegant hands as she held a pen poised above her notepad. She always took notes at the meetings, and had a flawless memory of what went on, in what order, and everything that was said. Her keen mind and sharp business sense had won her the reputation for being brilliant, but more than anything she was practical and had an innate, unfailing sense of what was right for her company. She had turned the profitable hardware store her mother had inherited years before into a model for international operations on a mammoth scale.

The Factory, as they had renamed it when it moved from its original storefront in a suburban locale outside Boston to an old empty factory building, was an astounding success, and Olivia Grayson along with it. She was the image of power as she presided over the board meeting. She was strong, innovative, and creative, and had started working at The Factory after school when she was twelve.

Her mother had been the daughter of a genteel family of Boston bankers who had lost everything during the Depression. Maribelle Whitman went to work as a secretary in a law firm, and married a young insurance salesman, who got drafted into the army after Pearl Harbor, and was sent to England in the summer of 1942, four weeks after their daughter, Olivia, was born. He was killed in a bombing raid when she was a year old. As a young widow, Maribelle moved to a modest suburb of Boston, and went to work for Ansel Morris at the hardware store, to support her daughter. For fourteen years, she helped him grow his business, had a discreet and loving affair with him, expected nothing from him, and brought up her daughter on the salary she made. And when she unexpectedly inherited his fortune, Maribelle wanted nothing more than to send Olivia to college, but Olivia had a thirst for business and no interest in college and academic pursuits. She had a passion and a love for commerce that drove her to take risks and make bold moves, and each decision she made catapulted the business forward to unexpected places and dizzying heights. Despite her youth, she made few mistakes, and had an instinct that proved her right every time. She had had the respect and admiration of her colleagues and competitors for years. Olivia was an icon in the business world.

And when Olivia went to work at The Factory full time, at eighteen, straight out of high school, three years after Ansel died, her visions had transformed the local hardware business into something her mother, and surely he, had never dreamed of. Her mother was running it then, Ansel was gone. And Olivia convinced her mother to add low-cost furniture with simple modern designs, not just the basic, ordinary items The Factory had sold until then. Olivia had added a fresh look and the excitement of youth. She brought a new design aspect, at low prices, to their merchandise. They bought bathroom fixtures from foreign suppliers, modern kitchen cabinetry, and appliances. Within a short time they were as well known for their innovative international designs as the reliability of their products, at astoundingly reasonable rates. Olivia used volume to their advantage, and kept their prices lower than anyone else's. Her mother had been worried about it at first, but time had proven Olivia right. Her instincts had been flawless.

Fifty-one years later, at sixty-nine, Olivia Grayson had created an empire that had reached around the world, and an industry that no one could compete with, although many tried. By the time she was twenty-five, Olivia had become a legend, and The Factory along with her, with its reputation for creative designs for anything for the home, from tools to kitchens and furniture, at rock-bottom cost. There was nothing for the home you couldn't buy at The Factory, and she traveled constantly to find new suppliers, products, and designs. Her empire was still growing, and her reputation along with it.

Remarkably, there was nothing harsh in her face as she sat in the familiar chair at the board meeting, flanked by her sons on either side. Both had joined the business, fresh out of business school in Phillip's case, and after getting a master of fine arts and graphic design in John's.

Olivia's mother had long since retired. The Factory was a product of Olivia's genius, and the enormous fortune she had made from it was her legacy to her children. She had worked a lifetime for what she'd built. Olivia was the embodiment of the American dream.

Although she wielded enormous power and her eyes were sharp, there was something gentle about her face. She was a woman everyone took seriously, yet she was quick to laugh. A discreet woman, she knew when to speak. And she listened carefully to fresh ideas, which then spurred her on to new creations, and even now she was always seeking to stretch The Factory into additional places and to greater heights than it had ever been before. She didn't rest on her laurels, and her passion and main interest was continuing to make her business grow. She still had the same excitement about it she'd had in her youth.

There were six members of the board, in addition to Olivia and her two sons, Phillip and John. She was the chairman and CEO, and Phillip was the CFO. He had his father's steady head for finance and had come to the company from Harvard Business School after he earned his MBA with honors. He was a quiet person, more like his father than his mother. Each of her sons had inherited a facet of her abilities, but neither combined them as a whole. John, her third-born child, was head of creative and design. John was an artist and had studied fine arts at Yale. Painting was his first love, but devotion to his mother had driven him into the business at an early age. Olivia had always known that with his artistic sense and training in design, he had much to offer them. He was more gregarious than his older brother and resembled his mother in many ways, although the money side of the business was a mystery to him. He lived for aesthetics, and the beauty he saw in the world. And he still spent all his free time painting on weekends. He was an artist above all.

At forty-six, Phillip was as serious and solid as his father had been. Phillip's father, Joe, had been an accountant and had helped Olivia run the business, quietly from behind the scenes. Phillip had inherited his financial accuracy and reliability, and none of his mother's creative spirit and fire.

John had inherited Olivia's innate artistic sense for design, and at forty-one, as an artist, he constantly brought new life visually into what they offered the world. He had enormous talent that he had funneled into The Factory, while dreaming of painting full time. Both men were essential to the business, but its life force was still their mother, even at sixty-nine. The Factory was still a family-held business, although they had had frequent opportunities to sell it and go public over the years. Olivia wouldn't think of it, although Phillip had been sorely tempted by some of the offers they'd had in recent years. Olivia insisted that The Factory was theirs, with its many stores around the world, and she intended to keep it that way.

Their enterprise was booming and continuing to grow exponentially. And as long as she was alive, she intended to see to it that there were Graysons at its helm. Her two daughters had no interest in the business, but she knew that her two sons would run it one day, and she had prepared them well. Together, she felt certain, they would be able to maintain the empire she had built, and she was nowhere near ready to retire or step down. Olivia Grayson was still in full swing, running The Factory and traveling around the world, just as she had done for almost fifty-two years. She showed no sign of slowing down, her ideas were as astounding and innovative as ever, and she looked ten years younger than her age. She was a naturally beautiful woman, with a passion for life, and ten times the energy of people half her age.

With her usual quiet, orderly style, she brought the board meeting to a close shortly after noon. They had covered all the matters on their agenda, including Olivia's concerns about some of the factories they were using in India and China. Phillip's main concern was their bottom line, which was healthier than ever. The products they sold at incredibly low prices were making them a fortune and were being distributed by The Factory around the world.

Olivia always wanted to know that their factories' practices were sound. And Phillip had assured them all again that morning that although they couldn't know everything about their Asian factories, they were using a reliable industrial investigative firm, and all appeared to be in good order. And the prices they were paying were leaving them the profit margins they had benefited from for years. Theirs was a model that their competitors envied and never succeeded in matching. Olivia had a magic touch.

John had also introduced a series of new designs that morning that they all knew would be snapped up by their customers in the coming months. The Factory was ahead of every trend, with sure instincts about what would sell and what their customers wanted, even before they knew it themselves. John had an unfailing sense for shape, design, and color. The combination they offered of low prices and high design, for items their clients were begging for, was unbeatable. They created a need and then filled it. The Factory leaped ahead financially every year.

The empire Olivia had founded was rock solid. And she knew her late husband, Joe, would have been proud of her, just as he had been in his lifetime. He had been the perfect mate for her. And he hadn't been surprised or critical when the business they grew together kept her from spending time with him or their children. They both knew it was inevitable that she'd be busy, especially when she was traveling, and even when she was at home. Joe had made up for it, with his more predictable schedule and less demanding financial duties in the firm. Trained as an accountant, he had been their chief financial officer until he died and Phillip stepped into his shoes. Olivia's mother, Maribelle, had retired from the business to take care of Olivia's children, shortly after Phillip was born, and that role suited her much better, and was less stressful for her. The business in Olivia and Joe's hands had long since outgrown her by then. Olivia had been the driving force of The Factory, and shouldered the responsibility with ease, despite the time it ultimately cost her with her children. She had tried to make it up to them as she got older, particularly in the last fourteen years since her husband's sudden death at sixty. He had died of a heart attack while she was away visiting new factories in the Philippines.

Joe's death had been a terrible blow to Olivia and their children.

Since then she had been more attentive to them, and made a point of taking her children and grandchildren on

a vacation together every year. She loved them, and
always had, and her husband, but she loved the business
too. The Factory was her passion and her life. It was an
all-consuming eternal flame that devoured her and sus-
tained her. Joe had understood that and never minded,
and her children also knew it, although some were more
accepting of it than others.

Their senior house counsel, Peter Williams, had been
at the board meeting that morning, to discuss some of the
issues that Phillip had raised, about what the financial
impact would be if they ever decided to shift from factories in Asia to different, more transparent ones in Europe.
They all knew it could hit their bottom line unfavorably,
and Phillip didn't recommend it. Olivia had wanted their
senior lawyer at the meeting. And Peter had voiced his
usual carefully measured and wisely weighed opinions.
She sought his advice on many subjects, and he always
counseled her sagely. He was conservative by nature, but
always practical in his suggestions, and he was creative in
helping them find solutions to sometimes dicey legal
issues. And inevitably there were some, in an enterprise as
vast as theirs. He had enormous respect for Olivia, and
had devoted the lion's share of his time to The Factory for
nearly twenty years. He never objected to the long hours
he had to spend on it, the sacrifices he had to make, or its

impact on his personal life. He had always been fascinated by the business, and the woman who ran it, and deeply impressed by her.

"What did you think of the meeting?" Olivia asked him as they waited at the elevator together. Phillip and John were still in the boardroom, and she had to get back to her office. Peter was heading back to his, a dozen blocks away. But as The Factory was his biggest client, he was at its main offices frequently. Olivia had moved the headquarters to New York from the outskirts of Boston forty years before. Her children had grown up in New York. Once they had opened branches in New Jersey, Chicago, and Connecticut, and on Long Island, New York was a more reasonable location for them than a sleepy suburb outside Boston. When they added the South, Midwest, and the West Coast, and eventually expanded their international operation, being based in New York made even more sense. Their offices filled an entire building on Park Avenue, and they had warehouses all across the country, and in Asia, South America, and Europe. Their stores had been international for thirty years. Olivia had been faithful to their old locations and maintained them but had added countless new ones. Worldwide, they now had close to a hundred stores, and every one of them was profitable and booming. Olivia had made few mistakes over the years, and corrected them rapidly when she did.

"I thought Phillip brought up some valid points," Peter answered her as they got in the elevator together, and she pressed the button for her office floor. Phillip and John's offices were on the same floor as hers. "I think we're keeping a close eye on any potential trouble spots. That's all you can do for now," Peter reassured her.

"I don't want to use factories with questionable practices." She echoed what she had said in the meeting, which was a mantra for her. She had a powerful social conscience that was in operation at all times. She had a strong sense of morality, as well as a good head for business. She was an ethical woman, with a kind heart.

"I don't think there's anything to worry about, that we know of.

And we're keeping our eyes and ears wide open," Peter said firmly.

"Are you comfortable?" she asked Peter directly with her piercing blue eyes. Nothing escaped Olivia's notice – it was one of the many things he admired about her. And she never sacrificed her ethics for the bottom line.

"Yes, I am comfortable," Peter said honestly.

"Good. You're my barometer, Peter," she said with a small smile.

"When you're not comfortable about our factories, that's when I'll start to worry." It was an impressive compliment coming from her.

"I'll let you know if anything changes. I believe that our sources are keeping us well informed. Do you have time for a quick lunch before we both go back to work?" She knew that he worked as hard as she did, and had as little idle time. They enjoyed talking business together and catching up on each other's news. Peter was sixty-three years old, married, with a grown son and daughter, and had had a rewarding career. They had fought many battles for The Factory side by side, and won.

"I can't," she said regretfully. "I have an interview with The New York Times at one-thirty, and a mountain on my desk to deal with before that." She dreaded the day he would retire. She relied heavily on his advice and clear-headed analysis of situations, and valued his friendship. She trusted him more than anyone else. And fortunately, he was vital and in good health and had no plans to retire for now.

"I would tell you that you work too hard, but I'd be wasting my time," he said with a rueful smile, and she laughed as the elevator stopped on her floor.

"Tell that to yourself," she said with a wave, as she got out, and the elevator doors stood open for a minute.

"When are you leaving on vacation?" he called after her, and she turned back as she answered.

"Not for another six weeks, in July." He knew about the birthday trip she took with her children every year. Each time she chose a different spectacular venue to entice them and entertain them. It was a tradition she had started after her husband died, and she knew Joe would have approved. It was something she did to try and make up to them for the father they had lost, and the time she hadn't spent with them when they were young. She knew she couldn't make up for lost time, but the trips she arranged for them were wonderful for all of them, and she put a lot of thought and effort into it every year. She considered it a sacred time.

Read the complete book – available now